The Exes

ANAM IQBAL

PENGUIN BOOKS

PENGUIN BOOKS

UK | USA | Canada | Ireland | Australia
India | New Zealand | South Africa

Penguin Books is part of the Penguin Random House group of companies
whose addresses can be found at global.penguinrandomhouse.com.

www.penguin.co.uk   www.puffin.co.uk   www.ladybird.co.uk

Penguin
Random House
UK

First published 2024

001

Text copyright © Anam Iqbal, 2024

The moral right of the author has been asserted

The brands mentioned in this book are trademarks belonging to third parties

Set in 10.75/15.5pt Adobe Caslon Pro
Typeset by Jouve (UK), Milton Keynes
Printed and bound in Great Britain by Clays Ltd, Elcograf S.p.A.

The authorized representative in the EEA is Penguin Random House Ireland,
Morrison Chambers, 32 Nassau Street, Dublin D02 YH68

A CIP catalogue record for this book is available from the British Library

ISBN: 978–0–241–66284–7

All correspondence to:
Penguin Books
Penguin Random House Children's
One Embassy Gardens, 8 Viaduct Gardens, London SW11 7BW

To the love of my life, Rameez,
for believing in me so much that
I started believing too

&

to my beautiful sister, Shanza,
for reminding me never to give up on
my dream to write

A Note on the Content

This story involves themes of cyberbullying, patriarchy, gender inequality, abortion, domestic violence, Islamophobia, classism, racism and mental health. I have tried my best to handle these aspects of the narrative with the utmost sensitivity and care. In accordance with your own lived experiences, some of these topics may be difficult to engage with. Please take care of yourself if you choose to journey into this story and remember that you are not alone.

Sending abundant love and light your way,
Anam.

Hello & Welcome to the UK's Leading Gossip Blog

To be the first to see exclusive footage, hear juicy secrets and enjoy my hard-hitting exposés about your favourite influencers, turn on notifications on all 'Mr Expose' platforms.

I know most of you are here for my scandalous speciality: THE EXES. If you live under a rock and somehow still don't know who they are, I recommend glancing over the following profiles before proceeding: ·

Karim Malik

Age:	17
Interests:	Business Ventures, Creating Viral Content, Gaming
Star Sign:	Gemini
Talent:	Ironically enough – Spotting Others' Talent
Best Friend:	Abeo Okon
Closest Connection:	Chloe Clark (long-time on–off girlfriend)
Ambition:	World-renowned Businessman

Chloe Clark

Age:	17
Interests:	Singing, Socialite Events, Photography, Fashion Trends
Star Sign:	Aries
Talent:	Singer-Songwriter, Guitarist, Lifestyle Photographer
Best Friend:	Felicity Wong
Closest Connection:	Karim Malik (long-time on–off boyfriend)
Ambition:	Popstar

Felicity Wong

Age:	18
Interests:	Dancing, Make-up, Skincare, Vlogging
Star Sign:	Virgo
Talent:	Dancer – Ballet, Ballroom, Contemporary, Street
Best Friend:	Chloe Clark
Closest Connection:	Karim Malik (spotted Felicity's talent before she did!)
Ambition:	Professional Dancer & Influencer

Abeo Okon

Age:	17
Interests:	Fashion, Modelling, Luxury Magazines, Travelling

Star Sign:	Taurus
Talent:	Textile Arts, Modelling, Fashion Stylist & Trendsetter
Best Friend:	Karim Malik
Closest Connection:	James Sawyer (First Serious Relationship)
Ambition:	Fashion Designer

Sanjay Arya

Age:	17
Interests:	Visual Art, Conceptual Art, Galleries, Philosophy
Star Sign:	Pisces
Talent:	Painting, Drawing, Digital Art, Printmaking
Best Friend:	No one in Particular
Closest Connection:	Bit of a Loner (Karim practically invented Sanjay via The Exes)
Ambition:	Artist

A Sizzling Summer Secret Spilled: Terminating the Last Remnant of a Relationship . . .

August is the month Londoners make the most of our elusive sun before the sweet sting of autumn sweeps over. All notable influencers from St Victor's School (who aren't already off jet-setting in exotic locations) are either roaming Mayfair to revive their wardrobes (after all, only three days until school starts!), brunching al fresco in Soho, or soaking up the sun in Hyde Park in their Alexander McQueen faille midi dresses and shorts that are trending this season (check my recent posts for Styling Tips and Who Wore It Best polls).

As for THE influencers – well, most of them have been surprisingly quiet as of recent. The Exes haven't spent much time together this summer; perhaps the tight-knit quintet needed a little space from each other? But don't worry – all the stuff they've failed to share online, I'll be a babe and dish out for them.

Felicity Wong has been pumping out dance and beauty content like never before on her TikTok – she's probably earned more than any other Ex this summer, and now officially has more followers on the app than anyone else in her clique (and in the country!). With the way her dance choreographies and East Asian skincare and make-up tutorials have been going viral recently, I can only see her following growing exponentially by the day, probably hour. Is she trying to outdo her fellow Exes? It's certainly working . . .

Abeo Okon has been shopping non-stop with his new beau and doesn't seem to mind spoiling him rotten. If the shelves at Hermès and Dior over on Bond Street look a little empty, now you know why. I must confess that Abeo may have inspired me to nab a few astonishingly colourful pieces from Versace; that man can style *anything*.

Rumour has it he's been approached by Burberry to model their upcoming collection. Now wouldn't that be iconic – something to keep your eyes peeled for . . .

Sanjay Arya has been holed up in his Notting Hill apartment/art studio: shirtless, cigarette in one hand, paintbrush in the other. It seems he's finally got the tortured artist look down to a T. Although he's shared some behind-the-scenes footage and glimpses of his artwork online (always with strange and deeply philosophical captions that no one seems to understand), most of it he's kept to himself. Is our famous teen artist already preparing his portfolio for university applications? Or perhaps he's planning to open his own gallery? Whatever you have to say about The Exes, you certainly can't say they lack ambition.

Now over to our fan favourites. It's been a whole month since our stellar couple posted anything on their socials, which, let's be honest, feels like *years* when it comes to them. Especially since they've always shared every single aspect of their relationship with us, leaving us screaming, 'Couple goals!' We aren't used to being stranded like this, Karim and Chloe! How rude. We thought we were a part of this relationship too *ugly crying face*.

Before their sudden disappearance, there were rumours about trouble in paradise, which rocked our world – we'd always thought the picture-perfect, lovesick couple would eventually make their way down the aisle, have children, and grow old together. Shame on you for selling us false dreams about love, Chlarim!

Although the YouTubers seem to have decided to keep their relationship under wraps recently, there's no escaping the all-seeing gaze of Mr Ex, and you darlings better brace yourselves because I have some piping hot tea to spill. Now, here's the thing: I have good news *and* bad news. We'll start with the good, of course, because you know I like to leave you with a sizzling bang (not that kind, you saucy rascals).

Lovebirds Karim and Chloe were holidaying in the French Riviera, soaking up the sun and *each other* while taking endless romantic strolls around the picturesque towns and private beaches (shout-out to @allieinwonderland for sending in the photos. You guys always have my back!). Don't mind me while I wipe away my drool after taking in Karim's tanned and deliciously toned beach body. I think we can all agree it's the ultimate summer dream to lick ice cream off those abs. Chloe's tanned midriff on the other hand – well, that brings us over to the not-so-good news.

An anonymous yet trustworthy source has confirmed that the passionate lovemaking at their romantic retreat left Chloe feeling a little . . . bloated. The reason she was seen arriving at London City Airport alone, puffy-eyed and red-faced, was . . . a positive pregnancy test. She has since been sighted at King Edward VII's Hospital and rumour has it she's chosen to go ahead with an abortion – the most surprising thing is that Karim is still nowhere in sight. I wonder what her Catholic parents will have to say about this. Talk about going straight from 'couple goals' to 'we're worried for your souls'!

Karim and Chloe have been in an on–off relationship for years, but they always, *always* find their way back to each other. If this relationship is truly over for good, what does it mean for The Exes? And, more importantly, what the hell does it mean for *us*? Even the thought of not seeing any more couples content from Chlarim gives me nausea – and I mean, worse than morning-sickness nausea. Should I give them a taste of their own medicine and stop posting about them for a while? They'll learn their lesson when they see the traffic on their platforms dwindling . . .

Heck, who am I kidding? Things are too juicy right now for me to go AWOL! Stay tuned for the latest news on the hottest kids in town!

Yours Unfaithfully,
Mr Ex

1

Gossip spreads like ink in water.

Sudden. Swift. Staining.

A single rumour has the power to change someone's reputation in a heartbeat.

'Some aunty caught her snogging a guy in his car,' Saliha whispered to me, lifting her chin in Hania's direction. We'd all secured summer jobs in Selfridges' beauty department, and Hania was working at the counter just opposite ours. 'Apparently they were in the Asda car park.'

Saliha snorted but my eyes instantly widened with worry.

'That is so messed up.'

My heart shuddered just thinking of all the ways Hania's relatives would be shaming her, how mortified she must be feeling and the endless gossip that would follow her. What bothered me the most about these rumours were the double standards – practically everyone in our community had spotted Hania's brothers with girls in the past and their parents probably hadn't even bothered to mention it once.

'Someone also sent Hania's mum screenshots from her private socials, and we've both seen how revealing those pics

9

are.' Saliha paused to raise her brows and then tucked a stray hair back into her hijab. 'I'm surprised she's even allowed to leave the house for work.'

I stared at Hania's red-rimmed eyes as she helped a customer.

Saliha laughed at my stricken expression. 'Obviously I feel sorry for her too, but we all know how risky stuff like that is in our community. She should've been more careful.'

'Should I let her know I'm here if she needs anything, or would that be weird since we don't really talk?'

Saliha grimaced. 'Definitely weird.'

'But isn't it worse to not say anything at all?'

'Do you *really* think she needs us, Zara?'

Hania was one of the most popular girls in our school. With her curvaceous figure, sleek black hair and doll-like features, she had everyone flocking around her like sheep.

'Guess not. I just hope she's doing OK.'

Saliha rolled her eyes. 'Everyone will move on when the aunties get hold of the next scandal. Do you reckon it was Imran she was caught with?'

I wrinkled my nose in distaste. With his temple fade trim, ear piercings and baggy tracksuits, my neighbour Imran Sayyid perfectly encapsulated the stereotypical 'rude-boy' image. He broke hearts left, right and centre, sometimes with as little as a wink.

As much as I tried to deny it, even I wasn't entirely immune to his charm. I'd had a crush on Imran in the past, but things were different now. Since turning seventeen, I was no longer fooled by the ridiculous bad-boy act. I was focused on getting through my final year of sixth form and heading towards a brighter future.

Hania suddenly looked right at us and narrowed her eyes as though she knew we were talking about her. Awkward!

We leaped into action. Saliha tried to duck behind the counter, her head whacking into its corner, and I walked right into a customer, knocking the palette she was holding clean out of her hand. Bits of colourful, glittering powder scattered across the white marble floor.

'I am *so* sorry,' I exclaimed.

From the corner of my eye, I could see our manager death-glaring at us – an expression we were used to by now. I shrugged it off and began clearing up the mess. Just a few weeks ago, I would've been jittery for the rest of the day after receiving a look like that, but this job had helped me to come out of my shell, to realize that there was no pleasing some people and it wasn't worth feeling anxious over them.

It got busier. Packs of girls came and went, and they all seemed to blend into one ...

The nineties flared jeans that were in again; Louis Vuitton Neverfulls; lip fillers from some place over on Harley Street; long hair with summery highlights done at hairdressers in Fitzrovia.

When things quietened, Saliha approached me with a mischievous look. 'Oh my God. I forgot to ask if you've read Mr Ex's latest post.'

I'd recently broken the habit of opening social media first thing in the morning, so I wasn't up to speed. With school starting soon, I didn't want to be glued to my phone, and it had taken everything in me to keep myself from being hooked on the one site that everyone at school checked regularly: Mr Expose's blog.

Mr Ex always had the juiciest gossip!

He exposed secrets about the top influencers in London that we all loved to watch, and he didn't spare the details.

His main victims were The Exes: the five teenagers who collectively ran one of the biggest YouTube channels in Britain. It was common knowledge that they'd chosen the name 'The Exes' to convey how quickly they moved on from styles, lovers, locations and scandals.

Although they do possess some talent, The Exes are basically just famous for being famous. They post silly pranks, daily vlogs and plenty of couples content.

They first went viral with the vlogs of their lives at St Victor's, an exclusive private school in West London, attended by the privileged kids of London's elite. I enjoyed watching their antics when I was younger, before I realized these were the people I'd be competing with for a space at a top university. They'd got a head start with all their years of a top-tier private education and the bank of mum and dad at their disposal. I'd have to work twice as hard to get the grades and opportunities that just fell into their laps.

From the moment The Exes entered the scene, they took the internet by storm. Their refined accents, lavish lifestyle, glitzy panache – it was as though the world had been waiting for them.

Saliha came up close, interrupting my thoughts. 'Apparently Chloe Clark just aborted Karim Malik's baby.'

I gave her a sceptical look.

'Oh there's evidence . . . photos of her leaving the hospital!' she exclaimed.

'That doesn't really prove anything,' I scoffed. 'It could've been for a blood test or practically anything else. Besides, a girl getting an abortion should *not* be the town's gossip. Like ever.'

Sal pursed her lips. 'Well, it's already out there now. And I doubt Mr Ex would post about it if he didn't have at least one reliable source.'

My brows shot together. 'Oh yeah, because British tabloids and gossip blogs share nothing but the *gospel truth*. We're literally in the era of fake news. And it's insensitive of Mr Ex to blast something like that if it *is* true – just imagine what state Chloe and Karim must be in.'

'They were together for such a long time,' Saliha continued, looking into space thoughtfully. 'I can't even picture them with other people. If they split for good, it's going to change The Exes forever.'

'I can't even imagine how Chloe must be feeling. Imagine every aspect of your relationship being available to the public! We're talking about an entirely different level of gossip here. I'd never survive – the whole world watching and judging my most intimate decisions.'

A shudder ran through me at the mere thought of it. My parents' judgements were distressing enough without the thought of my peers, the wider community or random trolls on the internet chipping in as well.

Sal's eyes widened. 'Can you imagine if this kind of news broke out among the aunties in our area?' She sniggered into her hand. 'They can't even handle bare shoulders and stolen kisses. They'd have a collective heart attack and be holding on to their dupattas for dear life.'

It seemed that even if you were incredibly rich and beloved, you couldn't escape the unfair expectations that society placed on girls and their bodies. I let out a sad sigh.

'Relax, Zara. These people live in a very different world from us. Scandalous news is normal for them. They choose to put themselves out there, and they know this comes with the territory.'

'They're human too!' I retorted. 'I know Mr Ex can be funny, but sometimes he's just plain awful. If the abortion news is true, he's provoking his hordes of followers to harass them on top of everything else they're going through. The Exes' comment sections must be looking unhinged right now.'

Saliha snorted. 'Oh honey, but that's how you know you've made it these days – when you've got haters. Just so long as you're still hustling from the hype. I'm gonna be that kind of a hustler someday. You just wait and see.'

Social media stardom really did seem to be the dream for everyone I knew these days. It was something I never really understood.

But in Saliha's case, with her sassy personality, soft Bangladeshi features and incredible modest fashion sense, I didn't doubt that she would one day realize her dream. Her Instagram had recently hit five thousand followers. She was even making some sales from driving her internet traffic to a website she'd set up called Saliha's Style, which sold jersey hijabs.

'Yup, just a few more crazy clickbait YouTube videos and you'll be up there with The Exes,' I replied sarcastically.

She glared at me for a whole two seconds before we could no longer hold our laughter in, mostly because I knew we were both thinking about her latest video, 'Super Spicy Noodles Mukbang'. After uploading it she'd glumly stated that two thousand views hadn't been worth practically burning her insides and prancing around like an idiot in pain for an hour.

'The Exes may use a lot of filters,' Saliha said. 'But you can't fake everything. The money, the travelling, the freedom. It *is* real. They get to shop rather than work here. Don't you want to know what it's like to have all of that?'

'Sure,' I murmured.

I'd imagined countless times what it would be like to be an Ex. Those daydreams of perpetual banter, romance and travelling had provided the perfect temporary escape from the suffocating reality of my home life, where I could never really let loose.

'Oh, another key piece of evidence,' Sal added smugly. 'Karim Malik hasn't posted anything on his socials in over a month. Now we all know why.'

My heart fluttered at the mention of him.

I'd certainly missed his presence on my feed these past few weeks. Karim Malik was so charming that I felt myself blush every time I watched his videos. As embarrassing as it was to admit it, I'd had my fair share of fantasies about him, like pretty much every other teenage girl who'd seen him online. He was even my screensaver at one point; when Mum had seen it, she'd said it was inappropriate and made me change it.

Saliha, on the other hand, was obsessed with Chloe Clark's style. When Chloe started wearing a classic pearl necklace, so did Sal. Even I felt the urge to grab one. I made a mental note to have a look in a high street jewellery store when I was paid at the end of the month. Anything from Selfridges would be out of my budget.

The Exes were leading all the current trends in fashion, beauty, lifestyle, content creation and everything in between. It was impossible to get away from the power of their influence, and by the time you managed to hop on to the latest trend, the next one was already in full swing.

When Mr Expose's blog had first gone viral, everyone had assumed he was connected to The Exes in some way, but it quickly became obvious that he was just an anonymous blogger with a similar name, who had a flair for dissecting their outfits, talents and lives.

Mr Ex immediately captured everyone's attention with his sassy and scathing exposés of the country's 'it' crowd.

Everyone wondered why The Exes even allowed Mr Ex's gossip blog to keep running. They were the children of England's elite, so surely they could have had it taken down with one phone call if they'd wanted to? Then the darker rumours began: people were convinced The Exes were staging the entire thing and running the blog themselves, doing it for publicity and views.

It wouldn't be the strangest thing someone had done in the cause of social media success. And it certainly made sense. How else would Mr Ex be getting access to all those private photos, videos and conversations? He seemed to know the most intimate details . . .

'Any new theories on who Mr Ex might be?' I whispered to Sal.

'Didn't you just say he's awful?' she quipped.

'Even though he's a feisty blabbermouth, he has a way of getting under your skin,' I admitted reluctantly.

Sal kissed her teeth. 'I'm sick of running around in circles with my ludicrous theories. But I'd bet all my scanty savings that Mr Ex is one of The Exes, most likely Abeo Okon – can't you just imagine him doing Mr Ex's voice perfectly? Anyways, I hope the snitch fesses up soon so I can shout *I told you so* from London's rooftops. You'll definitely have to help me capture that for my YouTube.'

The elusive, most-followed UK gossip blogger was so good at being anonymous that it seemed no one would know their identity until they chose to unveil it themselves, which they might never even do. And there was certainly no way of us knowing what *really* went on behind the scenes in the lives of the scandalous quintet. What we did know, however, was that The Exes were swiftly becoming the biggest influencers in the world, with the power to set and destroy trends with more sway than any celebrity.

Regardless of the rumours that spread about them, they would never really be harmed, because they'd already made it. All the world's luxuries and opportunities lay at their feet.

They were untouchable, happy, *free*.

Saliha was right.

I *did* want to know what it was like to have all of that.

Karim

2

Gossip doesn't bother me.

I was raised in it, surrounded by it before I even understood what my family name meant to others. The Maliks are known to be dashingly desirable, indecently rich, proudly intimidating.

We're the exclusive tea everyone wants a sip of, and, of course, everything people are too afraid to say directly to us is said behind our backs. But the hype only adds to our image and wealth, so we welcome it.

Whispers follow me everywhere I go, and I thrive despite them – *because* of them. I smile, wave, pose for selfies, all the while watching my social media accounts boom and the money roll in. All the while seeing my parents' businesses flourish and expand.

It's a good life.

Well, that's what I tell myself – it's the only way to survive the reality of being Karim Malik.

Behind the mask, the truth is that … this recent gossip feels different.

More personal. Sinister. In a way that makes me question the intentions of every single person I've ever met – even those

I've known for years. People are somehow getting their hands on deeply private information about me – the stuff I wouldn't even share with some of my closest confidants – and plastering it on the internet or, more likely, selling it to Mr Ex.

This gossip makes me feel paranoid and sick and drained.

I stopped reading the comments hours ago, but somehow the nasty remarks still drift in my mind. I need to talk this through with one of my friends.

But is there anyone I can truly confide in?

How do I know who I can trust?

I'll probably never confide in anyone about this, just like I never spoke to anyone about all the other emotions fluttering inside me, contained like moths in a sealed jar.

The loneliness was eating away at me.

It felt embarrassing to admit that I was so lonely; no one would believe me anyway because of who I am and all that I have.

But there was a gaping hole in my life that no amount of money, fame or respect could fill. A hole that seemed to be growing by the day, slowly swallowing me into its dark mouth.

I couldn't remember the last time I'd had a meaningful conversation with anyone. I couldn't remember the last time I'd showered, shaved, or even brushed my teeth. Had it been three days? A week? Time had lost all meaning, as had most other things.

Today was different though. I could no longer refuse to 'do life'. I had a meeting with the other Exes, one that would shape our future as a brand, as individuals, and, most importantly, as friends.

As I lay in bed wondering how the meeting would go, Mum rushed in and went straight for my floor-length curtains, sweeping them back. I groaned as the light flooded in and flung an arm over my eyes.

'Get up and get ready – you're going to meet your future sister-in-law today,' she announced. The hint of a Pakistani accent underlying her posh London enunciation was more prominent than usual; it intensified when she was stressed.

'Urgh. Mum!'

'It's afternoon, for God's sake. Get up and make yourself look decent, Karim. Today's food tasting with the Qureshis is important.'

Everyone at home had been going on about the wedding for a while now, but I hadn't given it much thought. The Qureshis, my brother's soon-to-be in-laws, had flown in from Lahore just yesterday, and my family had gone to the airport to pick them up. After dining at The Ritz, they'd dropped them off at their home in Bishops Avenue. I was the only one who had yet to meet my brother's fiancée and her family. Mum had complained that my absence had looked bad, and I knew she wouldn't let me off the hook today. Out the corner of my eye, I watched her come over and stand at the foot of my bed and then place her hands on her hips.

'Hai!' she cried suddenly.

I shot up in bed, rubbing the sleep from my left eye. 'What's wrong?'

'Your grimy socks just touched my feet,' she declared, a hand shooting to her head in distress.

It was common for Mum to be this theatrical – to act as though any dirty items around the house somehow came to life in her presence and were on a mission to get her. Even after seventeen years of living with her, I fell for it every time. I relaxed back into bed, grumbling irritably.

'Oh, the smell in here,' she continued. 'I'll have one of the maids place some diffusers around the room. Would you prefer Fresh Fig & Cassis or English Pear & Freesia?'

When I didn't respond, she continued speaking to herself. 'English Pear it is.'

She nodded as though she'd just made an incredibly important decision. When she looked at me again, a flicker of concern was present in her eyes. Had it not been for the Botox, creases of worry might've formed along her forehead.

'Do we need to book in a few sessions with your therapist?'

It was the way Maliks dealt with all problems: throwing money at them. We rarely spoke to each other about anything meaningful – we were all too busy wrapped up in our own lives. Speaking to a therapist could be helpful, but only if you told them the truth . . .

There was no way Mum had missed the news about the abortion; it was trending everywhere. But she'd likely assumed it was all fake gossip, as a lot of the other stuff turned out to be, not even worthy of being addressed. My parents didn't make time for me in their hectic schedules unless it was a life-or-death situation, and clearly this didn't cut it.

'No,' I grunted, pushing the duvet away. 'I'm fine. I was just about to shower.'

Now that I took her in properly, I realized how glamorous she looked. While I was in my room wasting away, her skin was glowing in a way that made her look half her age. She was wearing a floor-length silver gown encrusted with fine crystals and pearls. It was no doubt one of her own pieces; she was the owner of the world-renowned luxury Pakistani fashion brand Fouzia Faris, named after herself. The designer evening wear and bridal couture had carved its way into being a top choice for influential international shoppers, celebrities and brides. Visitor slots at our flagship store on Regent Street were always fully booked.

'Your father and I are heading out for afternoon tea with Sana and her family, but we'll be back soon. I need you to be present and on your best behaviour today. OK?'

'So, with Sana ...' I began awkwardly, unsure of how to refer to the girl from Pakistan who my parents had arranged to marry my older brother.

'You'll be expected to refer to her as Sana *baji*,' Mum said, a touch sharply.

I didn't even refer to my own older sister with such formality and respect, but I nodded in agreement.

'Does Sana baji speak English?'

My Urdu was appalling, so we wouldn't have much in the way of communication if she didn't.

Mum sighed dramatically, raising a hand as though she simply couldn't bear to hear me say another word.

'You've spent far too many of your summer holidays jet-setting with your friends. If you'd agreed to come on at least one family trip to Pakistan in the last six years, you'd have known the answer to that. And you'd certainly know a lot more about what your community is like in your motherland.'

She made to leave the room.

'You still haven't answered my question.'

'It was a stupid one,' she responded over her shoulder as she left.

Just as I stood and stretched, my sister strolled in.

'Urgh. The entire house smells of curry. With the amount of wedding caterers we've invited over today, it'll be a while before the smell goes away.'

In a sleeveless grey kurta from Fouzia Faris, Kiran looked great too and I suddenly felt even worse about my messy state. Just like our mother, she had an incredible eye for fashion; I usually asked her to accompany me when I met with designers and stylists for important red-carpet events. But that was also because I genuinely enjoyed her company, and I was much closer to her than to our older brother, Azad.

'Absolutely ridiculous,' she said, sitting at the edge of my bed and holding her phone up in my direction.

Staring back from the screen was a brown-skinned man with a large round face. He was wearing horn-rimmed glasses and had a rather bushy moustache.

'It's Sana's older brother. According to mum, he's a real catch. I think she's hoping to kill two birds with one stone and get me married off too.'

Kiran fake-retched.

'Did she give you any further details about him?' I asked.

'He's a well-established businessman in America apparently. Not that I care or want to know because I can't seem to get over his monobrow, which is like half his face. And the other half . . . well, let's just say I wish the monobrow and moustache were large enough to cover that too.'

I burst out laughing. And suddenly I regretted pushing her away for the past few weeks. Although there was a lot I couldn't speak to my older sister about, I felt less lonely with her around. 'I can't believe Mum thought you'd actually agree to *that*.'

'What *I* can't believe,' she said curiously, 'is that Azad agreed to an arranged marriage with someone from Pakistan. Would *you* ever do it?'

We locked eyes for a moment, then simultaneously snorted. With the kind of lifestyles we lived, it was unlikely that either of us would ever agree to an arranged marriage. Even the idea of someone else choosing one of our meals or outfits was unacceptable to us, let alone choosing our *life partner*. Azad was more traditional in his ways and closer to our parents. Kiran and I were the opinionated younger siblings who did our own thing and drove them slightly mad.

'Is it a full-on arranged thing?' I mused.

Kiran's brows shot up. 'Did you not ask him? He's your brother too.'

'I've been busy. Besides, you know how private he is.'

'Mum introduced them. They've been speaking for close to a year now. Azad had multiple business visits to Lahore, and they met up every time he was there. It may have been arranged to start with, but now it's something more.'

'Wow,' I replied. 'It seems everything worked out perfectly for him because Mum meddled in his love life.'

Kiran pouted. 'I'm next in line, now that I'm turning twenty-five, and practically past my shelf date according to everyone. Let's hope Mum doesn't try to dictate my marriage too. I could never deal with it. Too many prying aunties.'

'Who knows, it may be your only option,' I teased.

She showed me her middle finger.

I headed towards my walk-in wardrobe to pick something out. Every suit was ironed, scented and hung perfectly.

'What shall I wear?' I asked Kiran, who followed me in and settled into the bronze Casa Padrino baroque sofa. She used to spend hours seated right there, curled into its arm as we exchanged stories about our lives. I'd missed this.

'A black Tom Ford suit.'

'Hmm,' I grunted nonchalantly, even as I did exactly as she said.

Suit in hand, I turned to face her and saw pity in her eyes.

'Please don't,' I snapped. 'I'm not in the mood to talk about it.'

Kiran adjusted her dark hair around her pale face and gave me a concerned look that was identical to Mum's. She looked so much like our Pakistani mother, who was from Peshawar and Lahore. I, on the other hand, was told time and time again how much I resembled our Indian father, with his rich brown skin and sharply defined jawline. He was from Hyderabad, but he'd been born and raised in England and didn't have the same attachment to his heritage as Mum did. I related to him in that sense.

'Are you seriously going to walk on eggshells around me all day?'

'No, of course not,' she said unconvincingly, then sighed. 'It's just a difficult situation to be in. It was hard enough to deal with it in private, and now everyone knows.'

'I'm fine.'

'Have your PR team told you what to do?'

'Same protocol as always. Don't address the issue at all. Apparently it'll blow over just like everything else in the past.'

'It will,' Kiran declared, walking over to me. 'You know how quickly things move on the internet. Today is a day for family; I don't want you stressing about anything else.'

'But first I'm going to meet The Exes. We have things to discuss.'

'Now? You need to be here when the Qureshis arrive!'

'Don't worry, I'll be back in time,' I said impatiently, and raised my suit suggestively. 'Now if you don't mind, I'm going to change.'

When Kiran reached the door, she turned around to give me one last worried look before leaving.

It had been a while since I'd posted anything on my socials, and I knew my self-imposed sabbatical had gone on for far too long. It was time to get back to work. Even though I wasn't in the mood for it, I pulled out my phone and set it on a tripod to record a transformation video. I chose the new Stormzy song that was trending and recorded myself lip-syncing to the opening lines.

I wondered if anyone would be able to tell just how fake and forced my smile was. Well, they'd never been able to tell before, so the answer to that was a solid *no*.

After a quick shower and clean-shave, I donned my suit, ditching the tie and leaving the top two buttons undone. I attached silver cufflinks, clipped my Rolex on and ran a touch of organic honey-scented wax through my hair. I usually spent more time smoothing it out, creating my signature sleek Ivy League look, but I couldn't be bothered today.

I recorded the rest of the video and uploaded it without checking it through. I'd been creating content since I was thirteen; it was muscle memory now.

As I descended the grand staircase from the third floor, I stopped to take a few selfies for my Instagram story. They came out nice enough that I decided to upload one on to my feed as well.

Caption – *My sister was right. Our house smells of curry, but I kinda like it . . .*

I tagged Kiran in the post, knowing she'd appreciate the traffic. My account had hit twenty million followers recently.

When I reached the landing, I called to one of the butlers, 'You're driving me out. Grab the keys for the Cadillac. Alert the bodyguards too.'

I stepped out to find the London sky a bright, promising blue. The late-August sun instantly cast a warm glow over me. This kind of weather was rare enough that I usually savoured it, felt my spirit instantly rise with the heat, but not today.

My family's presence was the reason all the other dwellers of Upper Phillimore Gardens in Kensington had had to revamp their security systems. No paparazzi were allowed anywhere near this block. It was comforting to see the Malik family home, Number 5, loom tall and steady before me. It was a detached ten-bedroom, white stucco-fronted Victorian townhouse – classic.

This was my safe space.

Although I had security to keep unwanted people out of my life here, I knew that the moment I was sighted outside, the swarms would rush over, shoving and screaming and leaching.

I could already envision all the commotion along Oxford Street: the camera flashes that would leave me seeing double; the shouting that would sink into my mind; the crowd pushing to get closer and closer.

When the butler opened the car door and I settled into the warm red leather, the nerves kicked in. As The Exes, we had experienced our fair share of intense meetings over the years, but never over something like this: a secret with the power to break us apart.

A secret that was no longer a secret.

'Sir?'

'Selfridges,' I ordered.

As we got closer, my heart pounded.

On the outside, I appeared calm, collected. But on the inside, I felt anxious and exhausted. I caught sight of a random guy – grey backpack, rimless glasses, carefree grin – hopping on to a double-decker bus with a friend, lost in their conversation, utterly uninterested in the rush surrounding them.

I wondered what it would be like to be him.

Zara

3

The last hour of my shift passed agonizingly slowly, filled with forced smiles, repetitive conversations, a mind-numbing monotony.

I shuffled closer to Sal.

'I want to keep this job on weekends after school starts. Do you?'

'No way,' she replied, cocking a perfectly painted brow. 'This year's going to be tough. We need our weekends to revise, don't we?'

I didn't bother to respond.

She was right. But this job was my excuse to spend as little time at home as possible. Before I'd taken it, I'd never really been allowed out much. All my childhood memories were of being at home, doing homework, trying to get my two older siblings to let me play with them, and helping my mum around the house while we waited for Dad to come back from his shifts as a taxi driver.

Working here was my escape.

I finally had the freedom to explore the city I was born and raised in, yet still barely even knew. The commotion in

Leicester Square, the glittering lights of Piccadilly Circus, the street performers of Covent Garden . . . I wanted to experience all of it.

Money was the only reason Dad had agreed to let me take this job. This would be the hardest and most crucial year of my education, and although I always got high grades, the teaching at my state school wasn't very good; since I was competing with the smartest students in the country to study dentistry at uni, I wasn't going to risk it. I needed extra tuition classes in A-level maths, biology and chemistry to ensure I got the best grades I could manage. And tuition was *expensive*.

Becoming a dentist was something I'd been striving for ever since I met Aunty Seema at a wedding in my local community. I was fourteen and it was the first time I'd come across a woman so educated, eloquent and independent. She owned her own dental clinic, and her self-assurance was apparent in the way she carried herself and communicated with her husband and children. She was her own boss in every way, and everyone respected her for it, including my mum and her friends, even if they secretly judged her western clothing and modern lifestyle behind her back.

After meeting her, the seed of inspiration had taken root and never withered. *That* was the kind of future I wanted for myself.

I didn't feel comfortable asking my parents for money. This job was a better solution because I enjoyed being independent, and it wasn't something I would ever give up. Especially after seeing everything my sister was dealing with in her marriage.

'This was just supposed to be a summer thing,' Sal continued disapprovingly. 'If you carry on working on weekends, how will we find time to do our study sessions?'

'Don't worry, we'll still be study buddies,' I assured her. 'Our revision sessions are a necessity.'

'For *me*, not for you. You're the smartest girl in school. You'll get into whatever uni you apply to.'

'That's not true.' I was being humble – I knew full well that I was a top student in our school.

'Seriously though, you're an actual geek. I know it's important that we get into our dream unis but it's just as important to make memories in our last year of school together. We can't forget to have fun!'

'We won't,' I promised.

Saliha was my favourite person, the only one I confided in and really laughed with. I had other friends, but no one I hung out with outside of school. Of course, that was mostly because of all the curfews my parents enforced, but Mum never really seemed to mind much when I asked to go over to Saliha's. As rebellious as Sal was, she knew exactly how to behave whenever any elders were around. It really was an art.

We'd been best friends for as long as I could remember because we'd grown up together. We'd attended the same primary and secondary school, mosque lessons, and now sixth form too. While Saliha was a total extrovert, I was the quiet one who never let people get too close.

A large part of the reason Saliha and I had such different personalities despite our many shared experiences was the way we'd been raised. We'd been next-door neighbours for over ten years, and while her home was always full of people and laughter and love, mine was quiet. Strained.

'Do you want to do something after work?' Sal called to me while cleaning foundation smudges off the counter. 'The weather's amazing.'

I was searching our stock for a concealer shade but paused to give Sal an apologetic look. 'I wish I could, but I'm seeing my brother after work. He needs help with something.'

When we had mere minutes of our shift left to kill, I heard a shriek from our manager. Amy was usually as devoid of emotion as a zombie, so Sal and I exchanged a concerned look.

'Some of The Exes have just been spotted here,' she announced, radiating the air of someone brave enough to spill a state secret.

My stomach did a strange tumble.

Of course I knew The Exes also lived in London, but their London usually seemed to exist in a different dimension to mine. Even working at a luxury store like Selfridges, I'd never seen an Ex in person before. I locked eyes with Saliha, and we flew to each other like magnets.

My insides buzzed with excitement. These people seemed more dream than reality. I'd watched their videos for years, and now there was a chance I would see them in the flesh. It felt surreal.

As a large, noisy crowd spilled into our department, all the staff stopped working and either stared at the incoming mass of people or had their phones ready to capture some footage of what was going on.

'I think I see Karim,' Saliha hissed fervently, pointing ahead.

I looked to where she was gesturing.

It *was* Karim Malik.

The most handsome, charming Ex. The screams were ear-piercing as people flocked all around him. Through the dense crowd, I caught glimpses of him with stern security officers on either side.

To my astonishment, he didn't look like ... himself. Sure, he was still the sleek, gorgeous raven-haired guy I was used to seeing online, but something felt wrong. He had an intense grimace on his face, as though he was fed up with the world, and there were dark circles bruising the area around his eyes.

He looked utterly sick of the cameras, the people, the hysteria.

Saliha readied her iPhone camera as he passed by.

A girl ran through our make-up counter in an attempt to reach him, probably to nab a selfie. She managed to grab his arm for a second before one of his bodyguards scooped her up and hauled her back.

Karim scowled at the girl, and then glanced a little to his side. I was directly in his line of sight.

OMG, this is the moment I've been waiting for! Is he looking at me?

His eyes met mine and ...

Anger. Annoyance. Disgust.

I flinched.

The world moved on swiftly, bodies and colours swirling so rapidly I blinked to clear the fuzz from my brain.

It was all over within a heartbeat, but I couldn't seem to draw breath. The moment was stamped on to my mind, where I knew it would remain, probably forever.

Karim Malik, the subject of so much of my attention, had looked at me as though I was . . . trash.

He'd likely already forgotten my face; I was just another girl among the overbearing masses fawning over him. This encounter was a profound reminder of how big and powerful he was and how small and insignificant I was.

I had never before felt so conscious of my appearance, my ordinariness, my non-existent social status.

I had never before felt so worthless.

Karim

4

The rush was maddening.

It was quieter on the top floor, and I could finally breathe. I brushed away the bodyguards, making it clear I was going to enter alone. I walked into Alto by San Carlo, the rooftop bar and restaurant – our favourite spot at Selfridges.

The chatter and laughter instantly evaporated to an awkward silence. I didn't bother to greet them, only offered a quick analytical glance at their outfits, all carefully chosen to garner attention and set trends.

Ozwald Boateng blazers. Vivienne Westwood shirts and dresses. Alexander McQueen scarves. Multiple items of jewellery gracing their necks and fingers. Earth-toned Mulberry bags resting in their laps or at their feet.

Everything they wore was likely gifted. My delivery room was probably brimming with similar pieces, but I hadn't checked it this month. My mind was elsewhere.

Although the entire restaurant had been cleared for us, we weren't really alone. We were never really alone any more. I couldn't remember the last time I felt it was just us Exes together – not now that we always had our phones in hand, exploiting every moment and posting it for millions to gorge on.

'Why did you choose to meet here?' I challenged the group.

No one responded. It was an accusation more than a question.

'This conversation should take place away from the spotlight. In utter privacy, where we can be completely *honest*.' I emphasized the last word while looking at Chloe.

She suddenly found her French manicure rather interesting.

'Clearly there's a snitch with easy access to us,' Felicity answered tensely. 'It could be one of our cleaners. Or partners. Mr Ex seems to have plenty of snitches in his pocket. At this point, I wouldn't be surprised if he's inserted hidden cameras and microphones around our homes.'

'A random, last-minute location was our best bet for privacy,' Abeo added.

I pulled up a chair and got comfortable, leaning back and taking a moment to enjoy the London skyline the restaurant offered.

My entire life was in walking distance from here: my school, where I lived, the places that carried my most profound memories and secrets.

This was home.

But London was also beginning to feel like a stranger, always shifting and mutating, refusing to stay stable for even a moment. My city was the lover I couldn't figure out: sometimes I woke to tenderness and warm kisses, other times to a cold, empty bed.

When I turned back to the group again, they swiftly stopped exchanging loaded glances. I relished their muteness, their confusion at what to say or do. It was a pleasant change from their usual overconfident, carefree manner.

It would be an understatement to say I felt left out these days, so it was good to watch them squirm under the scrutiny of my gaze. Ironic, really: they were completely fine with having the world watch every aspect of their lives, and yet a single look from me had them reeling.

The Exes.

Chloe Clark. Abeo Okon. Felicity Wong. Sanjay Arya.

My best friends, occasionally my worst enemies.

'So calling a meeting here has nothing to do with the hype of us being spotted together in public after Mr Ex's latest post?' I asked sarcastically.

Abeo splayed his hands on either side of his blazer and waggled his fingers enthusiastically. 'Fair enough. I just couldn't bear the thought of not being papped in today's outfit. They always get the best candid photos for the gram.'

Felicity snorted and Abeo chuckled. But after seeing my expression, they swiftly suppressed their humour.

'What?' Abeo asked defensively. 'I like making sure my feed is fed.' He crossed his arms, his biceps straining the sleeves of his blazer. 'Besides, this is our job. It's what we do.' He looked right at me as he finished with, 'You're the one who told us to always think about business first if we want to become the best in the game.'

This was one of the things I admired most about Abeo. He could switch from being cheeky to discussing serious business in a heartbeat; he was the perfect influencer.

It was the truth. I had once said that. And meant it.

The social media space was competitive, with fresh talent popping up every day. We followed a set of rules to ensure we continued to grow the platforms we'd carved for ourselves.

Sunlight glinted off Sanjay's gold earring, and my eyes settled on its subtle, elegant *Exes* logo.

One of the rules was that whenever we were in public, regardless of the event, we'd wear at least one item from our own brand; it was the most natural and powerful way to drive sales. Today, I had worn our cufflinks, Felicity had chosen our white satin headband, Chloe our pearl necklace, Abeo our silk pocket square and Sanjay one of our earrings.

Chloe sighed and then said, 'Can we stop overanalysing things? We chose to meet here because we were in the mood for some nice drinks, seafood and a much-needed catch-up.'

I wish you'd be in the mood for some honesty occasionally, I wanted to hiss at her.

There was a lot I wanted to say to her, but I couldn't. Not right now, not when everything was still so fragile between us. A sarcastic retort was bubbling at the tip of my tongue, so I looked down at the food instead, trying to control my breathing.

There was a charcuterie board displaying an assortment of cheeses, marinated cured meats and Italian bread. The seafood platter was filled with rock oysters, tempura prawns and soft-shell crab.

My stomach clenched with hunger but the mere thought of consuming any of it made me nauseous.

'Look, Karim,' Abeo said impatiently, running a hand over his short-cropped Afro. 'It's time for us to start planning this month's content. We want you to be present in our videos again.'

I'd missed this – making plans with The Exes. I looked at Abeo, taking in his mahogany skin and full lips. He was the son of a British Nigerian businessman involved in property development throughout the UK and West Africa. His mother was an artist from France, and traces of a French accent occasionally peeked through when he spoke. His style was certainly a mixture of all these influences and gave him a sophisticated, alluring charm.

'Maybe it's time to take a step back,' I replied in a tired tone, 'and think about the direction we're all heading in.'

Abeo scoffed. 'The direction is obviously thirty million subscribers. We're only off by three million.'

It was a relief his clingy boyfriend, James Sawyer, wasn't there to egg him on as usual; I could almost hear him echo *thirty million subscribers* in the background for dramatic effect. They'd been joined at the hip ever since they started going out, and James simply tried too hard to be accepted as one of us, to be popular and seen. It was exhausting to witness, doomed as he was to fail.

For there could be no more Exes.

That was at least one thing we all still agreed on. Perhaps one of the only things.

'I'm sure you can all understand that I need a break. Especially since Mr Ex just posted about the abortion.'

I watched their expressions tighten as I finally brought up the issue more openly.

Chloe looked out the window, her nostrils flaring a touch. Her long blonde hair framed her in perfect sun-kissed waves. She always looked modelesque and camera-ready. I had once admired that about her. Now it only made me want to shake some sense into her, to tell her to let go sometimes, to stop caring so much about the stuff that didn't matter as much as the stuff that *did*.

When she turned back to us, she looked straight at me, her bright green eyes somewhat glassy. There were so many times I had run my fingers through her hair, across her lips, over her skin. But now the mere thought of any of that set me on edge.

'How did the news of the abortion leak?' Chloe whispered, her barely audible voice empty of its soft, melodious lilt for once. 'Only *we* knew.'

The Exes eyed each other suspiciously.

I analysed Chloe's expression.

A small, sickened part of me had thought that perhaps she'd been the one to tell Mr Ex. It would certainly keep her in the spotlight for a couple of weeks, right when she was trying to kickstart her singing career.

The tortured look on her face . . . no, it couldn't have been her.

But there were so many times I'd watched Chloe lie to Felicity about her whereabouts when we'd first started dating and wanted to keep it on the down-low. She'd been so convincing that even *I'd* almost believed she'd been enjoying family time the night before and not making out in bed with me.

'I didn't say anything to anyone,' Sanjay declared.

Felicity looked Chloe right in the eye as she said, 'Neither did I.'

It had never been this explicit – our suspicions of one another, the lack of trust between us.

'Obviously it was me then,' Abeo said with a manic smile.

'This is not the time to be sarcastic,' Sanjay replied.

Felicity sighed heavily as she took out a bottle of white nail polish from her handbag and began applying it to her thumb. 'I think it's stupid to start pointing fingers at each other.' Sanjay eyed her distraction distastefully and she shrugged. 'What? It's chipped in some places.'

I snapped. 'What the fuck is wrong with us? Are we incapable of having a single serious conversation about a very serious thing?'

Felicity snorted loudly. I gave her a death stare. She blew once over her polish and held her hands up in defence. 'I'm so sorry. Laughing at the worst times is basically my coping mechanism.'

Chloe smacked the table with a fist, making us all jump. 'I wish I hadn't told any of you about the abortion.'

I could feel the rage twisting on my face and didn't try to hide it. The fact that she'd told me *after* she'd done it . . . that she had almost decided not to tell me at all, had said that it was her body, her choice . . .

She had assumed I'd try to convince her to keep it, leading her to end her singing career before it had even taken off. She didn't even give me a chance to prove her wrong. I was still coming to terms with it all. She'd made so many assumptions about me, about us. I didn't think I'd ever be able to forgive her.

'If we're the only ones who knew,' I replied with deathly calm, 'then one of us five is a mole. Or one of us told someone else who can't be trusted.'

'I constantly feel *watched*, and not in a good way,' Sanjay said darkly, a stroke of sunlight suddenly streaming across his rich brown skin. 'There's stuff I haven't shared with anyone that's been posted on his blog. How the hell does he get access to it? Do you think he has people stalking us around the clock? Is he hacking our phones?'

Felicity's fingers tapped the table impatiently. 'I feel it too. I don't know whether it's just the fans being everywhere we go, but I always feel stalked.'

Silence.

Chloe combed through her hair with her pale, slender fingers. 'Whoever Mr Ex is, he definitely goes to our school. If we trace everything right back to the beginning, the way he described things in his earliest posts – where we eat, our classes, the events we attend – these aren't things he could have learned through watching our videos. He's from *our crowd*.'

Abeo nodded in agreement. 'And if we don't identify and stop him soon, he could really mess things up for us.'

'His recent posts are ruthless, and we're starting to lose money.' Felicity sulked. 'Two American brand deals have fallen through because of this . . . abortion controversy.'

I exhaled. 'Just imagine if the other stuff starts getting out.'

We sat in silence as the gravity of the situation settled in our minds. We all had our secrets. Plenty of them. Many which we hadn't even shared with each other.

Just a few months ago, Abeo and I had caught an early flight back from a brand event in Italy. We'd headed straight to his for a late-night swim only to walk in on his father relaxing in the jacuzzi with a naked woman who looked young enough to hang out with us. Abeo had told me to keep my mouth shut and we'd never spoken of it again. As an only child, he'd always been close to his parents; he'd never want his mum to find out, for his picture-perfect family to break apart.

As for Chloe, as well-established as her family were in England, they had relatives in Scotland who were still gang members, involved in the distribution of drugs throughout the country. The truth was that her roots were inextricably linked to that world; it was how the Clarks had amassed enough money to leave Glasgow and relocate to the heart of London in the first place.

Moving on to Felicity, the dance choreography she was *known* for, the very thing that had caused her TikTok to blow up, had been copied (albeit with slight alterations) from a dance group with a smaller platform. They'd tried to kick up a fuss to get credit for the dance routine, but their platform simply wasn't big enough to draw attention. Since then, Felicity had worked hard on creating original dance moves, but if people knew she'd stolen her most popular ones, they'd question everything she'd ever put out there.

And finally, Sanjay. During a stupid, drunken dare game a year ago, he had broken into our head teacher's garage and set his car on fire. The fire had spread to his house, where his wife and three children were sleeping. The fire brigade had come in time, no one had been injured, but the loss had been significant

43

enough that if Sanjay was ever exposed as having been the culprit, he'd likely find himself expelled, unwanted in any other school, and possibly even imprisoned.

If Mr Ex got a whiff of any of this, if he exposed it online . . .

There was far too much at risk for all of us – our reputations, our families, our *futures*.

Sanjay cleared his throat. 'He's so sharp, so careful about what he uploads. Always just enough to keep everyone guessing about who he is, but never enough breadcrumbs to lead us anywhere near his real identity.'

'Perhaps it's time,' I said coldly, 'that we sharpen up too.'

Everyone exchanged glances again. But this time, I felt included.

Chloe was The Singer.

Sanjay was The Artist.

Felicity was The Dancer.

Abeo was The King of Fashion.

And Karim Malik? Well, I didn't really have a talent like any of those.

My skill was recognizing what they all brought to the table, and utilizing it to produce addictive group content and merchandise. But that was the very skill that brought in the most views and revenue, that bound our friendship into a brand, forging a lifelong bond of secrecy, publicity and heartbreak.

'Let's end him,' I said, venom coating every word. 'Whoever the hell Mr Expose is, *he* needs to be exposed. And we're going to make it happen.'

Zara

5

Saliha and I walked towards Bond Street Station after our shift and I could no longer hold it in. 'Did you find it weird how Karim Malik looked at us?'

Sal's brown eyes met my darker ones as she frowned. 'I think everyone was weirded out by his death stares. And he was blinking so much – it was like he was winking a Morse code message to someone.'

I snorted loudly.

'Anyways,' Sal continued, 'where are you meeting your brother?'

'Notting Hill Gate Station,' I replied.

She hesitated for a moment, then asked, 'Did your mum agree easily?'

I shrugged. 'Not really. But I'm not letting my parents keep me away from him any more.'

A few years ago, my brother Farhan had told our parents that he was in love with Morowa, a Christian Ghanaian woman he'd met at university, and our very Pakistani, very Muslim dad hadn't approved one bit. Farhan bhai had always been strongheaded though, so he'd married her anyway.

Dad had disowned him. Threw him out like an old pair of shoes.

I often wondered whether Dad was really as cold as he came across. Surely he felt pain and loss too? He must still think about Farhan . . .

My brother had been a burst of colour within our home, always hiding behind doors to scare us, singing random Bollywood songs and laughing his annoyingly loud laugh. Dad had held him as a newborn, watched him grow into the kind, warm man he'd become. It made no sense to me how someone could throw away that bond so willingly.

But then again, it made complete sense.

This was what happened when you were obsessed with tradition, honour and reputation.

Even if Farhan bhai had become distant from us, at least he was in love and happily married. That was a lot more than I could say about my sister Aisha, who'd obeyed our parents' every decision. It haunted me every single day that Aisha baji had let herself get swept away in the storm of our parents' rules and expectations. She'd been stuck weathering it for so long now and there didn't seem to be any way out.

I wanted to become more like Farhan bhai, brave enough to make my own decisions and stick by them, because something in my gut told me that my future would look a lot like my sister's if I didn't . . .

'Have your parents seen their grandson yet?' Sal asked quietly. 'Zain's *so* cute. And he looks just like Farhan bhai!'

'No, they haven't. I did FaceTime Mum while I was babysitting him once. She didn't say anything, but she didn't hang up either. So . . . that's that.'

I knew Mum missed Farhan. He was her favourite child. Whenever I asked to go over to his place, she eventually softened up and gave me permission, even making excuses for me whenever Dad asked what I was up to. It was the only time she stood up for me in front of him.

Sal placed a soothing hand on my back. 'Is Farhan bhai's business doing all right?'

'It's been tough to set it up,' I replied honestly. 'But I think they're going to make it.'

Just over a year ago, Farhan and Morowa had opened Jashan, a modern Pakistani dessert shop in Ilford. They'd been advertising heavily on social media, and even Saliha had helped us get word out, but there were so many South Asian confectioners around, so the competition was fierce.

'They're bidding for a wedding catering opportunity today,' I continued hopefully as we entered the station and tapped through the ticket barriers. 'And they're short-staffed, so I'm helping out.'

'I hope it goes well,' said Sal. 'Their food is amazing and deserves more recognition.'

Jashan was going to be big someday. I could feel it. Farhan bhai had studied business and Morowa was a chef, and something about the way they worked together, combining their ideas and cultural worlds, told me that their difficult days would soon be behind them.

'If they get the job, I'll bring you some of Morowa's desserts to celebrate,' I said as I stepped on to the escalator descending towards the train I needed.

'Oh, they better get the job,' Sal called out just before she disappeared from my view.

Karim

6

'All we've managed to conclude is that Mr Ex is someone we know and probably a fellow student at St Victor's,' Abeo said with a scowl.

'Yes, that's literally it,' Chloe replied, eyes fixed on the small mirror in her hand as she reapplied a pink Chanel lip gloss. 'We should basically suspect all the people in our lives, even our friends.'

'Hmm,' Felicity pondered, absent-mindedly playing with her Hermès bracelet. 'I can't shake the feeling that he's *really* going to come for us this year, just before we all break up for university. I think that's why he's trying to reach out to us personally now.'

My stomach did a flip. 'What do you mean?'

Felicity exchanged a look with Abeo before meeting my eyes. 'Mr Ex has started sending Abeo and me anonymous texts.'

'Why didn't you tell me?' I asked incredulously.

'Erm . . .' Felicity's shoulders hitched up in an awkward shrug. 'You were a little busy?'

I let out a slow breath, irritation boiling under my skin.

'The texts have been playful so far,' Abeo explained. 'Only quips about him knowing where we are, who we're with – which, to be fair, everyone knows once we get spotted.'

Felicity coughed pointedly. 'But he seems to know our whereabouts *before* others do. And ... he's hinted he knows more. Like, secrets. We need to be careful because clearly he's not holding back on uploading sensitive info.'

'Has he asked you to do anything for him yet?' Chloe asked tightly.

The *yet* echoed in the silence around us, sharp and unwelcome, like a snake slithering its way around our circle, catching each of our necks in its snare.

'Whatever messages he's sent, I want to see them,' I stated squarely. 'We should try tracing the messages. Here, let me take a look.'

Abeo's brows shot up and he began adjusting his perfectly positioned silk pocket square. I realized that handing over your phone for someone to look through – giving them access to your private messages and photos and internet history – was like letting them into the deepest corners of your mind. There was a time we'd been so close we'd known everything about each other, but things were different now. I couldn't pinpoint the exact moment that cracks had formed in our friendship, but they had, and it felt like there was no going back.

'Is that OK?' I asked more gently.

There were half-hearted nods and murmurs of agreement. But I knew there would be excuse after excuse when it came down to actually showing me the messages. Perhaps I'd have to wait until Mr Ex reached out to me personally. There were so many ways he could blackmail me, ruin my reputation, destroy everything I'd built. Drawing breath suddenly became difficult; I unbuttoned my shirt further and inhaled deeply. This wasn't the time or place to lose my calm.

'He's getting nastier, isn't he?' Sanjay asked tensely. 'And with the way he keeps learning everything about us, it's like he's always one step ahead.'

'If he wants to keep playing with us, we need to show him that we're going to win,' I stated bluntly.

They all looked at me, as though waiting for instructions to follow. It was a situation I was used to.

I looked at their faces.

The diversity. The beauty. The talent.

Even this, I had cherry-picked. A stream of calculated decisions – deciding which of my friends would become members of The Exes. I'd selected the people who commanded attention the moment they walked into a room. The ones everyone loved to look at, speak about, get close to.

My father, Rohaan Malik, was the owner of the Malik Group, a transnational conglomerate with headquarters in all the major cities. He was one of the wealthiest men in the country, and although my mother had a way of coming across as soft and graceful, she was every bit the business shark her husband was. They may not have spent much time raising their children, leaving me with nannies and au pairs, but I'd still picked up my business savvy from them.

The Exes were my circle, my closest friends, and had been for years, but they were also a business decision. I'd been the first to see the potential in us banding together. We offered the real-life version of those sitcoms people grew addicted to – a group of best friends growing up together, experiencing life's different phases and chasing their dreams.

And just as I'd predicted, we'd blown up. Almost instantaneously.

I stood and buttoned my blazer. 'I have a family occasion to attend.'

Chloe's face fell. 'This is important.'

'I know, but I'm about to meet my brother's future wife for the first time. I can't skip this.'

'Oh my God,' Felicity squealed. 'Another Big Fat Indian Wedding? I loved all the clothes, food and dancing during Priya's events. Even our followers were obsessed!'

We'd had a blast during Sanjay's older sister's summer wedding festivities last year, and the content we'd captured had been a great boost for our platforms.

'This wedding's going to be both Indian *and* Pakistani,' I said, smiling, 'so be prepared for one hell of a winter wedding.'

'They're getting married this winter?' Abeo exclaimed. 'That's short notice. What's the rush?'

'I guess they're eager to begin their life together. In Islam, they need to get their nikah done before they can start living together and being more open as a couple. They're allowed to spend time together now but a lot of it is chaperoned, which I'm sure they find frustrating. Besides, I know you're just worried about the outfits.' I smirked at Abeo knowingly. 'Mum will obviously hook us up with the freshest Fouzia Faris drip.'

I gave them a swift nod and made for the exit.

'Can I talk to you?' Chloe blurted.

'Sure,' I replied politely, even though I really didn't want to. It just felt wrong to say no to her.

Chloe possessed a sensitive, volatile personality. She could go from being excessively happy about the simplest of things, like having a good cup of tea, to being an emotional mess because of the slightest inconvenience. When we were together, she'd had a way of dragging my mood around with hers. That was certainly something I didn't miss.

We walked out of earshot and turned to each other.

She wrung her fingers together anxiously. 'I wanted to apologize one last time and ask whether we can put everything behind us.'

As much as I didn't want to hurt her, I couldn't lie. Not about this. 'This isn't going to be like those times when everything went back to normal after a day or two. I need time.'

Her eyes filled.

'I just can't believe I found out from *Sanjay* that you reached out to him instead of me. That he's the one who convinced you to even tell me.'

Chloe couldn't look me in the eye. 'But we *all* go to him when we're in shit. He's got this chill, non-judgemental vibe. And I was just so . . . scared.'

Tears rolled down her face, and I just about kept myself back from brushing them away as I'd done a hundred times before. Anything I said right now would be the wrong thing to say, so I chose silence.

'We're scheduled to attend some events together,' she said, wiping underneath her eyes. 'Queen Charlotte's Ball, which is tomorrow. Then there's London Fashion Week and the Dior Couture Party. Are you still coming with me?'

I remembered all the events we'd enjoyed together over the summer, completely infatuated with each other, drunk on laughter and sunlight.

We'd attended Royal Ascot and Wimbledon, and then escaped to the French Riviera to be alone. Those first few days in Cap-Ferrat had been a dream; we'd decided to ditch our phones completely so we could just be in the moment, something that was usually impossible for Chloe.

We drank champagne, enjoyed panoramic views of the Côte d'Azur from our villa's rooftop, swam in idyllic coves and read books in the shade of palm trees; we ate at Michelin-starred beach restaurants and spent the nights wrapped up in each other's arms . . .

And then, one evening, everything shifted. Chloe became distant.

The following morning I'd woken up alone, every trace of her gone.

She'd texted to let me know she was back in London. I'd been confused and furious, but I'd tried to be understanding, assumed that perhaps something important had cropped up. But as much as I tried to contact her after that, she didn't respond.

Irritated with her vanishing act, I decided to stay in France alone for a while.

Mere days after I'd returned to London, Sanjay invited me over to speak with him and Chloe at his flat in Notting Hill.

That was when I'd learned the truth: not just that Chloe had been pregnant, but that she'd already had an abortion.

I was shocked. And hurt.

She'd kept me in the dark about something that concerned me so intimately, and what hurt just as much was that Chloe was clearly in the habit of keeping secrets from me. What other things could she possibly be hiding? All this secrecy and lying from someone who had once been my closest confidante was messing with my head.

'Karim?' Chloe pressed.

Once the memories started flooding in, they wouldn't stop. It was as though a fist had clenched around my heart and refused to let go. I had to honour our booked schedules as The Exes, but I didn't want to push things to go back to normal between us before I was ready.

'I remember promising to be your escort at Queen Charlotte's Ball and I'm a man of my word. But everything else . . . I think it'll be good for us to get some space from each other.'

Chloe nodded, looking deep in thought. When she met my eyes again, she smiled, and her shoulders relaxed a little.

'No one looks quite as dashing as you in white tie. People won't be able to keep their eyes off us.'

It was the kind of thing she used to say before we'd record our couples content. It suddenly became difficult to look at her and, from the way she was avoiding eye contact too, I knew I wasn't the only one feeling overwhelmed with all the memories we shared.

'So, I guess I'll see you tomorrow then,' she said awkwardly.

I nodded and watched her walk back to the others.

Felicity was demonstrating a new dance routine. Chloe took her blazer off and joined right in, giggling loudly as she messed up a move. As quick as that, she seemed perfectly fine.

It reminded me of just how manipulative and self-serving she could be when she wanted something. Sometimes it was difficult to tell what was real with Chloe, and what was only for the cameras and her personal gain.

'Ouch, what are you doing?' Felicity laughed as Chloe messed up another move and twirled right into her.

Abeo snorted. 'I recorded that. It'll be good for behind-the-scenes footage.'

It would be a while before I could join in with this sort of content creation again, if I ever managed to talk myself into it. The more time I spent away from it, the more ridiculous it all seemed.

Within seconds, we could block out our emotions, give the fans what they wanted to see, ignore the madness of it all . . .

And I was really starting to hate it.

When The Exes aren't Flirting, They're Fighting: London Social Season Set to End with a Bang

Nothing brings London's elite crowd together quite like The Social Season, and it's been marvellous this year.

You'll be pleased to hear that it isn't over just yet – Queen Charlotte's Ball is taking place tomorrow evening and, from what I've heard, at least four of The Exes will be attending. Before all the tragic drama unfolded between them, Karim was set to escort Chloe for her debut. Ironic that she'll be dressed all bridalesque and may not be seen with the groom we've always imagined her with.

Let's take a second to remember that our Chlo's a smart lass (with some rather street-smart Glaswegian roots!), and she thrives most when she's got a monopoly over the spotlight. Perhaps she realized she's been barking up the wrong tree this entire time and reached out to someone else to escort her. Someone whose family possesses Old Money (the *real* kind) and some sort of royal title – now *that* would make for the perfect escort to a ball (and would be an admirable social-climbing move).

Images of a dashing designer-clad prince riding a white stallion in search of Lady Clark are coming to mind, but perhaps I'm being a hopeless romantic; we all know this crowd doesn't quite do tender dates and innocent kisses. It's more likely for there to be a Cinderella-inspired sex-tape scandal or ball gown ripped wide open in the throes of passion. Either way, Chloe Clark's entrance (and more importantly, her *escort*) is something to look out for.

The feuding Exes have been largely absent from their YouTube channel, but they're still in sight elsewhere. Felicity Wong has been posting at least three TikToks a day (please note that if you do attempt to follow any of her dance tutorials, make sure you have plenty of space around you. I was bringing it so hard I almost fractured my left arm). I just love how *original* the routine is! But I'll refrain from sharing any clips of me dancing, just so you guys feel like you have a chance. Besides, I'm in no mood to break the internet . . . just yet.

Sanjay Arya has been active on his blog, sharing his latest artworks which celebrate South Asian Heritage Month. The richly hued figures in his art have a shapely, alluring quality – maybe he could pick up a thing or two about style from his own heritage (he practically lives in dull, paint-flecked *bin bags*)! Even Karim's posting content again, and although he still doesn't have a talent like the rest of the gang, he's topless in one of his recent posts. You know what that means: stop whatever the hell you're doing and go check it out.

Abeo had afternoon tea at The Savoy with his annoyingly chipper boyfriend. I mean, is it even legal to have that many teeth? With those pearly razors shooting out, isn't it some sort of health and safety hazard for Abeo to kiss him? Anyways, his dress sense has certainly improved since our Fashion King stepped in, and I guess it does make him less annoying now that he's ditched all those preppy denim dungarees. Goodness, that guy used to dress as though he was making a statement about not letting ugly garments feel left out.

Excuse me while I bite into some freshly baked scones from Soho's Secret Tea Room and browse the internet for this season's stellar white gowns. Catch my predictions for what the debutantes will wear over on Instagram. So far, it looks like it'll be a moment for Stella McCartney and Christian Dior this year. Oh, and do remember to get on your knees tonight and pray to the Good Lord that we aren't left revolted by a series of fashion disasters tomorrow. I'm still recovering from the outfits showcased at the Wong Summer Charity Gala that Felicity's parents threw. The guests may have been raising funds for charity, but it looked like *they* needed it just as much ...

This crowd may put on a good show for the world, but I hope they remember I'm an insider with a keen eye for how things look without all the filters. Stay tuned for a filter-free update on this Buzzingly Beguiling Ball.

Yours Unfaithfully,
Mr Ex

Karim

7

'You took *ages*,' Kiran scowled. 'They're ten minutes away.'

'I'm here and that's all that matters,' I responded tightly. 'You know I hate being pestered –'

The doorbell rang.

Kiran went to get it. Mum had made it clear that the butlers were to back off for the day and that we needed to step in to cater to these special guests ourselves.

When I saw the first person enter, my mouth fell open a touch. This was definitely not what I'd expected. She was perhaps one of the most beautiful women I'd ever seen, and her style was immaculate. She wore a sleeveless emerald-green kurta with intricate gold threadwork, and the jewels at her ears and neck matched it perfectly.

Her long brown hair was half-up and pulled back sleekly from her face to reveal small, round features. She didn't seem to be wearing much make-up and certainly didn't need it; her milky brown skin and green eyes possessed a mesmerizing quality.

Instantly, I could imagine her becoming a Malik.

Sana greeted Kiran warmly, then turned to me.

'Hello, nice to finally meet you,' she said in a posh American accent, making me blink. 'I'm Sana.' Well, I certainly didn't have to worry about not being able to communicate with her . . .

She extended a hand towards me, which I shook. She had a confident grip and a kind smile.

'This is Karim,' Kiran told Sana.

'Of course,' she said through a laugh. 'I'm not going to pretend I haven't come across your videos. They're great!'

'Thank you,' I replied. 'It's lovely to meet you.'

I greeted her parents and older brother and then we all made our way to the living room.

'I love the décor,' Sana said admiringly.

'Ah yes,' Mum said, looking pleased. 'I had my interior designers infuse natural, contemporary elements with a vintage South Asian edge.'

I looked around the expansive room and imagined I was seeing it for the first time. It was minimalistic and modern with plenty of natural light, and the few decorative pieces scattered about were striking and intentional.

Sana's parents were in the process of introducing their son when Azad appeared.

'As-salaam-alaikum everyone,' he said breathlessly, placing his briefcase near the sofa and smoothing a hand down his tie. 'Sorry I'm a bit late. My meeting ran over.'

'It certainly looks like you rushed over as soon as you could,' Mum said teasingly, and everyone laughed.

He looked down self-consciously, and I cringed a little. I'd never seen him so unsure of himself before – he usually carried the stoic grace and sophistication of our father. When he moved to hug Sana's father, he nearly tripped over his own foot and flapped his arms on either side to regain his balance.

Kiran snorted loudly and I pressed a hand over my mouth to keep in my own raucous laughter.

'Take it easy jaan,' Mum said with a knowing smile. 'Sana's not going anywhere.'

Azad recovered quickly and met each member of the Qureshi family with a hug, excluding Sana, to whom he modestly gave an awkward wave, making everyone chuckle once again. It was like I'd entered one of the romantic Pakistani dramas that Mum liked to watch.

'So, how's the product launch going, Sana beti?' Dad asked while Azad seated himself at his right.

'It's great,' she replied enthusiastically. 'My new lipstick collection was released just last month, and it's been a busy time with advertising and orders.'

As the conversation continued, I learned that Sana had studied accounting and finance at Lahore University of Management Sciences and set up her own beauty brand, named Sana Beauty, soon after. She had a social media ecosystem which boasted just under two million followers. Although that had nothing on the thirty million or so followers The Exes had on each platform, I knew the effort that went into building a brand online and I was rather impressed.

Sana Beauty products were currently among the bestselling make-up in Pakistan and had made her a millionaire in her own right, separate from her family's wealth, which was also significant. Sana's father was the owner of the Quresh Hotel Group, which had chains throughout Dubai and America as well as Pakistan.

Azad was helping Dad run the Malik Group and doing incredibly well at it. Together, Azad and Sana would be a real power couple. This wasn't going to be the imbalanced relationship I'd been imagining, where Azad would marry a shy, traditional girl with a completely different lifestyle and mindset. They suited each other, and in the way they kept exchanging glances, I could sense the chemistry between them.

I was happy for him.

But I also felt a strange emptiness settle inside me.

Although I'd had a handful of flings in the past, my only real relationship had been with Chloe. We'd dated on and off for years, but things had only become more toxic over time because we never seemed to be able to communicate well, which only increased our frustration and arguments.

In comparison, this relationship just seemed so wholesome, genuine, *right*.

I wanted to know what it was like to experience such a thing, to be with someone who understood me.

I'd always assumed that arranged-marriage introductions or dating girls from my own background wouldn't suit me, but clearly I'd made inexperienced assumptions. I could sense my mind shifting in this regard, realizing that maybe dating a girl who shared my culture was exactly the key to finding someone who understood me ...

'When I was growing up in Lahore,' Mum said, with a hand on Sana's mother's lap, 'Rahima was my best friend. We lived in the same area and went to the same school.'

'Then Fouzia moved to the UK for university,' Aunty Rahima continued in a strong Pakistani accent, 'met your dad, got married and forgot all about me.'

They both threw their heads back and laughed loudly. I fake-laughed politely with them, as did Kiran.

'We were still in touch here and there, especially on Facebook,' Mum said mischievously. 'And then, last summer, Azad and I went to Pakistan to prepare for the launch of my new collection. One day, we were out browsing in Emporium Mall when we bumped into Rahima and Sana. The rest is history.'

'Who knew our children would one day change our relationship from friendship to family?' Aunty Rahima pondered fondly. 'Subhanallah.'

Mum nodded heartily. 'And who knew that exactly a year from that first meeting we'd be planning their wedding?'

Sana looked down at her hands and for the first time I saw the hint of a shy, traditional Pakistani girl surrounded by people discussing her marriage.

'Not long to go now,' Aunty Rahima said keenly, and then turned towards her husband. 'To my surprise, Abdullah is pleased that the mehndi, baraat *and* walima functions will all be held here in London.'

Uncle Abdullah smiled and his thick moustache, which closely resembled his son's, curled upwards. 'We have so much family and far too many friends in Pakistan,' he explained.

'It would've been impossible to organize a wedding of less than a thousand people.'

Mum lifted her nose a fraction. 'We also have many people we could invite, but we don't let just anyone attend our events. We like to keep them *exclusive*.'

Aunty Rahima opened her mouth as though to say something but then decided against it.

It was a part of our culture to throw big weddings – all my cousins had done so in the past. It was a way of showing your status, how well connected and wealthy you were, and I could tell the pettiness among the elders was already beginning.

'Since time is of the essence, I've started getting things in order,' Mum said to Sana. 'As you know, I've arranged for the food tasting to take place now. Tomorrow, I've booked you in at my flagship store in Regent Street, so you can browse the bridal collections. Once you've chosen your outfits, we can visit the jewellers.'

Sana paused for a moment. 'I've already had some bridal outfits made in Lahore. I've also booked appointments with some bridal boutiques around Mayfair and Ilford Lane for later this week.'

Mum jerked as though she'd been slapped.

While some of the most influential people in the country had to go on the waiting list to visit the Fouzia Faris store, her future daughter-in-law was insisting on looking elsewhere . . .

I found myself praying Mum wouldn't break out into a dramatic tantrum or say something hurtful to Sana in response. I had a vivid image of her snatching a bunch of bridal gowns from Sana's reluctant grip, setting them on fire and shouting, *I'm doing you a favour!*

Mum and Kiran exchanged a look.

The look.

This was something they'd discuss between themselves later.

'Well, I'm always here to help if you need anything,' Mum said coldly, choosing to reel it in for once.

I let out an inaudible sigh of relief. Aunty Rahima fidgeted uncomfortably, and Dad's brows were a little too high.

'I'll check how the wedding caterers are getting on with setting up,' Kiran interjected awkwardly as she stood. 'They should be ready for us soon.'

'Of course, Kiran darling,' Mum said loudly, then pinned her gaze on Sana. 'As you can see, we like to arrange things *collectively as a family* over here.'

The first dig at her future daughter-in-law.

I'd been waiting for it.

And so the battle began.

Round one to Mum.

I glanced in Sana's direction. Her lips were pursed. She certainly wouldn't forget the comment anytime soon. I could already see a response sizzling inside her.

Majestic Malik Moments: The Big Fat Indian Wedding You'll Want an Invitation to (I know I do)

It's official.

I've just received confirmation that a wedding is taking place in the Malik family this winter.

Azad Malik (Karim's hunky older brother, in case you made the mistake of missing Karim's entertaining family vlogs!) will be marrying his Pakistani sweetheart, who just flew in from Lahore (check out @SANABEAUTY on Instagram if you want to get to know her). With the way she's posing and styling herself, perhaps we have some couples content coming our way from the older Malik brother! Out with the old, in with the new – things are moving forward fast and ferociously, just the way I like it.

This will undoubtedly be the Wedding of the Year, with a star-studded guest list, designer sarees galore (Fouzia Faris Boutique will certainly be pulling out all the stops) and all the glitzy glam expected from the majestic Maliks. Notable people from all over the world will be coming to participate in this ceremony – I'm talking about Hollywood meets Bollywood meets British regal charm – and we'll be hanging on to every last detail.

Malik birthday bashes, Iftar dinners and Eid parties have always proven to be unique and memorable – remember the seven-tiered cake by Rosalind Miller, and the matching Oscar de la Renta outfits the entire Malik clan once wore? All this excitement has built up my appetite for some spice, and I'm thinking about booking a reservation at Dishoom.

But there's that one question I'm sure is playing on all our minds: will all of Karim's besties be on the exclusive guest list despite the drama? The Exes have never failed to make an appearance in the past, but with all the cracks beginning to show in their clique, an Ex might just 'forget' to keep their schedule clear, or maybe some invites will get lost in the post this time.

Yours Unfaithfully,
Mr Ex

PS: Do you think it would be a bit much for me to run errands around Kensington and Chelsea in a red saree today? Perhaps power walking to some classic Bollywood song? TikTok couldn't even handle that. And neither could you. I don't think you guys will *ever* be ready to know who I am . . .

Zara

8

The white mansion stood grand and majestic, looming before us. Farhan bhai, Morowa and I stood frozen with bags of Jashan desserts in hand.

Farhan bhai took a deep breath and said, 'I hadn't realized they'd be this . . .'

'Loaded,' Morowa finished for him. 'The security should've been our first clue.'

Our catering van had been searched before we could even enter the street. Husband and wife shared a nervous look and, standing in between them, I felt the intensity of it.

'It's fine,' Farhan bhai murmured. 'We'll treat them like any other client.'

I could sense how much Farhan bhai wanted this opportunity. My nerves tightened at the thought of us looking out of place in such a grand environment, of us having to impress the kind of people who lived here.

'Let's not overthink it,' Morowa said, balancing the bags in her hands as she rang the doorbell. 'If they choose us, amazing. If not, then this will be a great learning experience.'

A man wearing a black and white uniform came into view. 'Hello. Are you here for the catering sampling?'

'Yes, we are,' Morowa replied, sprucing up her London accent to become as posh as his. 'We're Jashan.'

'Right this way, please.' His eyes roamed over us. I wasn't sure if I was imagining it, but his gaze felt judgemental.

We were led through a large foyer, past a winding marble staircase, down to the end of a long corridor and straight into what appeared to be some kind of . . . ballroom.

My breath hitched a little.

Crystal chandeliers descended from the arched golden ceiling. The light cast a warm glow across the perfectly polished dark-wood flooring. White pillars stood gracefully along the bronze walls and were interlaced with intricate copper mouldings and panels.

The butler led us to one of the smaller tables at the far end, gave us a tight smile and was off.

'This is really something, isn't it?' Morowa asked quietly, eyeing the competition.

From the mouth-watering aroma alone, I could tell the country's top chefs had been invited.

I glanced around nervously, and then looked down at myself. Farhan bhai had asked me to dress formally, and before leaving work I'd changed into something I'd *thought* was quite nice. However, this place was buzzing with men in laser-sharp suits and women in sophisticated cocktail dresses. I spotted Burberry suits, Gucci dresses, Christian Louboutin stilettos. Suddenly, my plain black blazer and trousers didn't seem to fit the fashion requirements.

Not to mention the state of my Primark heels, which had been passed down by Aisha baji. The shoes were comfortable, but I wished the left heel would stop wobbling that little bit with every step I took.

My thoughts were interrupted when my gaze settled on a familiar face. The moment I managed to put a name to it, my jaw dropped.

Kiran Malik.

Sister of Karim Malik.

My eyes still glued to her, I grabbed Farhan bhai's arm. 'You didn't tell me this food tasting is for the *Maliks*.'

I turned and found him just as shocked. 'I didn't know.'

Morowa nudged us both. 'Am I going to be the only professional one among us today? We need to play it cool. Stop looking like a bunch of fangirls out of their depth!'

We snapped out of it and got on with helping Morowa display an amazing assortment of desserts on the white and gold plates she'd brought. I watched in awe as she used syrups, sauces, chocolate shavings, powdered nuts and fresh flower petals to present each dessert as a unique, succulent swirl of colour and taste.

Despite the fierce competition surrounding us, Morowa's talent was too pure for anyone to ignore. The thought of how much business Jashan could get if any of the Maliks posted something positive about us online made my heart swell with excitement. Karim could be a smug, spoilt brat for all I cared – just as long as Farhan bhai benefited from this incredible business opportunity.

My eyes kept trailing back to Kiran, who was making her way around the ballroom, greeting people, laughing prettily.

She was even more beautiful and ethereal in real life. It was another one of those dreamlike moments, like the first instant I saw Karim in the flesh, before he'd ruined it. Kiran was the reason I'd gotten into make-up – the first beauty tutorial I'd attempted to follow was hers.

Her sleeveless kurta complemented her modelesque frame so perfectly . . .

Oh no.

She was looking right at me. Walking straight towards our table. Her knowing smirk told me that she'd noticed me ogling her and that she was used to it. I felt the urge to hide. Being here was making me feel completely out of place.

'Hi, how's it going, guys?' she asked in a surprisingly kind voice.

'Good, thank you. How are you doing?' Morowa replied confidently.

'Great! I just wanted to let you know that before the tasting, my team will be over to discuss some details. Thank you so much for coming today, the Maliks really appreciate it.'

She nodded and turned to leave.

'I want to assure you,' Morowa said quickly before she went, 'that we've got many vegan and gluten-free options, and that we take great pride in catering to all dietary requirements.'

Morowa was using this as a chance to really sell our services, and I was silently urging her on.

'We offer healthier, lighter and, in my opinion –,' here Morowa gave a cheeky grin –, '*tastier* dessert options.'

Kiran laughed softly and began to analyse the plates we had on display. 'I love what you've done here! So minimalistic and aesthetic. It feels French, but with traditional South Asian desserts.'

She looked deep in thought as she browsed our display. 'Oh yeah, I remember you guys now. My assistant came across your socials, and I instantly knew we had to invite you.'

Morowa positively beamed.

'I'm looking forward to this food tasting,' Kiran added with a little wink.

Karim

9

'Have you planned much else for the wedding then?' Mum asked stiffly.

'Not yet,' Sana answered. 'I'm just in the process of hiring a London wedding planner.'

It was an obvious message to Mum to back off. Clearly Sana would prefer to arrange her wedding according to her own tastes, with no interference.

'Hmm,' was all Mum said.

An awkward silence ensued.

It was becoming abundantly clear that Sana wasn't going to be a traditional Pakistani daughter-in-law. She would not be busying herself with people-pleasing, allowing others to take control of her life or placing the desires of her in-laws above her own. She was an independent, successful woman, and she would not be moulded into anything else just because she was getting married.

This quality was exactly what I'd want to see in the woman I married in the future – my family could be *a lot*, with their opinions and assertiveness, and it was important to stand your ground in their company. Ironically enough, showing us

Maliks you weren't always going to do things as we demanded was crucial to gaining our respect.

I wondered whether Sana's response would have been deemed strange if she'd been raised here in London, and I didn't think so. Mum had assumed certain things about Sana because of her upbringing in their motherland. But we all knew that if Sana was to survive in this world, in *our* world – with all its cameras and crowds and criticisms – she had to have a backbone, and she'd just shown that she did.

Kiran walked in and nodded at Dad, who stood up eagerly to announce, 'The caterers are ready for us. Shall we?'

Dad led the way into the ballroom and, as soon as I took in the delicious aroma, my appetite came back in full measure.

After browsing and sampling for two hours, we'd chosen most of the wedding menu.

For starters, we'd gone with tandoori chicken tikka, masala prawns and aloo chaat. For mains, it was Hyderabadi biryani, Lahori lamb karahi, butter chicken and matar paneer korma. Accompanying these dishes were freshly baked butter and garlic naans, mint chutney, green chilli achaar and cucumber yogurt raita. We only had desserts and drinks left to choose.

While everyone was busy tasting more finger foods, Kiran leaned over and whispered, 'What do you think of Sana?'

'Perfect for Azad. What do you think?'

She wrinkled her nose. 'I like her. I just don't *know* her yet. Azad certainly seems infatuated though.'

'Mum's not going to like her favourite child's attention being so wrapped up elsewhere,' I said. 'Hate to say it, but I think there'll be a stereotypical mother and daughter-in-law scuffle.'

Kiran made a face. 'I'm so not ready for that.'

'I wasn't expecting the American accent. Did they used to live there?'

'No, she went to an American school in Pakistan.'

I glanced across the stand and caught Sana's brother staring at Kiran for what seemed like the tenth time, and I found myself imagining what he'd look like with neater brows and no moustache.

Not too shabby, I realized.

He'd lost quite a lot of weight compared with how he'd looked in the old photo Kiran had shown me earlier and it had given his face a nice structure. Uncle Abdullah had explained that Adil was twenty-seven, three years older than Sana. He lived in New York and managed the American chains of the Quresh Hotel Group.

The moment Adil realized I'd caught him ogling my sister, he looked away flustered, tilting his plate of kebabs so that some mint chutney slipped on to his shirt in the process.

I turned back to Kiran with a grin. 'Have you noticed Adil eyeing you up?'

'Multiple times. What a creep!'

'If he worked on his style a bit, I could see him being your type. Perhaps he just needs to pay a visit to my barber over in Westminster. That guy works wonders.'

Kiran pinched me in the side, making me yelp. 'Perhaps he needs a full body wax, but what is it to me?'

'It seems he's already half in love with you, darling sister.'

'He's *not* my type, OK? He looks like something shipped straight from Shaadi dot com. And since when did *you* become a rishta aunty? I'm getting enough pressure from the elders. I don't need you joining in.'

'Just helping you keep your options open.'

Kiran huffed. 'Let's teach him a little lesson about staring, shall we?'

She looked right at Adil as she slowly, sensually took a bite of her seekh kebab and then licked the chutney from her lips. Adil's eyes widened a fraction and he turned to his parents, almost as though he was afraid they'd caught him doing something inappropriate.

I nearly choked on the samosa I was eating.

There was no way Adil would be able to handle her.

'What an amateur,' she murmured in a bored tone, but I saw Adil already sneaking glances at her again.

My blazer pocket buzzed. I pulled out my phone to see a text popping up from Abeo.

> I have an inkling about who Mr Ex could be. When can I see you?

I immediately put down my plate and made to leave.

'What is it?' Kiran asked. 'Where are you going?'

'I'll be back soon,' I replied absent-mindedly.

'How do you always manage to get out of everything?' she called after me. 'It's so unfair.'

Zara

10

'They're heading our way,' Farhan bhai whispered urgently.

My heart hammered in my chest as I noticed the Maliks were only two tables away.

Morowa waved to grab my attention. 'Make sure the information cards on that side match the right desserts.'

I'd already checked the left side of our set-up multiple times, but I obliged.

Our table was currently filled with a colourful array of puddings and confections. On the side I was examining, there was rose rasmalai, apple kheer, pistachio milk cake, carrot halwa trifle and saffron kulfi served with miniature gulab jamuns. Morowa's side included even more mouth-watering options.

Kiran walked over to us first.

A sharp voice came from behind her. '*Where* has Karim wandered off to?'

Kiran turned to face the glamorous, glowering middle-aged woman in a stunning gown. Having come across 'The Malik Family' Instagram page, I instantly knew she was her mother – Fouzia Faris. Many aunties from the local community, including Mum, wanted to purchase her designer kurtas and sarees, but none of us could afford them. I always imagined that maybe I'd save enough to buy my bridal gown from there in the future though. Off the rack, of course.

'He'll be back soon,' Kiran replied.

Fouzia's nostrils flared. 'We need to show a united family front to the Qureshis! I told him to be on his best behaviour today. And why do you keep wandering away from me as well?'

Kiran huffed loudly. 'Relax, Mum. I'm just ensuring our schedule goes to plan.'

Ignoring what her daughter had just said, Fouzia took a step towards her. 'I need you to stay at my side, to speak up whenever Sana attempts to make all the decisions. I can't be the one to step in every time. I don't need the label of monster-in-law just yet.'

'Just yet?' Kiran exclaimed. 'Don't you mean *ever*? Please just calm down!'

Farhan bhai and I exchanged a wide-eyed look. Did they not realize we could hear them?

'Look, Mum,' Kiran said in a falsely bright tone, steering Fouzia towards our desserts, probably to distract her. 'This is exactly what we need. Such a unique, elegant presentation. Visibly grease-free. They have vegan and gluten-free options as well.'

Fouzia surveyed us first, and then looked down her nose at our display. She seemed to have instantly decided she didn't like what we had to offer.

'It's certainly ... different. Some of our guests will be

coming from India and Pakistan, and I don't think they'll appreciate something so unfamiliar.'

'But the wedding is both British *and* South Asian, as are *you*,' I blurted defensively.

Suddenly everyone fixed their gaze on me. Fouzia's eyes were wide, and I could tell she wasn't used to being challenged. But there was no backing down now: my blabbering mouth had got me into this mess, and it was the only thing that could get me out ...

'What I meant to say is that I think this is exactly the aesthetic that will represent your family well,' I continued. 'It's a *Malik* wedding – people will expect something extraordinary. You can't be typical and just plonk down gulab jamun or laddoos in front of your guests when it comes to dessert.'

Kiran laughed loudly, but her mother didn't seem the least bit amused.

Fouzia grimaced at me, making me shrink, and then her eyes found our name card. 'I haven't come across Jashan before. When were you established?'

Morowa gulped. 'Last year.'

She scoffed. 'There's no way. I cannot take a risk at my son's wedding with such an inexperienced team.'

Farhan bhai flinched next to me. The glow on Morowa's face vanished.

'Why are we starting our dessert tasting with *them*?' Fouzia asked Kiran incredulously. 'I want to begin with the most well-established pâtissiers. If you're going to do the job of our assistants, arrange that.'

Fouzia linked her arm around her daughter's and began leading her away. 'You need to be more realistic, Kiran,' she told her. 'Newer, smaller businesses won't understand the logistics of catering for a big wedding. That company's inexperience was obvious enough from their lack of proper uniform and their amateur appearance. As I always tell you, first impressions matter.'

Kiran turned to give us an apologetic look before she was whisked away completely.

Farhan bhai released a long, disappointed sigh and turned to me. 'What was that tone, Zara? That is *not* the way to get new customers on board.'

'But she was being so dismissive about our display,' I argued.

'It doesn't matter,' he scolded. 'You must always be patient with customers.'

'I'm sorry,' I whispered, knowing he was right. 'I was only trying to help.'

Farhan bhai put an arm around Morowa and they took a deep breath together. 'We still have the food tasting,' he said hopefully. 'They can't send us away before they've even tried our desserts. And even if this doesn't work out, we'll have other opportunities in the future, right?'

Morowa nodded but her eyes were a little glassy, and that made mine fill instantly. It was my fault – I'd *ruined* this for them.

So much effort had gone into preparing for this opportunity: the limited funds that had been spent on buying the best-quality ingredients, on paying for a babysitter, fuel, and much, much more. Farhan bhai and Morowa's hard work – years and years of testing and tasting recipes, of late nights and animated chats about their dreams, of spending their hard-earned savings on this business – had been rejected so carelessly.

Money meant nothing to these people. I hated it – the way they had so much in comparison to us, the way we were under their thumb, literally scrambling for this one opportunity.

I needed some air, otherwise I'd either scream or burst into tears.

'Be right back,' I murmured as I left, not knowing where on earth I was going.

Everything was a blur of stoic waiters, sleek dresses and sparkling laughter. It almost felt as though I was moving in slow motion and couldn't get away from it all fast enough.

In the corridor, I took deep breaths and wiped my tears away. No one else was here, and I was glad for the space.

I began to pace.

Both my siblings were struggling in their own ways, and I was powerless. I loved them so much and wanted to help them, but I never knew the right thing to say or do. I wished my parents would step in to support them, to fix our family, but they refused to do anything, and we were all just becoming more distant from each other.

Everything was falling apart.

My heel wobbled. My stupid cheap shoes. My knees felt weak, and I leaned on the closest thing to me – the side of a grand piano. Focusing on my breathing, I looked straight ahead.

The Quran.

My heart stopped.

The holy book was encased in an acrylic glass cube. It was displayed open, and the ancient pages seemed to hold the weight of the entire universe, the answer to every question I'd ever had, the secret behind every emotion I'd ever felt.

Mum had always taught us that the Quran held the literal words of God, that it was our root to connecting with Him, to understanding everything about our existence and purpose.

I wiped my eyes and began making out the Arabic text. Some lessons at my local mosque had taught me to read Arabic, but I didn't understand it well. I stared at the curve of the letters, the smooth lines, the symbolic dots.

It had been a while since I'd prayed.

Perhaps I was angry at God. It was hard to believe in a God who was all-powerful and yet let bad things happen to good people. I couldn't help but feel that God had brought me into this messy, heart-breaking world and then left me all alone.

Still, I found myself whispering in my heart.

Please, Allah. Just fix everything. Not for me. But for my sister. For my brother.

I began to feel lighter.

Let my sister find happiness and be safe from all harm. Let my brother's business do well so that his family has enough income. Please open my parents' hearts and minds so that this family has a chance at being one again. Bring us all under your divine goodness and protection.

'What are you doing here?'

I jumped and looked up in the direction the voice had come from.

None other than Karim Malik was walking down the grand staircase, fixing his cufflinks as he descended. Everything from his sleek black suit to his slick hair held the perfect image of refinement that I was so used to seeing online. If it hadn't been for the look on his face, he'd have had the air of a perfect gentleman. But his brows were knitted with disdain at the sight of me.

He was looking at me as though I was a thief, when all I'd been doing was praying for my family.

Every other emotion zapped out of me.

I was left with only rage.

Karim

11

Abeo refused to tell me anything over the phone. I'd just have to wait until this ridiculously elaborate food tasting was done and he could finally come over.

Annoyed, I headed downstairs to rejoin Kiran. On the way, I noticed an unattended waitress staring at our décor, eyeing it as though she planned to take something with her. This was why I didn't like having strangers in the house.

'What are you doing here?'

She looked up sharply, then her expression darkened.

'Taking a moment to admire your art. As you can tell from my clothing, I'm *working* at today's food tasting. What did you assume I was doing? Stealing something?'

Taken aback by her bluntness, I didn't know how to respond. I reached the landing and walked over to her, keeping a little distance between us.

'Well?' she pressed.

'Erm, actually I –'

This was certainly a first. I wasn't used to stammering around girls.

She scoffed. 'You people look down your nose at anyone

86

who doesn't have millions of pounds or followers. It's sickening. Not everyone's obsessed with you and your belongings. Get over yourself.'

She stormed off.

I felt my face redden as I chased her. 'Excuse me? What did you just say to me?'

'The truth,' she said simply, half-turning towards me.

My skin felt hot with indignation. 'I'm going to have you and your entire company thrown out right away. What's your name?'

Her eyes grew wide.

It seemed she'd finally remembered where she was and who she was talking to. She turned to face me but slipped hard on the marble floor.

Instinctively, I reached out and wrapped an arm around her waist. Her hands, which had been flailing seconds ago, gripped my shoulders.

The last thing we needed was the drama of our foyer being covered with a waitress's blood – Mum would absolutely lose it.

This close, I was forced to see her. *Really* see her.

Her soft brown skin possessed a warm glow; it reminded me of a burning candle – how it illuminated everything in its presence, how it felt impossible to look away once the sway of the flame had caught your attention. Her dark eyes were lined with smudged kohl, and they seemed heavy with anger and sadness. I found myself wanting to know why.

She cleared her throat.

I snapped out of it.

As I moved to lift her, my hold on her waist tightened and she looked away. I could sense she wasn't comfortable being touched this way, that the bounds of her modesty were being tested. In one swift move, we were standing right in front of each other, mere inches apart. She was a whole head shorter than me and had to lift her chin up to meet my gaze.

My arm was still wrapped around her. Her grip was still deep on my shoulders.

She smelt like . . . spice and sugar.

I glanced down to see what had made her fall.

A broken heel.

'Looks like you need new shoes.'

She took a sharp step away from me, removed her other heel as well, and took a slow, deep breath.

'And looks like you –' Her voice had come out hard, cold. But it seemed she was out of angry comebacks because she let her shoulders sag and said, 'Should lend me some superglue.'

Surprised, I began to chuckle, and her shapely rose-hued lips lifted in a secret smile. Suddenly we were both laughing. Her laugh was so pure, so childish, that it softened something inside me.

I usually knew exactly how to behave in any given scenario; I'd been trained to deal with all kinds of social situations, and knew when to be charming, reserved, apolitical, and everything in between.

But in this moment . . .

'What's your name?'

'Look –' she raised her hands in surrender – 'I'm just having a really tough day. Don't take it out on the rest of my team. I'll leave. Let them stay.'

'No, I'm not kicking you out. I was just . . . curious.'

'OK, may I ask your name first?'

My brows shot up.

She snorted. 'Oh, you're assuming that I already know who you are?'

'Don't you?'

She folded her arms. 'Isn't it nice to be able to introduce yourself once in a while? And for people to get to know you in person rather than assume they know you from what they've seen online?'

No one spoke to me in this way. Honestly, I didn't know how to answer, so I gave her a smile instead.

'You look better when you smile,' she said softly, and then lifted her brows. 'When you looked at me last time, you had such an angry, arrogant expression. It was unsettling.'

'Everyone expects me to always have a smile on my face, but it can be hard sometimes, especially when I'm not in a good place,' I admitted, surprised that I felt so comfortable being so open with a stranger. 'Hold on. Last time? We've met before?'

'You don't remember, do you? I'm not surprised. Forget it.'

I raked through my mind for any trace of her. To my astonishment, there was something there, but it was blurry, as though I was seeing it underwater.

'Karim, we need you back *now*,' Kiran called as she rushed into the foyer. 'Mum's not happy with your disappearing act.'

She paused to eye me and the waitress with curiosity, and I sensed a tinge of disapproval that she was the source of my distraction. The girl must have sensed it too because she made to leave, but I stood in her way, wanting more time with her. I threw a peeved look at Kiran.

'I'll be right there,' I told her, looking pointedly towards the door.

'Please just hurry,' Kiran whined as she took the hint and left us alone again.

'So, your name?' I prompted.

'You'll find, Mr Karim Malik,' she whispered gently, looking down at her hands, 'that even these days, some people value their anonymity.'

When she finally looked up at me, slowly, hesitantly, I realized I was holding my breath. The sound of my name on her lips continued to echo in my mind as she turned to leave.

This time, I didn't stop her.

I waited in the corridor, perfectly still, almost frozen, and found myself hoping she'd look back, sure that she'd do so at least once.

She stopped before turning the corner and tucked a strand of hair behind her ear.

Her body shifted in my direction, but she paused, as though deciding whether or not to look back at me. And then, choosing not to, she disappeared.

Zara

12

'You look like you've seen a ghost. Are you OK?' Morowa asked worriedly.

'I just had the most Bollywood moment of my life,' I whispered, 'and it was with *Karim Malik* of all people!'

'What?!'

'It's our turn to present,' Farhan bhai interrupted, nodding towards the swiftly approaching Malik-family entourage. 'Listen, Zara, I don't know where you ran off to, but I need you to stay focused now. We already look short-staffed. And remember to be polite and patient.'

'Sorry – yes, of course,' I mumbled.

Karim spotted me. He gave a subtle nod in greeting, and I swiftly looked away, busying myself with placing extra spoons near plates. A mask of professionalism slipped over my face.

Just so long as I reined in my sharp tongue, we still had a shot at this.

'Hi. Welcome to Jashan Desserts,' Morowa said brightly.

'Thank you,' Kiran replied warmly. 'Let's proceed with the food tasting!'

Morowa began to point out the different desserts and I could feel Karim's eyes on me. I wasn't going to give him the satisfaction of seeing me flustered over him, so I turned towards Morowa. But I couldn't stop the way my skin blazed under his gaze. I gripped the spoon I was holding until my knuckles turned white.

If only there was a way to stop feeling so self-conscious . . .

'What do you think, Sana?' Kiran asked a beautiful petite woman who'd grabbed a plate from Morowa's side of the table.

'It's really tasty,' Sana replied pertly. 'Oh my God, I could actually finish this entire thing right now.'

'Please go right ahead.' Morowa laughed. 'That's our mango and passion-fruit pudding. The thin coconut flakes and raspberry sauce add a nuanced texture and tang to the creamy organic pudding.'

'Well, I've never been to a South Asian wedding where they served such a dessert,' Fouzia said tightly, narrowing her eyes in Sana's direction.

'I actually think it's great when people have the courage to break barriers and bring something new to the table,' Sana responded, not bothering to even glance in Fouzia's direction. 'It shows the chef's confidence.'

'Yes, I agree with Sana,' Azad Malik said quickly, halfway through a pudding himself. 'This is by *far* the best dessert I've tried today.'

I recognized Karim's older brother instantly. Even if I hadn't seen him in Karim's vlogs, I would've spotted that they were related through their matching features and style.

Kiran gushed, 'I knew you guys would like these desserts.'

'Why don't you introduce your team to us?' Karim asked Morowa.

I finally looked back at him. The fluttering feeling in my chest expanded until it reached my fingertips and toes.

'Yes, of course,' Morowa replied happily, and proceeded to introduce herself and Farhan bhai, but Karim's eyes never left mine, as though nobody else's name or presence even mattered. When she finally revealed my name to him, his lips curled at the edges.

'Zara Khan, eh?'

'Yes,' I replied sharply, feeling strangely exposed.

He walked right up to me without any concern that everyone's eyes were now on us.

'What would you recommend?' he asked softly, reaching for my hand.

I froze.

His finger trailed across the side of my hand as he plucked the spoon from my grip.

Ignoring the tingling sensation his touch had left, I replied, 'Everything our chef makes is incredible. I guess it depends on your personal taste. What do you like?'

'Hmm . . . I like it when I have to work a little harder to get a taste.'

I swallowed.

It didn't feel like he was talking about desserts.

I had no idea how to respond but the silence was stretching out, so I went with whatever came to my mind and pointed towards the tropical cheesecake near Morowa.

'The flavour in this cheesecake is unique and not easily detectable. The cream cheese is a blend of five exotic fruits and a touch of honey. It might take you a while to pick apart the flavours, if you manage to do it at all.'

He smirked at the daring edge to my tone, picked up the dessert and put a spoonful in his mouth. He closed his eyes and murmured in satisfaction before opening them and looking right at me.

'Mango. Pineapple. Passion fruit. Coconut. And . . .'

His brows creased as he struggled to place the last one.

'Guava,' I finished for him. 'You're good, but not quite good enough.'

Two could play at this game of double meanings.

A slow smile curled his lips as he held my gaze. 'Beautiful. I'm interested –' he turned to his brother – 'in having them cater.'

'I agree!' Sana responded enthusiastically. 'Let's proceed with them for the mehndi, and possibly the walima?'

I couldn't believe it.

The Maliks began trying more of the desserts, grabbing them eagerly, murmuring their satisfaction and compliments. Morowa and I exchanged a look of sheer disbelief and joy.

'May I get your company card?' Karim suddenly asked Morowa, who grabbed one from the table and handed it to him.

'Are everyone's contact details on there?'

'Yes,' Morowa replied. 'My husband's number is at the bottom left and mine is on the right.'

'And what about Miss Khan?'

Morowa looked at me and stuttered for a while, unsure of what to do. Instead of letting the awkwardness linger,

I grabbed a pen, took the card from Karim's hand and jotted my number on the reverse side.

When I handed it back to him, he threw me a roguish grin.

And so, Karim Malik had my number. I was too stunned to know how to feel.

I wanted to look busy, to organize the desserts or the cutlery, but I couldn't seem to move or steal my gaze away from his.

Karim took another bite of the cheesecake and murmured contentedly. I felt the vibrations of that murmur reverberate along my spine. Then he put his plate down and whispered, 'I'll be seeing you, Miss Zara Khan.'

It sounded like a promise.

13

'It's just an inkling,' Abeo said as I let him into my house. 'It's not like I've *actually* figured out who Mr Ex is.'

'Spit it out already,' I demanded.

Instead of responding, he took his shoes off and jogged up the winding staircase to my room. He didn't say anything until the door was closed behind us.

'OK, so this has been going on for a while now,' he began, a touch breathless. 'I've noticed that random bits of information I share with James end up on the blog.'

My eyes widened. Abeo was accusing his boyfriend of over a year – his first proper relationship, a guy he was *really* into – of being the abominable Mr Ex.

'As I say, it's just an inkling. But I think it's worth looking into.'

'James?' I asked in disbelief.

'Don't tell the others yet. I could be completely wrong. Mr Ex has many ways of getting info on us. He could've learned the same things from somewhere else.' Abeo bit his lip, looking conflicted. 'And James doesn't have the fashion sense and witty way with words that Mr Ex does.'

I nodded slowly. 'I mean, James loves gossip – so maybe he's just talking more than he should and information is reaching Mr Ex that way.'

Abeo gave me a look. 'Either that or James is a *really* good actor. He may have been downplaying his confidence and style this entire time. And he may have been playing *me* from the moment we met.'

We stood in silence for a while.

I felt chills skitter up my spine at the thought of such pretence, at the fact that the person tormenting us could be someone we believed we *knew*, someone who was switching masks all the time, changing faces so effortlessly.

'I'm sorry, Abeo,' I said eventually.

He continued to stare into space for a few moments, then shrugged and collapsed on to my bed.

'You know how quickly I'm capable of getting over guys. I just want to know the truth now.'

I went to lie down next to him. 'So do I.'

He turned to face me. 'What do we do?'

'Whoever Mr Ex is, he deserves to be put in his place. And if it's James, then so be it.'

'I agree.'

'No emotions getting in the way then?'

Abeo's brown eyes went blank. 'None.'

I could practically see his scheming mind at work, his ruthless side pushing away everything that could distract him.

'I'm going to pretend everything is normal between me and James, but I'll be keeping a close eye on him. It might be hard to do that all the time though. Do you think we should get private investigators involved?'

'Hell no,' I hissed. 'Imagine paying a bunch of strangers to investigate our secrets. They could sell them. They might even blackmail *us* for money. We could end up having more than one Mr Ex in our lives. I don't trust anyone. No, this we do alone.'

Abeo scowled. 'It isn't fair that we have to go at it alone when Mr Ex gets plenty of help. His followers send him so much footage on us, and his comments section is always full of up-to-date gossip about us.'

'But he's anonymous. There's nothing at stake there – not for him, and not for the people getting in touch with him. We're public figures. Our *everything* is on the line.'

Abeo sat up, crossed his legs and turned to face me. 'Listen, there's something you should know. I want to tell you before I chicken out and lose the courage.'

A dark feeling pooled in my stomach as I also sat up and looked at him.

He took a deep breath, then let it all out. 'I told James about the abortion. When I went over to see Chloe a few days ago, she looked really upset and when I asked, she told me everything. I met James that evening and . . . it just poured out of me. I guess I needed someone to talk to.'

I gave him a cold look. His eyes were raw with regret.

'I'm sorry, Karim. I should've known better.'

Despite the sting of betrayal, I wasn't going to push Abeo away too. I already felt disconnected from the other Exes. I had to pick my battles wisely.

'It's done now,' I snapped. 'There's nothing that will undo it. Just be *extra* careful with what you tell James in the future.'

'I will,' he said, looking beyond relieved at my decision to let it go. 'So, this means either James leaked it,' he said thoughtfully, 'or the others haven't been honest about who else they told. I guess the real question is: do you trust them?'

'I honestly don't know who to trust any more.'

'Is there anyone *you* suspect?'

'Well,' I said slowly, giving him a sly look. 'You're the only guy I know who has a *great* sense of fashion, and who loves boys, gossip, drama –'

Abeo scoffed and tried to push me off the bed, making me chuckle. My phone buzzed and I pulled it out of my pocket.

An anonymous text.

'Hold on,' I said, my heartbeat spiking. 'I think Mr Ex just texted me for the first time.'

'What?' Abeo barked, then grabbed my phone and proceeded to read aloud:

> We all want to see you as Chloe's Prince Charming one last time.
> I quite like the thought of seeing you together again, arm in arm.
> I'm sure things between you two are already tense and awkward.
> It wouldn't help if she learned of your tryst with that leggy brunette.
> We both know you were rather forward . . .

He looked at me in disbelief. 'What the heck does that mean?'

I buried my head in my hands and mumbled, 'I might have made out with a random girl at a private party a few months ago.'

Abeo kissed his teeth disapprovingly.

'Chlo and I were on a break then,' I said defensively, lifting my head.

'These excuses won't work! Do you have any idea how bad this makes you look? Especially right after the abortion news.'

'I don't know if it really counts as cheating if –'

'Does she know?'

I shook my head.

'Would you ever tell her?'

I shook my head again.

'Do you *want* her finding out?'

I gave Abeo a hard look. 'Obviously not.'

'Well then, it's bloody cheating.'

With a deep sigh, I stood and began pacing, my feet comforted by the softness of the plush wool carpet.

'Chloe cannot find out about this,' I said. 'She'll turn this whole thing round on me and make me look like the bad guy. We can't let her have any ammunition on me right now. I guess this is Mr Ex's first threat. Chlo and I were planning to go to the ball together anyway, but now Mr Ex will think it's because of him and I hate that. He isn't the one in control here.'

'Isn't he?' Abeo asked with narrowed eyes.

I continued to pace in silence.

'Urgh, you're going to think I'm gross,' he said suddenly, falling back on to my bed. 'But Mr Ex kinda . . . turns me on. He's so dark and unpredictable, and he's got a real sense of humour on him. He clearly knows his fair share about style too. That's the kind of guy I've always wanted. Why am I more attracted to James after the possibility of him –'

I grabbed a pillow and used it to smack Abeo a few times. He screwed his face up but didn't try to protect it, almost as though he knew he deserved it. When I was done, he groaned, grabbed the pillow, and buried his face deep into it.

'Yeah, yeah. I know,' he said in a muffled voice. 'It's stupid. Ridiculous.'

Abeo's phone began to ring. He looked at the screen and said, 'It's Noah. Shall I pick up?'

Chloe's younger brother was only one year below us in school and had a habit of spending more time with us than with people his own age. Noah was an awkward kid with an easy laugh. He'd come out to his Catholic parents recently, and Abeo was helping him through the process. Just because I needed space from the Clarks for now, it wasn't right for me to drag Abeo away from them too.

'Yeah, answer it.'

I zoned out while Abeo advised him on what to wear at the ball tomorrow.

'That kid's got a thing for me,' he said matter-of-factly when he hung up. 'He tries to hide it but it's obvious. He's a sweetheart and all, but it's *never* gonna happen. You know

I don't like sweet guys. I really don't want to break his heart, so I hope he never tells me or makes a move. I think he's too shy to do that anyway. So, back to Mr Ex –'

'Can we start dealing with all this tomorrow?' I cut in abruptly.

'Yeah, let's savour this bit of peace while we can,' Abeo agreed. 'The moment school starts, things are gonna get wild. I can just feel it.'

We lay side by side again, staring at the ceiling, lost in our own thoughts. I was the first to break the silence.

'Have Chloe and Sanjay been hanging out more?'

Abeo didn't respond for a while. I could tell he was choosing his words carefully. 'Yes, they have. Much more than usual.'

Chloe had chosen to confide in Sanjay, and that was redefining our circle, changing loyalties, altering the factions within our group.

Something twisted in my gut, but I replied casually, 'Well, Chloe's always switching besties. She seems to get bored of them quicker than her designer bags.'

Every term at St Victor's, Chloe Clark would choose people to boss around – those she'd have at her beck and call to do everything from taking her photos, to helping her with homework, to picking up her dresses from exclusive boutiques around London. She knew that most students in our school would do pretty much anything to become a part of her clique or get a single mention on her social media. In fact, most of them would go out of their way for something as little as a compliment from her.

But it was obviously different with Sanjay. He was one of The Exes. She couldn't boss him around in that way. He was her equal.

'Are you actually up for the ball?' Abeo asked.

'Not really.' Just the thought of it was enough to give me a headache.

'It might be fun. Could feel like old times again.'

'Things will never be the same. Not after this summer.'

Abeo propped himself on his elbow. There was a touch of pity in his eyes that I despised. I was used to people looking at me with respect and envy, occasionally fear.

'It's obvious you've been feeling a little left out recently,' he said. 'But you need to remember that you're not just an Ex, you're *The* Ex. The pioneer. No one could ever push you out. Only you can choose to leave. And if you were to do that, the whole thing collapses. We're no longer The Exes.'

I tried not to let it show, but I was grateful for everything he was saying. I needed to hear this. Instead of responding, I just nodded.

My thoughts returned to Zara Khan, as they often had since the moment I'd caught her in my arms. For a second, I wondered whether to tell Abeo about her, but decided against it. None of The Exes knew her, she wasn't a part of my world, and I loved that.

Being around her, even for a brief moment, had felt so refreshing, different, *real*. I wanted to see her again.

Abeo rolled on to his back again. 'Mind if I sleep over?'

'Not at all. That's one thing that'll definitely feel like old times.'

He exhaled slowly. 'You want to know what I'm thinking?'

'What?'

'Mr Ex is going to be there tomorrow. There's no way he would miss an event this big in our social calendar.'

'Well then, I guess our hunt for Mr Ex begins at Queen Charlotte's Ball.'

14

When I stepped out of Barking Tube Station, the scent of fried chicken hung in the air, a group of boys in baggy clothes lingered around the local barber's, and a drunk man was swaying outside the off-licence. As I made my way home, a woman approached me, asking for some spare change.

Barking was the less refined, more laid-back younger sibling of London's West End, and it was home.

Farhan bhai had offered to drop me off but I didn't want to risk Dad seeing him. It was unnecessary stress for everyone involved.

Thoughts of Karim Malik chased me with every step: the feel of his hands on my waist, his smouldering smile, those dark eyes. My head spun with the impossibility and reality of it all – and I couldn't wait to tell Sal. But how on earth was I supposed to convince her that Karim had my number when I barely even believed it myself?

As I unlocked my front door, balancing the box of victory treats I'd promised Sal in one hand, a sense of dread rattled through me. It was late, way past my curfew, and Mum wouldn't be happy. There was no way she'd let me go over to

Sal's at this time of night, so she'd get her desserts tomorrow, and I'd have to tell her everything over FaceTime.

'As-salaam-alaikum,' I called out as I entered. 'I'm home.'

Mum stepped into the corridor wearing her heavily stained yellow apron and a dark grimace.

'Walaikum-assalam, you're lucky your dad isn't home to see you walk in at this time,' she replied in Urdu.

'Farhan bhai's appointment ran longer than expected,' I explained in our mother tongue; it was the only language I spoke with my parents because they weren't fluent in anything else. 'I know you won't ask, so I might as well just tell you: Jashan got a *really* big opportunity.'

Her expression softened and I ran to her, enveloping her in a tight embrace. I was open with her in a way I could never be with Dad. Although she and I struggled to communicate at times because of how different we were, at least there *was* a line of communication.

With Dad, there was nothing.

She gave me a kiss on the forehead, then gestured towards the kitchen with her chin. 'Come help with dinner. Go change first.'

I went upstairs to my room and put on a shalwar kameez, which Mum insisted should be the only thing I wore around the house. Apparently, Dad liked to see that I'd retained as much of our culture as possible because that somehow made me a better person. When I came back downstairs, Mum told me to cut onions and then wandered off to the living room, probably to peer out of the windows into our neighbours' or continue watching one of those Pakistani dramas she was addicted to.

As I got to work, it was impossible to think of anything but Karim and how he could possibly message me soon . . . maybe even call . . .

'Stir the curry, you lazy girl,' Mum shouted, rushing back in. 'You're always lost in your daydreams. Your dad will be home soon. You know how annoyed he'd be if I served him burnt food!'

The excitement zapped right out of me.

Mum was always so worried about meeting Dad's expectations that it drove her into the worst moods, which were always directed at me since I was the only one she could openly express herself to.

A touch of anger bubbled in my stomach as she pushed past me. Everything about this cramped house was starting to irritate me.

Saliha told her parents everything, regardless of how gossipy or inappropriate it was, and it was fine because they loved to laugh together and share their life experiences. I couldn't remember the last time I'd shared anything meaningful with my parents, let alone laughed with them. I thought about how it would feel to speak to my mum about anything I'd experienced today . . .

She simply wouldn't get it. She'd scold me for speaking to a boy and then confiscate my phone to check everything on it.

We'd been raised in different countries and possessed contrasting outlooks on just about everything, and that meant there was an insurmountable gap between us.

Usually I kept my mouth respectfully shut, but today I just couldn't. 'I was busy cutting the onions like you told me to. You didn't say to keep an eye on what *you're* cooking.'

She tutted loudly. 'I don't know how your future in-laws are going to deal with you.'

Every conversation with her seemed to lead back to marriage – a constant reminder that this wasn't my real home, my real family or even my real life. Since I was a girl, everything *real* would begin after marriage.

'I've finished cutting the first two onions. What shall I do with them?'

'Put them on my head,' she snapped sarcastically. 'They're obviously for the second curry, so start making it. We're having chicken karahi.'

'Don't you always criticize my cooking every time I try to make something?' I retorted. 'Besides, I have revision to do now that school's starting.'

Mum's death stare caused my stomach to tighten.

'You'll need these cooking skills later in life even more than your education, and then you'll thank me. Besides, why were you out for so long if you have schoolwork to do?'

I exhaled slowly to calm myself, then inhaled the pungent smell of spices and caramelizing onions. 'I already told you. I was out for work, and then for Jashan's appointment.'

'You can do all this going out after you're married.'

'Go out with my future husband?' I blurted sarcastically. 'Oh, like how Aisha baji's husband takes her out?'

'Javed has to work,' Mum said sharply. 'He's providing for your sister and their two children, so he doesn't have time to take her out.'

'Why are you always defending him?' I screeched. 'Baji has

told you again and again how badly he treats her. Do you not *hear her?*'

Mum began kneading the dough for rotis as though I hadn't said anything at all. I felt the urge to grab a plate and smash it just to get a reaction from her. As always, she preferred silence whenever I brought up the fact that my sister was trapped in an abusive marriage.

When Dad had first arranged it, baji was only twenty-two, a fresh graduate trying to figure her life out. She'd always been a good, obedient daughter and easily gave in to the pressure to marry Javed even though she wasn't attracted to him. I'd tried to talk her out of it, but she'd brushed me off as the naïve younger sister who knew little about the world.

But this much I had known even at thirteen – you should only marry someone who understands your mind and soul, someone you cannot wait to begin a life with.

Javed had been an overseas student from Pakistan at the time, and he was the son of a cousin who was close to Dad. And that was all that Dad had really thought about: the fact that *he* liked the guy, and how the marriage would please his relatives. There had been no discussion of how compatible the couple were, what their aspirations were, and whether there was any real connection between them.

The marriage had been for the sake of the relatives who were nowhere to be seen now that baji was severely depressed, and struggling to raise two children on her own because her husband was always absent. And it was even worse when he was home, because then she didn't feel safe.

'I mean it, Mum,' I pressed. 'Why don't you ever take baji's situation seriously?'

She placed a rolled roti on to a flat pan, looking perfectly unbothered. I wondered whether she truly felt no concern for baji or if she'd just mastered keeping every emotion hidden from her face, exactly as Dad preferred it.

Aisha baji had mentioned divorce to Mum many times in the past, but her response was always the same: it would be a source of shame for our family, it was important for children to live under the shade of their father, and no one would marry a divorcee, especially one with two children, so if she did divorce Javed, Aisha baji would be alone for the rest of her life, with no support, because she certainly wouldn't be given permission to return to this house.

I knew these weren't really her own words, they were Dad's. Mum had no real say in anything; she accepted Dad's expectations and decisions as her own. I couldn't blame her entirely: this was what happened when a girl was deprived of an education, married off far too young and lived her entire life dependent on a man who didn't respect her as an individual in her own right.

But I just wished Mum would take the blindfold of submission off her eyes and look at the true state of her family and realize why it had become like this.

'How would you feel if her depression actually led her to suicide?' I asked sharply.

'Oi, besharam!' Mum shouted, calling me shameless, because apparently it was wrong to talk openly about something as haram and taboo as suicide. 'Aisha is lucky to have a man who hasn't left her and who doesn't harm the children. If you ask me, she's being ungrateful. You know what, it's my fault.' She pointed the rolling pin at my face. 'I've spoilt you girls. If I'd raised you to focus on your responsibilities more, neither of you would have time to think about all these extra things.'

I scoffed. 'So this is somehow *our* fault now? And *that's* the benchmark you've placed? That he doesn't harm the kids! He may hit her, but he doesn't leave her! *That's* what you want for your daughter? For both of your daughters?'

Mum must have seen something unyielding in my eyes because she looked away swiftly and said, 'Just go upstairs and do your schoolwork.'

We'd only end up having an even more heated argument if I continued this conversation, which would lead to a few days of silent treatment until one of us caved. I was sick of the whole routine. It achieved nothing: Mum didn't even try to understand where I was coming from, and I certainly couldn't agree with how she was handling the situation with Aisha baji. With either of my siblings.

Rushing up to my room, I grabbed my textbooks and got into bed.

I had a missed call from Sal, but I wasn't in the mood to talk to her any more. I tried calling Aisha baji, but she didn't pick up. She rarely responded to my messages or calls any more, always found an excuse not to talk to any of us. She'd once told me it made her feel lonelier to know we were all aware of her situation and yet did nothing to help her.

I felt useless, and I hated it.

Flicking through my textbooks and revising for exams always made me feel better; it reminded me that this didn't have to be my life, that hard work and good grades could open doors to a different future for me. I skim-read a few pages from my biology textbook, only half-absorbing the information in my tired, agitated state.

Eventually, the squeak of the front door opening pierced the silence, and I heard Dad's heavy footsteps.

As hungry as I was, I'd skip dinner tonight. I didn't want to see either of my parents.

I thought I'd be awake for hours, feeling the weight of a home broken by irreconcilable differences, but the tiredness of the day pulled me into the dark, and I craved to fall into it.

To be taken away from this place.

Karim

15

Having Abeo sleep over was exactly what I'd needed to get out of my slump.

He was ruthless, focused. He hadn't let me sleep in past seven.

After a quick breakfast, we'd gone rowing in Wandsworth and then brunched at his home in Mayfair, where I'd attempted to trace the anonymous text Mr Ex had sent me.

Nothing worked.

This guy knew exactly what he was doing, and it seemed even my tech knowledge wasn't advanced enough to identify him.

We'd concocted a plan for tonight. The other Exes would also be attending Queen Charlotte's Ball, but we'd decided not to let them in on it, for now. And the rest of our time had been spent creating and uploading content: a gaming video, a vlog, and a clip of us getting ready for the ball. Regardless of what went on in our lives, work didn't stop, and none of us could take a lengthy break from building up our brand and followers.

Abeo shot me a confused look. 'Shall I upload this on to The Exes' TikTok or my personal one?'

'Definitely the main account,' I responded, adjusting my white bow tie until it sat just right.

'Damn,' he grinned, showing me the video. 'We look *good*.'

When Abeo and I arrived at One Whitehall Place, the ball was in full swing.

Partners and parents in white tie and glittering gowns were milling about the hall, which exuded Victorian grandeur. The high ceiling was lined with sparkling chandeliers, and the red carpet matched the crimson curtains draping the floor-length windows, which overlooked the Thames.

As a waiter whizzed by, Abeo grabbed a glass.

'I'm going to look for James. Coming?'

I shook my head and he left.

As I stood alone, I could sense people watching me. Usually I wouldn't think twice about it because I'd practically grown up in the public eye, but their gaze had taken on a sinister undertone now; I couldn't divorce it from the omnipresent glare of Mr Ex. All I could think about was that these people were either relishing the salacious gossip he spread about me or feeding information to him themselves. I felt the urge to get away from them all.

At least my brooding expression was deterring selfie requests.

Zara Khan would never ask me for a selfie. I couldn't picture it. The thought made me smile.

A flash.

I blinked.

A figure in a black suit curled behind a pillar just before I could see his face.

It was a mistake – he hadn't meant to use the flash. But an ordinary fan or photographer wouldn't have then hidden in such a way. Which could only mean that he was neither . . .

A tap on my shoulder. I started.

'What's happening?' Abeo asked.

'Someone just took a picture of me,' I replied distractedly. 'By mistake.'

Keeping my eyes peeled, I rushed over to the pillar. But by the time I reached it, there was no one there.

'It wasn't James. He was with me the whole time,' Abeo said, catching up to me. 'Look – he's coming over now. Remember what we spoke about? Act normal.'

James came up to us with a wide grin. 'Nice to see you.'

I gave him a tight smile and pretended to be interested in his excessive chatter. After a while, Noah joined us too, and when he went in for a hug, I embraced him. Not his fault that I'd broken up with his sister.

'Is it all right?' Noah murmured self-consciously, looking down at the kilt he was wearing.

'You look great,' I reassured him quickly, my mind still fixated on that flash.

Someone clattered a spoon against a glass, and the hall swiftly fell silent.

'The formal procession is about to begin,' the host announced. 'Escorts must prepare for the arrival of the debutantes.'

I walked towards the hall's entrance, Abeo and James in tow.

'Do you know what Felicity's wearing?' James asked Abeo.

'Of course,' he replied matter-of-factly. 'I chose her entire look myself. Carolina Herrera gown and diamond jewellery from Van Cleef & Arpels.'

'I helped put my sister's look together,' James responded. 'Jenny Packham gown. Pearl jewellery from Dior.'

Abeo pursed his lips.

Fashion really brought out his competitive side. He opened his mouth to respond with what would undoubtedly have been a feisty comment, but then something caught his eye. 'Sanjay, what are you doing here?'

'This is unexpected,' I agreed. 'I didn't realize you had a deb to escort.'

'Neither did I,' Sanjay replied sheepishly. 'One of Chloe's friends needed to replace her escort, and she volunteered me.'

He chuckled awkwardly and scratched his neck, avoiding our eyes. It was weird seeing Sanjay with slicked-back hair and wearing a fitted suit. We were so used to his heavily oversized outfits stained with paint. But he looked ... good. Really good. James was openly checking him out. It was clear we'd all forgotten how well he could clean up.

'Oh wow, the girls are here,' James said, and everyone's eyes snapped in the direction of the debutantes, who were elegantly entering.

Chloe was right at the front, as expected.

Her white satin gown flowed down her body like water, accentuating her modelesque physique. A slit up one leg added the perfect touch of sensuality. The light caught on the sheen of her glossy blonde Hollywood waves.

I felt slightly breathless.

Chloe Clark was mesmerizing, infectious. She always had been. With every year that passed, the power of her beauty and charisma only seemed to intensify.

As she approached me, her full red lips lifted into a smile. I smiled back, then caught her bright green eyes. And that was when I realized – she hadn't been looking at me at all.

Zara

16

'Tell me the whole thing again,' Sal pressed.

I'd already repeated everything that had happened between me and Karim Malik many times over, yet it still hadn't lost its thrill. I didn't think it ever would.

'*Again?*' I grinned, rolling on to my stomach.

'I want *all* the deets.'

'I've literally told you everything. That's all that happened.'

'So far.'

Sal waggled her brows suggestively and I giggled, hugging my pillow tight to my chest. I'd told her that he hadn't messaged or called yet, and she'd said he was just trying to play it cool, that there was no way he wouldn't reach out after the Bollywood-level moments we'd shared.

'Why are we doing this over FaceTime?' she asked. 'Can't you just come over to mine with those treats you promised? At least then we can gush properly.'

'Mum gave me a massive list of chores,' I grumbled. 'Dad's friends are coming over for dinner today. You'd think they're coming to inspect if there's any dust behind the TV.'

'She did give you permission to come over though, right?'

'Yeah, but I can't stay for long because I still have to finish cleaning.'

'We literally have to ration our time together!' Sal replied irritably.

'I'll come now. Oh my God, you're going to love the tropical cheesecake. I believe it was Karim's favourite.'

I hung up the phone to the sound of Sal shrieking like a wild animal. I put on a white T-shirt and the thinnest tracksuit bottoms I owned, as the September sun was still hot.

A few minutes later I was sitting on her bed, and we were devouring the desserts in rapturous silence because they were that damn delicious.

'I've got more news,' I told Sal. 'Farhan bhai secured an amazing deal for catering the desserts at the Malik mehndi *and* walima functions!'

'Congratulations!' she squealed. 'I just knew Jashan was gonna make it big.'

'Mum acted as though she didn't care when I told her yesterday. But I saw her on her prayer mat earlier today and she was crying. Tears of gratitude for once. I could tell.'

'I'm so glad things are finally looking up. Maybe your parents might even reach out to your brother now?'

I shrugged as I snuggled into her side. I felt completely and utterly calm. I regretted not calling her the previous night; I should've because she always made me feel like everything would be just fine.

'I'm going into a sugar coma,' I muttered through a stifled yawn.

'Me too,' Sal replied, scrolling through her phone, and

suddenly bringing it close to my face. 'Have you seen this yet? It's going kinda viral!'

It was a video of Imran Sayyid's fitness journey.

I found myself blushing a little as I watched clips of him doing push-ups, throwing fists at a punching bag and lifting a barbell into a smooth biceps curl. His six-pack was visible through the sweat-soaked grey vest clinging to him.

'He's in *really* good shape now, right?' Sal exclaimed. 'Only one day till school starts. With how much both his muscles and his followers have grown, girls will be all over him.'

'Nothing new there. I don't know how much more popular he could become.'

Imran was in the same clique as Hania, and although he'd been seen with plenty of girls in the past it had certainly never damaged *his* reputation. His family's reputation, on the other hand, had been irreversibly tainted when his eldest brother had been imprisoned for selling Class A drugs.

Most of our local South Asian community had started whispering and keeping their distance from the Sayyids. My mum had stopped speaking to them soon afterwards, only lingering around long enough to glean bits of gossip that she could share with the other aunties.

My parents had made it clear that I was to stay well away from Imran. It was silly of them to even mention it because they didn't allow me to speak to *any* boys. But they'd probably felt they needed to make it extra clear because the Sayyids' house was exactly opposite ours and they'd allowed me to play football with Imran when we were children.

In the last year of primary school, things changed. The

boys had become taller, leaner, more aware of the fact that we were girls. Although they didn't leave us out of football, they started treating us differently, making comments about our ability to play as well as them. One boy even stated that we should sit every game out in case we were injured and got the boys in trouble, to which Sal responded by showing him the middle finger, tackling him and scoring a goal.

Something else also changed: I began to notice just how attractive Imran Sayyid was, how good his tanned arms looked in T-shirts, how my heart thundered whenever he came close.

While Sal remained carefree, I started behaving differently around the boys, no longer shouting sarcastic comments or moving my body recklessly; I became quieter, more reserved.

Imran and I attended Quran classes at the same mosque, but since it was segregated I never really saw him, apart from maybe a few glimpses here and there near the entrance, but it would be considered inappropriate and immodest for us to stand about chatting, not that I ever tried, and he never attempted to reach out to me either. I sometimes thought I saw his gaze settle on me, but I could never be sure because I purposely kept my eyes fixed on something else if I sensed he was nearby.

The last time I'd spoken to him was a year ago, when I was walking down a corridor at school; he'd tapped my shoulder and extended a hand towards me, holding my library card, which it turned out I'd dropped. I'd murmured my thanks and he'd given me a quick wink before strolling off. It had been the smallest, most meaningless interaction and yet my heart had pounded wildly, and I hadn't been able to concentrate much for the rest of the day.

Although Sal always took a few minutes to chat to Imran if she happened to spot him on our road, I never dared to. The last thing I needed was for my parents to catch me speaking to him, and anyway, Imran Sayyid just screamed trouble. A whole load of handsome, overconfident, rebellious trouble.

'You don't have a crush on Imran, do you?' I asked Sal, who was still staring at his biceps on her phone screen.

'Oh, hell no!' Her eyes snapped to mine. 'Roadman ain't my type.'

'That's the spirit.'

There wasn't a single girl we knew who'd come out of something with Imran Sayyid with dry eyes.

'I know we've barely chilled, but Mum will get annoyed if I'm not back soon,' I said reluctantly.

Sal made a face but immediately stood, threw her hijab on, then pinned it into place. She walked me to my door so we'd have a few more minutes together.

'Saliha Begum,' I sang as I hugged her. 'You're literally the most perfect best friend and sister a girl could ask for.'

'Sisters for life,' she said with sass, and then looked over my shoulder and began to wave. 'Speaking of the devil . . .'

I turned and –

Imran Sayyid.

He was grabbing his gym bag from the boot of his black Volkswagen Golf GTI. When he noticed us, he lifted his head a fraction in greeting.

The middle Sayyid brother, Saqib, had done well at university, studying economics at University College London and getting himself a high-flying job in Dubai soon after graduating. He sent his family back plenty of money, which was how Imran had been able to buy himself a car and indulge in the flashy lifestyle he currently enjoyed. I'd heard he'd even fine-dined a handful of girls from school.

'It's been a while,' Sal said with a smile. 'What you been up to?'

'Jus' this and that, innit,' Imran replied, swinging the gym bag over his shoulder. The motion emphasized the perfect shape of his biceps.

He'd grown in height and muscle density – perhaps even in sex appeal, if I dared to admit it. I gulped a little, scolding myself for my inappropriate thoughts. His gaze found mine and I abruptly began to study Saliha's hijab.

'What's happenin' with you, mate?' he asked, locking his car and strolling over to us until he stood at the edge of the pavement. Sal walked closer to him, too, and tugged me along with her.

'Oh, you know, jus' this and that,' she said, imitating him.

He chuckled.

It was a soft, deep sound that left my nerves in jumbles.

'We're planning to revise our notes for maths and chem tomorrow,' Sal said. 'Wanna join us?'

'Calm,' he replied, looking genuinely interested.

My insides grew hot with annoyance at Saliha. I wished she'd asked me first. How could I focus on studying if Imran Sayyid was in the same room?

'I've still got the notes Saqib made,' Imran said. 'He did real well in his exams. I'll share 'em with you guys.'

'That would be amazing,' Saliha replied eagerly, and then looked at me.

123

There was a pause as though they were both waiting for my input. I looked at Sal with my *what are you doing?* eyes.

She gave me her *stop being weird* look in return.

When she turned back to Imran and smiled, I was still staring at her hijab pin, clueless of where else to look. I knew I'd come across as a complete weirdo if I kept gawking at her head though, so I dared a glance in his direction.

He was looking straight at me.

I held my breath.

Karim

17

'Noah looks great in a kilt, right?' Chloe crooned into my ear. 'He was quite insecure about wearing it but I'm glad Abeo convinced him. Thank you for escorting me, by the way. It feels right to do this with you.'

My left hand was in hers and the other rested on her bare back. In the centre of the hall, we danced as though floating – poised, fluid, perfectly synchronized, the result of years of attending elitist galas and celebratory balls. We'd been trained and polished to play the part, to gain the approval of high society.

There were many other dancers, but none who were being watched and recorded like us. I knew Chloe's personal photographer was currently capturing footage for her socials. Mr Ex would certainly be pleased, thinking he'd caused this little Chlarim reunion; he was probably staring at us this very moment. The thought made my skin crawl.

'You're the smoothest dance partner I've ever had,' she continued. 'Let's promise to always save each other at least one dance at whatever ball we attend, OK?'

I didn't bother to respond – I wasn't in the mood to feign happiness.

She moved back a little and gave me a warm smile. 'This makes things feel a bit more normal, right?'

'We have to be dancing for things to be normal between us?'

She laughed softly. Usually I cherished that sound; today I didn't. I'd noticed the way she'd looked at Sanjay, and the way he had looked back.

'Not dancing necessarily. Just doing the things we did when we were friends.'

It was strange that even though she was in my arms, my skin touching hers, I felt distant from her. Disconnected.

'Do you *really* think we can be friends?'

Chloe's eyes widened in surprise. 'Of course. Don't you?'

I looked away and focused on the dance – twirling her here, waltzing around once, lifting her, coming together again. Her eyes met mine and I noticed her face had fallen. I didn't want to deal with this.

'Would you please excuse me?' I walked off before she could respond.

It would be better for both of us if we gave each other space. I grabbed a lemonade and took a sip.

This was a rather scandalous move: to leave your partner stranded on the dance floor. I could feel the whispers gathering in volume around me. It made me want to start a scene wild enough to really give them something to talk about.

Sanjay broke off his own dance with his debutante and went over to Chloe. They couldn't make it more obvious that something was going on between them. Abeo was still dancing with Felicity, but his eyes were trying to catch mine, to check whether I was OK. I turned away, wanting to be left alone.

The music began to fade out, and the host gushed, 'Such elegant dancing from our debutantes and their partners!' She paused for the clapping to settle. 'May I please have all the debutantes join me on stage? We shall now reveal the Deb of the Year.'

As the girls made their way forward, Abeo came to stand by me. 'What happened between you two? Is the Mr Ex plan still on?'

I noticed that Sanjay still stood exactly where Chloe had left him, choosing not to join me and Abeo like he usually would have done.

'Nothing.' I shook my head. 'And yes, of course it is.'

'I don't think anything's happening between them,' Abeo said, eyeing Sanjay pointedly. 'He's just helping her get through this difficult time as a friend.'

The host cleared her throat before saying, 'The Deb of the Year award goes to ... Chloe Clark.'

More applause broke out.

Chloe's expression held the perfect amount of surprise and joy. Picture-perfect and deeply likeable, despite all the controversy that was surrounding her right now. She smiled prettily as the mic was passed to her.

'Thank you so much. As a token of gratitude to everyone who put this incredible event together, I would like to sing a song I was inspired to write by my charity work. The bulk of this song was written in the Poets' Corner in Westminster Abbey.'

She began to sing with chilling beauty, and the anger inside me started to fade. Chloe Clark felt most real when she was singing, and I could tell everyone else was savouring the moment just as much as I was.

I'd been there when she'd first started writing songs; we'd been thirteen-year-olds stuck in her bedroom for hours on end, working on lyrics and tunes. I'd played the piano while she sang at the top of her lungs . . .

The truth was that I still loved her, I always would. But if I wanted to see her flourish, I had to let her go. Our on-and-off relationship had been toxic and unhealthy for both of us. And perhaps Abeo was right: maybe I'd misinterpreted what was happening between her and Sanjay.

I had to handle my emotions with Chloe better. If I kept on pulling stunts like this, it could damage our friendship irreversibly.

'Maybe we should let the others in on the plan,' I whispered to Abeo.

'No. Don't back out now,' he replied, his expression stern. 'We need to do this. Mr Ex never takes a day off, and we can't afford to either.'

The applause was roaring when Chloe's song came to an end. With guidance from the host, she cut the luxurious six-tiered pink cake. Felicity and Chloe then joined Sanjay in the centre of the hall. Abeo moved towards them, and I followed suit.

'That song was the highlight of the evening,' Sanjay complimented.

'Thank you,' Chloe beamed.

Abeo widened his eyes a fraction as he looked at me. And I knew it was time.

A staged fight, sparked by Abeo. That was the plan to prise out Mr Ex.

He would want to be as close as possible, to hang on to every single word that passed between us. Abeo had a personal videographer in place to capture every moment involving him tonight; if anyone was lingering particularly close, trying to capture anything, we'd be able to see it in the footage.

'So, how are things going between you two?' Abeo said, looking between Sanjay and Chloe, his tone confrontational. 'It seems Chloe's moving on much quicker than Karim. Right, Sanjay?'

It hurt – even though I was the one who'd concocted the plan, who'd chosen the exact words that were coming from Abeo's mouth.

Colour rose high on Chloe's cheeks and her mouth quivered. 'Have you been drinking, Abeo?'

'Nope,' he responded, freestyling now. 'I'm just saying what the world is thinking. You certainly know how to move on from someone you claimed to have loved for years. Oh, you didn't answer my question, Sanjay. Don't you think it was quick?'

Sanjay clenched his jaw.

'I'm sure you don't mean that, Abeo,' Felicity murmured, eyes wide.

'I most certainly do,' snapped Abeo. 'While Chloe's busy making eyes at Sanjay and trying to get a reaction from Karim, our content creation is stalling. Maybe she's done with our group content and wants to use these scandals for clout just in time for the release of her big single?'

Chloe's eyes filled. She wasn't used to hearing Abeo be so harsh. Certainly not towards her anyway. Her mouth opened as though she was about to say something, but then she closed it again and rushed away.

'Screw you,' Sanjay growled at Abeo before going after her.

'What is *wrong* with you?' Felicity raged.

Some people approached Felicity to ask for selfies, and she used it as an excuse to get away too, throwing Abeo a filthy look.

'I'll check the footage tonight,' Abeo told me. 'Hopefully something's been captured.'

'Mate, I think she's really hurt,' I said. 'I don't want her thinking you're the bad guy. I'm going to find her and explain.'

'I'd apologize personally, but I don't think she'll want me anywhere near her right now. I hope she understands.'

I headed swiftly down the stairs, my chest tight with discomfort. I could make out Chloe's voice from a room on the right.

'No one ever says anything to *him*,' she complained loudly between sobs. 'All the hate comments are directed towards me. Karim gets *nothing*. And I'm the reckless, shameless slut.'

'It's OK,' Sanjay said soothingly. 'It's all going to blow over soon.'

'If a man chooses his career, he's smart and ambitious. But if a girl does, she's a selfish, evil bitch.' She cried deeply and it stung. Perhaps we'd gone a touch too far. 'Why do I feel like I'm losing everyone?'

'Chlo, you're not. Things will go back to normal soon. And you'll never lose me. I'm right here. I'll always be here for you.'

'Thanks, Sanjay. Nobody gets me like you do.'

That stung too. I decided to ignore it. She was upset.

'Karim embarrassed me on the dance floor tonight,' she said tearfully. 'I'm trying, but I just don't see things getting better.'

'It's not just you – these days, he's pushing everyone away.' Sanjay paused. 'Maybe he's figured out about us.'

My head pounded.

'I thought we were being subtle.'

'Subtlety isn't your strong suit,' he quipped, and she gave a watery giggle.

I'd had enough. I barged in.

Chloe's lips wrenched apart from Sanjay's as they jumped away from each other.

Seeing them together was like a fist slamming straight into my heart.

'Oh, Karim,' Chloe said desperately. 'It's not what you think.'

Hurt became fury. 'What?' I spat venomously. 'That you got with one of our best friends mere *weeks* after we broke up, after having an abortion you didn't even tell me about.'

She choked on a deep sob. I couldn't care less. Not any more.

'It was traumatic for you too, right?' I posed as a genuine question. 'Or maybe you didn't really care about that either?'

Sanjay stepped towards me with a hand raised, as though trying to tame a wild animal. 'Please, Karim –'

'Don't say my fucking name,' I shouted. 'You *knew* how I felt about her. Eye-opening to see what kind of a brother you really are.'

Sanjay could no longer meet my eyes and I faced Chloe again. 'We were together for *years*. We've been in love since we were kids.' My voice suddenly got louder. 'It's like the most important relationship of my life meant *nothing*.'

They both flinched.

It felt as though the ground was shaking, but I realized every part of *me* was quivering – with disgust, anger, humiliation.

I took deep breaths to steady myself, and I knew when I next spoke it needed to be calmly. 'I can't have people in my life that I don't trust, and I don't trust either of you. I'm done with you both.'

'Karim, please,' Chloe begged, mascara dripping down her face. 'I'm so, so sorry. Please don't do this. What about The Exes?'

'Don't let this ruin our years of friendship, bro,' Sanjay murmured, looking close to tears himself.

'I don't hate either of you,' I said, surprising myself with the emotion breaking out in my own voice. 'I just don't want anything to do with you. Be together, if that's what you want. Just stay the hell away from me.'

A Frenzy of Unfollows: Are The Exes Actually Becoming Exes?

A Fancy Ball? Stellar Fashion Face-off? Intense Exes Drama? Count me in.

It seems the end of London's Social Season meant the end of some friendships too. Queen Charlotte's Ball contained some rather tragic fall-outs between The Exes, a scorching heartbreak and, most devastating of all, fashion disasters which made me want to hurl my guts out.

After ditching Chloe mid-dance, Karim thought he'd gotten the upper hand. But our defiant diva went on to win Debutante of the Year, sing with chilling eloquence and *hook up with Sanjay Arya*! All in one night. Is this situation too morally questionable for us to be proud of our fellow feminist for not letting a man bring her down? My morals are always a little questionable but even I'm a tiny bit confused right now. Someone managed to snap Chloe in Sanjay's arms after the showdown, and I can confirm they looked mighty cosy . . . (photos have already been posted across my socials).

One thing is perfectly apparent now – while Karim is still heartbroken as ever, Chloe is already back in the game. Throw a spritz of Dior's Pure Poison over our shining new couple, swathe them in the freshest Balmain drip, add a slow-mo edit to a video clip of them looking into each other's eyes, and you know they've entered the scene to *kill*. Is it just me or is Sanjay suddenly looking rather hot? And I mean carefree, artistic, wildly-in-love Leo from *Titanic* hot. Move over Karim and make some space for our new crush! But remember to be careful, Sanjay, you wouldn't want to get so hot that you start setting things on fire, would you?

Right now, Chloe is making all the other mean girls we know look . . . nice. And yes, that includes the unforgiving Upper East Side girls of New York, the social-climbing heiresses of Singapore, and the pompous Parisian models who rule the fashion world. Barely recovered from her abortion, little Ms Clark has thrown away her childhood love and blossomed into a woman capable of . . . well, pretty much anything apparently. And yes, I did get chills while typing this, and you should've got them while reading it.

Karim Malik unfollowed Chloe Clark and Sanjay Arya on *everything* earlier today in a groundbreaking move indicating the separate directions their social media may now be heading in, for the first time ever. London Fashion Week is just around the corner. The famous quintet would always be seated next to one another and dressed in matching designerwear, but things might be different now. I sense change on the horizon! I don't know about you guys, but this year I'll have my eyes on The Exes more than the catwalk.

Stay tuned for my ratings of the Best & Worst Dressed from Queen Charlotte's Ball. Love her or hate her, Chloe Clark took the crown – a vision of elegance in that Stella McCartney bridal gown, she literally looked ready to walk down the aisle to commit to her one true love forever (yes, the irony is killing me too). As for whether *I* love or hate her . . . well, the truth is I'm still deciding. At least she isn't being boring this season, right?

Now, may this be a reminder to all you doting darlings. Love is probably the right choice. But lust will always be more fun.

I lust you all.
Yours Unfaithfully,
Mr Ex

Zara

18

'How's your summer job going?' Imran asked.

'All right,' Saliha responded nonchalantly, as though it wasn't the most popular guy in our year she was talking to. 'How are your parents doing? I haven't seen them in a while.'

'All good,' he replied, running a hand over his expertly faded beard. 'Yours?'

'Quite annoyed these days, to be honest. Our neighbour on the other side is causing more trouble than usual – throwing her rubbish in our garden, stealing our parking spot, having screaming matches in the middle of the night.'

'Yeah, Jessica's real charmin',' he said sarcastically, looking towards her house. 'She's shouted bare racist stuff to my mum over the years.'

He snorted when Saliha's mouth fell open in utter disbelief, and I thought about Imran's mum.

I hadn't interacted with his family much and all I knew about them was gleaned from hearing Mum chatter away on her endless phone calls.

His mum was a seamstress who'd stitched sarees, salwar kameez and lehengas for the local South Asian community until the middle Sayyid son had begun sending her enough money that she'd stopped taking orders. His father was disabled and rarely seen in public. However, my bedroom window faced their home and I occasionally caught sight of Imran manoeuvring his father's wheelchair to his car, helping him settle inside and driving off somewhere – most likely to the hospital, because he didn't seem well enough to be going anywhere else.

I occasionally glimpsed other things through those curtains too: Imran walking around his bedroom, working out, sitting at his desk . . .

Imran suddenly turned to me. 'Zara, right?'

My heart skipped a beat.

I nodded, a little surprised that he'd got my name right. With the kind of people he hung out with at school and the number of girls he'd spoken to by now, I thought any memory of me would be a long-buried, distant thing.

'Ain't you the one who aced her GCSEs?' I didn't bother to respond, and he tilted his head to one side appraisingly. 'Can't go wrong if I'm with the smarty-pants, innit? Give me your Snapchat.' When I furrowed my brows, he smiled and added, 'I'll send over some photos of my brother's notes. I've already got Sal on Snap.'

I paused.

'That would be great,' Saliha answered for me, and then squealed. 'This is going to be amazing, guys. Saqib did insanely well!'

Urgh. She was right though. Having access to Saqib's notes could help me achieve the grades I needed to get into university. I unlocked my phone and reluctantly looked up at Imran, who was towering at least a foot over me.

'Your username?' I asked.

'I'm not your man.'

How very appropriate – I could only imagine the number of girls he spoke to who needed that reminder. I couldn't help the way the corners of my mouth curled upwards. I noticed his smile deepen as mine did, and I looked away quickly.

Every time our eyes locked, I felt a strange connection. But I wasn't foolish enough to believe that I was the only one who felt such a way around him. Such flirtatious antics were probably how he got girls to fall for him, and I wasn't going to be one of them.

I began to type: *imnotyourman*.

It felt a little strange to add him. My parents didn't believe in mixed-gender friendships and would've preferred to have sent me to an all-girls school had there been one close by. There was no way they would've given me permission to communicate with any boy on my phone, but it *was* for the sake of my education . . .

He accepted the friend request there and then.

Wow. His Snapchat score was the highest I'd ever come across.

If anyone ever wanted to see proof of Imran's popularity, this was it. My score was pathetic, practically non-existent. Saliha was the only person I really went back and forth with on the app, and I usually preferred to call or FaceTime her.

I put my phone away and turned to Sal. 'I've got to go before it gets too late. See you tomorrow.'

Before leaving, I forced myself to meet Imran's gaze. He looked right at me, no hesitation or softness in his eyes. He made me feel so ... *seen*.

'Bye,' I said quietly, at which he nodded once, before winking at Sal and walking off himself.

From all the shoes in the entrance area to our house, I knew Dad's friends were over. There were no ladies' shoes, which meant I wouldn't be expected to say salaam; in fact, in this case Dad would prefer for me to make myself scarce, which I was more than happy to do.

When I re-entered my room, I saw that Imran's windows were wide open.

He suddenly came into view.

Topless, tense and flexing. I watched him admire the progress of his physique in his full-length mirror while he listened to fierce British rap, which I didn't recognize but knew Saliha definitely would.

I dared to go closer, until I stood at the edge of my window, staring at the muscles rippling on his smooth brown back as he moved. I could even make out the reflection of his defined abs from this angle. I inhaled slowly as I watched him.

His form was impeccable, literally good enough to get him signed with a top modelling agency. It was only a matter of time before his Instagram *really* blew up. I abruptly remembered the caption he'd written under a workout clip he'd posted.

The only thing that clears my mind when I'm stressed.

There were no further personal details, there rarely were on his account, but that had been enough to get me wondering what stressed out the cocky, carefree Imran Sayyid.

I'd come up with three possibilities: his imprisoned brother, his father's ill health, and having to live up to the middle Sayyid son's academic and career achievements.

Imran suddenly turned and looked right at me.

I practically threw myself on the floor. I lay there for a long moment, blood pounding, teeth clenched, heart thudding.

He must have noticed my reflection in his mirror from the moment I'd begun looking at him. He'd probably known the entire time I'd been checking him out.

'Oh, you idiot,' I groaned, running my hands over my face.

My phone pinged. I crawled to my bed and grabbed it.

It was a Snapchat notification from Imran.

A part of me wanted to wait, to play it cool before opening the message, but I couldn't do it, not after this. It would be impossible to focus on anything else until I'd somehow cleared the air. As I unlocked my phone, my head buzzed with all the possible clarifications I could send.

I was just cleaning my window.

I heard a sound coming from the street.

I wanted to talk to you about the chemistry notes.

They all sounded fake and stupid. I cringed, wishing Sal could be with me right now. She'd know the right thing to say. I took a deep breath and opened the chat.

I thought I'd give you a close-up too.

There was a video. I tapped it. It was a mirror-selfie-style clip of him flexing his biceps and then zooming in on his abs and slowly slanting down to the V-cuts that disappeared into the band of his tracksuit bottoms.

My mouth hung open as I decided what to say. I started typing, not wanting to make it look as though I was putting too much thought into it.

> There really was no need for that. I was only trying to find a way to tell you to turn down the music. You should be more mindful of your neighbours. Maybe this is the behaviour that drives Jessica to her bouts of racism

He sent multiple laughing emojis, which made me smile and feel a touch calmer.

But then:

> Yeah right. You keep telling yourself that, Khan

> And you keep telling yourself everyone's obsessed with you, Sayyid

He started typing something, then stopped and began again, almost as though he'd changed his mind about how to respond. It felt good to know that I was somehow putting him on the spot too. Then he sent the message.

Here are some notes on organic chemistry. I found
them helpful. Let me know what you think

It was weird to realize that the guy who always came across
as rebellious and blasé in school actually cared about his
education; perhaps Saqib had made more of an impression on
him than his eldest brother had.

Six photos arrived and I screenshotted them immediately,
not wanting to miss the chance of having access to any scrap
of information that could help me, especially related to
chemistry, which I found the hardest.

'Zara, come down,' Mum called in Urdu from the bottom
of the stairs. 'Help me with dinner.'

'Coming,' I called back, and quickly messaged one last time.

Thanks. I owe you.

After putting my phone on my bedside table, I drew my
curtains, not even daring a glance in his direction, and then
changed into a pink floral shalwar kameez, covering my head
loosely with the matching dupatta as Mum did. As I draped
the scarf around my neck, a flurry of Snapchat message
notifications arrived from Imran. Curiosity got the better of
me, and I opened the chat.

That quickly huh?
No girl has ever said that to me so soon
I'm kinda speechless
I guess I should say . . . thank you?

What was he was talking about? I scrolled back a little and practically yelped.

Instead of *I owe you*, I'd accidentally messaged *I love you*.

Cheeks hot and heart frantic, I began replying.

Oh my God. I meant I love you.

Urgh. It happened again. What the hell was wrong with me?!

I meant
I OWE you.

He disappeared from the chat, not bothering to reply. I didn't blame him. With all my staring and now this, he probably thought I was some weird loser who was obsessed with him.

I tried to call Sal to commiserate. She didn't pick up.

Not knowing what else to do, I buried my face in my pillow and screamed. I couldn't believe I'd messaged Imran Sayyid *I love you* within the first ten minutes of our first real conversation. Not once, but twice. I could never show my face again.

I was going to die of embarrassment.

Karim

17

I had a long, intense workout at my local gym.

Lifting the heavy weights and feeling the sweat bead on my skin had been the perfect escape. The rage and pain turned to exhaustion, then fizzled into something else. Something much easier to handle.

I sat in my car, wondering what to do next.

Abeo and Felicity were probably still at the ball; they'd been trying to get in touch with me for two hours now, but I'd put my phone on silent and ignored them. There wasn't a single thing either of them could say to make me feel better right now.

I found myself thinking about Zara Khan again.

The way she'd spoken to me had been so refreshing. I had an inkling *she'd* know the right thing to say in this moment. Without thinking too much, I called her. The ringing went on and on. Just when I thought she wouldn't pick up, she did. I froze, my head pounding with nerves in a way I wasn't used to.

'Hi. Calling to find out whether I managed to glue my shoe together?'

I chuckled. 'How did you know it was me?'

'I don't usually have unknown numbers call me. In fact, I never really give my number to anyone.'

'Well, I'm glad you gave it to me,' I replied tentatively, stretching my fingers over the cool leather of my steering wheel.

'And I guess I'll know by the end of this convo whether *I'm* glad I gave it to you.'

'So, I only get one convo for you to decide if I'm worth getting to know? What a way to put a guy under pressure.'

She paused for a moment. 'Something tells me you know how to handle the pressure just fine.'

'What are you up to?' I asked, remembering her soft brown skin and kohl-smudged eyes. I wished I could see her right now.

'Hiding in my room from everything and everyone.'

I laughed, loving her honesty and the fact that she wasn't bothered with trying to appear cool and busy on a weekend. 'I'm practically doing the same thing in my car right now.'

'Oh really? I assumed you'd have something more exciting to do on a Saturday night.'

'Don't go making assumptions about me now. Didn't you say people should get to know me themselves rather than assume they know me from whatever they see online?'

'Wow. Already quoting me right back to myself? I feel like a wise old philosopher now.'

'So how about it?' I asked, heartbeat spiking. 'Shall we get to know each other with no assumptions involved?'

She snorted a little. 'Do you really think you can manage it?'

'Why should it be any harder for me than it is for you?'

'Because your London is very . . . inaccessible and exclusive. Snobby, to be blunt. And mine is open for anyone who wants to step into it.'

'Even me?'

It seemed Zara was at a loss for words because the truth was that I couldn't just go anywhere I wanted in our city, especially to the parts where she probably hung out; most places would require security and careful planning. She laughed nervously, as though acknowledging that.

'OK, fine. I see what you mean. It's not so simple. What if I introduce you to my world and you introduce me to yours? But we both swear not to be judgemental in any way at all.'

'World?' I asked curiously. 'You make it seem like we're from different planets. We live in the same city.'

'But I doubt you've experienced much of my London. And I certainly haven't set foot in yours.'

'Let's do it,' I replied keenly.

Somehow, I knew that seeing her, being around her, would be the perfect distraction from the chaos of my life.

'Why don't you tell me the things you like doing and maybe I can plan a first date?' she asked tentatively. 'Oh . . . I didn't mean *date* date. Unless of course it is. But it doesn't have to be. I don't know if –'

'It's a date,' I said through a smile, finding her nervousness endearing. 'Definitely a date.'

She cleared her throat. 'OK, cool. Great. Nice. I mean . . . cool.'

We laughed at the same time, and I sensed a deeper crack form in the ice that was breaking between us.

I turned my car on and began to drive home, taking the long route as we continued our conversation. We spoke the entire journey, even as I walked up to my room and jumped into bed. There were no awkward or silent moments, and it almost felt like I'd known her for years. We stayed on the phone for many hours into the night. There was just so much to say and hear.

I wanted to know everything about Zara Khan.

Zara

20

I knocked on Saliha's front door with a grin so wide I probably looked manic to anyone passing by. I couldn't wait to tell her everything.

I would've texted her some details by now, but it was more exhilarating to gush over Karim in person, and there was so much to fill her in on because I'd spoken to him until about three in the morning.

My smile vanished the moment the door swung open.

Imran Sayyid.

How did I forget Sal had invited him to join us for this revision session?

'Hey.' He gave me a slow perusal.

I did the same back.

His fade was so fresh it made me wonder if he lived at his barber's. I was used to seeing him in a T-shirt, but he'd changed it up today by pairing it with dark jeans instead of joggers.

'Hey,' I repeated.

He gave me a lopsided smile. 'All right?'

Wait. This was the first time we'd spoken since he'd caught

me checking him out in a half-naked state, after which I'd accidentally professed my love for him. I cringed.

He moved to one side and held the door open for me. As I walked past him, I realized he could've left me more room.

My shoulder was practically scraping his chest when I paused and raised my brows, signalling that his cheap flirty tricks wouldn't work on me. The glint in his eyes told me that he wouldn't stop anyway.

'Great, we're all here,' Sal said, appearing in the hallway, completely oblivious to the weird energy between me and Imran. 'I've put all the notes on the dining table. Shall we?'

'I'm ready, fam,' Imran replied, following her. 'Dunno about Zara. She's tryna distract me already.'

I was about to fire out a defensive response, but Saliha had already left.

Imran chuckled before saying, 'Keep up, slowcoach.'

Sighing irritably, I shut the door and chased after them.

While I set up my books and stationery on the table, I was acutely aware of Imran's presence opposite me, of how his eyes would occasionally try to catch mine or linger on my hands, lips, neck. Nerves fluttered around my stomach.

'So,' Saliha began, 'school starts tomorrow.'

Imran leaned back in his chair, placing his well-built arms behind his head as a cushion. 'It's weird, innit? Summer's flown by. I'm lookin' forward to goin' back though.'

'Course you are,' Saliha jeered. 'Can't wait to go back to chirpsing the galdem, right? The girls literally throw themselves at you.'

'Why you talkin' like the chirpsin' stopped during summer?'

Saliha smacked his arm and giggled but I cast him the most disgusted look I could muster. I hated the way he always got who he wanted, that he didn't think twice before breaking their heart. He was probably the guy who'd ruined Hania's summer and moved on the very next day while she was a complete mess. I despised his attitude.

'What's up with you?' Saliha nudged.

'Oh nothing,' I replied casually. 'I'm just allergic to fuckboys.'

For a second there was pin-drop silence, and I thought that perhaps I'd really offended him. But then he rocked his head back and laughed. Saliha joined him and, shortly after, I did too.

'Whoa, Zara,' Imran said, face bright with humour. 'Didn't know you had it in you.'

'Well,' Saliha sighed, 'she's on to something. You've gotta admit you're a bit of a wasteman.'

I secured my hair into the bun I liked to make when studying. 'Someone had to say it to your face at some point.'

'I appreciate the honesty,' he said, his voice dropping to a lower register. 'Tell me, am I the guy your parents warned you about?'

Imran leaned forward, muscles flexing as he placed his elbows on the table and planted his chin on his fists, coming even closer to me. Although there was a whole table between us, it felt like his face could've touched mine. My heart thudded wildly.

Saliha finally sensed the weird vibe between us because she cleared her throat noisily and said, 'OK, let's start recapping chemistry first.'

'Saqib's notes are sick for Year Twelve chem,' Imran said casually, zapping out of the moment.

'Great, let's do it.' Saliha turned in my direction and subtly widened her eyes, making it clear we'd discuss Imran later.

In between revising, Saliha and Imran cracked jokes and shared stories. I was quiet the entire time, trying to retain as much knowledge as possible.

'I'm getting hungry,' Saliha said around two hours in. 'I'll get us some snacks.'

'I'll come with you,' I said quickly, not wanting to be left alone with Imran.

'Nah, you guys carry on,' Sal waved.

I felt Imran's eyes focus on me, but I refused to look up from my notes. Perhaps if I looked busy, he wouldn't attempt to strike up a conversation.

'You're a quiet one, ain't you, darlin'?'

No such luck.

'Don't call me darling. And I only speak to people I feel like speaking to.'

'Oh yeah, I forgot, you prefer lookin' at me, innit?'

I avoided his gaze.

'I ain't complainin'. I like lookin' at you too. But you've seen more of me than the other way round.'

'And that's exactly how it's going to stay.'

He made a puppy face and looked like a child for a second before his devilish grin came back. 'I'd argue that's unfair.'

'I would argue that we've come here to study, and you should focus on doing that rather than winding me up.'

'Hmm, that ain't entirely true. I came here to study *and* see you.'

My stomach somersaulted.

I remembered the time he'd passed me my library card: the kindness, the wink, the way I'd felt. A part of me was exhilarated that my childhood crush was saying this to me, but I stamped that part down. Imran Sayyid was a player, the most dangerous and experienced kind. I wasn't going to buy into this.

'Yes, I'm sure you were just as eager to see me as you are the –' I put on a sarcastic tone – '*galdem* you were busy *chirpsing* all summer.'

He snorted. 'It's bare funny hearin' you talk like that.'

'Like what? Like you? Now you know how you sound.'

'Look,' he said, his voice suddenly quieter, as though sharing a secret. 'I gotta say it – if you were so allergic, you wouldn't have been eyein' me like that from your room.'

'You really need to get over that, OK?'

'And you need to get over yourself and admit you're kinda into me.'

My mouth fell open. OK, if that's how he wanted to play it. 'Goodness, you're cocky. You've gone through this entire routine with multiple girls before me, haven't you? But I need to clarify to you that I'm *not* going to fall for your typical plan.'

'What if I admit I ain't got a plan with you?'

I looked at him suspiciously. 'Oh, there's always a plan with guys like you. You're going to flirt with me for a while, then *convince* me to get it on with you, and right after I give in, you'll drop me for another girl. And then you and everyone else at school will call me a slut.'

Imran looked surprised for a second, maybe even offended. And then a mask of careless humour crept on to his face. It seemed he was good at hiding his true thoughts and emotions.

'So, you're admittin' I *could* convince you to get it on with me?'

I scoffed. 'Thanks for admitting your intentions are purely physical.'

'You haven't really given me a chance to explain what my intentions are. Being purely physical with me came from your mouth, not mine. Did you just give me a glimpse of what goes on in your mind?'

I blushed. Heavily.

'I'm not going to let anyone get in my way this year,' I responded tightly. 'I need to get into university so I can move far, far away from all of *this*.'

His gaze fixed on me, as though he was trying to figure me out. 'Far away from what exactly?'

I'd given too much away. Personal information. About how I was feeling, what I desperately craved, the kind of life I was currently trapped in at home . . .

'Nothing,' I said coldly. 'At this rate, *you*.'

I put my earphones in and looked down at my notes.

Thankfully, he didn't attempt to speak to me again. But the curiosity that had sparked in his eyes didn't seem to leave me alone either.

Zara

21

The study session was more productive than I'd predicted. In three hours, we managed to go through most of the chemistry notes and large chunks of maths. As soon as I decided to move on to biology, my phone buzzed.

A text from Karim. My heart leaped.

> I can't stop thinking about you. If you're up for it maybe we could meet today? I'm already out. I could drive to East London now if you're free . . . I just need an address of where to pick you up

I grabbed Saliha's arm. 'Can I speak to you outside, please?'

Imran looked between us for a second and then went back to scrolling on his phone – something he'd been doing on and off for the past hour, in between tapping my shoes with his, throwing glances in my direction and asking me questions about chemistry.

Saliha followed me into the corridor.

'Karim's saying he wants to meet.' I swallowed, showing her the text. 'We spoke on the phone for ages last night, and I told him to come down to my part of town at some point so I could show him around. I didn't realize he'd want to come *now*.'

'Holy shit! This is insane,' Saliha squealed, her eyes glued to my phone screen, but I was too busy thinking through the logistics to be excited.

'My curfew is eight,' I said. 'That's two hours from now. Just about enough time for a date, right?'

'Do it!'

I gave her a death stare. 'Wearing this? I *sleep* in this hoodie sometimes. But if I go back home to get all dressed up, Mum will know something's up, and she won't let me out again.'

Sal kissed her teeth comically. 'Karim Malik really doesn't understand the struggle for brown girls, does he?' Her eyes softened as she caught my tense look. 'Listen, sis, you can go up to my room and borrow whatever clothes and make-up you want.'

I wrung my hands together nervously.

'Not that you need to change anything,' Sal added sweetly. 'You've got an effortlessly beautiful look going on. I think he'll like that you aren't trying too hard just because you're meeting *him*. Text him back and say it's on! Remember to tell him to pick you up in the street behind ours so no one sees you guys.'

The panic suddenly struck deep. 'What if someone *does* see us and tells my parents?' My heart stopped at the mere thought. 'What if something happens and my mum suddenly needs me and tells me to come back right away?'

Saliha snorted. 'No offence but your mum is on the phone so much that she barely knows what's going on around her. The only thing that woman needs is her gossip buddies. As for the nosy aunties in the neighbourhood, just put your hoodie over your head. You'll basically look like a boy, which means a free pass to do anything you like, including hopping into a random guy's car.'

'Right, OK,' I replied, slowly registering everything Sal had just said. 'I could actually get away with this.'

'You most definitely can. And you will. And *I* will live every moment vicariously through you. Oh my God, Zara, you're going on a date with *Karim Malik*!'

We locked eyes for a second, and then we were squealing, hugging, jumping up and down.

'Hold on,' I said, breaking away, serious again. 'I've never been on a date before. What do I even do?'

'Just think of it as chilling with a friend. Be exactly as you are with me. Well, maybe not *exactly* because you should defo throw in some flirting.' When I widened my eyes, she gripped my shoulder soothingly. 'You're going to be just fine, sis. Now text him to come and get you already.'

With a grin, she left me in the corridor alone. My hands felt clammy as I texted Karim the street name. He messaged back almost instantly.

I'll be with you shortly

My stomach clenched nervously.

I went straight up to Sal's room to refine the natural make-up look I'd done earlier, darkening my mascara and putting some blusher on. By the time I'd finished getting ready, packed my things and said my goodbyes to Mr and Mrs Begum, I heard another ping.

'I think he's here,' I whispered to Sal.

'You better not keep him waiting then,' she murmured back mischievously. 'And send me your live location.'

I nodded, then turned to Imran. 'Thanks for the notes. They're really good. I'll see you later.'

'Why you leavin' so soon?' he asked in a disappointed tone.

'Something came up,' I replied, feeling a strange sense of satisfaction that he wanted me to stay.

'You look nice.' He winked, then his gaze dropped to my lips. 'I like the gloss.'

My belly swooped low. Imran Sayyid was noticing me so closely with that dark, unwavering gaze of his and it was making me feel things I didn't want to feel.

'Thanks,' I muttered, looking away quickly.

I could tell from the corner of my eye that he found my shyness amusing. Another excited hug from Sal and I was off into the warm early-evening breeze, my body zinging with nerves.

As I turned into the next street, I stopped dead in my tracks at the sight of a pearly white Ferrari. It was completely out of place among the middle-class terraced houses, with middle-class cars parked out front.

I hugged my hood tighter around my face. People would surely be looking out of their windows at the glorious revving of the luxury sports car. It was so easy to imagine Imran and his friends drooling over it. I practically jogged up to the car, pleased to see that it had tinted windows, and jumped in.

'Let's get out of here,' I said, barely registering Karim's presence and snapping on my seat belt.

The aroma of rich, leathery oud filled my senses and left my mouth watering. He even *smelled* rich and famous.

Karim laughed. 'You're rather eager. You haven't even informed me of where you'd like to go.'

Although I'd spoken to him only recently, it suddenly registered with me just how posh he sounded, how different his speech and style was to the people I'd been sitting with minutes ago.

'Erm,' I replied nervously, looking out the window. 'Please just start driving and I'll tell you on the way.'

'OK,' he said gently, and moved out.

'Turn left now,' I said, feeling calmer as the distance from home increased.

'Rather bossy, aren't you?'

I finally turned to him properly. He was in formal clothes, but he'd shed his blazer and unbuttoned his white shirt, so it revealed a bit of his chest. His sleeves were rolled messily but his hair was slicked into shape neatly.

His side profile was exquisite – his jawline, the slope of his nose, his shapely lips. *He* was exquisite. And then it hit me like a ton of bricks – I was sitting in a white Ferrari with Karim Malik.

'Oh, shit.'

He looked at me. 'What's wrong?'

I cleared my throat. 'Nothing.'

Karim glanced at me, and I felt the urge to throw myself out of the car.

'You look nice.'

I raised my brows at him. 'Don't you dare.'

'What?' he grinned that heart-stopping grin I'd seen a million times in his videos.

'I was studying at my friend's place. You didn't give me much of a heads-up, so it's basically your fault I look like a mess.'

He laughed. 'I was being honest, actually. I've never been on a first date with a girl who was dressed so casually. I like it. It looks like something you'd lounge in in your bedroom . . .'

So, this was definitely a date. I gulped a little.

'Well, thanks,' I replied awkwardly. 'And you look really . . .'

The words *classy*, *sexy*, *hot* came to mind. That's where my brain stopped working, and I certainly wasn't going to blurt any of those out.

'Aren't you going to finish that sentence?'

'Nope – I'll leave it to your imagination.'

'All right. Well then, I'll go with ravishingly handsome.' We stopped at a traffic light, and he faced me completely. 'Perhaps even irresistible. I'm close, aren't I?'

I shook my head but couldn't help smiling at the same time. We locked eyes and I felt my breath catch.

'You're taking me around your London then?'

'Since I have a curfew, I can only show you a fraction of it today. You'll have me home by eight, right?'

'Yes, Cinderella,' he said with a smirk. 'I'll have you home on time. That's a promise.'

'Just to be clear, you're not an arrogant prick, right?'

Karim knocked his head back and laughed loudly. I joined in. It felt good to hear him laugh, and to know that I was the reason.

'If I was an arrogant prick, do you think I'd own up to it?'

'I guess you'd be too much of an arrogant prick to admit you're an arrogant prick. It'll just be difficult to hang out with you if all you do is this . . .' I paused to screw up my face and put on a posh accent. 'Urgh this place is filthy. Must I really park my darling car next to these common cars owned by common folk?'

Karim laughed loudly again. 'Wow. You really have a lot to learn about me.'

'You have a lot to learn about me too.'

'I'm looking forward to it.'

Something deep inside me that had grown still and silent over the years began to flutter, slowly at first and then with a ferocity that left me breathless.

It felt like hope.

Karim

22

As I drove, it suddenly hit me that I couldn't remember the last time I'd been so fully present in the moment with someone.

In Zara's presence, my mind didn't wander; I wasn't thinking about The Exes, Mr Ex, or any of the scandals circulating about me online.

Everything with Zara felt alarmingly real and rooted. She hadn't attempted to record anything, hadn't even glanced at her phone once. Somehow, I had known that meeting her would be like this; something in my gut had told me she was exactly who I'd been searching for.

'I don't think I've thanked you yet for helping my family get the catering deal,' Zara said after a short, comfortable silence. 'It's a life-changing opportunity for my brother's company. It means more than I could tell you in words.'

I looked over at her. When her dark eyes met mine, my stomach lurched as though I'd missed a step.

'That's OK,' I replied. 'They serve incredible food and got the job through pure talent. So, where are we going?'

'Just keep driving to my instructions,' she said coyly. 'You'll see soon enough.'

When we arrived, I parked in the spot she suggested and noted that the area *did* look quite rough. Then I asked, 'What now?'

She grinned. 'We're going to the arcade. And when we're hungry, we'll go and savour my local fish and chips because it's the best in the world.'

Her excitement was contagious. I couldn't recall when I'd last visited an arcade. It must have been *years*. We'd stopped going to busy places like that to avoid being bombarded by fans; for a long time now, we'd chilled only in the most exclusive places around London.

'Just remember what you said about not being an arrogant prick,' she said, jumping out before I could get her door.

'I don't actually remember making any promises of the sort,' I replied with a smirk. 'Just give me a second.'

I went around to the boot, rummaged in my gym bag for a bit, then donned a cap and hoodie.

'Just in case the paparazzi come for you, right?' she teased.

'I'd really prefer not to talk about that ... stuff,' I replied quietly.

'OK, I see. Anyway, I'd rather talk about how I'm going to beat you at air hockey.'

As easy as that my smile returned, and my heart felt lighter too.

'So, you're competitive then?'

'I can be.' She threw me a sly look.

As we walked, I noticed that on the opposite side of the street a group of boys were hanging around the off-licence. They were eyeing us closely, then turned their gaze towards my car. I pulled out my phone, texted my live location to security and sent them a picture of where I'd parked my car.

Zara eyed the boys. 'Maybe we should just go somewhere else?'

I scoffed. 'What happened to not being a snob about parking with the common folk? Don't worry, it's taken care of.'

'Those guys just scream trouble,' she whispered anxiously.

I felt the urge to reach for her hand, but I didn't. It felt too soon for that.

When we entered the arcade, its loud music, dim lights and blitz of colourful gaming machines made the outside world fade away. The interior was a little time-worn and grimy, but I liked it.

Zara grabbed some spare change from her pocket and began to insert it into the air-hockey game.

'Wait, I've got it,' I said quickly, ever the chivalrous guy who paid for everything at dates.

I pulled out my Gucci cardholder and removed one of my bank cards.

'There's no cashpoint around here,' she said with a shrug. 'It's cool, I've got it.'

She inserted the coins, went round to the other side, and we started to play.

Zara was so sharp and fast with her disk that she didn't miss a single hit, and I was barely hitting the puck in time as it zipped around the slippery surface of the table. She scored goal after goal and won the first game easily.

I pretended to wipe sweat off my forehead. 'I see you aren't going easy on me.'

'You'll get there,' she replied smugly. 'Round two?'

I nodded, bracing myself as she inserted more coins. I poured my entire being into the next game; nothing else in the world existed right then. I stretched my stance, arms moving wildly across the table. I got my first goal in. I wasn't modest about it and punched the air hard while whooping loudly. She gave me a look but there was a smile tugging at her lips.

After that, I really got the hang of it.

When I won the second game, I looked right at her and, with satisfaction, said, 'You'll get there.'

She narrowed her eyes and pursed her lips. 'Oh, it's so *on*.'

I didn't feel the time pass as we worked our way through the arcade, throwing ourselves into one game after another. I loved her playful competitiveness. I lost games gracefully, but when she did, she made cute grumpy faces and said we *had* to play again.

When I finally got round to checking my watch, I remembered I didn't have long left with her. I didn't want the evening to end. I didn't want to leave her world so soon.

Zara

23

It was impossible not to be open with him – we laughed loudly, swore colourfully, placed bets and jumped around like a pair of careless kids.

I didn't quite realize when it happened, but at some point he stopped being Karim Malik and just became a normal guy. A guy I was having a great time with. I no longer felt like an awkward introvert – I was fun and relaxed and carefree. Maybe this was the Zara I was supposed to be, if things in my life had been different, if my family had built up my confidence rather than slowly tearing it down.

When we walked towards his car, still giddy from playing in the arcade, I noticed Karim nod at a man parked just behind him. He was clearly Karim's security guard, who he must have alerted earlier. The man looked at me carefully, no doubt surprised that Karim was hanging out in a place so different to his usual haunts, with a girl who was definitely different to his usual type.

'The chippie is just a two-minute walk from here,' I said, then suddenly felt a little insecure and added, 'but I understand if you wanna leave now.'

'No way!' he exclaimed keenly. 'I was promised the best fish and chips in the world.'

A small smile settled on my face as I led us towards the restaurant. The aroma hit us before we entered, and my mouth watered intensely. But as we went in, I felt a fresh wave of insecurity. I'd never really noticed before, but the place was small, with mismatched chairs, and the floor and tables could've used some cleaning.

I turned towards Karim, half-expecting him to be grimacing behind my back, but he looked perfectly calm as he took the place in.

'Where would you like to sit?' he asked casually.

'Maybe a table near the back,' I replied, trying to match his calm energy.

It seemed he was taking our agreement to not be judgy seriously, and I was going to give him the benefit of the doubt. I chose the cleanest table; it still had a ketchup smear and a few crumbs scattered across it, but I hoped he wouldn't notice.

Karim came round to my side and I turned to him and said, 'Oh, sorry, would *you* like to sit here?'

'No, I'm getting the chair for you.'

I couldn't control my giggle and suddenly *he* looked like the insecure one. His gesture was just so unexpected; no one had ever done something like that for me before.

'That's so kind, thank you,' I said quickly, reassuring him. 'But I was going to let you sit down while I go and order.'

'No, you treated me to the games, so I'd like to get dinner,' he said firmly, then looked towards the man waiting near the till. 'Erm. They don't come to you?'

I shook my head and snorted. 'They don't take card payments either. Only cash.'

'Seriously?' Karim looked baffled. 'I didn't even realize there *were* restaurants in London that are cash only.'

'Don't worry, it's on me. Shall I just order you what I like?'

He gave me a lopsided smile. 'Sounds good. Thank you so much.'

I ordered two large portions of fish and chips, complete with mushy peas, curry sauce, tartare sauce, and two ginger beers. The food came quickly, and when I dived in without hesitation, Karim followed suit. This meal wasn't meant to be eaten with patience and grace.

'It's good, right?' I asked, putting extra salt and vinegar on my chips.

'Oh my God, so good,' he replied through a mouthful, something I could tell was uncharacteristic of his usual manners.

I couldn't quite believe I was having my favourite meal with my favourite influencer. This was just bizarre. No one would ever believe this, unless they spotted me . . .

'By the way, if you see me randomly dive under the table, don't be too alarmed,' I said, suddenly panicking slightly.

His brows shot together uncomprehendingly. 'Why would you do that?'

'Let's just say, I can't have any aunty or uncle from my community seeing me out with a guy.'

Karim looked at me thoughtfully. 'Well, I don't want anyone seeing me and then screaming it to a crowd. So *I* may be the one doing the diving.'

'I find it much easier to talk to you than I thought I would,' I admitted, breaking the succulent fish with my fork. 'For some reason it feels like I've known you for ages.'

'Same. I haven't had this much fun in a long while.'

His words pulled at my heartstrings, making them strum and sing.

Karim's forehead creased. 'Can I ask you for a favour?'

Curiosity tugged me to edge a little closer to him. I nodded.

'Please don't go on my socials or read about me online. I don't want it to affect how you see me. You were right: I do sometimes wish I could introduce myself to people *myself* rather than them assuming they know me because of everything on the internet.'

Easy enough. 'It's a deal. I was planning to cut off from social media anyway, so I can focus on my A levels.'

Karim looked relieved. 'So, this is your London then?'

'Just a small bit of it. What do you think?'

'I like it – more than I thought I would. But that might have something to do with my escort being so damn attractive.'

I blushed and looked down, unable to meet the intense look in his eyes.

'Is it my turn to show you around *my* London now?' he asked.

'Erm.' I widened my eyes a little. 'I don't know if I'll ever be ready for your London. To fit in there, it seems like you need the right kind of contacts, status, wealth. But I guess you can tell me what it's *really* like.'

'I'll let you decide that for yourself . . .'

Excitement flushed my cheeks, but then I noticed the clock behind him and felt another wave of panic. 'I have to be home in ten minutes.'

'Don't worry, I'll get you there,' he said, pushing his plate away and standing.

We rushed to his car, and he swiftly drove me back to the street he'd picked me up from.

'I don't feel like dropping you home,' he whispered after parking up.

My spirits lifted until I felt like I was floating. 'And I don't feel like going home.'

We leaned into our headrests and looked into each other's eyes. It didn't feel strange or uncomfortable. I didn't feel the wave of shyness or insecurity that would usually make me turn away, curl back into my shell. He stretched a hand towards me, and I felt tense for only a moment before he gently tucked a strand of hair behind my ear. I closed my eyes and savoured the fluttering sensation that lingered from his touch.

I walked into my house, greeted my parents, only half-listening to a lecture from Dad about how I'd been going out too much, had a shower and got into bed, but I wasn't *really* there.

In my mind, I was still with him.

Karim

24

The first day back.

I walked through the gates of St Victor's School knowing that things would be different this year, and yet I still hoped The Exes would be waiting for me at our picnic table like they always used to.

It was empty. The other tables were full of high school students and sixth formers, but the table right in the centre was left abandoned. Everyone knew it was ours, whether or not we used it.

We'd created so many memories at this school, and they hung vividly before my eyes: me explaining our weekly schedule to The Exes while we lounged around our picnic table; Chloe eating an apple as she leaned against my locker waiting for me after class; Sanjay sneaking in a quick smoke as he drew hilarious caricatures of us during lunch; Abeo waiting for our teacher to turn away before throwing gossip-filled notes at my head; Felicity pulling out a camera at the most inappropriate times to capture content for our vlogs.

And, of course, everyone else watching us from afar, taking note of everything we did so they could emulate it, finding any excuse to talk to us or sit nearby, trying to earn invites to our exclusive events or get a mention on one of our platforms. Their stares would be the same as ever this year, but what they saw now would be very different; there could be no hiding the divisions that had formed between us.

All these memories that I held so close to my heart suddenly felt like something to forget rather than to reflect on.

'Hey, Karim. Over here.'

It was Abeo. Felicity waved at me from beside him. They were standing by one of the stone pillars that lined the marble corridor leading to the grand entrance.

'Goodness gracious,' Felicity said, getting straight into it, 'the ball got rather tense! Chloe filled me in on what happened between you guys, and I just want to be clear with you that I don't support what they're doing at all. It's way too soon and so disrespectful. Did you manage to cool off on Sunday?'

I nodded.

My Sunday with Zara had been perfect. We were texting non-stop now; she was addictive. Although the sting of Chloe and Sanjay getting together was still there, it seemed distant now, already in the background.

'I was going to apologize to Chloe just after the ball,' Abeo said, 'but when Felicity told me what happened, I didn't bother.'

'Did you guys notice the cryptic messages she's been posting everywhere online?' Felicity hissed. 'Talk about playing the victim.'

I sighed. 'I unfollowed them, so I have no idea what either of them are up to.'

Abeo's eyes widened. 'That's a big move.' None of us had unfollowed each other before this. 'I obviously get it but ...' He looked at Felicity pointedly.

Felicity stuttered before saying, 'I hope you don't expect us to unfollow them too? We've got to think about our collective platforms –'

'No,' I cut in. 'I would never ask you to do that. I just really didn't want to see them on my page any more.'

'Understandable,' Abeo said, nodding.

'They barely have anything in common,' Felicity huffed. 'Chloe always thought Sanjay was basic, and he always thought she was fake. Just watch how they barely even last two months. They've messed up The Exes for a meaningless fling.'

Abeo glared at something in the distance.

I followed his gaze.

Chloe and Sanjay were walking in our direction, hand in hand, black and white uniforms crisply neat, expressions fierce. It was almost as though time slowed when Chloe's eyes cut into mine, communicating only one thing: *I don't give a shit any more.*

My heart clenched, but my face betrayed no emotion. We both turned away from each other at the same time.

'The nerve!' Felicity screeched.

'Let's not do this right now,' I muttered, massaging my temple with a hand.

Abeo nodded. 'There are far too many eyes on us. Let's not give them anything more to talk about. Did you notice that neither of them were wearing any Exes icons?'

'What does that mean exactly?' Felicity snapped. 'Are they even Exes any more?'

They both looked at me.

An idea flashed in my mind. 'We need a meeting with them about the brand, and you're going to arrange it, Felicity.' She opened her mouth to argue but I stopped her with a look. 'They'll listen to you. You're the one with the least animosity towards them.'

'*Obviously* I care about our brand and income,' Felicity said, 'but I hate being caught in the middle.'

'Karim's right though,' Abeo chipped in. 'Before getting our managers and PR team involved, we need to figure out what *we* want. We haven't uploaded anything as a quintet for a while now.'

'But our followers are still going up,' Felicity said with a shrug.

Abeo snorted. 'I guess it's true what they say – there's no such thing as bad publicity.'

Felicity threw her head back and whined, 'I *really* don't want to talk to them. I just want to be in a dance studio doing ballet until I drop.'

Abeo placed a hand on her shoulder. 'Perfect! Azad's mehndi is coming up and we need you to start working on the choreography for it.'

'I've already started that . . . and I did it for a group of five dancers.'

I cleared my throat. 'I've got plenty of cousins who'd be happy to fill in the remaining two spots. There's no way Chloe or Sanjay will be a part of my family celebration.'

The bell rang and we separated.

Chloe and I were in the same form for registration and I'd usually sit with her, but today the seats on either side of her were filled with girls who stared daggers at me while she completely ignored my existence, gazing into a mirror and applying lipstick. It seemed she'd already chosen her cronies for the year.

I walked past them all and took an empty seat near the back. Classmates stole glances in my direction, whispering agitatedly. The scandals over the summer had provided enough gossip for the rest of the year. I ignored them all.

There was only one reason I was still in school, despite earning enough through my social media to not have to worry about working, and that was the University of St Andrews. My parents and siblings had studied there, as had my grandfather. While Mum and Kiran had studied history of art, Dad and Azad had done computer science, and that was exactly what I wanted to study too.

This was more than a family tradition. It felt like something I had to accomplish for *myself*. I planned to stay focused in school, keep up my grades, and not let any of this gossip get in the way of my dreams.

At lunchtime, I sat with Abeo in an empty classroom, our lunch trays before us, my head floating with trigonometry, university applications, and worries about whether The Exes brand would survive all of this drama.

Felicity suddenly burst in, lunch tray in hand. 'They've agreed to come,' she groaned.

She sat down facing us and stuffed a spoonful of peas into her mouth.

'Did they agree easily?' I asked.

She gulped her food down and rolled her eyes. 'They were quiet for a sec and then began whispering. After making me wait around for a good few minutes – on an empty, growling stomach, may I add – they said yes. Who the hell do they think they are? I'm so done with them.'

We ate our lunch in silence, each of us lost in our own thoughts. Mere seconds after we'd finished, the door creaked open. Chloe entered first, her expression steely and defensive. Sanjay followed close behind her with a sheepish look on his face.

'You wanted to see us?' Chloe asked me sharply.

My insides darkened at her bluntness. It was a show; it had to be. She couldn't be so cold, not after everything we'd been through together.

'Yes,' I said, gesturing for them to join us. 'Thank you for coming. We wanted to discuss the future of our brand.'

She looked flustered at the kind, professional stance I was taking, unsure of how to proceed.

I was the unspoken leader of The Exes for a reason, and I wasn't going to let personal quarrels break up a brand worth multimillions.

Zara

25

'Urgh, bunch of rude cows,' Saliha hissed, glaring at the girls who'd raced past us to grab the last few seats in the lunch hall.

'Excuse me?' said the tallest one, glaring back.

'It's OK,' I said quickly. 'I'm sure there's space elsewhere.'

Saliha kissed her teeth and strutted off, her steaming tomato pasta bobbing on her lunch tray with each forceful step.

Until this point, it had been the best first day back ever. I'd filled Sal in on every detail of my date with Karim Malik and we'd been giggling non-stop. She had been in such a chipper mood, but now she was cranky as hell because she couldn't stand the arrogant way all these popular girls behaved.

There was an obvious hierarchy in our school, and although it could be fluid at times, with people moving around between the different cliques, there was a consensus on who was popular and who wasn't. I hated the way the overconfident loudmouths at the top assumed the rest of us were passive side characters who spent our time admiring them when in fact we were just busy living our own lives.

Sal's sudden shriek of irritation made me jump.

'I was literally standing right next to those seats,' she protested. 'It's an unspoken rule that if you're standing that close, they are *your* seats. You'd expect them to have more respect for sixth formers.'

'Will you stop ranting already? Don't let them ruin our lunch.'

'That girl is Hania's younger sister, Alisha,' Sal said. 'There are rumours that *she* was the one dating Imran over the summer. No wonder she's suddenly so confident. She thinks she's become popular through association.'

I couldn't help but glance back and look at the girl properly. I saw it – both her resemblance to Hania and the reason Imran was drawn to her. There was a particular look he generally went for, and she encapsulated it entirely. Her dark hair was long and glossy, her heavy make-up accentuated her doll-like features, and she knew exactly how beautiful she was.

'Apparently they stopped seeing each other because Hania's parents wouldn't allow either of their daughters out the house after Hania was caught with that other guy. He was from another school, by the way.'

I sighed, an indignant flare sparking in my chest. 'Let me guess – they still gave their two sons complete freedom to do whatever the hell they wanted.'

My gaze flicked over to Imran's table, where Hania and her twin brothers, who were in the academic year below ours, were also sitting. They were all part of the same crowd and were always the loudest in the hall. The most watched too.

'Obviously,' Saliha hissed. 'They were uploading new content on their socials every day. Racing their crappy cars, going to the gym in the middle of the night, chilling in shisha bars.'

'It's so pathetic. Wherever Imran goes, all his boys follow,' I said, looking at him. 'I have no idea why any girl would willingly hang out with them. They have absolutely no respect for women.'

Imran suddenly looked right at me. I froze.

He'd barely acknowledged my existence at school before. We'd talked more during our study session at Saliha's than we had in ten years of school together.

To my surprise, he nodded a greeting at us, then called us over with a tilt of his head. The others from his table turned to face us.

I gulped, hating the attention.

'Shall we just go and sit there?' Saliha asked tightly. 'I'm hungry. I'll start a riot if I don't eat right now.'

I opened my mouth to say *no*, but she was already sauntering over.

'You girls strugglin' to find seats?' Imran asked. 'No problem. I got you.'

His eyes lingered on me and I looked away sharply. I wanted to have a chilled-out lunch with my best friend, not be thrown into the midst of this judgemental clique where I wouldn't be able to relax for a second.

Imran turned to the two boys opposite him. 'You guys are done, so bugger off now.'

The moment they left, Saliha sat down and said to Imran, 'Your girlfriend was pretty rude to us just now.'

His brows furrowed. 'Girlfriend?'

'Alisha.'

'She ain't my girlfriend,' he said, eyes flicking to me. 'You gonna sit?'

Without a word, I took a seat and began eating my pasta. I'd decided I was going to be as reserved as possible.

'Hold on, what did you just say about my sister?' Hania snapped. 'I heard you mention her name.'

There was pin-drop silence around the table for a few seconds before Sal spoke up.

'I just mentioned she was quite rude to us and took our seats from right under my nose, and then had the nerve to be smug about it.'

'And I said we ain't seein' each other any more,' Imran chipped in nonchalantly.

'Stop bitchin' about my sister,' Hania hissed, and then stared at her brothers. 'You two could stick up for her as well. She's your damn sister too.'

It was obvious they weren't in the habit of defending their sisters either at home or anywhere else.

Hania grabbed her tray and stormed off, her two best friends trailing close behind. I inhaled deeply. Great. We all had biology together and I'd probably have to deal with passive-aggressive comments spoken *just* loud enough to be overheard ...

'Girls are too sensitive, man. They go crazy over the smallest things,' said one of Hania's brothers, snickering with the other boys. It was the larger twin, and I felt the urge to slap his round, haughty face. I could only imagine how unsupportive he would've been when Hania's summer had turned to hell.

'Excuse me?' I hadn't planned to speak up, but it had been impossible for me to hold back.

'What?' he barked at me.

'Your comment was sexist and stupid.' The words came out of me cold and venomous. 'At least she has the guts to stick up for her family, which is a lot more than you have the guts to do.'

'Oh,' Imran hooted and flicked his wrist. 'You got told.'

All the boys on the table began laughing, jeering and throwing around taunting comments.

'Man's getting gunned down today.'

'She put you in your place, fam.'

My hands started to feel tense and clammy.

The larger twin made a face at me and said, 'Maybe you should keep your typical Paki nose out of other people's business, you little nobody.'

The boys around him began laughing so hard they were struggling to catch their breath, pushing into each other and smacking the table. Only Saliha and Imran remained serious.

'That's out of order, man,' Imran said harshly. 'Apologize now.'

Hurt crept deep inside my chest, squeezing tightly, until tears pricked at my eyes. I took a deep breath. I wasn't going to let any of these people see how much this was getting to me.

'You all right?' Imran asked me.

I avoided his gaze and didn't bother to respond. He was as bad as the rest of them. He'd goaded his friends to do this – all the times they'd objectified and belittled girls in the past had enabled this.

As I stood, something in my expression made everyone around the table go instantly quiet.

'You have nothing real to say to me in response to me calling you out for being sexist and spineless and so you're attacking my physical appearance and being racist. You're Pakistani yourself, so I don't understand why you'd say something like that.'

The snickering resumed almost instantly. I scoffed in disbelief.

'This is what you guys do, isn't it? When you can't handle a girl calling you out for your bullshit you start putting her down in any way you can.'

'Bunch of weak, spineless tossers,' Saliha spat. 'Your muscles aren't fooling anyone.'

Saliha made to stand too but I pushed her shoulder down. 'Please stay and eat properly. I'll see you later.'

'Zara, wait,' Imran called after me.

I didn't stop, not even as he jogged up behind me.

'Don't take those guys seriously,' he said, and then stuttered a little before continuing. 'You're so beautiful and smart, and everyone knows it.'

I turned to him, my face stripped of all emotion.

'Stop pretending you give a shit about me. I'm sure you've all spoken to plenty of girls like that in the past, both behind their back and openly humiliating them to their face in front of everyone. Just go back to your boys and keep laughing blindly at their sexist, racist jokes.'

His brows creased with annoyance and he opened his mouth to respond, but I spoke first. '*Please* stay away from me.'

I walked into the girls' toilets, locked myself in a cubicle and finally let the tears fall freely. I checked my phone to find that Karim still hadn't responded to my texts from earlier. I closed my eyes and imagined I was with him.

Far away from here.

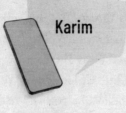

Karim

26

Everyone sat in silence for a while, staring at different corners of the room like they'd all sworn to appear as disinterested as possible.

It was strange. Our lunchtimes had always involved non-stop chatting, stomach-aching laughter, and excitement for all the things we had planned for the weekend ahead.

'OK,' I said finally. 'We need a realistic schedule for our collective channels. For obvious reasons, it may be difficult to create content together. So we should start posting separately. The goal should be keeping our joint platforms active.'

Felicity raised a hand. 'I don't get it. We post separately on our personal channels anyway. The Exes page is meant to be us doing videos *together*.'

'I was just coming to that. From now on, create content with whomever you want from The Exes, and plan a new schedule with them. Abeo, Felicity and I can post on Wednesdays and Sundays.' I looked over to Chloe and Sanjay with the most professional mask I could muster. 'You guys need to decide when you'd like to post and let us know.'

Abeo cleared his throat. 'But our collective-lifestyle vlogs get the highest engagement. Which means we still need to have a presence together, as The Exes.'

'I think you're right,' Chloe added. 'We should still do the occasional vlog or video all together. We didn't work this hard to build up this brand only to let personal things affect it.'

Abeo gave her the filthiest look I'd ever seen, making me smirk a little.

'Yes, exactly,' I replied. 'Let's confirm an uploading schedule by tonight over WhatsApp. We can start doing whatever feels natural and easy, and perhaps with time we can start shooting things together again.'

'I'm happy with that,' Chloe said, and then turned to Sanjay. 'Seems good, right?'

I ignored the lingering smile they shared.

Felicity pretended to puke, and Abeo failed to contain his snort.

'Another thing we need to address is events,' I continued. 'London Fashion Week will begin in a few days, and we've always attended together in the past. I think we should do the same this year.'

'That seems perfectly reasonable to me,' Felicity said. 'I only have one condition: no gross public displays of affection from *any* of us.'

'What is that supposed to mean?' Chloe asked sharply.

Felicity shrugged. 'No need to get defensive. I was only stating a fact. Literally no one on this planet wants to see either of you canoodling. You look like a pair of inconsiderate clowns.'

Chloe stood up, her face twisting with offence.

'Hold on, please,' I said, raising my hands in an attempt to calm her. 'That was wrong, Felicity. You should say sorry.'

To my surprise, she instantly mumbled a half-hearted apology.

'We're here right now to protect our brand,' I reminded them. 'Can we please be adults and focus on that? I'm the one most affected by . . . everything. If I can look past it, the rest of you can too.'

Everyone looked down, no longer able to meet my gaze, and Chloe took her seat again.

'We can't let Mr Ex take control of our narrative. *We* need to be in control. And that means sticking together.'

'There's something else you guys should know,' Chloe murmured. 'I received my first text from Mr Ex last night.'

'Do tell,' Abeo prompted, not sounding particularly sympathetic.

'Erm, I don't know if you guys have noticed, but Mr Ex has been dropping hints in his blogs about . . . my roots. He's basically threatened me. If I don't post a photo of myself wearing an outfit from his merch collection on Instagram by tomorrow, he's going to start exposing my family history.'

'Are you going to do it?' I tried to keep the judgement out of my tone.

Her silence said it all. It was unthinkable that Chloe would wear an outfit of someone else's choice without charging thousands for it. Even more unthinkable that she would basically be putting money directly into Mr Ex's pocket.

'This is him testing the waters,' Felicity said quietly. 'He wants to know whether he can control us. Very soon he's going to start ordering us to do the stuff he *really* wants us to do.'

Felicity was right. This was only the beginning. Soon Mr Ex's demands would start to really feel like threats.

'I'm still trying to trace his messages,' I said darkly. 'It might take me a while longer. As for now, we need to show a united front.'

Sanjay cleared his throat. 'The Exes is only going to work if we change the rules. The old ones won't work for us any more.'

'It's true,' Chloe said, locking eyes with him. They'd obviously discussed this between themselves earlier.

I averted my gaze from the pair even as I spoke to Sanjay. 'Well then, what do you propose?'

'That we have more freedom over how we represent our brand. And even if we do attend events together, we stick together only at the start of the occasion before doing our own thing.'

'Essentially what you're saying, Sanjay,' Abeo said tightly, 'is that you want all the benefits of being in The Exes and yet don't want to make an actual effort to be a part of the group.'

Chloe looked flustered. 'That isn't what he's trying to say –'

'Is your name Sanjay?' Abeo cut in darkly, then turned to him. 'Are you letting her talk for you too now?'

Sanjay looked peeved.

Before he could answer, I said, 'I understand where you're coming from. And if you'd prefer to spend less time together as a group during events, that's fine.'

'I just think that if things are this tense between us,' Sanjay explained, 'we should give each other some space. It would be better than to risk creating a scene like the one at Queen Charlotte's Ball.'

Abeo and I exchanged a look. The others still didn't know it had been staged, and it seemed that neither of us wanted to tell them. All the resulting tension between us certainly felt real enough.

Felicity scoffed loudly while looking at Chloe. 'I know what this is about. You guys are doing an iconic couple look for London Fashion Week, aren't you?'

'And what if we are?' she asked nonchalantly.

'That's something you and Karim used to do together,' Felicity cried. 'Do you have any idea how painful this must be for him? I just can't believe you're this selfish. You know what? I hope someone breaks your fucking heart just as badly one day and that you have no one left to turn to.'

She stormed out.

'That day doesn't seem far off to me,' Abeo murmured before exiting as well.

We sat in stunned silence, and then Chloe spoke, her voice thick with emotion. 'I'm never going to get any of you back, am I?'

She sniffed, trying to steady herself. 'I'm not trying to be selfish. I just feel like there's no going back to how things were, and I need to at least try to move forward. Either that or I'll just fall apart and never . . .'

My gaze locked on Chloe's, and those glassy green eyes shared a hundred unspoken things with me.

I can't stand the thought of losing you forever.

I don't want to hurt you.

I hope you'll forgive me for everything.

Sanjay shifted uncomfortably. 'Shall I give you guys some privacy to talk?'

'No, you stay,' I said swiftly. 'I'll go.'

Dapper and Daring: Is There an Iconic New London Fashion Week Couple in Town?

For the past four years, we've seen Karim Malik and Chloe Clark grace London Fashion Week with a stellar couple look. Do you guys remember last year's His & Hers Burberry Vintage Check suits? The slicked-back wet hair and flawless skin – they looked angelic. It was iconic, and plastered *everywhere*, so how could you possibly forget it?!

But sadly, some things have changed. So have some people. As well as those they hold hands with while in public. Burn! Ouch. A spritz of Tatcha Dewy Skin Mist could provide some much-needed relief.

This year, Sanjay Arya stepped into Karim's classic Tom Ford Oxford shoes, and didn't really have much trouble filling them. He had a roaming hand at Chloe's waist the entire evening, and both were clad in matching oversized black Saint Laurent blazers baggy enough to fit Karim in their pocket.

But the most attention-grabbing thing about their look was the heavy liner, which smudged almost halfway down their eyebags (do I sense a new viral make-up trend?! Get on it, beauty bloggers! It's time to get your dishevelled emo on!). It almost looked like they'd just rolled out of bed, and after *very* little sleep. After all of this, we have to admit: there is indeed an iconic new couple in town with eyes only for each other!

Chlojay? Sanloe? Chlanjay? Urgh. Doesn't have the same ring, does it?! Let's just call them the Controversial Couple – CC for short.

To everyone's surprise (I almost dropped my tea when I saw it!) The Exes showed up together, awarding the world with the charismatic group photos we love so much. But the moment after the shots were taken, they went their separate ways – talk about FAKE. The quintet have clearly broken off into two factions: although CC were keeping their distance, their eyes kept lingering back to Karim Malik and his crew, who were whispering non-stop.

Are The Exes just going to fake it till they make it? I think so ... but how long can they really keep this up?

My prediction is not very long at all.

Yours Unfaithfully,
Mr Ex

Zara

27

'I haven't ridden a bike in years,' I squealed as Karim threatened to let go of the handlebars completely. 'Keep hold of me!'

It was Sunday, and we were riding Boris Bikes in Hyde Park. I'd shortened my shifts at Selfridges, so I was able to sneak in some time with Karim before I was expected to be home. Although this was only our second date, we were constantly texting or FaceTiming each other now, and it all felt so natural.

Even in tapered jeans and a simple white T-shirt, Karim emanated a sophisticated aura. He'd donned Ray-Bans and a black Gucci cap, and we'd found a secluded pathway scattered with towering trees; no one had spotted him, and it was so quiet here it almost felt as though we had the entire park to ourselves.

'We aren't far from my place,' Karim said, a glint in his eye. 'Perhaps we could go pick up the tricycle I used when I was five?'

I laughed out loud, attempted to smack his arm, and then squealed again as the bike shifted too much to the left. He helped me regain my balance and kept me upright while I pedalled.

The way my near-falls made my heart dive had nothing on what his mere presence did to me. Around him, I felt giddy. As though every second I was falling deeper into something I'd never rise from, and would never want to, because there was none of the darkness or pain I was used to waiting for me at the bottom. With Karim, there was only light and happiness.

'My brother taught me how to ride a bike in our local park when I was ten,' I told him, 'but I haven't ridden one since then, so I guess –'

I let out an unladylike yelp as my left foot slipped right off the pedal.

'Don't worry, I've got you,' Karim whispered, coming closer, surrounding me with his signature scent of rich, leathery oud.

I breathed in deeply, savouring it. Our eyes connected in a flurry of heat and anticipation, our mouths dangerously close.

'You're easily distracted, aren't you?' he murmured, and I noticed the way his eyes swooped to my lips.

'Only when you're around,' I replied, quickly looking away, my heartbeat frantic.

It still alarmed me how open I'd become with Karim. The Zara who spoke for hours about things as meaningless and meaningful as the foods I liked to eat, the places I hoped to visit someday, the way my favourite music made me feel . . .

Despite all our differences, he somehow understood me. And maybe I understood him too. The *real* him that the world didn't get to see, that he'd told me even his friends barely got to see any more. There was so much about his life that had turned out to be different from what I'd expected. A lot of the time, he felt just like me: alone even when he was surrounded by people.

'You can do it,' he urged, easing his grip again. 'I'm barely even holding you up. It's all in your head. I'll let go a little now.'

'Don't you dare,' I warned. 'I need you to hold tight.'

Karim wound his arm around my waist and squeezed gently over the fabric of my blue T-shirt, his fingertips dipping into the sensitive skin on the side of my stomach. 'Like this?'

His hand, slowly stretching upwards, caressed me so smoothly that I found myself arching into his touch.

These were experienced hands that knew exactly where to touch, the places to spark sensation. These hands had touched the beautiful Chloe Clark, in places a lot less innocent . . .

A mix of discomfort and jealousy shot through me, and I stiffened suddenly. He suddenly went from being Just Karim to being *The* Karim Malik – world-famous influencer, my celebrity crush, an Ex. He must have sensed my unease because he immediately backed off.

'Shall we do something else?' he asked quickly, holding the bike steady as I got off.

I'd already told him I'd never been in a relationship before and was quite closed off with boys because of the religious and cultural values I'd been raised with. He'd been perfectly respectful of that, had said we didn't need to rush anything, and we planned to move at a speed that worked for both of us. But somehow it still felt like . . . I wasn't giving enough.

Chloe Clark had given him everything: it was all too easy to remember those clips of him kissing her deeply, touching her openly, going on dates in luxurious places abroad, attending extravagant events with *very* public displays of affection. And here I was: seventeen, sneaking out for a simple park date, totally inexperienced with guys.

And not even entirely sure if I was interested in becoming more experienced at this point in my life . . .

I opened my mouth to say something, anything, but then closed it again, at a loss for words.

He gave me a knowing look, almost as though he could sense my inner turmoil, and took my hand.

'Let's take a walk,' he said warmly. 'It's a gloriously sunny day in London, and you know what that means – we make the most of every minute.'

Karim

28

'Are you all right?' I asked.

She nodded but gripped my hand a little tighter than before. We walked through a shaded pathway speckled with towering trees, and my thumb gently stroked the back of her hand.

'Could we speak about some . . . stuff?' she asked quietly.

'I'm great at talking about stuff. I love stuff. It's actually my favourite subject.'

She smiled a little. 'It's stuff related to . . . us. It's about where this is going, and my views on relationships outside of marriage.'

The word *marriage* flared up like a warning sign in my mind. No girl had ever brought up the topic before, not even Chloe, and we'd been together for a long time. I tensed up but tried not to let it show on my face.

'Go ahead,' I replied anxiously.

'I told you before that I don't give my number out to any guys, and I meant it. I don't usually do this either.' She gestured to the space between us. 'Date anyone, I mean.'

She ran her fingers through her hair and sighed. 'I guess what I'm trying to say is that our boundaries and expectations are probably very different. Maybe we should talk about them?'

'I don't have any expectations, Zara.' I rubbed my neck awkwardly, unsure of how to proceed with this conversation. 'Let's just see where this goes naturally, OK?'

She stopped walking, pulled her hand out of mine and crossed her arms.

'I'm from a more conservative background than you. If my parents or *any* elders knew I was here, with a boy, all alone . . .' She widened her eyes and remained frozen like that for a few seconds, letting the message sink in. 'They've raised me with quite strict Islamic values. And honestly, I do still hold those values close to my heart.'

It suddenly occurred to me just how different our lifestyles and concerns were. I was used to not labelling things when I spent time with a girl. I went out on casual dates whenever I felt like seeing someone; I kissed or touched them if they wanted it too and it felt right in the moment. But Zara hadn't experienced any of these things, which meant that everything she went through with me would be a first for her. She wasn't only thinking about what felt right for us; her mind was also filled with the expectations of her parents, community and God. I felt a sense of responsibility settle on my shoulders; I really cared about her and didn't want to do anything to make her uncomfortable.

'I'm sorry. I feel like I've been a little oblivious to some parts of you. Why don't you tell me what *your* expectations and boundaries are?'

'Honestly, I'm just figuring them out now,' she replied nervously.

'That's OK,' I said, trying to reassure her. 'Just communicate with me.'

Some of the tension across her forehead eased away. 'All I really want to communicate right now is that I've never been physical with a guy before. And right now, I'm not sure I want to be until marriage.'

'That's perfectly fine,' I replied. Despite the sinking feeling in my chest, I respected her decision completely.

'Also, I do want to spend more time with you but it's hard in between school, work and the curfews my parents put on me. I'll try to see you whenever I can, but I just need you to understand that I don't have the same freedom you do.'

I nodded. 'Got it. I would never put you under pressure to see me. We always have FaceTime, right? I love those goofy faces you make at me.'

A small smirk appeared at the corners of her mouth and my heart leaped. I loved making her smile.

'Are you sure I'm not too different to what you're used to?' she asked in a small voice.

'You're perfect, Zara. You're the one I want.' I hesitated. Maybe we were having this conversation because she was now second-guessing this entire thing and where it would go, but the thought of not seeing her any more set me on edge. 'What do you want?'

'You,' she replied simply, and I exhaled in relief.

I found us a quiet spot underneath an English oak tree, and we stopped to enjoy the view of the Serpentine, taking in the sparkling lake, the bright blue sky, the majestic greenery.

Zara spread her arms out, smiled widely and took a deep breath, as though a weight had lifted off her. 'I love it here. I can't believe I've been in London my whole life and never come here before.'

It was beautiful that she found pleasure in the small things. Everything about her was beautiful. It was only our second date, but I could sense how deeply I was falling already.

'What's your favourite memory?' I asked.

She gave me a curious look.

'Everyone has that one vivid memory of pure happiness. What's yours?'

Her head tilted as she contemplated, and then her eyes lit up.

'I have an amazing best friend, Sal. You're going to love her, trust me. She's such a fan, by the way. So last summer we spent a lot of time doing each other's make-up in my bedroom. My summer playlist was on repeat, which she found super annoying, but I loved! We laughed so much, over the silliest things. I helped her shoot the weirdest YouTube videos and it was hilarious. Still not as funny as all the prank calls we did! I was just so grateful that she'd come over to chill with me even though she was allowed to go out and I wasn't –' She paused as her eyes found mine, her expression suddenly tense. 'It probably sounds boring. I bet your favourite memory is of some epic holiday with your best friends –'

'Sal sounds incredible,' I cut in. 'Spending your time with a true friend is better than travelling all over the world with fake ones.'

I didn't want to dampen the mood by talking about The Exes and our drama. But I knew if I ever wanted to talk about any of it, she'd listen with patience and no judgement. With her there was no risk of my words reaching millions of people; they would stay only between us. And I cherished this trust I felt between us.

'Your favourite memory is beautiful,' I said. 'Thanks for sharing it with me.'

She smiled softly, and my eyes darted to her full, glossy lips again. She was the most conservative girl I'd ever gone out with, and I knew to respect her boundaries, but I had to admit it was getting hard. I was so attracted to her and felt the constant urge to touch her, kiss her. Even if I couldn't do that just yet, maybe I could get closer in other ways.

I moved to stand in front of her. I reached for her hands, and she let me place one on my shoulder, and interlace my fingers with those of the other. As I led her into a slow dance, her mouth fell open and she looked around self-consciously.

'Karim?' she gasped, her eyes wide. 'What are we doing?'

'Making your new favourite memory.'

In one quick movement, I gripped her waist and lifted her, twirling her on the spot. She giggled and held on to my shoulders, her hair flying forward.

'Do you think this has potential?' I asked with a grin.

Instead of responding, Zara closed her eyes. She stretched her arms out carelessly. I continued to twirl her, my face full of the sunrays coiling through the leaves above us, my blood thrumming with the knowledge that I would never forget this moment.

This was for me, for her.

There were no cameras, no crowds, nothing to show or prove.

When I slowly set her down and she opened her eyes, I noticed they were bright with unshed tears.

'What's wrong?' I brought my forehead lower, connecting it with hers.

'Nothing,' she whispered. 'For the first time in my life, everything feels just right.'

Zara

29

He'd done it – he'd created my new favourite memory.

We were lying on a picnic blanket he'd brought, our bellies full of the homemade scones, strawberry jam and clotted cream his personal chef had prepared. And our Londons were beginning to blur . . .

'This can't be real,' I murmured.

'What can't be real?'

'You. Us. Those perfect scones.'

He chuckled, and the sound was like music to my ears. 'What do you mean?'

'Maybe you're used to living in a fairy tale, but I'm not.'

Karim turned towards me and set his head on his fist. 'Actually, neither am I. I'm just good at making my life *look* like a fairy tale. But it's something completely different to really *feel* it. You're showing me that.'

'I wish we could stay out here forever,' I said with a lazy sigh, 'but I need to get going. I've got homework due in tomorrow. Urgh, I'm not looking forward to going into school.'

'Tell me about it,' he said with a grimace, as he lay down again. 'It's been a weird start to the school year.'

I'd seen clips of St Victor's School in his vlogs. It was sleek, grand and equipped with all the latest technology. I imagined him walking around the pristine corridors, being treated like royalty by all his classmates, getting taught by some of the best teachers in the world.

'Oh yeah?' I said through a smirk. 'It must be so horrible to study at the most prestigious and sought-after school in the country! Too many people vying to be at your beck and call? Too many state-of-the-art facilities to choose from that it makes your head spin?'

He nudged me a little, the corner of his mouth lifting. 'Knock it off.'

'Do you think you'd notice me if we went to the same school?'

There was so much I was asking here . . . whether he could sense that I was unpopular, whether he would still notice me if I was surrounded by numerous gorgeous and sophisticated girls, whether I was attractive enough for him to want me despite all the other options.

'I don't know,' he answered. Although it hurt a little, I was glad he was being honest. 'But I do know that I'm very grateful we met, that you put me in my place so damn well in our first conversation.'

I burst out laughing, and all of a sudden there was no more hurt.

'I really needed that,' he said simply. 'I really needed *you*.'

His eyes found mine and I held his gaze, didn't flinch away from the intensity of how it felt, the things it did to my heart.

'I like to think that we'd always have found our way to each other,' I whispered.

He reached for my hand. 'Then let's just think that.'

'You slow-danced with Karim Malik in Hyde Park?' Saliha squealed.

Sighing dreamily, I drew my curtains to give us some much-needed privacy because Sal was now leaping around my room so enthusiastically that her scarf was barely hanging on to her head.

As I did so, I spotted Imran sitting at his desk, chewing the end of his pen, deep in thought.

Our eyes locked.

My breath caught in my throat.

I felt my cheeks warm.

He'd messaged me on Snapchat a few times since that mess during lunch, but I hadn't responded. His messages were surprisingly kind and thoughtful, but I didn't like the way left my nerves in a jumble. My emotions felt so out of my control around him, so I'd decided to limit our interactions, starting by ignoring him and skipping out on our revision sessions.

A subtle smile lifted his lips as he ran a hand over his beard.

How could I find such a simple gesture so damn charming?! What was wrong with me?

He attempted to mouth something to me, but I swept the curtain between us. I felt a little guilty about brushing him off like that, but this wasn't the time to think about Imran Sayyid.

This was the time to gush about how it felt to literally get swept off my feet by *Karim Malik*.

'Oh my God, he's such a gentleman!' I exclaimed. 'He held and twirled and lifted me so *perfectly*.'

Sal pretended to pass out on my bed, and I giggled as I joined her.

'This is exactly how me and Karim were lying on his picnic blanket approximately an hour ago.'

Saliha's eyes widened until I thought they'd pop right out. 'No one from school would believe this unless they saw the cold, hard evidence.' She waved her phone at me, where I'd sent her the selfies.

'We only took those for memories,' I said. 'Please don't show anyone.'

She sat up and crossed her legs. 'You know I'd never. The thought of your photo getting into the wrong hands is enough to give even *me* a panic attack. Your parents would completely lose their shit.'

'Don't even go there.'

'Holy cow! When did you go from being boring ol' Zara to actually having a life? I didn't think I'd *ever* see the day.'

I pulled a silly face and we laughed, but then her expression clouded and looked strangely . . . off.

'What is it?' I pressed.

'You haven't been keeping up with Mr Ex, have you? There's a lot that's going down in Karim's personal life right now.'

'What do you mean?'

I only half-wanted to know. I could tell Sal was about to bring me back to reality.

'Chloe was caught getting it on with Sanjay mere days after the abortion news was leaked. Then they attended London Fashion Week as a couple. If anything, I thought Karim would be a heartbroken mess right now, not ... What I'm saying is, The Exes just seem so twisted.'

Irritation prickled across my face.

'Karim isn't twisted like the others. He's different,' I replied defensively. 'You should know, you're the one who's been obsessed with him for ages.'

'Zara, I don't see how that's possible. That's his social circle, has been for *years*. I just don't want it to be a case that you're a rebound. Or a distraction. What if he's speaking to about five other girls too right now?'

I shook my head. 'It's different between us. I know it is.'

'This is Karim Malik we're talking about! Whenever he wasn't with Chloe Clark, he was a total player.'

That had done it – the seed of doubt was planted.

Perhaps it had already been there, because all of this was far too good to be true, anything exciting in my life usually was. Saliha's words had simply given my insecurities a face and then thrust them into the light.

She was only being protective, but I still felt some resentment kick in. I hadn't wanted my little bubble of bliss to pop so soon. But if the roles were reversed, I'd have warned her of the same things. Probably much sooner.

Sal gave me a worried look. 'These people look good on camera, but the truth is we have no idea what they're really like. I just don't want you getting hurt. Please be careful.'

'You're right. About everything. I promise to be careful.'

'Did anything happen between you guys?'

I cocked a brow. 'I told you *everything* that happened. You know I'd tell you straight away if I had my first kiss.'

An unexpected image fell into my mind – Imran Sayyid wrapping his hands around my waist, pulling me close so our bodies pressed together, lowering his head until his lips met mine . . .

I'd fantasized about this a thousand times – having my first kiss with the first boy I'd ever desired, the very one that had awoken feelings of lust within me, and the thought of kissing him always left my heart pounding, my head rushing. But this was a secret, forbidden thought that I'd never even share with Sal, that I'd never admit aloud to *anyone*.

'Zara?' My attention snapped right back to Sal, who was still looking concerned. 'This has all happened so quickly. I guess I'm worried about you . . . changing.'

'Boys will come and go but you will *always* be my best friend,' I promised.

'Good,' she said fiercely, giving me a bear hug.

'By the way,' I said as we came apart, 'Karim wants to show me a glimpse of his world too, and I'm nervous.'

Although Karim remained disguised whenever we met, it was still such a risk. There were so many people out there interested in his love life and all it would take was one snap of us together for my life to crumble before my eyes.

'Obviously you'll have to be cautious – Mr Ex lives in that world. And so do some of the bitchiest, wealthiest influencers in the country. You've got to watch your back.'

I exhaled. 'I know. I've told Karim I don't want to risk being seen with him, and he's being careful. No one has spotted us so far, but I'm just worried about how he plans to pull off taking me to one of his events while keeping my identity anonymous. And how on earth am I supposed to socialize and fit in with all those famous influencers?'

'Never feel pressured into doing anything. Just remember you can always say no, *even* to the iconic Karim Malik,' Sal said reassuringly, and I nodded. 'Also, why did you skip out on yesterday's study session?'

I paused awkwardly for a second. 'I just thought I'd be more productive alone. More focused.'

Sal rolled her eyes. 'Was it because of Imran?'

'Not at all,' I replied too quickly. Who was I kidding? It was impossible to lie to Sal. 'OK, fine. Maybe a little.'

She gave me a knowing look. 'There's *definitely* something there between you guys, isn't there?'

'Hell no! Why would you think that? There *is* something between me and Karim though.' When I looked at her, she had a wide Cheshire grin on her face. 'What is it now?'

'Well, well, well. From having nothing going on with *any* guy, to having two of the hottest guys ever chasing you? You're my inspiration, boring ol' Zara!' She laughed loudly as I covered my face with my hands. 'Imagine how cool it would be if you actually did have your first kiss with Karim Malik!'

'Oh my God, you're being so hot and cold about him! But yeah, I know. Argh!'

And then we were squealing and giggling again.

I blasted my summer playlist, and we danced around my room wildly, singing along at the top of our lungs.

Karim

30

'You seriously want to admit to our followers that your most iconic dance routine ... isn't actually *yours*?' Abeo asked in disbelief.

'It's ridiculous, I know,' Felicity conceded, toying with a piece of sushi wedged between her chopsticks. 'But maybe it'll prevent Mr Ex from blackmailing me.'

It was early in the evening, and we were at Felicity's Belgravia apartment, lounging in the living room on a food break in between content creation. We had the place to ourselves because Felicity's parents were in Hong Kong.

'Mr Ex is already controlling *Chloe Clark*'s wardrobe,' Felicity snapped incredulously. 'Maybe it's smarter if we all just spill our secrets ourselves. At least we'll be free from blackmail threats then.'

'Free and fucking cancelled!' Abeo announced, then took a dramatically deep breath. 'I don't know what drugs you're on today, girl, but I recommend you sober up before you do some dumb shit. And bring us all down with you.'

Felicity began to pace around the room. 'I'm so sick of this stuff from my past chasing me all the time. I *love* collaborating with different dance groups, but I don't do it any more because I feel so paranoid that they all secretly know I'm a fraud and don't respect me.'

'Maybe you're overthinking this,' I reasoned. 'Maybe those dancers you stole the moves from have forgotten all about it and you need to move on too.'

Her face fell, as though I'd uttered something ridiculous. 'Plagiarism isn't the kind of thing dancers just forgive and forget. Haven't you noticed the hints Mr Ex has been dropping about my oh-so-*original* dance routines?'

She ran her hands through her silky black hair as though she was about to pull it all out. 'Do you think it's really too late for me to just give those dancers credit?'

'Oh honey, it's like four years too late,' Abeo exclaimed.

Felicity suddenly paused and stared out of the window, her expression looking like she was a million miles away. 'If I have to do *one* more thing in exchange for him not ruining my reputation, I think I'll really lose my mind.'

'What?' I asked tersely. 'What did he ask you to do?'

Felicity jumped and turned to face us, as though she'd seen a ghost. She knew she'd said too much. A cold shiver crept through me; whatever it was, I could tell it was bad.

'Show us the messages,' Abeo demanded.

Felicity tapped her foot nervously, avoiding our eyes. And it suddenly became clear just how many secrets the three of us were keeping from each other as well.

'This is something I need to deal with alone,' she said in a conclusive tone.

A strained silence fell.

'Has Mr Ex sent *you* any new messages?' I asked Abeo.

He shrugged. 'Only the occasional flirty texts. Completely meaningless.'

'You've been ignoring them, right?'

'Obviously,' Abeo replied too confidently, scrolling through his phone with a nonchalance that appeared artificial.

Felicity and I exchanged a look.

Every Ex seemed to be playing their own game with Mr Ex, and each of us was playing alone, which made us all that much easier as targets. We'd be more powerful together, but the gaps between us just seemed to be widening.

I hadn't even told them about Zara yet, and I didn't really want to. I liked there being a part of my life that was just for *me*. Something people couldn't meddle with.

'Shall we just get back to shooting the vlog?' Felicity drawled.

It was obvious none of us were really in the mood to continue shooting. Content creation had become such a chore – even hanging out together had.

Still, we got up, fixed our faces and our moods, and got back to work.

Zara

31

'I've never been to a Halloween party before,' I said nervously, taking in all the spooky decorations adorning the shops around Camden High Street.

'It'll be fun,' Karim responded, 'and it's the perfect way for me to introduce you to my world.'

I crossed my arms against the cold wind. 'I don't really like big crowds.'

'Abeo's Halloween parties are quite exclusive. They can get busy but it's never really a full house.'

'I know.' I smirked when Karim's brow shot up. 'I've obviously watched The Exes' videos before. They're rather difficult to miss, especially the Halloween ones. They always go viral. You guys go all out with your costumes.'

Karim chuckled. 'I *was* going to tell you what I'm planning to go as, but I think I'll keep it a secret for now. Come to mine first and we'll go together. Around ten should be good.'

I stopped dead in my tracks and stared at him. I had no idea whether his expression shifted in response because I could barely see his face behind the dark sunglasses that hid his eyes and the cap that shaded half his face.

'What's wrong?'

'Do you really think I'd ever get permission to leave my house at that time?'

'Have you never snuck out before?' Upon seeing my expression, he laughed. 'Oh, come on, live a little. Sneaking out is basically a rite of passage for teens. You need to try it at least once. What's the worst that could happen?'

'You really don't know my parents,' I replied quietly. 'There's a *lot* that could happen.'

'There's no pressure, Zara.' His voice was kind. 'If you're able to make it, amazing. If not, there's always another time.'

He lifted his sunglasses to wink at me and my heart fluttered.

Over the past month, we'd met every weekend. While sharing meals or strolling through parks and museums, we exchanged endless stories. These stolen moments with Karim in the most beautiful corners of London were what I most looked forward to. It was as though my life was always in black and white, and colour surged into everything the moment I met him again.

We reached Camden Tube Station and lingered outside it.

'Thank you for lunch – that pasta was amazing,' I said as Karim drew close to me. I shifted uncomfortably and looked down at my feet. I'd sensed him wanting to kiss me a few times now. He was always a complete gentleman, but I could tell he wanted me. I wanted him too.

And what if he lost interest in me if I didn't let him take things further? How much longer could we go on like this?

'Let me know when you get home, OK?' Karim murmured, tucking a loose strand behind my ear. I loved it when he did that.

I looked up at his tall frame, his gorgeous face, his deeply alluring lips.

As ever, I felt the urge to grab him and forget all boundaries. As ever, I didn't.

Guilt seared through me even if I did something minuscule like hold his hand. My parents' warnings were instilled so deeply within me that they constantly lingered at the back of my mind, creating a barrier between us.

'I always do,' I said through a smile.

He smiled back, knowing we'd be sending each other messages back and forth the moment I got off the Tube.

'I'm looking forward to seeing you tomorrow – hopefully,' he said, going in for a goodbye hug.

'Hopefully,' I responded, savouring the feel of his arms wrapping around me.

As he let go, he kissed me gently on the cheek. It was the first time he'd done that. It felt electric.

'I hope that's OK,' he said gently.

'More than OK.'

His answering grin made me swoon.

The entire journey home, I fantasized about what it would be like to kiss Karim. I craved feeling his hands on my body and his lips on mine. I imagined that I had turned at the last second, so instead of kissing my cheek, his soft lips had met mine. I'd been *so* curious for so long now – what would it feel like to be kissed, to shun all boundaries and just close the distance between me and the boy I wanted more than anything else in the world? And every time I met Karim, I felt my self-control slipping a little more.

The sharp rev of a car snatched me out of my thoughts as I entered my driveway.

Imran hopped out of a BMW filled with his friends. He was laughing as he fist-bumped one of them and shut the car door.

I couldn't help but check him out.

His skin fade and beard were blended flawlessly as ever, and his gorgeous features were creased with humour, which only made him look more charming. His tracksuit bottoms screamed comfort and his well-defined biceps were visible through his grey hoodie . . .

While Karim's style was more classic and refined, Imran's appeared effortless, as though he could've rolled out of bed like that, and still managed to look so damn good.

The moment I caught his eye, he jogged towards me. I turned away instantly.

'Zara,' he called. 'Hold on a sec.'

His friends in the car noticed me too and began rolling down the windows.

'Oi, Zara,' one of them said. 'You brushed up nicely this weekend.'

I always dressed up a little extra when I saw Karim, taking time to perfect my natural make-up look and pick out a stylish outfit. Suddenly my fitted jeans felt too revealing. To be fair, even if I'd been in a burka their wandering gazes would have made me uncomfortable.

'Shut up, man,' Imran answered back for me.

He caught up to me, and the frustration on his face was clear.

'You haven't responded to my messages in weeks now. At least hear me out.'

'My parents are inside,' I retorted, pointing to the front door. 'I don't need you getting me in trouble.'

'I'll keep my voice down,' he whispered, gesturing to his friends to leave. They drove off, and I felt I could breathe a little easier. 'You gonna give me a chance to talk now?'

I crossed my arms. 'Talk about what?'

'About how you've been blamin' me for something I didn't even do.'

'Fine, I haven't been responding to your messages, it's true, but it's not like we were best friends before this. Why does it even matter to you?'

Imran stuttered. 'Honestly, I don't know. I just can't seem to stop . . . thinkin' about you.'

I rolled my eyes. 'I already told you – you can't seduce me with your usual tricks.'

His gaze darkened.

A muscle in his jaw twitched as he nodded in the direction of the road. 'I literally just *chased* you. I never chase girls. I'm trying here, Zara.'

I lifted my hands in mock excitement. 'Oh wow, I'm the luckiest girl in the world. Imran Sayyid is chasing me. What an honour.'

He took a step towards me and suddenly all the humour faded, replaced by an intensity that made me stand very still.

While holding my gaze, he kept coming closer until I was tilting my neck all the way back to look up at him.

I swallowed slowly. 'My parents might –'

'I don't care.'

It was impossible to draw breath, to think straight.

With Karim, things felt safe and slow, as though I had some semblance of control. But with Imran, it was like all rules and limits became meaningless. If he knew I wanted him but was holding back, he'd simply take my hand and walk me through every boundary himself, until we'd broken them all.

It was kind of intoxicating.

'What do you want from me?' I whispered.

'I want –'

His gaze lingered from my eyes to my lips to my neck, and back up again. Then he shook his head and broke away. Something told me that he didn't share his feelings very often, but he wanted to try with me.

As he walked away, I felt the urge to hold him back. It was only after he'd left that I realized I had lifted my hand to stop him, but it had been a mere second too late.

Zara

32

'It's impossible to live with him!' Aisha baji cried in Urdu.

'Calm down! Stop crying.' This was Mum's pathetic and typical attempt at comforting her. It seemed my family's motto was: *never express emotion even if your world is falling apart*.

I tiptoed closer to the living room to eavesdrop, my chest tight with fear.

Dad's trainers lay outside the door, which meant this conversation was taking place in his presence. Although Aisha baji had previously opened up to Mum about her situation, she'd never mentioned her marital problems to Dad directly. He still knew plenty about what she was going through because Mum confided in him, but he'd done little more than tell Mum to pass word back to Aisha to be a better wife, to work harder to keep her husband happy.

'Allah tests everyone. This is your test!' Mum exclaimed.

Rage sparked its way through my nerves. I hated the way my parents corrupted our religion and twisted it into whatever suited them. The truth was they wanted their daughter to continue suffering so *they* wouldn't have to suffer the whispers of the local community about the shame of a divorced daughter or the damage it would do to their family relations in Pakistan.

'Listen, beti,' Dad said solemnly. 'You have two children together now. You need to think about what's best for them.'

'That's exactly what I'm doing,' Aisha baji whimpered. 'He's so aggressive towards me around the children. He's always swearing and shouting. They're getting older now, and they understand much more. I don't want them to grow up thinking these things are OK.'

'I'll talk to Javed soon,' Dad replied dismissively. 'It's time for me to go to work now. You should go home.'

I saw red. After the beautiful day I'd just had in Karim's presence, I'd forgotten the reality of the home life I was going back to. Years of hatred and despair eddied inside me as I barged into the room.

'Go home?' I screeched in Urdu. 'Even after you know what she's going home to? And what are you going to call Javed over for? Biscuits and tea? All while you pat him on the back and discuss the morning's Pakistani news? If one thing's clear by now, it's that you're too spineless to stand up for your own daughter in front of that filthy man you proudly call your son-in-law.'

Everyone was standing now, and they looked at me as though I'd lost my mind. Saniya and Abbas stopped playing with their toys and stared up at their loud, angry aunty. A wave of guilt enveloped me; I didn't want them to witness yet another fight.

'Stop it, Zara,' Mum hissed, and I detected fear in her eyes; she didn't want me to rile Dad. 'Is this how you speak to your father?'

'It's the truth,' I hissed back. 'And my religion teaches me to stand up for truth and justice.'

That shut them right up.

I scoffed. 'I don't know what you've been learning but it definitely isn't Islam if you think it's OK to sit back and watch your daughter's husband beat her up and ruin her life.'

'Please be quiet, Zara,' Aisha baji cried. 'You're only making things worse.'

'Oh, so you do have a voice,' I said sarcastically. 'Why don't you raise it for once?'

'Just *stop it*,' she sobbed.

My own eyes welled, and my voice cracked with sadness as I said, 'Tell Mum and Dad that they married you off to a scoundrel and don't have enough interest or backbone to help you now that you and your children are suffering.'

'Oi!' Dad roared, making everyone jump, then he pointed a finger straight at Mum. 'Look at how disrespectful you've raised your daughter to be! Look at the shameless way she's dressed!'

My clothing had nothing to do with any of this. I felt the urge to scream.

All the bitterness I'd ever felt towards Dad wrapped around my tongue and came out in a venomous question. 'You're always going to find a way to blame a woman, aren't you?'

'Living under my roof,' he barked, eyes popping, 'and *this* is how you talk to me?'

Mum glared at me wildly, signalling to me to shut up, but I was done with walking on eggshells around the truth, with seeing her bending to Dad's will at every turn instead of saying and doing what *she* wanted. I wouldn't be controlled by my family in that way any longer.

'Why do you always divert the topic? Answer the real questions here. Why aren't you helping your daughter out of an abusive marriage? Why can't she just stay here with us? Are you so worried about what your relatives will say that you can't even help your own daughter and grandchildren?'

He bellowed again and raced towards me with a hand raised.

I froze, my entire body trembling with fear.

Aisha baji held on to his arm at the last second, shielding me from his wrath. 'Just leave, Zara!' she cried.

I shook my head. 'I don't want to leave you alone.'

'I've told you not to come here to discuss your problems, Aisha,' Mum snapped. 'This is the result when daughters come back to their father's home after getting married. Go back to your own home and we'll come to see you and Javed soon.'

Dad huffed loudly and left the room. Instantly, all of us could breathe easier.

'Don't bother,' Aisha baji replied quietly.

I'd just said everything to our parents that she didn't have the courage to say herself, and she'd just witnessed that it had made no difference at all. She packed Abbas and Saniya's toys and left with them. My heart ached for them.

'I'm going to have words with you about how you're dressed,' Mum spat at me. 'The nerve of you to go out like that. Is this how we raised you? What will people say about our daughter's character?'

'That's right, Mum,' I replied coldly. 'Care more about what people say than about the truth of what's going on in your life. It's done you a lot of good so far, hasn't it? Estranged son. Abused daughter. Another daughter who probably has a similar kismet in store.'

'Be quiet, you disrespectful girl!'

There was a mixture of irritation and fear on her face; she was worried about the kind of trouble my sharp tongue and reckless honesty would get me into. I wished she could see that silence and obedience clearly got a woman into enough trouble too.

I ran upstairs, wrapped myself in my duvet and cried until I had no more energy to give. I stared into space blankly, feeling empty and broken. After a while I called Saliha.

We were on FaceTime for hours.

Karim tried to call me, but I ignored him. I just needed my best friend right now. I couldn't confide in Karim about how embarrassingly awful things were at home; his family was so picture-perfect.

I told Saliha everything. After listening, she attempted to distract me with funny stories of the guys who slid into her DMs, but nothing could lift this dark weight.

Today was the first time Dad had heard me truly express myself, but instead of hearing the pain and sorrow in my voice, he'd only heard disobedience. Whether I obeyed his rules or not, I knew I'd never be good enough for him, and maybe that was because I was a girl. If I'd learned anything from Mum's scolding and gossiping over the years, it was that girls were regarded as a burden: their body, behaviour and future were too unreliable, always laced in hardship and shame.

Daughters were difficult to raise, difficult to give away, difficult to take back.

It made me want to disappear.

'Zara?' Sal prodded, pulling me from my thoughts. 'Where are you lost?'

'Nowhere.'

'Come on, it'll be OK,' she said softly, her forehead creased with worry. 'Are you sure I can't come over?'

I shook my head.

'And you can't come over here either?'

'No, if I step out the house right now, I feel like my parents will tell me never to come back. If only I had someplace to go, I would leave myself.'

'You can just stay here,' she offered.

I gave her a half-smile. 'You know I can't do that. Your parents have enough children to deal with as it is.' I sighed. 'Karim invited me to the iconic Exes Halloween party tomorrow night. Shall I just do it? Sneak out and go to see his world? You're the one who told me to make memories this year, right?'

'Oh, Zara. Maybe not the kind of memories that could get you into *serious* trouble.'

I opened my mouth to argue but she cut in, 'It's been a stressful evening already. If you still want to do this Halloween thing tomorrow, I promise I'll help you come up with a plan. But for now, you need some rest.'

'OK,' I whispered, my heart already set on what I wanted. When we got off the phone, I finally texted Karim back.

I don't want to spend my whole life afraid of living. And this seems like the perfect time to make a change – tomorrow I step into your world.

Karim

33

After picking up my costume, I drove straight to Mayfair to help Abeo with the party prep.

His family's mansion had been transformed into a vampire's lair: coffins lay askew, bats hung from the ceiling, cobwebs coated the opulent furniture, towering candles lit the length of the vast dining table, which held bowls of fake blood.

'As ever, the décor is impeccable,' I told him, genuinely impressed.

He looked smug. 'It really is perfect, isn't it? Everything's right on track, by the way. Security will check the face of every single person coming in. The cameras have also been adjusted to ensure there are no blind spots. We'll have footage of everyone entering and leaving.'

I nodded. 'So, by tomorrow, we'll have a list of all the possible people Mr Ex can be.'

'I feel like he's still going to get away with it, and there's a part of me that kinda wants him to.'

'What's that supposed to mean? I thought we –'

The look on his face stopped me short. That was fear in his eyes.

'I haven't told this to anyone else,' Abeo whispered, 'but just a few days ago I received an envelope. Inside it were photos of me making out with James at his place in Kensington. And, er ... they don't leave much to the imagination.' He cleared his throat, looking uncomfortable. 'The last thing I need is for Mr Ex to release a sex tape of me. If we rile him enough, who knows what he'll do. Let's face it, he has way too much stuff on us now. It's impossible to get the upper hand.'

I took a deep, unsteady breath.

'Does James have security tapes of his entrance?'

'I told him to check them, but he didn't find anything.'

Blood pounded in my ears. 'Was there a note or anything with the photos?'

'Yeah,' Abeo said gingerly. 'He basically implied he would've shown me a better time than James.'

'We can probably rule out James being Mr Ex then. But it just doesn't add up. He was the strongest contender on our list.'

'I don't get it,' Abeo said thoughtfully. 'I don't know whether Mr Ex is flirting with me or threatening me. Just when I think I finally understand him, he pulls something I'd never expect. It's kind of ... thrilling.'

Holding Abeo by the shoulders, I got close up to him and looked him dead in the eyes. 'I don't know what's going on between you and him, but you need this reminder: he is *not* good for you. With everything he has on you, he could destroy you in a heartbeat. He's a messed-up stalker. You need to detach.'

'I know, and I will,' he replied, but his promise didn't seem to reach his eyes.

Mr Ex had clearly got under his skin.

'The moment we discover his identity, the ball will be in our court,' I explained. 'We can threaten him then – we'll tell him if he wants to remain anonymous, he'll have to quit talking about us on his blog.'

'Do you really think he'll let it go that easily? He could make a serious profit from releasing what he has on us.'

'He wouldn't want the world to know his identity. While he's anonymous, he's witty and entertaining. The moment everyone knows who he is, he'll just be a bully.'

'You're right. Holy shit. I can't believe he's going to be in my house in a few hours.'

'It'll be just like every other year. He's come to *every* Halloween party you've ever thrown. How else could his blog have listed all the gory, juicy details of everything that went down?'

'We better get him this time, Karim. The longer this goes on, the more stuff he digs up on us.'

'Don't worry, we will. How are things going with James? Is he your date for tonight?'

'Oh, he's just a time pass now,' he replied with a shrug. 'I'm trying to keep some distance between us. I guess he is my date tonight though.'

Unease crept through me. I had a feeling Abeo had his eyes set on someone else entirely, the last person he should've been interested in. I knew how much he loved a thrill, especially when it involved a dash of romance.

226

'I'm bringing a date too,' I told him.

'Who?'

'Just someone I like.'

We could both keep secrets from each other.

His eyes narrowed. I gave him a little nod of farewell before leaving him to his thoughts.

This was why I constantly craved Zara's energy and company. Between us, there were no lies, no secrets, no double meanings. We never doubted each other's intentions or honesty; I could be the most authentic version of myself, knowing that she was also showing me who she was down to the core.

I'd met so many beautiful girls in the past, but there was something different about Zara that drew me in: she was outspoken and brave and would never let my status stand in the way of reprimanding me if it was needed, and yet she was soft and thoughtful and always ensured I was doing OK. Perhaps she was the only person in my life who truly checked in on me, not to make sure I was well enough to carry out my duties to my brand or to other people, but for *my* sake. She saw me without the layers of fame and wealth, and she still wanted me.

That meant everything.

It surprised me that I'd fallen for her so deeply in such a short amount of time, but everything between us just felt so right, as though we were fated to meet and be together . . .

Although I was nervous about introducing her to my world, my crowd, I knew it was something that would have to happen eventually. We couldn't stay in our own little bubble forever if we really wanted to make this work. I just had to protect her from the vultures that always came for me; I had no choice but to deal with them, but I never wanted to expose her to their viciousness. She wasn't someone who liked gossip; I loved that about her and planned to keep our lives as drama-free as I possibly could.

It sometimes felt a little strange that I'd become closer to Zara Khan than to any of the people I'd known for years, but it also made perfect sense: I'd outgrown them, and I was growing into her, our essence entwining until we saw each other better than anyone else in our lives.

Zara

34

Karim arrived to pick me up just before ten. I told him to wait a street away, just like last time.

'You look like you've seen a ghost,' he joked as I got into the car.

I sank lower into my seat. 'Let's get out of here before I change my mind.'

He laughed as he drove off. 'You really are a daredevil tonight! Getting right into the Halloween spirit – I'm so proud of you. Every kid has to sneak out at least once in their life.'

My insides twisted with discomfort.

I texted Sal quickly, knowing she'd be waiting to hear from me.

> I'm with Karim now. I really hope I don't get caught!

She responded almost instantly.

You won't, sis. Your parents will be knocked out cold soon. You deserve this night out to forget about everything and enjoy life! Just remember to be careful. Love you. Send me pics. But remember to not let anyone else snap you!

I sent her lots of heart emojis.

'Is everything OK?' Karim asked. 'You seem tense.'

'I had a fight with my parents last night. A big one. If they find out I've snuck out tonight, it'll probably be the end of my relationship with them.'

'Oh, come on. As much as parents love telling us off when we screw up, they're never angry for more than a few days.'

I looked him dead in the eyes. 'My parents are built a little differently.'

He reached for my hand. 'I can drive you back right now if you want.'

'No,' I replied firmly, lacing my fingers through his. 'Trust me, I'm less stressed here than I am at home.'

When we reached the Malik mansion, Karim led me to his sister's room, as she was going to help me get ready. Kiran opened the door and squealed with excitement. 'It's *you*! I remember you from the food tasting!' She beamed. 'I thought, wow, that girl is gorgeous – I'd love to do her make-up. And here you are! I'm so glad Karim's finally made a normal, drama-free friend.'

'Your make-up is incredible,' I replied just as enthusiastically. 'I've been watching your tutorials for years. This is literally a dream come true.'

The three of us settled on Kiran's massive bed and Kiran started on my make-up, and as she applied it she spilled all the tea on how intense the one-upping was getting between their mother and her soon-to-be daughter-in-law.

'Monster-in-law and bridezilla are understatements,' she said. 'Azad is stuck in the middle of this wild tug of war. I won't be surprised if they pull his arms right off before the wedding even takes place.'

Karim knocked his head back and laughed loudly, making me giggle.

Kiran was such easy company; her down-to-earth vibe made it feel as though we were old friends. It felt disorientating being in this magnificent mansion again but this time as a friend of the Maliks instead of as a waitress. The truth was, I'd never imagined being invited to hang out with such people rather than work for them.

'All right, Karim, it's time for you to leave because we're about to put our costumes on,' she said as she finished putting the last curl in my hair. She nudged his leg, and he rolled off the bed.

'See you in a bit then,' he said with a wink.

I gave him a little wave.

'Good riddance,' Kiran grunted. 'Now us girls can finally get down to real business. Do you mind if I choose your look?'

'Go ahead!' I'd be completely lost if she left me to figure out my ensemble. I'd never dressed up for Halloween before, not even as a child; Mum and Dad had referred to it as *haram nonsense*.

Kiran disappeared into her walk-in wardrobe and, not knowing whether she intended me to follow, I lingered.

'Well, come on then!' she exclaimed, and I practically sprinted in after her.

The coats, trousers, bags and shoes were colour-coordinated and organized with such precision that I could hardly bear the thought of picking anything out and removing it from its rightful place.

'This is going to be perfect,' Kiran squealed, giving me a handful of black velvet and satin items.

I went back into her room to change. When I returned to show her, she gasped.

'You're a vision! And I'm a visionary.'

She grabbed my shoulders and steered me towards a full-length mirror hidden in her wardrobe.

My mouth fell open.

I'd been transformed into a dark fairy ... and I looked exquisite.

A fitted, floor-length black dress. Velvety feathers crowding every inch. Dark satin gloves grazing my elbows. Wispy wings at my back. Hair styled in loose, glossy waves. Bold red lips. Heavily blackened eyes hidden behind a filigree mask.

I loved the anonymity.

'Thank you so much!' I said, genuinely delighted.

'No problem at all. Now I could really use some help to get into my Superwoman costume.'

While she did her final touches, I took a few mirror selfies to send to Sal, who blew up my phone telling me how epic I looked.

Karim was waiting in the foyer dressed as Batman. As we approached the grand staircase, he looked up to watch me descending, like they do in the movies.

A half-smile formed on his lips as he took me in, and I found myself blushing.

'You look incredible,' he said as I reached him.

'Of course she does,' Kiran said, coming up behind me. 'Meanwhile: Batman? How predictable.'

'Still not as predictable as you.'

She punched his arm as we left the house.

By the time we arrived at Abeo's house, the party was in full swing. My mouth grew dry. Sensing my apprehension, Karim wrapped a comforting arm around my waist. A guard stopped us and asked for our names. We were told to remove our masks, and my stomach clenched with discomfort.

'No one's looking,' Karim reassured. 'It's just for security purposes.'

While we lingered near the entrance, Kiran began hugging people and was swept into the crowd.

'I'm right here,' Karim shouted over the music, holding my hand tightly. 'The moment you want to leave, we'll walk out.'

I tried to relax a little. This was Karim sharing his world with me – and I wanted to show the same openness he'd offered me. I loosened my shoulders and let the beat of the music sink into my bones.

'Do you want to dance?' he asked.

'Sounds fun,' I replied.

Within seconds I was jumping and swaying with the crowd, singing the lyrics at the top of my lungs, grinning at Karim so deeply I thought I'd never feel sad again. It was as though I'd been waiting to let loose like this forever, and the dancing and singing poured out of me so naturally I stopped caring about whether people were watching and judging me.

It was just us. Karim and me.

When the DJ slowed the music down a bit, Karim wrapped his arms around my waist and pulled me into a slow sway. I rested my chin on his shoulder and let my body inch closer to his and move in sync. That was when I realized how many people had their phones pointed at us, and I was finally able to hear what they were saying over the music.

'She must be his new girlfriend!'

'Wait till Chloe sees.'

'Who is she?'

'That girl's kinda hot.'

Karim turned to the crowd with a clenched jaw, about to say something. But this was out of his control.

'It's OK,' I told him, 'no one can see my face, so –'

'No, it's not OK!' He grabbed my hand. 'Come with me.'

As Karim manoeuvred us out of the crowd, trying to shield me from the cameras, someone moved in front of us, blocking our path.

Chloe Clark.

'Hi,' she said drunkenly to Karim. 'Aren't you going to introduce us to your new friend?'

Sanjay was at her side. They were dressed as Mr and Mrs Incredible. As expected, she looked beautiful, but something about her haughty tone and expression made her instantly unlikeable.

'Hey,' Karim replied aloofly. 'We're going to get something to drink. See you guys later.'

Chloe switched her attention to me, clearly not taking the hint. Her bright green eyes narrowed with curiosity. 'I'm sure you already know *exactly* who I am. But who the hell are *you*?'

'The dark fairy,' I said coldly. I wasn't going to let anyone ruin our night. 'I think Karim should get me a drink now. If I'm made to wait any longer, I might just cast a particularly dark spell on you.'

I brushed past her without waiting for a response.

Karim

35

Zara led me away, handling Chloe's rudeness with grace. Just as we reached the drinks stand, the disco lights switched off, plunging Abeo's mansion into pitch black.

'Hey, guys,' the DJ announced, 'this next song has been requested by . . . erm . . . a Mr Ex.'

My head snapped up.

Death metal music punctured with sharp screaming blasted on. People started panicking, shoving and shouting as they tried to manoeuvre in the dark.

'Stay away from the crowd,' I ordered Zara, guiding her to a corner. 'I need to go and check what's going on. I'll be back soon.'

Zara let go of my hand reluctantly.

In between flashes of light from people's phones and hard shoves from every direction, I managed to reach the staircase and scanned the room for Abeo. It was impossible to see more than a wild mass of people crashing into each other. I got to the first floor and tried the lights, but they weren't working. They must have been switched off at the mains.

I tried to call Abeo, but he wasn't answering. I switched on my phone torch and began looking for him.

Someone grabbed my arm. I tried to pull it away, but it was being held with a firm grip.

I turned to find the face of Venom mere inches from mine, dark elongated eyes, long, sharp teeth, tall and lean physique. There wasn't a single inch of the guy's face or body on display. Yet somehow I knew the person behind the mask had a wild grin on their face.

Mr Ex.

'I'll make a deal with you,' he said in a deep, familiar voice that I still couldn't quite place. 'Tell me the name of the girl you came with, and I'll leave you alone for the rest of the night.'

'I'm not telling you shit,' I hissed.

'Perhaps I should pay your date a little visit then. She can tell me herself.'

I gritted my teeth. 'Don't you dare go anywhere near her.'

He chuckled in a low, husky voice and I went for him then. But he was quick and dodged to the side. I barely managed to shove him before stumbling myself. I turned around quickly, ready to attack again.

But he was already slinking into the shadows. I jogged forward, trying to keep an eye on him, but I couldn't see much in the gloom.

I carried on down the main corridor, passing vampires and demons and witches, my heart pounding in my ears, my eyes searching wildly for Venom.

Ah! There he was – standing outside Abeo's bedroom. He was pressing someone up against the wall, his hand wrapped around his neck. As I neared, I realized it was Abeo he had in a chokehold. But Abeo didn't seem to be struggling; in fact, he was smiling, his bloody fangs resting on his lower lip as he closed in for a kiss. Mr Ex's neck swooped lower too. My stomach somersaulted.

'Abeo?' I called out in disbelief. 'What the fuck?'

Mr Ex didn't waste a second. He merged with a passing group of witches and instantly disappeared, not giving either of us a chance to get to him.

'Listen, I can explain!' Abeo exclaimed.

'I don't have time for this right now,' I said irritably. 'He threatened my date so I need to find her. Did you manage to identify him?' Then I added in a harsher tone. 'You clearly got close enough to.'

'No, I didn't. Maybe I would've been able to if you hadn't interrupted.'

'Would you actually tell me who it is if you knew?'

'I'm still on your side, Karim. Look –'

I didn't bother sticking around to listen to his excuses, and headed for the stairs in a rush, uncomfortable with how long I'd left Zara alone. Someone clutched one of my biceps. I pulled my arm away aggressively, thinking that Mr Ex had come for me again.

But it was Chloe, and she was about to fall down the stairs. I quickly caught her and heaved her up against the banister.

'Sorry,' I said quickly. 'I didn't realize it was you.'

'It's OK,' she replied, swaying a little. 'I was looking around for you.'

She took my mask off and threw it over the rail. Then her fingers were stroking down my neck, my chest, lower and lower . . .

I grabbed her hands. 'What do you think you're doing?'

'It was a mistake to leave you. We belong together. Things haven't felt right since we broke up.'

She sprang forward to kiss me. I looked the other way, and her lips caught my cheek instead.

'Stop!' I yelled, shaking her. 'You're with Sanjay now. Get a hold of yourself.'

'Who's that girl you were with? Is she helping you get over me?'

'You need Sanjay to take you home,' I said tightly, letting go of her. 'I'm going to look for my date.'

'You miss me too, don't you?'

'No. I've moved on, Chloe. And so have you.'

'You're lying,' she whispered, trailing kisses down my neck. 'I know you're still in love with me.'

I tightened my grip on her arms, pushing her away. 'Why are you doing this? Haven't you messed with The Exes enough? Haven't you *hurt* me enough?'

'I never meant to hurt you.' Then her lips were on mine, pushing me back, leaving me nowhere to turn.

The lights came on in a blinding flash and then there was a roar so loud it overpowered the chaotic music. I pulled away from Chloe to see a crowd had formed around us and people were staring. The way we were elevated on the stairs, standing in everyone's line of sight, it was as though we were on a stage. People started heckling:

'Was this the surprise the lights were switched off for?'

'Took you guys long enough!'

'We knew Chlarim would never really be over!'

My eyes sought out Zara and found her exactly where I'd told her to stay. Her mouth was agape in shock; the pain of betrayal shone in her eyes.

From out the corner of my eye, I saw Venom following my gaze until he found her too. With a steady prowl, he began making his way towards Zara.

I peeled Chloe off me and ran towards them.

36

Karim drove me home. The silence was deafening, so I decided to break it. 'Is it all true? Everything with Chloe ... the abortion?'

He clenched his jaw tightly but nodded.

Sal's warnings echoed in my mind; she'd been right about everything.

'So, what are you doing here with me? Am I a rebound? A distraction? A fling?'

Karim shook his head but remained silent.

'Will you *please* talk to me?' I snapped.

'I'm over her,' he said, sounding desperate. 'I want nothing to do with Chloe. If it wasn't for our joint platforms and brand, I'd probably never speak to her again.'

Although Karim and I weren't officially in a relationship, hadn't put a label on whatever it was between us, I'd simply assumed that we were exclusive, that he felt as strongly for me as I did for him. It was a stupid assumption to make about a guy like *Karim Malik*.

Hadn't the whole reason we'd started dating been to show each other our worlds? How could I have forgotten how many girls fanned around him and how intense his relationship had been with his gorgeous ex who was still throwing herself at him?

I took a deep breath before asking, 'Have you been seeing other girls in the time you've been dating me?'

'No. It's been only you, Zara. It *is* only you.'

'So, if we're exclusive, why were you kissing Chloe Clark at an event where you took *me* as your date?'

'I didn't kiss her. She kissed me. And I pushed her away.'

'You didn't seem to be pushing her away. You were holding on to her.'

'That's only what it looked like. I was trying to get away from her on a flight of stairs, for crying out loud. Please, Zara. You have to believe me.'

I was silent for so long that Karim reached over for my hand. I let him grasp it but didn't hold his in return. His slightest touch felt so good, so *right*, that it made my eyes fill.

'I'm so sorry for all of this,' he said. 'I forgot how manipulative my world is. I wish I'd never brought you into it. I screwed up. After this you'll never want to see me again.'

'I wish it was that easy.' I turned to face him. We stopped at a traffic light, and he met my eyes. 'I wish I cared so little that I could just forget about everything between us and move on, but I can't. You're the best thing in my life right now.' My voice broke on the last few words, and I turned away from him.

'I'll do anything to win back your trust, Zara. Just tell me what to do.'

I was quiet for a while. What *did* I want from him?

Anxiety trickled along my bones, making me freeze. It was nearly one in the morning. I hadn't received any texts from Sal to alarm me, but there was still a risk of getting caught and losing my parents' trust and respect forever. Well, even more than I already had. And what if everything was irreversibly ruined between me and Karim? Was I really about to lose everyone in one night?

'There *is* something you can do,' I said, trying to keep my voice even. 'I want you to tell me *exactly* what you feel for me. The plain truth.'

'That's what you want?'

I nodded. 'I want to see if this thing is worth fighting for. If it isn't, it's better we become strangers again. And if it is . . .'

'Then?'

'If it is, then maybe it's time to be more realistic. We lead such different lives. We're practically opposites in every way.'

He scoffed. 'Either way we break up?'

'I didn't know we were ever together.'

'Stop that. The only reason I didn't ask you to be my girlfriend ages ago is because of your values. I didn't want to make you uncomfortable. You *know* what this is. This is what it feels like when you're deeply connected to someone, when they understand your soul. You don't experience this with just anyone. It's extraordinary and rare and precious.'

'Well, I wouldn't know. I've never been in a relationship before.'

'This feels like more than a stupid high-school romance,' Karim said impatiently. 'Like – Zara, I can imagine you as my wife.'

A sharp silence fell between us.

'Sorry, that just came out,' he said sheepishly. 'I didn't mean . . . I know we haven't been speaking for long . . . it's just because I know marriage is what you want. . . but we're still so young and –'

'Stop waffling. I get it.'

I hadn't wanted that to sound so icy, especially after he'd practically admitted he was *really* falling for me, but I was still processing seeing him with Chloe . . . What if he was just telling what I wanted to hear?

'Isn't that what you wanted?' he replied calmly. 'For me to tell you exactly what I feel for you?'

My stomach was in knots.

'Yes.'

He sighed quietly before saying, 'Being with you feels like . . . fajr. The time between dawn and sunrise when the world is sleeping, and you rise to pray and savour the blessing of that moment. You feel like that stillness and purity in my loud, flashy life.'

My eyes filled.

It was the perfect thing to say, and it was impossible to be angry with him any more.

'After everything I've been through – being dissected in the public eye, the toxic relationships and friendships, the abortion – I've learned what I want and don't want. And I know I want *you.*'

We arrived at the street near my house, and he parked up.

'I feel like I just poured my heart out,' he said nervously. 'Oh my God, I've said too much, haven't I? I'm freaking you out!'

'No, Karim,' I replied reassuringly. 'I needed a moment because you just said the most beautiful thing anyone's *ever* said about me.'

He exhaled his relief before saying, 'And that doesn't even *begin* to cover what I feel for you.'

I instinctively reached for his smooth, clean-shaven cheek and traced my fingers down it, exactly as he'd done to my face so many times. He froze and I held his gaze. It was the first time I was touching him in such a way, and it was the most intimate thing I'd ever done with a boy.

'It's only fair,' he said, tilting his head to kiss my fingertips, 'if you tell me the truth about what you feel for me too.'

'You're certainly flashy.' I nodded suggestively at the Ferrari logo on his steering wheel. 'And your world is definitely loud, perhaps a bit too loud for me. But somehow, you make me feel safe. When I'm with you, it's just me and you. That's all that matters. You make me feel less invisible, more *loved*.'

My eyes widened with panic.

'I didn't mean to imply that you're in love with me ... or that *we're* in love,' I blurted. 'It's too soon to –'

'Stop waffling. I get it.'

My grin immediately stretched wide to match his. We reached for each other's hands at the same time. The warmth of his touch radiated all the way to my heart.

'You were right about the boyfriend thing, by the way,' I said. 'I don't want one. I just don't like that label and what it implies. And I'm still not ready to be intimate like ...' I blushed, unable to finish the sentence about us getting physical. 'But maybe if things go well between us, then in a few years … the wife thing … won't seem so far-fetched.'

Karim reached for my cheek and traced a thumb down it so gently I barely felt it. I shivered.

'You're worth the wait.'

My eyes flicked to the dashboard. 'It's one in the morning! I need to get home *right now*. Please could you help unclip my wings?'

'Of course,' he replied, and I faced the other way.

Then his hands were shifting my hair to one side, caressing the nape of my neck as they went. I'd never been so aware of my body, so conscious of someone's proximity to it. He began unpinning the costume, his fingers working gently, slowly. I closed my eyes and sank into the sensation of being touched so tenderly. It was becoming difficult not to throw myself at him.

When I opened my eyes, I caught my reflection in the window and barely recognized myself.

The black mask, the red lips, the wild hair.

But maybe it was time to get used to this girl staring back at me; perhaps she was my true self, finally finding her way out. I liked this girl – she was confident and fierce. She looked in control of her life and her future.

Karim tugged the wings off in one swift move, making me gasp a little, and then whispered in my ear, 'Is that OK?'

The hairs on the back of my neck stood up. I wanted him to take off more than just the wings. I faced him, every part of me craving his touch.

'Is it strange that I feel even closer to you after this whole thing?'

'No,' he replied. 'I feel the same.'

'Can I get a goodbye hug?'

As we embraced, I grabbed a chunk of his hair and pulled tightly, snapping his head back. A groan of pain escaped his lips.

I came in close. 'I don't want you thinking you'll get away with things so easily with me. Just so we're clear, if you ever kiss another girl while we're together, I'm going to make sure you regret it.'

'That is so hot,' he murmured with a smirk.

'Just making sure you know I'm *well* worth the wait.'

I moved back before either of us could give in to temptation.

'There's one thing I want to ask before you go,' Karim said as I opened the door. 'There was a man dressed as Venom standing near you. Did he speak to you?'

Confusion creased my brows. 'Yeah, he's an old friend of yours, right? He said you'd sent him to check on me. He introduced himself and then asked for my name.'

'Who did he introduce himself as?'

'Venom.'

'Did you give him your name?'

I made a face. 'Of course not. I found him a bit creepy.'

'Thank God,' he sighed.

'Is everything OK?'

He nodded and started up his car. 'Please text me when you get in.'

As I snuck back into the house, I panicked over the tiniest squeak or creak. It wasn't until I was in my bedroom that I finally took a deep breath. I couldn't believe I'd actually pulled it off!

When I got into bed, ready to text Karim and Sal, glaring blue lights flashing outside my window caught my attention.

I got up and peered out. An ambulance was parked across the street. Imran came into view, talking to two paramedics, who were rolling a stretcher his father lay unconscious on.

And I witnessed something I thought I'd never see – Imran Sayyid crying.

Halloween Heat: Two-Timing Trysts in Mayfair Mansions

Oh, the nerve of making out with your ex in front of your new girl. The drama of seeing your girlfriend get back with the ex she left for you. There really is a reason they refer to themselves as The Exes.

As the images reveal, Karim Malik showed up to Abeo's annual Halloween Party with a Dark Fairy that we are yet to unmask. All we know about her so far is that she's fun, sexy and glamorous – everything a man could possibly want, especially on Halloween night. I don't know about you guys, but I'm so ready for an unveiling ceremony. Maybe that could be the idea for the Exes' next video?! Everyone: leave comments across their socials to let them know it's what we want to see! We'd basically be doing them a favour – none of their content has been particularly engaging recently, so perhaps it's time for the fans to demand what they want.

From what I can see of Ms Mysterious so far, she's somebody perfectly capable of carving out a space for herself (with chic style) and ruffling feathers (did you notice the velvety black ones on her dress?! Meow). With her svelte physique, olive skin and dark hair, the new girl is giving me some hardcore Selena Gomez vibes, and I'm all the way here for it; although the world could certainly avoid another heart-shattering, soul-crushing love triangle. We will never quite get over that one, will we?

Chloe, however, struggled to handle seeing her old flame with a new girl. That Ex seriously acted out by practically flinging herself at Karim, and as entertaining as it was, it was not a classy move. Even in her custom Louboutins and carrying her gold Judith Leiber clutch, she came across as a jealous, incredible mess – for the first time her outfit was *not* on point; Mr & Mrs Incredible simply didn't go with CC's vibe, especially since commitment isn't their strong suit.

Goodness, Chloe, if you wanted a silly little fling, you should've chosen one of those guys who hang around the pubs in Covent Garden and Kentish Town Road, drinking beer and watching footy. Was it really worth messing up ... well, *everything*? For us and for you. The Exes simply aren't the same – it's obvious from the half-hearted YouTube vlogs and basic TikToks that never feature the quintet together any more. Something's missing, and everyone knows it's Chloe's self-respect. Burn!

Karim Malik, on the other hand, isn't entirely innocent in this. Or is he? Did Chloe throw herself at him or did he instigate it? I guess we'll never really know for sure. Does all of this mean there's hope for a Chlarim reunion after all? Or is this Dark Fairy going to cast a spell on Karim's heart and ensnare him completely? Even after Chloe's attempt to sow discord between them, Karim and his new love interest were seen leaving together, so maybe this girl is in it for the long haul ... I guess only time will tell.

My skin-tight Halloween outfit totally slayed all others this year; I was oozing sex appeal all night. I know Abeo would agree ... What do you reckon I went as? Leave your guesses in the comments section below. Impatiently awaiting your replies.

Yours Unfaithfully,
Mr (S)Ex(y)

Karim

37

'They barely even lasted two months,' Abeo hooted derisively.

Abeo, Felicity and I were sitting in the lunch hall, catching up. The whole world had now witnessed me and Chloe kissing, with Sanjay standing in the crowd and looking on in disbelief, then storming out.

'This was bound to happen since they're polar opposites,' Felicity said. 'But I just can't believe she tried to get with you again, Karim. The disrespect and nerve!'

Abeo snorted. 'I had a feeling she'd get bored of Sanjay quickly. Chloe likes adventure and spontaneity, and his favourite thing to do is sit in silence and paint. But to get bored *this* quickly?'

'Did you check out the footage from last night?' I asked Abeo, steering the conversation elsewhere.

'Not yet. Haven't had the time. But I have an awful feeling it'll be as pointless as it was at Queen Charlotte's Ball.'

'We know he came as Venom,' I said. 'We need to check the security footage from the entrance. The guards would've made him take his mask off. I can come over after school and we'll look over it together.' I gave Abeo a pointed look. 'Besides, there are other things we need to talk about.'

He appeared annoyingly unbothered when he said, 'Yeah sure, come over.'

'What did James come dressed as?' I still had a hint of suspicion about him; his height and build certainly matched Venom's. But his voice ... 'And was he with you the whole night?'

'He came as Count Dracula as well. Tried to steal my thunder and everything. And he decided to stick himself to me like glue. I think I spent most of the night trying to get away from him.'

'Is that *really* what you spent most of the night doing?'

Abeo gave me a hard look, and I narrowed my eyes, knowing I had to reel it in until after school, when we were finally alone. I understood Abeo better than the others, and so I knew he wasn't coming from a bad place; he was just attracted to the guy's danger. But if the other Exes got a whiff of what was going on between him and Mr Ex, they wouldn't be so forgiving.

'Who was that girl you were with?' Felicity asked me suddenly. 'You didn't introduce us. Are you like ... officially together?'

I nodded. It was a little strange that I hadn't introduced her to my friends, but I preferred it this way. Zara wasn't the type to chill with this crowd anyway; that much was obvious from last night.

'What's her name?' Felicity pressed on. 'Wasn't she annoyed about what happened?'

'It's Zara. She was at first, but we talked it out and she knows we have something real. I'm relieved it survived the stupid stunt Chloe pulled.'

'Wait, what's her *full* name?' Felicity asked. She raised her hands in surrender when I gave her a look. 'Sorry, I don't mean to pry, I'm just wondering if I could find her Instagram and see the face under that gorgeous mask. Goodness, I sound like such a stalker.'

'Leave it alone,' Abeo groaned. 'It must be nice to have something away from all the drama. I'm happy for you, bro.'

I gave him a tight smile. 'Thanks.'

'Things will be so awkward for Sanjay now,' Felicity said. 'I don't know if he has any friends left. At least Chloe will still have her group of twittering suck-ups.'

As if on cue, Sanjay entered the hall, lunch tray in hand. The sound of whispered chatter swept across the spectating crowd, and it intensified as Sanjay came straight towards our table.

'Oh no he didn't,' Abeo exclaimed in sing-song disbelief. 'I swear if this guy thinks he's going to sit with us . . .'

When Sanjay got close enough, he leaned down and whispered, 'Look, there's something you guys should know. Chloe's all over the place. She *isn't* stable. She's been drinking heavily, behaving recklessly. Ecstatic one second and crying her eyes out the next.'

He took a step away, turning his body towards the exit.

'I'm not sure what's going on with her,' he added, 'but I don't want to be involved. If you guys still care about her . . . I just thought you should know.'

It was obvious Chloe had hurt him too. She'd broken his heart and left him completely isolated. He was a loner before I'd welcomed him into The Exes – an invitation he gratefully admitted had changed his life – and I found that I didn't want him to go back to that loneliness. I knew his heart: he wasn't a spiteful person; he was passionate, and it was that passion that had brought him close to Chloe, not a desire to cause me or anyone else harm.

'Sanjay,' I said. 'Come sit with us.'

He hesitated. 'Are you sure?'

I nodded. 'How long can we really avoid each other?'

Felicity and Abeo glared at me. Sanjay timidly sat next to me, and an awkward silence fell, not just on our table but all around us. It took me a moment to realize it wasn't because of me and Sanjay.

Chloe had just entered the hall alone, holding a lunch tray. It seemed even the suck-ups didn't want to be seen with someone who was currently being shamed online for her promiscuity. Perhaps they were enjoying this moment of dethroning the long-standing Queen Bee. Chloe looked right at our table, astonished to see Sanjay sitting with us.

'You predicted it, Felicity,' said Abeo. 'Lo and behold, she has no one left.'

'Slut!' someone shouted.

Raucous laughter filled the hall, swiftly expanding and spreading.

Noah stood up, red-faced. He opened his mouth to say something to protect his sister but then looked around and realized he wasn't quite confident enough. It was difficult to watch him freeze up like that.

'You're cancelled!' a guy yelled.

Chloe burst into tears, put down her tray on the closest table and ran out, covering her face as she went.

'I think you should go after her, Felicity,' I said. She began to argue but I cut in, 'Chloe's still an Ex. And she's your best friend. Are you really going to let people treat one of *us* like that?'

Her eyes shone a little. 'Fine, I'll go and talk to her. You're a good person, Karim.'

Felicity stood before I could say another word.

'Shut up!' she roared. 'If I find that any one of you has been slut-shaming Chloe Clark, I'm going to name and shame you on my personal TikTok tonight. Yes, the most followed account in the damn country. Everyone will know you're a sleazy bully. The whole world will despise you and we'll see who's cancelled then.'

A sharp silence fell upon the hall instantly.

'I bet you've all been enjoying the fake news Mr Ex has been spewing about us, haven't you?' Felicity cried. 'I wonder how you'd like it if *your* life was being twisted and sold as entertainment? How you would feel if your most private moments were being taken without your permission and splashed in front of everyone to gossip about?'

She took a deep breath to steady the emotion in her voice. 'It's easy to sit around and judge us. To slut-shame the girls in our school for exercising the same bodily autonomy that boys do. To laugh at all the things that are going wrong in the lives of the people you've always watched.'

By the last word her voice was hard. 'But I want you to remember exactly who you're dealing with: we're The *fucking* Exes. And don't you forget it.'

Then she walked out, and no one dared to speak above a tense whisper for the rest of lunch.

Karim

38

The second text I received from Mr Ex came while I was en route to Abeo's place.

> Zara
>
> A sweet name.
>
> But has she got a face meant for fame?
>
> How about we make a deal . . .
>
> Send me a pic of your new beau
>
> And I'll keep one of The Exes from falling *real* low.

I felt sick.

How the hell did he know her name? And what secret was he planning to reveal if I didn't comply? Abeo's sex tape? Felicity's choreography theft? Sanjay's destruction of our head master's property? Some crime attached to Chloe's mobster family?

Or maybe something else entirely?

This so-called *deal* with Mr Ex could irreversibly destroy any of my friendships with The Exes. None of them would understand why Zara wanted to remain anonymous so desperately and they wouldn't forgive me for not sharing a simple pic to save all that we'd built together.

When Abeo opened his front door, I thrust my phone in his face.

'Only you, my sister and Felicity knew her name. How the hell did he figure it out?'

Abeo's eyes narrowed as he finished reading the text. 'It wasn't me. And I don't think Felicity or your sister would snitch either.'

Everyone in my life was watching their own back with Mr Ex because they all had secrets to hide, an image to protect. I simply couldn't trust anyone at this point . . . I couldn't rule out anyone I knew being *him*. The thought sent shivers through my body.

'So did he just conjure up her name with his psychic powers?' I hissed.

'Now, first things first,' Abeo replied calmly. 'Don't talk to me in that tone. Let's sit down and discuss this like adults.'

I scoffed. 'Adults? Not starry-eyed, lovesick little boys? Are you sure you can handle that?'

Instead of retorting, he flounced over to the sofa and gestured for me to join him. The whole place had been cleaned, and every trace of last night's Halloween escapade had been removed. Abeo had his diplomatic face on, so I decided to fix mine on too.

'Whatever's going on between me and Mr Ex,' he said tightly, 'is *not* what you think.'

'Why don't you go ahead and clarify what *is* going on?'

'I've made him believe I have feelings for him. It's giving me a glimpse into his mind, even access to some of his decision-making.'

I rubbed at my head, at a loss for words. 'Huh.'

Abeo grunted disapprovingly. 'Do you seriously think I'd jump ship and abandon the people I've grown up with, who I love? For a fling with our *unhinged stalker*?'

My cheeks burned.

'You guys do have this ... chemistry,' I said awkwardly. 'He's always complimenting you in his posts while ripping the rest of us down. I thought that maybe you got sucked into his advances.'

He shrugged. 'I have chemistry with lots of guys – you should see the kind of hotties that slide into my DMs. Regardless of what I may feel for Mr Ex, I'll never forgive the way he's tormented us all.'

'Why didn't you just tell me?'

Abeo gave me a look. 'I wasn't sure if my charm was even going to work on him.'

'Well, did it?'

His grin was broad. I shouldn't have underestimated him.

'If you hadn't interrupted us,' he continued with a wink, 'I may have been able to unmask him yesterday. Anyways, let's distract Mr Ex, shall we? I'll make sure your new girl comes off his radar.'

He opened his phone and began typing. I leaned over and saw that he was writing an email to Mr Ex's official contact account.

Haven't you had enough fun messing around with Karim's love life? Give the guy a break and leave his new girl alone.

We sat in silence, waiting for the reply. I jumped a little when Abeo's phone pinged with a new email. It had been barely five minutes. I leaned over his shoulder and read the response with him.

Nothing comes for free in this world, darling. A deal means an exchange. If your dear Karim can't handle this one, tell him to offer up something else that could capture my interest. I won't always soften up just because you're involved, honey.
Yours Unfaithfully,
Mr Ex

'We already knew he wouldn't let us off easily,' Abeo said. 'The guy trades in secrets. So, if you want to protect Zara, give him something juicy.'

I began pacing, thinking about what I could give up . . .

Then it clicked.

'Tell Mr Ex I'll give him exclusive footage and insider details from my brother's wedding. He'll get the photos before any other reporters or social media pages. Even our own.'

Abeo's eyes widened with glee. 'You *genius*!'

He tapped out a message. I continued to pace, my stomach in nervous knots.

'It's done,' he said smugly.

'That was bloody close.' I collapsed on to the sofa, rubbing my eyes.

'Any idea about what he meant by one of us falling *real low*?'

I sighed deeply. 'No. He's clearly got something big up his sleeve. Since he's your secret lover, why don't you ask him and see whether he dishes?'

Abeo nudged me. 'I just saved your ass, so how about a little thank you? Oh, and I looked through the Halloween security tapes before you got here. Mr Ex snuck in with a large group of people, and the guard didn't realize when he slipped right past him.'

'He's a slippery little prick, isn't he?'

'Slippery maybe,' Abeo said with a half-smile, 'but he definitely didn't seem little.'

I could only keep a straight face for a second before we burst out laughing.

'You need to chill or Mr Ex might just become your new man,' I warned. 'He'll be stalking you from the proximity of your bedroom.'

My phone buzzed. Zara was calling. A surge of protectiveness swept over me, but I didn't plan on telling her what had happened in case it stressed her out. The situation with Mr Ex had been handled.

For now, at least.

'I'm going to take this,' I told him, and went out to the corridor for some privacy.

'Hey.' She sounded upset.

My stomach clenched with unease.

'Zara? What happened?'

'It's about a guy I know from school. His father passed away.'

'I'm so sorry. That's awful.'

Her voice quivered. 'I was so horrible to him in the days leading up to this.'

'What do you mean?'

'The boys he hangs with were making sexist jokes, so I basically told him I didn't want to be friends any more.'

I ached to comfort her, to hold her to my chest. 'It's OK. You couldn't have known something like this would happen to his dad. And obviously it *isn't* right if the people he hangs with make jokes like that.'

'But it wasn't even him directly. I don't know what to do. Should I reach out or do you think he'd rather not hear from me right now?'

'Definitely reach out, Zara,' I said firmly. 'Losing a parent is the most devastating thing someone can go through. It's much bigger than petty disagreements.'

'You're right – that's perfect advice. How are you so perfect?'

I chuckled as I leaned against a wall. 'I'm definitely not. You'll discover that yourself in due time. I really miss you.'

'I miss you too.'

'When can I see you again?' I asked keenly.

'Erm . . . I actually wanted to ask whether you could attend the funeral on Friday. I'm not sure if we'll even see each other because it's segregated, but it'll give you a chance to pray jummah in my local mosque. I know I'm asking you to skip school, but for some reason this janazah feels important to me. I want you there.'

I couldn't even remember the last time I'd prayed in a mosque ...

'I'll be there.'

She needed me right now, and I wanted to be there for her.

'How are you holding up?' I asked. 'How's everything else going?'

'Home is as awkward as ever. Let's not even go there. School feels pointless; my teachers just aren't very good, so I basically have to teach myself everything. I'm still saving up for tuition lessons. I want to start them early next year. I'm currently focusing on completing my university application.'

'Have you decided what you're applying for?'

'Dentistry, for sure,' she replied instantly. 'All I need is *one* offer; I don't even care what uni I get into. What about you?'

'Computer science. And I *definitely* care about what uni I get into. It's got to be St Andrews.'

'It feels like there's a lot in store for us, doesn't it?' she said softly. 'University gives me a sense of hope.'

'Me too, Zara. Me too.'

The mosque was beautiful.

The place was packed for jummah, but I managed to find a space near the middle.

There were rows and rows of men and boys, sitting shoulder to shoulder, facing the mihrab, listening to the khutbah being delivered by the imam on the importance of charity. He was the only one standing, and he spoke with such eloquence that he held everyone's full attention.

I felt waves of peace envelop me.

When the adhan was announced and everyone stood in response to the call to prayer, an unexpected surge of emotion clogged my throat. The melodious recitation penetrated all my barriers, directly piercing my heart.

As the prayer began, everyone moved as one, synchronized in their postures, oration and faith. And I was a part of something so much bigger than myself, something that simultaneously stretched throughout history and to the furthest parts of the cosmos, reality and existence.

Shortly after jummah, the body of the deceased was brought out, fully shrouded in a white cloth and positioned in an open coffin. It was placed in front of the imam.

The one thing guaranteed about this life was death – the time we had here was so fleeting, meant to be used wisely, lovingly.

That knowledge was humbling.

Since I'd met Zara, I'd begun doing things that were helping me grow as a person. She inspired me to tap into my deeper thoughts and spirituality in a way no one else did, and it was making me fall hard for her. I couldn't imagine life without her any more.

As the prayer for the dead came to an end, I headed towards the shoe racks with the crowd. I heard a few whispers of my name, and I instantly tensed. Perhaps it was naive to have hoped the people coming here wouldn't notice me.

I ducked my head, eager to get into my car as soon as possible.

Zara had made it clear we wouldn't be able to speak here. I hoped to get at least one glimpse of her, but it certainly wouldn't be considered modest for me to gawk at the women's side of the mosque in anticipation.

'As-salaam-alaikum. You're Karim Malik, aren't you?' a man said, placing a hand on my arm. 'Can I get a selfie?'

'Walaikum-assalam, yeah, sure,' I replied quietly, hoping it wouldn't attract too much attention.

'I'm a big fan too,' a young boy said. 'Could I also get a selfie?'

I smiled and obliged.

Far too many people were starting to notice, so I swiftly hunted down my shoes from the racks and slipped them on.

At the exit, I witnessed all the emotion the family members had contained while inside. The wails and cries of the mourners sliced uncomfortably through the usual city sounds.

Women were pouring out of the ladies' section of the mosque.

My heart dropped when I spotted Zara.

She was in a black abaya and hijab, and her face was wet with tears. She looked so different to every other time I'd seen her. She looked . . . distraught. I tried to get her attention, but her eyes were fixed ahead. I hated that I couldn't console her.

I followed her gaze and my eyes landed straight on a guy who was holding on to the shrouded body, crying his heart out, refusing to let go.

The whispers and prodding intensified around me until everyone had learned that Karim Malik was among them. And then it seemed that only the immediate family of the deceased were still focused on the funeral; everyone else was looking at me, pointing in my direction, trying to get closer.

But not Zara.

Her eyes never left the man mourning.

'How do you know the guy whose father passed away?' I finally asked Zara.

We'd been on the phone for a while; I could tell she was no longer in the low mood that had taken hold of her since the funeral. That meant it was the right time to weave in the question that had been eating away at me. I wasn't used to feeling jealous, and I knew I was petty and selfish to feel it at a time like this, but I couldn't help it.

'Imran? He's from my school,' she replied dismissively, but I didn't plan to drop it so easily.

'And you're friends?'

Zara was quiet as she thought about this, and I sat up in bed. Did she pause because they didn't talk much or because she saw him as something more than friends?

'I guess so,' she said finally.

Her curt answers irked me.

'What does that mean?' I pressed. 'How can you not be sure if you're friends?'

Zara yawned softly. 'We're just . . . from the same community. Thank you for coming to my local mosque today – I have so many memories in that place. I'd love to see where you read the Quran when you were growing up.'

I stuttered for a moment. 'I didn't go to the mosque much growing up. Still don't, to be honest.'

There was an awkward silence.

'Oh. So where did you read the Quran? Just at home with your parents?'

It surprised me a little – the matter-of-fact way in which she'd said it, as though it was simply how she expected things to be.

'I can't read the Quran, but my dad taught me how to pray a few years ago in Ramadan. It was a nice way for us to bond because I don't really see him much due to his hectic work schedule. Everyone in my family is usually quite busy throughout the year, but in Ramadan things slow down for us all and we have iftar dinners together most evenings and spend time talking about Islam and what spirituality means to us. If I'm completely honest with you, my family only focuses on faith during Ramadan, and we aren't so practising during the rest of the year.'

'I see,' she replied lightly, but I could sense her disappointment.

'Thank you for encouraging me to come today,' I added quickly. 'That's the first time I prayed jummah at the mosque this year and I think I'll try to do it more often now.'

'First time this year?' she asked in astonishment.

I remained quiet for a while. I could sense her judgement, and doubt began niggling at me again. Perhaps she secretly longed to be with someone who'd grown up with the same values and lifestyle.

Someone like that guy . . .

'Have you ever liked Imran?' I blurted. The question was out before I could contain it. 'Sorry – you don't have to answer that if you don't want.'

'It's OK, I don't mind.' She cleared her throat. 'I did like him at one point, just a little childhood crush a long time ago, but nothing ever happened between us. He's not my main childhood crush though.'

'Who is?' I sighed, imagining another good-looking, well-built lad from her community.

'Karim Malik from The Exes, obviously. I had his picture as my phone's background, wrote his name in love hearts in my diary, bought a T-shirt with his gorgeous face on it – wore it a few times too.'

I threw my head back and laughed heartily. She joined in, and we didn't bring up that other guy again.

Zara

37

I stood on Imran's doorstep, lasagne in hand and worry in my gut.

It was a few days since his father's funeral; he'd stopped coming into school and hadn't responded to any of my Snapchat messages.

A khatam was taking place at the Sayyid house today: all the women from the local community were congregating to read the Quran and make a collective prayer for Uncle Sayyid. It gave me the perfect excuse to go over and check on Imran.

I was steeling myself to knock but a few women came up behind me and beat me to it. They eyed me blatantly, staring at my plain shalwar kameez, the silky dupatta wrapped loosely around my head, the tray of food I was holding. This attire and the fact I'd clearly spent a significant amount of time in the kitchen today should have meant I fitted right in with them, but I still felt like they didn't approve of me.

The door opened and the aunties greeted Mrs Sayyid as though they were the most concerned friends, but I knew about all the gossiping that went on behind her back, especially about Fawad's prison sentence.

'As-salaam-alaikum, Aunty,' I said to her. She looked like she'd aged a decade in a matter of days. I spoke in Urdu, the only language she knew. 'I'm so sorry for your loss.'

'Walaikum-assalam,' she responded, giving me a warm hug. 'Thank you for the food. There was no need.'

'It was no problem, Aunty. Where shall I put it?'

She pointed me towards the kitchen, placing a gentle hand on my elbow, then left me to it.

My heart ached for her. I'd always been fond of Imran's mum; she was so soft and sincere. Thankfully there were no aunties lingering in the kitchen, so I didn't have to force any awkward conversations. After placing my tray among the other food, I pulled out my phone.

I called Imran, deciding that if he didn't pick up on the first go, I'd leave. But he answered straight away, and my heart leaped.

'I'm at your place,' I said quickly. 'I brought you some food.'

Imran was quiet for a few long moments, then said, 'I'm coming down.'

I nervously paced the length of his small kitchen that closely resembled mine, and then Imran was standing before me. He didn't say anything and neither did I. He was in his typical tracksuit bottoms and white T-shirt, but it wasn't crisp like it usually was; it had the air of being slept in, perhaps for days. His eyes were red-rimmed but still as piercing as ever.

He looked me over once, then said, 'What did you bring?'

I pointed to the lasagne, and he immediately got to work. He took out two plates and then cut us both a slice. With a plate in each hand, he made to leave the kitchen.

'Come with me,' he said over his shoulder.

My eyes widened. 'To the living room? With all the aunties?'

It was only girls and women in there, and they hadn't even started eating yet. This would look beyond weird, for me more than him. Men were never judged as harshly as women for doing something inappropriate.

Imran shot me an *obviously not* expression, then gestured towards the stairs with a tilt of his head.

My mouth grew dry. 'To your room?'

He didn't bother to answer and carried on, barely glancing back at me before disappearing.

This was a scandalous move.

If any aunty happened to see me entering his bedroom . . .

But given the circumstances, I didn't feel able to refuse him. I rushed behind him, straight up the stairs and towards his room. I paused outside, took in the dark look in Imran's eyes, and began second-guessing my decision.

He cocked a brow. 'What's the delay, Khan?'

The sound of a flush from the bathroom spurred me into action, and I practically sprinted into his room and shut the door behind me before anyone could see us.

'That was close,' I breathed.

He shrugged as though he couldn't care less, grabbed one of the plates from his bedside table and settled into bed, leaning against his headboard as he ate. I waited for him to say something. He didn't.

'How are you doing?' I asked tentatively.

'How do you think?'

He was grieving, obviously, so I had to overlook his tone, but it still felt harsh.

I looked around his bedroom. It was large and surprisingly organized; I'd always imagined him to be messy. A wide wardrobe, with a full-length mirror for a door (the very mirror he'd seen me checking him out in), stood on one side. I walked over to the window and looked across the street into my own bedroom. It felt surreal to be standing on this side.

'There's never anything interesting to see. You always draw your curtains while changing.'

Heat flushed my cheeks. 'It seems like you want to be alone. I'll just leave.'

'If I wanted to be alone, I wouldn't have made you a plate,' he said, pointing to it with his fork.

'I'm not hungry. I'll see you later.'

In one swift move, he stood, fetched the plate and walked over to hand it to me. 'It's really good. You should have some.'

I don't know whether it was the compliment or the sudden softness in his eyes, but I accepted it. Imran looked at the foot of his bed suggestively.

'It's OK,' I said. 'I don't mind standing.'

'Just offerin' you a seat,' he murmured. 'Wasn't an invitation for anything more.'

My breath hitched. He walked around me, pulled out the chair from underneath his desk and placed it in front of me.

'Thanks,' I said quietly, then sat down and began to eat.

We ate in silence for a while until he suddenly said, 'I'm sorry I'm being a bit –'

'It's OK,' I replied instantly.

'No, it's not. You already don't like me and I'm makin' it worse.'

'What makes you think I don't like you?'

Imran opened his mouth to say something, then closed it again. He looked me up and down, smirking a little. 'You look good in traditional clothing. It suits your personality.'

'What's that supposed to mean?' I asked defensively, noting his swift change in topic.

'You're just such a . . . good Pakistani girl – always getting perfect results in school, listening to your parents, following the rules.'

I gave him a hard look. 'You'd be surprised.'

'Oh yeah? What you tryna tell me, Khan?' His brows shot up. 'That you're not such a good girl? It's risky to tease a guy with a reputation like mine. In his own bedroom, might I add.'

I averted my gaze from his, my heart racing. His room was suddenly starting to feel rather . . . cramped.

'I wasn't teasing you. And you can't be as bad as your reputation makes you out to be.'

'Don't be so sure.'

My silk dupatta slipped off my head and I instantly pulled it back up, placing it higher than before, hoping it would remind him of the boundaries between us. I finished my slice quickly, stood up and placed the plate carefully on his desk. I wasn't going back into the kitchen in case I bumped into anyone; the plan was to leave as quickly and quietly as possible.

'I'm sorry,' Imran said. 'I think I'm just trying to distract myself.'

My heart melted a little. 'Is it working?'

'For the first time since Dad passed away my mind is elsewhere.'

'Then keep doing it,' I said with a smile, pleased that he was finally opening up to me. 'If it's helping with your grief, I'm willing to put up with more of your inappropriate comments.'

He chuckled.

'Come on then. Hit me with some more of your tacky flirt lines.'

'It doesn't work like that,' he said with a grin. 'The tacky flirt lines have to come naturally.'

'What else can we do to distract you?'

I regretted the words the instant they left my lips. The look in his eyes made it incredibly clear what kind of thoughts were racing through his mind.

He stood and walked over to me confidently, no hesitation at all, until a mere arm's length remained between us. I stepped back, until I could feel the wall behind me, knowing I'd partially brought this upon myself.

'I did say it was risky to tease me in my own bedroom.'

My heart thudded uncontrollably but I kept my tone even. 'I didn't mean it like that.'

He laughed softly. 'You wouldn't have looked at me like that if it hadn't crossed your mind too.'

I gestured to the small space left between us. 'We aren't what you think we are.'

His head tilted to one side. 'We are. You're just not ready to admit it to yourself yet. Earlier I said you don't *like* me. I didn't say you're not into me.'

My dupatta slipped off my shoulder again.

Imran picked up the edge of it. Just as I thought he was going to gently put it back in place, he tugged it instead.

I gasped as I unwillingly stepped towards him, holding on to it tightly so the entire thing wouldn't glide away into his grasp. He was so close that I could see the specks of stubble growing around his beard.

Slowly, he draped the scarf over my shoulder, his knuckles purposefully grazing my collarbone and neck just before he let go.

The soft touch of the fabric on my body broke the spell of the moment, spurring me back into action. I moved towards his door, but he stood in front of me.

'Imran,' I warned.

'I'll stop the moment you tell me to,' he said simply. 'Just tell me you're not the least bit interested in me, and I'll stay away. I'll never try comin' close to you again.'

The word *never* echoed in my mind, cold and unwelcome. His head tilted lower, his eyes locked fiercely on to mine, and the words I was trying to say seemed to be stuck in my throat.

'Say you don't want me, Zara,' he whispered, daring me, coaxing me, his lips getting dangerously close to mine.

My voice box had apparently become redundant.

'Jus' tell me to stop,' he murmured, edging closer every second.

I took a small step back, but still couldn't seem to speak.

'Refuse me. It's so simple.'

And I stood there like an idiot, letting him slip a gentle hand to the nape of my neck and angle my chin higher with a slight tug of my hair. I held my breath, then gulped, then opened my mouth to speak but still nothing came out. My heart stammered as he made the final move towards my lips. Unable to do anything else, I closed my eyes.

The anticipation kept rising and then . . . nothing. Because I suddenly felt the absence of his touch, of his presence.

My eyes flickered open, and I saw Imran standing a whole foot away, hands in pockets, grinning. 'I knew it. I just wanted you to know it too.'

What?

Anger suddenly replaced every other emotion. He'd forced out the feelings that I'd buried deep, and he'd thrust them in front of us both so openly, so carelessly.

'You were trying to prove a point?'

Imran shrugged, looking so annoyingly smug that I wanted to slap him.

I hated him. I hated that some inescapable part of me wanted him. I hated that when I was with him my brain stopped working.

'I'm leaving now,' I snapped, still embarrassingly breathless.

'Just so you know – next time I won't hold back,' he murmured. 'And now we both know neither will you.'

Imran's curtains were parted, and I could see inside easily. He was wearing a black thobe and standing in prayer, a white topi covering his head.

I just couldn't figure him out. There were so many layers to him – all of them concealed under humour and flirtation. He rarely showed me the real him; a few glimpses slipped out here and there, and I liked them more than I dared to admit.

And then there was Karim.

I can imagine you as my wife.

I imagined Imran saying those words, and I imagined liking it; I imagined a whole lot more – daydreams that included willingly removing my dupatta and throwing it on his bedroom floor, closing the small space that always seemed to linger between us, roaming my fingers hungrily over his hard chest, inhaling his luscious scent as I went on my tiptoes and pressed my lips against his . . .

'Stop it, Zara,' I scolded myself aloud as I got into bed.

I couldn't have feelings for Imran. I was with Karim. *The* Karim Malik, who everyone wanted. It wasn't right. I should've refused Imran straight away . . . but it had been so hard . . . and what if it happened again?

The sound of a sharp bang woke me.

I hadn't even realized I'd fallen asleep. I got up and looked around, completely dazed. And then the fireworks erupted again.

I'd forgotten it was Guy Fawkes Night.

I approached my window for a better view.

It took me a few seconds to realize Imran was also standing at his window, looking at the same fireworks. His eyes caught mine and my heart stopped. He looked down at his phone, and I used it as an opportunity to escape his gaze and rush back to bed.

My phone pinged with a message from him.

Cute pjs. You look beautiful.

Butterflies rose and fell in my stomach.

Then he was calling me.

I began to panic. What would we even talk about? But that didn't stop me from picking up.

'Hi,' I said uncertainly.

'Hey,' he replied in a voice so deep and husky it made me swoon a little. 'Come to the window so I can see you. Don't worry, I won't make any inappropriate comments. Unless you secretly enjoy 'em. If so, own up now and I'll let 'em flow freely.'

I didn't bother answering him, but I did go back to my window, grabbing the seat from my study desk to settle in. I looked right at him when I asked, 'How are you?'

He sighed and scratched the back of his head. 'I'm feelin' bad. I scared you off earlier. I'm sorry. I really did appreciate you comin' to check on me.'

'Don't worry, I'm fine. I'm not so easily scared off.'

Imran chuckled. 'You practically legged it out of my room, Khan. So don't give me that bull.'

I showed him my middle finger, only making him laugh louder. 'I wasn't scared of you. I was uncomfortable with ... what could have happened.'

'Nothin' would've happened without your permission, Zara. I made that clear. That's not me.'

Goosebumps covered my entire body. Imran had a way of getting into my mind, under my skin. He was across the street, in another house, yet I felt his presence so strongly he could've been right next to me.

I cleared my throat. 'I didn't want anything to happen.'

'Do I still need to convince you that you did? Because I'm up for the task.'

It became impossible to speak, so I didn't answer, but Imran's words left an exhilarating anticipation lingering in the silence between us.

'How's your mum doing?' I asked, changing the topic entirely. Safe ground.

'She's all right. It's hard. She's lost her husband, and two of her sons are never able to see her. It's just me. I hate thinkin' about her spending so much time alone.'

'I'm really sorry. Let me know if there's anything I can do. She doesn't know me that well but maybe I could come over occasionally to see her. I'm not good at making Pakistani food – but I could bring other stuff. Cakes and pies.'

He was quiet for a while, and I thought maybe I'd said something wrong.

'That's real kind of you, Zara,' he said eventually, his voice thick with emotion. 'She'd love it. Mum always wanted a daughter.'

'No problem,' I responded warmly.

'You know what? It may seem that my dad passed away from heart disease, but it wasn't really that.'

My mouth grew dry. 'What do you mean?'

'After Fawad bhai got sent to jail, Dad stopped takin' care of himself. He came to this country to give his children a better life, and worked damn hard in factories, restaurants and taxis to provide it. Then his eldest son made friends with bad people, got caught up in messed-up things and ended up destroying his dreams for his family. Fawad bhai went to jail two years ago but Dad never really got over the humiliation and heartbreak of it. And it all eventually caught up with him.'

His voice quivered a little and I felt my throat close up.

'And that's what's killin' me,' Imran continued sternly. 'If Fawad bhai hadn't made such stupid decisions, things could've been different for my family. Now we're all scattered. Dad isn't with us any more. Fawad's in jail. Saqib's in Dubai, and plans to stay there, probably so he can run away from everything here. He only came back for the funeral, left two days later and probably won't return for a long time. I'm the only one with Mum now and I don't even know how to console her sometimes. It just doesn't feel like we're a family any more.'

I took a deep, unsteady breath. 'I'm so sorry, Imran. You should know that it's not only you who feels like that. Trust me.'

And then I told him about the issues in my family too, how we all lived so close but were so far apart that the distance between us could never be crossed. I told him about how my parents had emotionally blackmailed my sister into an arranged marriage, how it had turned out to be abusive and yet they weren't letting her leave it because that's how much they cared about their reputation.

I told him that my brother never came over any more because my dad had disowned him for marrying a Black woman, and that my mum was heartbroken she could never see her son but wouldn't dare question her husband's decision. I told him about how suffocated and misunderstood I felt all the time in my own house, how sometimes I wanted to disappear altogether.

I found myself telling him things I hadn't even told Saliha or Karim because deep down I knew they'd never understand what it was like to belong to a broken family. I told him things I'd never dared to say aloud.

We talked long into the night, and when dawn broke, we were still looking at each other.

A Sinister Side to Karim Malik: Extreme Times Leading to Extremist Views?

We all know the past few months have been rather intense for Karim Malik. An abortion. The heartbreak of losing his childhood sweetheart. Betrayals from close friends. A steadily decreasing follower count while the other Exes continue to shine and grow . . .

I mean, jeez. That guy has been through it.

But I don't think any of us saw it coming to *this*. The heart-throb influencer was recently spotted at the East London Mosque. None of us had expected him to take a *religious* stance as a response to all his woes. Photos have emerged of him praying among the congregation, and I'm wondering whether there's reason to be . . . concerned.

I mean, who's going to be creating content for us if he starts praying five times a day? And what kind of content should we be expecting if he suddenly starts showing more interest in fasting than fashion, or maybe even in fast fashion – ew?! Speaking of which, the guy's outfits have been all over the place recently (who on earth pairs a striped D&G shirt with a Céline houndstooth jacket?! And why is he glued to those cheap-looking whitewashed jeans from The Exes' collection?). It's as though he isn't even a teen fashion icon any more . . .

It certainly seems his thoughts are occupied elsewhere these days. Maybe there are other factors that pushed Chloe Clark away – it may be the case that we've been harder on her than we should've been. And so, my darlings, the plot thickens. Throw in some unhinged behaviour and a few more unusual detours from Karim and maybe this will turn into a BAFTA-worthy thriller. You know I'll have the popcorn ready.

In other news, Felicity Wong's family is broke. Yeah, I just pulled off the sticking plaster there. There was no easy way of putting that out there. In an embarrassing turn of events, it has been unveiled that the funds from the Wong Charity Gala in Hong Kong this past summer were actually *kept* by the Wong family as a means of paying off their piling debts. What a shameless thing to do – in the name of charity?!

Poor Abeo – he travelled all the way to Hong Kong to attend his friend's event and donated generously. Don't worry, boo, your fashion game is still the strongest on the scene, so at least you still have that to comfort you. The Wongs, on the other hand . . .

And one last thing on Felicity – she's more of a blabbermouth than you'd expect. She was the one who tipped me off about the Chlarim abortion situation. I know, I know. She's one of The Exes and she's Chloe's best friend. How could she?! Well, we all have our reasons . . .

I'm no longer holding back, and I KNOW you're all here for it. Stay tuned for more upcoming dirt on the people you hate to love and love to hate.

Yours Unfaithfully,
Mr Ex

Karim

40

The latest post from Mr Ex hit differently from the previous ones.

It was an attack on my whole identity. And the comments section was so Islamophobic – so full of racist and hurtful jabs – that I felt tears pricking at my eyes.

I went to look for Dad. Only he would know the right thing to say in this situation. I raced to the living room and stopped dead in my tracks.

Cousins, aunties and family friends I hadn't seen in months – some of them in years – were lounging around the room, talking, laughing, dancing to the dhol. Wedding decorators had been busy adorning the house with lights, marigold garlands and colourful drapes. The place was littered with multicoloured pillows and golden trays bearing henna cones and mouth-watering mithai. When they saw me enter, family members began saying salaam and coming up to hug me.

I greeted them warmly but quickly made excuses about needing to be elsewhere. It was great that the wedding festivities were officially starting but I just wasn't in the mood to be around people. Not right now.

As I made to leave, Kiran ran up to me and grabbed my arm. 'I was just coming to get you. It's time for you to learn the mehndi dances. There are only three weeks to go, and everyone else already knows the choreography.'

'Not right now,' I snapped. 'Where's Dad?'

'Karim! I'm working so hard to get everything together for the wedding. The least you can do is occasionally be present. Even your friends are more involved than you. Felicity has been coming over regularly to help with the dances.'

'Oh, right. Well, Felicity is no longer invited, and she won't be coming here again. In fact, none of The Exes will be at the wedding.'

'What?' Kiran positively screeched. 'But I *need* her. Can you please delay all the drama between The Exes until after the wedding?'

Anger rose from the pit of my stomach. 'Have you not checked Mr Ex's latest blog?'

Kiran's eyes widened. 'No, I haven't been on my phone much today.'

'I'm so glad you get a break from the online world, sis,' I said bitterly. 'Unfortunately, I'm not so lucky. Felicity told Mr Ex about the abortion. She's probably the one who informed him about Zara's identity too.'

Kiran gaped. 'Are you for real?'

'Abeo texted me as soon as the blog released. He's siding with Felicity because of how Mr Ex was supposedly blackmailing her. So clearly I can't trust either of them, and I don't want them anywhere near me. I've blocked Felicity.'

'I can't believe this is happening,' Kiran breathed, holding her head in disbelief. 'You're all best friends!'

'*Were*,' I corrected her. 'Things are different now. Apparently now The Exes are a group that spill information on each other to protect their own backs, and I don't want any part of it.'

Before she could respond, I stormed off.

I entered Dad's home office without knocking and was glad to find him at his desk.

One look at my face and he pushed his laptop screen down. 'What's wrong?'

'Have you seen the things people are saying about me online right now?'

He shook his head. Of course he wouldn't know. He watched the news and read economics journals first thing on a Saturday morning; he didn't scroll through social media feeds.

'People are implying I've become an extremist,' I said through gritted teeth. 'All because I decided to go to a mosque to pray on Friday.'

Dad's expression softened and he gestured for me to sit.

'You'd think I committed a heinous crime. People are telling me to stop trying to Islamize Britain, to stop preaching a violent religion to the children I influence, to go back to my country, to stop promoting terrorism. All I did was *pray in a mosque.*'

My voice had become louder with each word. I stopped to take a deep breath, to calm down.

'Listen to me, Karim,' Dad began, 'I'm not going to sugar-coat things. There is a lot of Islamophobia out there. Some people may try to distort the faith we hold dear, and to misrepresent who you are as a person. You cannot let them get inside your head. If you do that, it'll get to a stage where you won't be comfortable being yourself. You'll become somebody you feel you have to be. It won't be the real you.'

'I've never received hate like *this* before. Death threats. It makes me want to never go near a mosque again.'

Dad leaned forward, his face tense. 'You cannot let complete strangers with highly misinformed ideas of your religion dictate what you believe in and how you live your life.'

I frowned. 'I know, I know. It just feels like maybe things would be easier if I wasn't ... Muslim.'

It had been impossible to meet his eyes as I'd said that. Guilt and shame crept over every inch of my skin, and I instantly knew I didn't mean it.

I felt the pressure of labels and disappointment from both sides: people from my community thought I wasn't Muslim *enough*, and others found me to be *too* Muslim. All I wanted was the freedom and space to choose my own relationship with my faith.

'You're allowed to express yourself, Karim,' Dad said, surprising me with the gentleness of his response. I'd expected anger, admonishment. 'I'll never judge you for anything you say to me in this regard. But you need to make your decisions based on good intentions and truth, not fear.'

'It just doesn't make sense to me ... Why do so many people hate us?'

'It's not just us. Hatred of people from different backgrounds has existed for as long as humanity has. All of it stems from a place of ignorance and a dangerous superiority complex. People not bothering to understand others. People believing their way of life or appearance is better than others'.'

'I hate it,' I whispered.

'As do I.'

Dad placed both palms flat on his desk as he said, 'Just promise me you'll remember this: we believe God is the most merciful, the most loving. Believing in Him is what has made my life so worthwhile; my belief has been my backbone and strength through all of life's trials. Don't let go of your belief unless it enriches your life more to do so, which simply isn't possible. Trust me. You can always go ahead and try it, and find out for yourself.'

My heart clenched. 'Sometimes it feels like this entire life can be taken away from me in the blink of an eye – for saying the wrong thing, for being seen in the wrong place. You're telling me to be myself, but will I ever be accepted for who I am?'

For the first time, Dad's expression seemed sad. 'It's likely that you'll experience more Islamophobia and racism in the future. I've experienced it, and so did your grandfather.'

He looked outside his window, and I was sure his eyes filled a little. 'Your grandfather fought in the Second World War for Britain. I was married in this country and my children were born here. Our family contributes to the British economy, culture and charity sector copiously, and so we are accepted in this country. This is our home.'

I scoffed a little. 'We have to justify our acceptance in this country through all of that? I'm pretty sure there are people who do very, very little to contribute to this country and yet it would never be questioned whether they belong here simply because they possess the right skin colour or religion.'

Dad was quiet. I almost felt bad for putting him on the spot like this. He'd always had a quick, easy answer to everything I'd asked him in the past. Now he studied my face carefully, and I looked right back at him. And the seconds ticked on by.

When he smiled, it was an unguarded, heart-wrenching thing. 'You're growing up, Karim.'

The wrinkles had deepened around his forehead and eyes. His hair was speckled with more white than black now, as was his beard. How had I missed how much he'd aged?

We were sitting here talking about my grandfather – perhaps one day I'd be sitting with my son and talking about my father, trying to explain this same unexplainable thing to him. A vicious cycle of unbelonging that bound us together over the generations, an elusive dream we all had to belong right where we were, an inherited fear that perhaps we would never really belong anywhere.

Emotion clogged my throat and I didn't know what to do other than rush over to him. He stood and embraced me for a long time. I felt more connected to him than I had in a long time.

'I'm going to the Remembrance Day Charity Gala this evening,' I said into his shoulder. 'Will you and Mum be there?'

'Of course,' he replied warmly. 'We go every year, don't we?'

'I'll wear a poppy for Grandad,' I said quietly, and felt him smile.

Karim

41

It was a well-established tradition for The Exes to attend the Remembrance Day Charity Gala as a quintet, all clad in sharp black evening wear – top hats for the men, fascinators for the women – and to be fundraising for veterans and war refugees.

I made my own way to the Gherkin – this year's location – not bothering to notify the others. I couldn't care less if I saw any of them there. The Exes were all two-faced, backstabbing liars and I wanted nothing to do with them.

Upon arrival, I lingered with my parents for a while, making small talk with their friends. Then I excused myself, got a drink and walked towards the glass dome roof to enjoy the panoramic views of the city. I took a few photos for Instagram, including one where my reflection was visible in the glass.

Dad was right. This *was* home. Even if I sometimes felt a little out of place here, I wouldn't allow some people's hatred to make me feel like a stranger in the city I was born and raised in.

My thoughts returned to Zara, as they always seemed to. I imagined her standing next to me, holding my hand. Even the thought of her was enough to quell the loneliness threatening to engulf me. I had lost all my best friends, but I still had her.

'No one rocks a suit quite like you do.'

From the reflection in the glass, I saw it was Chloe. She was in a sleek black gown, her hair pulled back in a low bun, a beret angled on one side of her head, three poppies pinned over her heart.

'Or a top hat,' she added. 'You look great.'

'As do you.'

'But you haven't even seen me,' she whispered, taking a step closer.

I faced her and took another sip of my drink. I didn't say anything, only looked her up and down once, then gazed straight into those intense green eyes that had made me feel so much – possibly every emotion a human could experience.

'Now you have,' she crooned.

I turned back to the view of the city, choosing silence again.

She cleared her throat, blatantly uncomfortable with my dismissive attitude. 'I finished recording my first album yesterday.'

'Congratulations,' I replied. 'It's what you've always wanted. I'm glad your dreams are coming true.'

'Not all of them.'

A leaden silence fell.

'I really wanted you there, you know,' she murmured. 'I just didn't know how to ask. Would you have come, Karim?'

I exhaled deeply, already exhausted with this conversation. 'Honestly, I don't know. It's something we always spoke about, and our history isn't meaningless. Maybe for the sake of that, I would've shown up. Or maybe it would've just been too hard for me in the end.'

Chloe took a small step closer to me, her heels clanking delicately against the black tiles. 'I think about it every day, you know. What our baby would've –'

My cutting glare made her stop short, but there was a sincerity in her glowing eyes.

'Would've?' I found myself prompting.

'Been like,' she finished softly. 'They would've grown up to become a person in their own right, with their own thoughts and hobbies and experiences. Our child would've been a living, breathing piece of us both, but something more, something better.'

Her voice cracked on the last word.

A strange, indescribable emotion filled my chest – the restlessness you feel when you misplace something dear to you.

She pulled a tissue out of her black Chanel clutch and dabbed just under her eyes. 'It's driving me crazy, you know – thinking about what our baby would've been like.' She laughed softly. 'I don't think it'll ever stop haunting me.'

I wanted to tell her that it haunted me too, that she wasn't alone in feeling that, but I couldn't seem to speak.

'Karim, I never really told you how sorry I am. But I am. For everything.'

I found myself closing the distance between us, so we stood exactly side by side, staring down at the city because it was too damn hard to look at each other while we talked about this.

'Of course I forgive you, Chloe. It was an impossible choice. You did what you believed was right for yourself, for your future. I'm also sorry for being hard on you at a time that was so hard in itself. Maybe it's my fault too. Clearly I did something wrong if you felt like you couldn't turn to me.'

Chloe gripped my shoulder and shook her head, her red eyes wide with distress. 'That's not true. You were my best friend and the most amazing boyfriend. No one's ever been there for me in the way you have. And now I know no one ever will. I took you for granted, and it's the biggest mistake I've ever made.'

I didn't know what to say. It was obvious she wanted me back, but our lives were gradually shifting further apart. I could no longer imagine a future for us – sometimes not even as friends, let alone anything more.

'I'm finally getting therapy, by the way. I know you were encouraging me to go for ages. I'm trying here, Karim. I want to do better. To *be* better.'

'You already are. The fact that we're having this conversation proves it.'

Her smile was wide and infectious. 'Thanks for sending Felicity after me at lunchtime, by the way. I don't know what I would've done without her. I was *such* a mess.'

And the warm feeling was gone. 'I can't believe she's the one who leaked the news about us.'

She sniffed loudly. 'Felicity confessed to me shortly before Mr Ex posted the news online. It's not what you think. Things have been really hard for her this year.'

'Things have been hard for *her*?'

Chloe flinched. 'Please just hear me out. All her family's businesses in Hong Kong went bankrupt. The Wongs had to sell most of their assets. She's literally the sole person supporting her family right now, and they have massive costs just to maintain their lives.'

'The Wongs can't be doing that bad,' I sneered. 'Felicity gets paid *generously* from our social media platforms and merch, not to mention her own separate earnings.'

'It's not just that, Karim. Felicity had no choice but to do whatever Mr Ex told her to do because he discovered the one secret that could destroy her family's reputation. Obviously Mr Ex played Felicity for as long as he wanted and then revealed the news anyway. She's devastated. So is her family. They feel unable to show their faces to anyone.'

I finished the last of my drink. 'She should've told us what was going on.'

'Mr Ex told her not to, and he has a way of finding out everything, doesn't he?'

'The abortion is the most traumatic thing we've ever been through, and Felicity went and told Mr Ex as though it was some salacious gossip, all to save her own ass. I would *never* have shared something so sensitive about her with Mr Ex just to save myself. And I don't think you'd ever do it either! Are you seriously going to let her off so easily?'

Chloe exhaled slowly. 'Don't you think she's been through enough? She was the most bubbly, carefree person before all of this happened. Haven't you noticed how much she's changed?'

I scoffed. 'All of us have changed. A little too much. I need space from you guys for a while.'

'You will forgive her eventually though, right? You have to. She was being *blackmailed*; her family was being threatened. None of this is her fault.'

I'd heard enough and made to leave.

Chloe grabbed my arm, holding me in place. I looked down at her hand and then at her face. She removed her grip instantly, her eyes widening at whatever darkness she saw tainting my features. There was still a barrier between us. It would take a lot more than one heartfelt conversation for it to come down.

'This is probably a bit late, but I also wanted to say sorry for what I did at the Halloween party.'

'For that, I don't accept your apology,' I replied coolly.

Zara was the only person in my life I trusted wholeheartedly, who saw me for who I was. Chloe had tried to rip that away from me too, to leave me completely alone.

'You hurt a lot of people by kissing me. It isn't cute for you to play with everyone's emotions.'

Chloe's lower lip trembled. 'I didn't mean to. I was drunk and dealing with a lot of strong emotions. I thought you'd understand.'

I shook my head in disbelief.

'What happened to us, Karim? The truth is, we all still love each other. Despite everything. And we need to stick together. We can't let Mr Ex win.'

I brought my face close to hers and let malice coat each word. 'What if I told you it isn't Mr Ex? What if it's The Exes? We're growing apart because we failed to give each other the respect we deserve.'

'*No*, it's all Mr Ex,' she insisted desperately. 'He's been threatening us separately and creating divides between us so that we don't communicate with each other. He's been blackmailing Sanjay, stating that he'll expose the arson attack if he doesn't produce artworks for him. Sanjay has to paint for him whatever he demands, and it sometimes takes hours, *days*. Then he has to post the art to whatever random addresses he's given, and Mr Ex makes *so* much money from selling Sanjay's original pieces.'

Despite everything he'd done behind my back, I found myself feeling a little sorry for Sanjay. Art was his passion, his life, and Mr Ex was poisoning that too.

'Mr Ex has been controlling my wardrobe for weeks now,' Chloe continued, 'which is affecting so many of my brand deals. I can't even shop any more without being overcome with anxiety. And when I'm anxious I find it so hard to sing well, to produce content, to function at *anything*.'

She leaned closer and cast her eyes around the room before whispering, 'Abeo told me about his sex tape. He also mentioned that Mr Ex tried to get information on . . . your new girlfriend.'

I wasn't going to speak to her about Zara, and the look I gave her made that perfectly clear.

Chloe held up a hand. 'OK, let's not go there. But what I'm trying to say is that he's been blackmailing us *all* this year. He divided us so we wouldn't band together and come for him. Don't you want to work together to get back at Mr Ex? To take revenge for all the fear, bullying, blackmail and sleepless nights?'

As much as I wanted to destroy Mr Ex, I couldn't stomach the thought of spending time with any of The Exes right now.

'No,' I said. 'The only thing I want is to steer clear of the people who I once loved but who betrayed me.'

I placed my glass on a tray held by a passing waiter and walked away. I would swing by my parents, inform them I'd already made my donation online, and head home.

As I scanned the hall, my gaze met Abeo's.

He was standing with Felicity on one side and Sanjay on the other. I gave Felicity a cutting glare. She flinched. But then a cold mask arranged her pretty features into aloofness. Chloe walked over to them and joined the entourage. Dressed in the sharpest black suits and dresses, wearing the most graceful hats, they all eyed me with identical cavalier expressions. The people I'd grown up with. Who were once my entire world.

They were easily the most beautiful and influential people in the room; they fitted next to each other as seamlessly as a puzzle, and their bond appeared unbreakable to any onlooker – even to me, despite knowing how many fractures there were between us all.

A thought crossed my mind: with their graceful appearance and the epic view of London in the background, it was the perfect moment to capture a new profile picture for our socials, even with me absent.

My heart froze over as it hit me that I simply didn't fit with them any more. It was as though I was looking at complete strangers.

I didn't know whether it was Mr Ex's planning or the hand of fate or my very own decision, but one thing was very clear. There was a new order in The Exes.

And I was the odd one out.

42

Late November brought with it an abundance of excitement and nerves. Catering for the Malik wedding was the biggest opportunity Jashan had ever secured and we were all hopeful that it would go so well that it'd be the first of many big successes for the business.

'I can't believe the mehndi is today,' Morowa said tensely as we drove to the event in their van.

'To be fair, it was a fairly short-notice wedding,' Farhan bhai replied. 'I'm just glad we're prepared. Inshallah it'll be great.'

'Oh yeah, it was super short notice,' I chipped in. 'Karim was telling me about how crazy it drove his family to try and arrange everything in time.'

Farhan bhai looked at me sideways from the driver's seat. 'You've been speaking to Karim Malik quite a bit then, have you?'

I shrugged, trying to appear nonchalant. 'I guess we've become friends.'

'That's just one more perk of this job, isn't it? A hot, famous new friend.' Morowa giggled. I couldn't help but join her.

'Just friends, right?' Farhan bhai enquired in a sharp tone.

It was a reminder for me to keep a respectful distance from boys, to remember the boundaries I was expected to maintain. Although he was just showing some brotherly protectiveness, I felt my cheeks grow hot.

Karim and I spoke on the phone for hours every night, and we found every opportunity to see each other, especially on weekends, even if all we did was go for a drive and catch up in his car. He was definitely touching me for longer – still innocent touches at my back, my face, my neck, but they felt so good I barely suppressed the urge to ask for more. I kept wondering the same thing: how could it be wrong when it felt so *right*?

And he was becoming more open and vulnerable with me now, sharing pieces of his mind with me that left me feeling as though I knew his soul intimately. Since Mr Ex's Islamophobic post, he'd experienced a wave of hate online and I'd tried my best to be there for him, to listen to his fears and worries, and to soothe them away in whatever way I could.

He often felt lonely and misunderstood. As did I. Something undeniable connected us. I'd started confiding in him too, sharing snippets of my struggles at home, because he was a constant presence in my life, dependable in a way that others weren't.

Imran was infuriatingly on and off whenever we spoke. The first thing that came to my mind when he read my messages but didn't bother to respond was that he was either speaking to other girls or bragging to his mates about how close he'd come to kissing the goody-two-shoes Zara Khan in his own bedroom.

I hated how insecure he made me feel.

When we did talk, it was amazing. And when we didn't, it was devastating.

My emotions with him were too overwhelming, a roller-coaster ride I just wanted to get off.

If my first kiss had been with him, I would've hated myself right now; I'd have felt like I'd given up something precious to someone who simply didn't value it. I was so grateful he'd stopped when he had, and I'd decided I would never let him get so close to me again.

Things with Karim, on the other hand, were stable and progressing in a way that felt natural. Incredible.

'Of course, Farhan bhai,' I said matter-of-factly. 'Just friends.'

Morowa began discussing details of the catering with my brother, and I was glad about the diversion. I pulled down the sun visor and began judging my appearance in the mirror.

Karim had officially invited me to the wedding, and so I was going both as part of the catering entourage and as a guest, and I'd certainly dressed up for the occasion. When I'd informed Farhan bhai that I wouldn't be wearing the black and white Jashan uniform, he'd been a little hesitant at first, stating that I should've maintained a professional distance from our clients, but he'd come around.

Instead, I was wearing one of Aisha baji's old outfits: a lightly bejewelled beige Anarkali suit with pearl buttons down the centre. I still remembered the way Aisha had looked when she'd worn it on Eid many years ago – her smile infectious, her long black hair flying as she ran in the garden, raising her dupatta above her head. That same dupatta was now pinned to my shoulder, and I loved the way it made me feel connected to her, even as my heart felt heavy because she was never that happy or carefree now.

I'd done a soft make-up look that was characteristic of traditional mehndi glam: my skin was glowing, bronze-gold eyeshadow swept across my lids, and I'd chosen a rosy-pink lipstick. My hair was out in loose waves and peeking through were the dangly gold-and-pearl earrings I'd borrowed from Sal, the only jewellery I was wearing.

When we arrived at the Natural History Museum and parked up, I looked at Morowa and grinned.

'What an iconic venue for a wedding!' I beamed.

'It's a Malik wedding,' she replied. '*Everything*'s going to be iconic.'

As we were about to enter, Farhan bhai said to me, 'Since you look like a guest, I think you should just sit with your friends. But do keep an eye on the dessert service and let us know if everything is going smoothly.'

'Are you sure?' I asked.

'Yes,' Morowa said firmly, squeezing my hand. 'Have fun tonight. We're all going to live vicariously through you while we work.'

They left to join the rest of the catering team and I approached the entrance tentatively, knowing I was quite early for a guest.

'Zara, you're here!'

Kiran walked towards me with arms outstretched. Karim was at her side.

They looked breathtaking.

Kiran wore a voluminous bright yellow lehenga with a sleeveless, cropped choli. Her hair was slicked back in a low bun wrapped with a gajra. Karim was in a sage-green and gold sherwani, with a gold resham scarf hanging loosely around his neck.

They deserved to be on the cover of *Asiana Wedding* magazine.

'You guys look amazing!' I enthused, hugging Kiran. 'I'm not too early, am I?'

'You look gorgeous, babe. Other guests will be arriving soon,' Kiran replied, already sauntering off to see to a task. 'I hope you've got your dancing shoes on today!'

Karim gave me a mischievous smile. 'You're going to see me do a dozen dance routines today. I learned the choreography for all of them in the past week, so no judgement if I mess up.'

'You're going to be great. I can't wait!'

'By the way, you *are* dancing tonight. I'll come and grab you myself if I have to.'

'Don't you dare,' I warned, punching his arm.

He came closer to me and trailed his thumb softly down my cheekbone. 'You look amazing, Zara. I don't know how I'm supposed to focus on anything when you're here looking like this.'

I blushed, then ran a hand from his shoulder down to his chest, stopping at his heart, enjoying the feel of the smooth threadwork under my fingers. 'I love this look on you. You should definitely rock it more often.'

'If this is what you're into, you better not be surprised if I turn up to our next date in something like this.'

I giggled and he ran his fingers through the silken fabric of my dupatta. 'And I'd really like for you to wear something like this for me in the future.'

Karim's eyes darkened in a way that suggested it would be only for him, that we'd be alone, and I wouldn't be wearing it for long at all. I swallowed, every part of me thrumming with exhilaration.

He took hold of my hand and led me into the main entrance.

The Victorian architecture and Romanesque arches of the Hintze Hall were as glorious as ever, as was the blue whale skeleton suspended from the ceiling, but other aspects of the space had transformed it into a marker of South Asian heritage. Lamps and candles, multicoloured flower arrangements and umbrellas, vibrant garlands and drapes.

The grand staircase led directly to an ornately decorated floral stage; there was a large dance floor surrounded by mehndi trays bearing henna cones and sweets; and a purple iridescent glow adorned the hall, creating an aura of opulence and otherworldliness.

'It's stunning,' I breathed.

Karim began introducing me to his family and friends. It felt so easy to bond with them over our excitement for the event. I didn't feel like an introvert at all. This was the first time I'd hung out with a large group of people and still felt seen, heard, respected.

It was strange to me – the fact that I could feel so invisible in my own world and yet here, surrounded by such wealthy influencers, upper-class society folk and complete strangers, I could feel so . . . accepted, so *myself.*

Karim

43

It was as though we'd entered a nineties Bollywood film in the heart of modern-day London.

The two dhol players created such an upbeat ambience for Azad bhai and Sana baji's entrance that everyone longed to start dancing the moment the bride and groom took their seats on the multicoloured, brightly lit stage.

After a quick welcome speech from my parents, the DJ announced that the dance performances would take place as a contest between the bride's side and the groom's side, with the latter kicking off the show.

My stomach was in knots throughout the entire first performance, but, more than anything else, I cared about impressing Zara. After the smoothness of the first dance routine, my confidence kicked in. I loved seeing Zara in the front row, seated with my cousins, clapping me on, cheering for everyone.

On the bride's side, an endless entourage of Sana baji's cousins and friends had flown in from Pakistan, having rehearsed some spectacular moves to the latest trending music, and they were incredible.

We were keeping up well though.

Kiran had encouraged our side to prepare comedy performances as well: it added an extra layer of entertainment to watch aunties and uncles don masks of the bride and groom's faces and dance to classic Bollywood songs.

Some of the girls from the bride's side had tried flirting with me during the performances. It had been fun, but I only had eyes for Zara. I couldn't wait to be near her again.

When the final dance performance finished, Kiran and I grabbed Azad bhai and Sana baji, and soon everyone was on the dance floor. It was the most beautiful mayhem. Everyone moved with such joy, as though not a single disagreement or hiccup had taken place in preparation for this day, as though everyone was happy from the heart, and always would be, for this new bond that had been made.

I danced with my parents, and I couldn't remember the last time I'd felt so carefree and light-hearted. Mr Ex and The Exes may as well have disappeared altogether from my life.

When I'd given my family enough time, I went to look for Zara. She was still sitting, grinning openly as she looked at everyone having a good time. When she spotted me approaching her, my hand outstretched, her eyes widened with panic.

'Oh, come on,' I shouted over the music. 'It'll be fun.'

I took her hand and pulled her towards me. She rolled her eyes dramatically and then laughed as we were swept into the crowd. I didn't stop until we were right in the centre. I held on to her waist and danced with her to the beat of the drum, to the bhangra, to the fresh remixes of classic Bollywood songs.

We jumped and swayed and sang along to the cheesy love songs at the top of our lungs.

Maybe this was the happiest I'd ever been.

Only when I was dying for some hydration did I pull Zara away from the crowd, grab a bottle of water and escape to a secluded corner hidden behind a row of colourful drapes and suspended marigold garlands.

'Want some?' I asked breathlessly after taking a long swig.

She nodded, took it from me and began to drink. I watched her closely as she knocked her head back, closed her eyes and swallowed. My gaze fixed on her smooth neck, the glistening gold on her eyelids, the subtle sheen of sweat on her forehead.

Everything about her compelled me to draw closer.

Zara smiled as she handed the bottle back to me. I returned the smile as I placed the bottle on the floor and moved nearer to her. We were both still breathing heavily. I got so close that we no longer had to shout over the music. I was towering over her a little and she lifted her chin to meet my gaze.

'You were right. That was a lot of fun.'

'It was,' I murmured, tucking her hair behind an ear so I could see her face better. '*You're* a lot of fun.'

She lowered her gaze demurely and it tugged at my heartstrings. When she looked up at me again, I noticed a fire burning in her eyes.

'You know what you said about imagining me as your wife?'

My stomach in knots, I nodded.

'I thought you should know that I can imagine it too. And I can definitely imagine wearing something like this again. Just for you.'

Desire shot through me so fiercely it almost made me weak at the knees.

This was the girl I wanted to take home with me, to wake up to every day, to speak to about all my deepest fears and dreams.

'You're driving me crazy, Zara,' I breathed, curling a hand around her waist.

Usually, she would stiffen at my touch, but today she was different. She melted into it, drawing closer, lowering her lashes, lifting her chin, parting her lips.

I placed a hand gently on her face, slowly trailing it down to the back of her neck, and I tightened my hold of her waist, pulling her closer. The desire I felt for her was reflected in her own eyes and I couldn't hold back any longer. I gradually tilted my head lower, knowing this was her first kiss, giving her enough time to pull back whenever she wanted.

'I've never felt so safe and seen,' she whispered, her breath tickling my lips.

Light spread through my body, a heat that felt like coming home to a crackling fireplace after a long, cold day outside. 'Neither have I.'

And I meant it. The world saw me through the carefully curated content I put out to entertain it, but Zara saw the real me, and I knew my every emotion and thought was safe with her. Always would be.

'You're perfectly right for me,' I said.

She smiled, then repeated, 'You're perfectly right for me.'

'Is this OK?'

Zara nodded. And then I kissed her.

My lips pressed against hers gently. I could tell she was tense, so I kept it soft. It was as though my lips were barely touching hers. I could tell she was holding her breath. My fingers were caressing her waist and neck lovingly, holding her close, showing her how much I wanted her.

I broke off the kiss and looked at her.

Her eyes were still closed, and I leaned lower to trail kisses up her neck. She gasped a little, stiffened for a second, and then moved her head back to give me better access. I brushed my lips to the centre of her throat, then made a little circle with my tongue there, and she moaned.

The sound had a different impact on us both.

I tried to recapture her lips with mine, but she moved back self-consciously, her hands pushing my chest away. Her eyes were wide with worry, as though she'd expressed something she shouldn't have.

'It's OK, trust me,' I said, holding her gaze. 'It's the sexiest sound I've ever heard.'

She breathed deeply for a few seconds, and I was afraid she was pulling away from me, but then she smiled and bit her lower lip. The hands which had just pushed me away curled into the material of my sherwani and tugged me close again. I almost stumbled into her, and we both burst out laughing.

'We can stop if you want,' I offered.

'No,' she breathed. 'Let's do it again. And this time I'm going to try kissing you back.'

We both reached for each other this time, and our lips met with an intensity that I felt somewhere deep inside my chest.

I parted her lips with mine and went in with a deeper kiss, biting her lower lip.

When I first put my tongue in her mouth, she inhaled, freezing a little.

But then she found my rhythm and began copying my movements. She breathed and moaned into my mouth, hands roaming over my chest and neck, tiptoeing higher as though she couldn't get close enough.

Lust curled around my body, making me want to unbutton her dress, touch her everywhere, feel her bare skin against mine. I pulled back and looked into her eyes.

'We should stop now,' I said firmly.

She looked hurt for a second, then she realized why I'd moved away, and she smirked.

'You're a quick learner,' I said, grinning down at her.

She stuck her tongue out. 'You're a good teacher.'

I was about to respond when the flash of a camera caught me off guard. Zara froze, eyes widening until she looked frantic.

'What was that?' she asked in a panicked tone. 'Was someone taking photos of us making out?'

I rushed towards the area the flash had come from, but there was no one there. An uncomfortable feeling took root in my heart, washing away the excitement and desire I'd felt moments ago.

Zara caught up to me. 'Someone just photographed us, didn't they? Oh my God. What if those photos end up online?' The blood had drained from her face.

We'd hired plenty of wedding photographers and videographers, some to capture social media footage, others to prepare a traditional South Asian wedding trailer and photo album. It was probably one of them . . .

I knew it was wishful thinking even as I considered it as a possibility.

Those photographers would've been out with the crowd, capturing the bride and groom and their loved ones celebrating with them. They wouldn't have come to a secluded corner to take photos of the groom's brother with his tongue in a girl's mouth.

It was probably a nosy, meddling guest . . . someone who wouldn't think twice about giving Mr Ex some juicy new gossip . . . or maybe it was the menace himself . . .

My hands grew clammy as I realized what this meant for Zara. It was hard enough to be swept into the limelight, but to be splashed in front of the public eye for the first time in *this* way. I was barely able to protect myself from the scrutiny and hate online. How on earth was I going to save *her* from it?

It was getting hard to draw breath.

The DJ announced that dinner would be served shortly, and it was time for everyone to take their seats.

I turned to Zara and held her hands in mine. 'I've got to go back to my family now. Let's just get through this evening, OK? Don't worry, everything will be fine.'

She nodded, but I could see in her eyes that she didn't believe me.

London's Lustrous New Love Story: Our Dark Fairy Unceremoniously Unveiled

Astonished. Intrigued. Turned on.

That's how the events of the past few days have left me feeling. Somehow, all at once.

Despite the very public Halloween smooch, it seems that Chlarim are truly old news, because Karim Malik officially has a new love interest. And yes, perhaps she isn't quite as alluring behind-the-mask as I'd anticipated and doesn't possess the star-power of her modelesque famous beau, but she's managed to capture the heart of the ultimate Ex, and so she's officially on our radar too.

Sources have confirmed that the lady passionately locking tongues with Karim (photos shared below) is named Zara Khan, a seventeen-year-old student from East London. There's limited information available about her on the internet, and no active social media accounts I could direct you to (she might as well be from another planet!). But some helpful fans from her sixth form have sent over old school photos and some footage of her. With a non-existent fashion sense and little camera presence, it seems the saying *opposites attract* is applicable here: Karim has done a full 180 in his choice of girl – or rebound, should I say.

But then again, I guess it's too soon to say whether or not this is a *real* relationship. Whatever the case, even I must admit they were a sight for sore eyes all wrapped up in each other's arms (and faces) at the scenic Natural History Museum. Decked in their bedazzling South Asian attire, they looked like a couple from an old Bollywood film, just not as conservative. Love was truly in the air, as was splendour, because the Maliks got everything right in the first wedding event for Azad Malik and Sana Qureshi.

And so, Halloween's Dark Fairy was finally unceremoniously unveiled. The girl who cast a spell over Karim Malik's heart may not be perfect, but she's definitely unique and interesting. I'm positively intrigued – and ready to dig deeper.

Let me know your thoughts in the comments section.

Yours Unfaithfully,
Mr Ex .

44

My first kiss had been nothing short of a dream.

It had taken place amid music, dance, history, art and the celebration of love.

Things with Karim felt so *right*, and I'd melted when we'd both expressed exactly that to each other: *You're perfectly right for me.* Those words were now imprinted on my soul. So when he'd closed the distance between us, I hadn't held back any longer.

I wanted him.

And I wanted him to know it.

No more boundaries or overthinking or hesitating.

His lips were so soft, meeting mine again and again, leaving me wanting more. His smooth hands caressed my neck, hair, waist, back, until it had become impossible to think about anything but his touch.

And when he'd kissed my neck, and my lips, moved his tongue against mine, tightened his grip on my body . . . it was ecstasy.

But, of course, things could never go right for me – there was always a catch. Something to pull me down to reality whenever I dared to be happy. I still felt the shock of that flash; my life could literally be over because of a single picture. In my community, once a girl's reputation was brought into question, it left irreversible damage. And since I'd been caught with none other than Karim Malik, it would likely reach an international audience.

I wanted to check my phone to see if anything was already circulating online, but I simply didn't have the guts. My hands started shaking the moment I picked it up.

Group family photos were being taken on the main stage and Karim was smiling broadly, completely at ease. The photographer said something, and they all laughed – the perfect image of a beautiful, happy family.

Either Karim had a good poker face, or he was genuinely already over it. I knew he was doing the right thing for his family, but I still felt resentment surge over me.

Karim wouldn't be affected by this photo at all.

Everyone had seen footage of him kissing Chloe Clark – and other girls he'd had flings with. His family didn't care about his liberal lifestyle. If these photos got out, it would simply look like he'd hooked up with a new girl at his brother's wedding and was finally moving on from his complicated ex.

But it would destroy me. The guilt was already becoming overwhelming.

'Zara,' said a voice.

I didn't turn towards it, didn't even respond. I was frozen, unable to do anything but feel the panic inside me grow and grow and grow.

A hand nudged me.

'Hey,' Morowa said, bringing her face close to mine and giving me a comforting smile. 'Are you OK?'

I felt the urge to cling to her. Instead, I simply nodded, putting on a brave face, even smiling a little.

'I'm leaving now. Do you want a lift home?'

I stood instantly.

She came closer to talk to me more easily over the loud music. 'You can stay if you want, it's up to you. I'm not sure whether your parents gave you a curfew –'

'I want to leave now.' I allowed her to guide me to the exit.

Karim was still occupied, his eyes fixed on the camera, and so he didn't see me leave. I couldn't face saying goodbye to anyone.

It was a quiet drive home. My phone was on silent, but it vibrated on and off throughout the journey: missed calls from Saliha, Aisha baji and, surprisingly, even one from Imran. I threw my phone to the bottom of my bag. I could barely breathe. Surely this string of calls was an indication that people were starting to find out . . .

Arriving home, I noticed the living-room lights were on.

The second I unlocked the door, I knew something was terribly wrong. The air felt suffocating. My gut instinct told me to turn around and leave – but where could I run to?

A hushed, heated conversation was taking place. All I wanted to do was go to bed and not rise again until this had all blown over, but the living-room door whipped open, sharp as a lash.

'Come here, Zara.'

One look at my mum's red-rimmed eyes and I knew – the photo had already reached my parents.

I followed her in.

Dad was standing there, staring daggers at me. I didn't have the courage to meet either of my parents' eyes, couldn't even find my voice to say salaam. Every part of me was trembling with dread. I felt tremors skitter down my limbs, making me weak at the knees.

'Is this the day we raised you for?' Dad barked in Urdu. 'Was this your way of showing the world the values we gave you?'

'This is what happens when you give a girl too much freedom,' Mum spat. 'From the way you started answering back and dressing, I should've known something like this was going to happen. You shameless wretch.'

She sauntered over to me and waved her phone in my face. I saw screenshots an aunty had sent her on WhatsApp. Not just one photo, but image after image of me kissing Karim Malik, all taken from Mr Ex's blog. Close-ups.

Sensuality and desire oozed out of the photos so clearly that I felt like people were seeing me naked. It was humiliating, degrading.

My heart shattered.

The most precious, passionate moment of my life had become either entertainment or disgrace for the world to consume. I attempted to say something, to somehow find the words to explain.

'Mum –'

It took me a second to realize she had slapped me.

The sting came gradually and then all at once. I faced her with tears crowding my eyes, feeling utterly helpless.

'*Besharam ladki*,' she hissed.

Shameless girl – the words crowded the chamber of my mind, where I knew they'd echo forever. It was obvious she was only getting started. I held my breath in anticipation of the next blow. I just didn't know whether it was going to be physical or verbal.

'We've never been so embarrassed. Everyone we know is seeing our daughter do *this*. No one has ever dishonoured our family like this before.'

She looked me up and down with such disgust that I felt like absolute filth. I'd crossed a boundary with her today. Usually, I saw her love and concern gleaming behind her admonishment. Not this time.

'You've left your own father unable to speak to his relatives without drooping his head in shame. It would've been better if you'd just died.'

'Mum!'

She slapped me sharply with the back of her hand, and Dad harrumphed in the background as though pleased. This time, I didn't bother facing her again. I turned away from my parents and let the tears fall.

'Don't you call her that any more,' Dad roared at me. 'And definitely don't call me your father. You're dead to us. The doors of this house are closed to you. Make sure you don't show us your face in the morning, or ever again.'

'You're lucky that all we're doing is disowning you and kicking you out,' Mum added. 'If I was caught doing anything like this, my dad and brothers would've *killed* me.'

They walked past me, went up the stairs to their bedroom and closed the door behind them.

I don't know how long I stood there, feeling the life drain out of me. Somehow, I eventually made it to my room and finally looked at my phone. I ignored all the missed calls and texts and decided to open my social media so that I could have an idea of the damage . . .

It was . . . everywhere.

The photos and video clips of me and Karim kissing were plastered all over Mr Ex's socials, with engagement so high the images were being pushed by the platforms. It was practically going viral. Memes and slow-motion romantic edits of it were already popping up.

Even though I knew it wasn't a good idea, I flicked through the comments section.

Everyone seemed to have an opinion about me. About every inch of my appearance – my features, my clothing, my hair, my jewellery, my weight, my height, my skin colour. And most of it was nasty. Apparently I was the awful, ugly homewrecker who had come in between Chlarim, the perfect couple who would always be in love and were fated to be together forever.

It got worse, more *real*, when I came across the comments left by people I knew personally: students from my school, girls I'd taken mosque classes with, local aunties and their sons or daughters. Words like *slut*, *shameless*, *disgusting girl* swam before my eyes again and again, filling me with a sharp, nauseating anxiety.

Before this, I'd practically been non-existent on social media. Nothing had prepared me for this onslaught. Goosebumps covered my entire being as I read each painful, awful thing directed at me. I'd never felt so exposed, vulnerable, hated.

I didn't know how to deal with it.

People had started to discover my official Instagram account. It was on private and I only had about a hundred followers, but in the past hour I'd received five thousand friend requests.

This was getting too much for me.

There was only one person who could advise me right now, for he'd been through all the highs and lows of social media himself, and he was literally going through all of this with me.

I tried calling Karim.

He didn't answer.

Feeling completely stranded and broken, I curled into a ball on my bed and bawled my eyes out. The darkness that always seemed to linger around the edges of my life was devouring me whole right now, eating away all traces of hope and light left in me.

The voices in my head kept repeating what seemed to be the final truth about my existence: I was a shameless, disgusting girl who'd destroyed everything, who deserved to die. Things would never be OK again, not after this.

My phone started ringing. The tears blurred my vision so much that I could barely see anything as I picked it up.

'Karim,' I cried into it. 'I really need you right now.'

A deep, soothing voice answered. 'It's Imran.'

Zara

45

'You're all over Instagram. It's pretty intense. Are you OK?' Imran asked.

I couldn't breathe. I tried to exhale slowly to steady my voice, but a flood of sobs broke out instead.

'I'm not OK,' I cried. 'I'm not OK. I'm not OK.'

I kept repeating it.

And I couldn't seem to stop.

Imran was saying something to me. It sounded pacifying, kind, but it was incomprehensible to me right now. I was so sure he'd hang up, but he stayed, continued to listen to me echo the same thing as though I'd lost my mind.

I'm not OK.

After some time, Imran became silent, my voice grew hoarse, and the tears clinging to my lashes dried. Now that all the emotion was gone, cried out of me, I felt numb.

'This will never go away. I won't make it through this,' I said lifelessly, declaring the finality that I felt.

'Yes, you will. Stuff moves quickly online,' Imran reasoned. 'This will all blow over in a week tops.'

Rage gripped my soul. 'My parents have disowned me.

Mum slapped me twice, then basically told me I'm a shameless whore who's better off dead. Will that also blow over?'

He stuttered a little, then fell silent, as though he didn't know what to say.

I sneered. 'I've already told you about how my family is, haven't I? I've dug my own grave, so I might as well jump into it.'

'Zara! Don't think like that!' he exclaimed, but I ignored him.

'We both know that if a boy from our community did something like this, people would just find it cool, maybe even romantic or funny,' I said bitterly. 'His parents would probably just tell him off lightly. But I'm a girl. It's different for us. There's no coming back from this.'

'It *is* harder for girls in our community,' Imran admitted gently. 'It's completely unfair that girls are made to carry the weight of their family's honour, that they're shamed for doing the things that guys get away with like it's nothing. And I'm not going to act like I know how that burden feels.'

He took a deep breath and continued in a firmer tone, 'But I want to remind you that you can be the change, Zara. You can choose to heal from this and have an incredible future where you refuse to let people's judgements dictate how you feel about yourself and your life.'

His words were soothing, but they sounded distant, like he was describing an unrealistic dream I'd never be able to reach.

'I'm all alone now. I have nowhere to go.'

'That's not true,' Imran said frantically. 'Come to your window.' When I didn't respond or move, he said more forcefully, 'Either do it or I'm going to come to your house this very second, break down the door and bring you over to mine. I don't care what your parents say or do.'

Not having the energy to deal with the nightmare of yet another scandal, I walked over to the window and stood there. Imran looked at me, and his expression shifted from worry to something that looked like pity. I hated it.

'You need to trust me and listen to me, all right?'

I simply nodded, too tired to speak or argue.

'You're going to change first. Put on something comfortable.'

I probably looked like an awful mess, my hair tangled, mascara bleeding down my face, my outfit crumpled awkwardly. But I couldn't care less. It was soothing to have someone tell me what to do. It meant I didn't have to use my brain. I couldn't even be bothered to draw the curtains; I just about had the energy to unpin my dupatta, so I began to undress straight away. I remembered the time he'd made that comment about not being able to watch me change behind the closed curtains. Apparently, this was his lucky day.

'Zara,' he murmured, 'draw your curtains first.'

Ignoring him, I carried on undoing the pearl buttons down the centre of the dress. If my face and body were up for the world to stare at and criticize, then what did this matter? Nothing really mattered any more. My cleavage was on show now, as was half my bra.

'Stop it,' Imran said sharply. 'Draw your curtains.'

'It doesn't matter,' I replied coldly. 'I'm a worthless slut now, remember?'

I looked up and met his gaze fiercely. We stared each other down for a while. His eyes didn't stray from mine for a single beat. Whatever that look was on his face right now, it certainly wasn't arousal or excitement. Eventually, I gave in and dragged the curtain across, hiding myself from view.

Imran kept giving me instructions, and I followed them all: tie your hair back, take your make-up off, drink some water, put some socks on, wear a warm jumper. He didn't mention anything about me kissing a world-famous influencer, and I was grateful for that.

Others tried to get in touch with me in between – Saliha was messaging non-stop, Aisha baji tried calling three more times. But for some reason I wasn't in the mood to speak to anyone but Imran. There was a stability and calmness about him that I needed right now.

And then it was like Guy Fawkes Night all over again. I sat on a chair, staring at him from my window, holding my phone close to whisper to him. He was wearing a black vest, which revealed his toned arms and part of his chest. I looked at the faint mess of hair in between his pecs; not too long ago, I'd imagined touching my way down his chest, getting on my tiptoes in front of him. I remembered the time in his bedroom . . .

'Where were you?' I asked him. 'You disappeared on me.'

His eyes narrowed. 'Let's not talk about that right now.'

'I want to know.'

Imran ran a hand through his hair in the way I realized he did when he was nervous. Then he took a deep breath and spoke quickly. 'I got a little scared, all right? I realized I was gonna fall for you if we spent too much time talkin'. And we're only teenagers. I'm not ready for any of that.'

I certainly hadn't expected *that* to be his response; I didn't even know how seriously to take him. It was still far too easy to imagine him speaking to twenty other girls in the time since he'd stopped showing interest in me.

'You aren't the girl I'd want just a casual fling with. I want . . . the real stuff with you. And my dad dyin' is the only real thing I can handle this year.'

'That would've been perfectly easy to communicate to me. You chose to ice me out instead.'

'I'm sorry, I was an idiot. Communicatin' isn't my forte. You were right when you said we weren't really friends before, so I thought maybe it would be easier if we stopped speakin'.'

My eyes felt itchy with exhaustion. I rubbed them and checked the time. It was nearly three in the morning.

'Well, in that case,' I said through a suppressed yawn, 'we can totally go back to being strangers. We've ignored each other for years while studying in the same school and mosque, so it shouldn't be hard.'

'No way. I admit that I was an idiot, Zara. I'm not disappearing on you again.'

'I find that hard to believe.'

'At least give me a chance. Let me be here for you right now. I can tell how much everything's gettin' to you. I'm not leaving you alone.'

I didn't say anything. It was hard to communicate how much his presence right now meant to me without my voice breaking, and he'd heard enough of me crying for a lifetime.

'Things will get better, Zara. There'll be a day when you look back at this incident and feel nothing.'

'It doesn't work like that for brown girls, and you know it. I'm ruined. I don't know where on earth I'm supposed to go from here.'

'Pack your things,' he replied simply. 'You can stay at mine.'

Despite everything – all the stress and mania and fear – the mere thought of sleeping under the same roof as Imran Sayyid did strange things to my heart, my breath. And there was no way I was risking that temptation; I no longer trusted myself. I didn't want to feel desire ever again. It was the root of this whole mess.

'I'm going to call Sal,' I replied, my shoulders already sinking at the looming absence of his voice.

'OK. Just know that you have my home if nothin' else works out.'

Hearing the word *home* on his lips was enough to make my chest tighten with yearning and pain.

The tears began anew, and when Saliha picked up the phone, she heard me crying like she never had before.

I opened the door to let her in. She held me close to her for an hour, a decade, a lifetime, and then she came upstairs to help me pack.

'Saliha Begum,' I croaked. 'You're literally the most perfect best friend and sister a girl could ask for.'

'Sisters for life,' she whispered.

I allowed myself to smile a little.

Karim

46

We got home from the mehndi in the early hours of the morning, and everyone was exhausted.

Mum and Sana baji wouldn't stop complaining about the pain their heels had left them in. Adil was gawking at Kiran as usual. Dad looked like he was ready to crash right there on the living-room sofa. I could barely keep my own eyes open.

The Qureshis had wanted to go straight home, but Mum had talked them into coming over for karak chai and chatter. A few cousins and family friends had also come to ours, so there were still some guests to entertain.

'How do you think the event went?' Mum asked everyone keenly.

'Amazing,' Aunty Rahima replied enthusiastically. 'What fun we all had!'

'It's a night I'll always remember,' Sana baji chimed in, leaning her head against Azad bhai's shoulder. 'It was my dream mehndi. Thank you to everyone who helped make it a reality.'

These were the only people who seemed to have the energy to talk, because everyone else was either silently scrolling through their phone, drinking chai, or gradually dozing off.

'We better start the preparations for the baraat and walima functions straight away,' Mum said seriously. 'Those events are much bigger and only one week away.'

'There's no way this event would've been successful without all of your contacts, suggestions and tailors, Aunty Fouzia,' Sana baji said gently. 'Thank you so much. I'm sorry if I was a bridezilla at times.'

'And I'm sorry if I was a monster-in-law at times,' Mum replied with a wink.

I smiled, enjoying the warm, happy mood my family was in.

'So, Karim beta,' Aunty Rahima said. 'When is it going to be your turn, eh? Seeing your older brother's wedding must have planted a little seed in your mind too.'

Mum cackled along with her and then raised her brows. 'My older son let me choose his bride, and I'm sure my younger son will do the same when his time comes.'

'Not a chance.' I laughed. 'If it's OK with you all, I'm going to turn in for the night.'

I lugged myself up to my room, planning to call Zara as soon as my phone came on; I'd captured so much epic wedding content that the battery had died a while ago. Zara hadn't said goodbye before leaving and I wanted to check in on her. I stuck the charger in my phone and got into bed, waiting for the phone to turn on.

The sound of my phone vibrating woke me. I checked my watch – it was nine in the morning. I picked up right away, preparing to apologize to Zara for disappearing.

I heard Abeo's voice instead.

'It's Felicity,' he said. 'She had a serious car accident last night. Chloe told me.'

'What?' I squawked, shooting out of bed.

'Late last night, Felicity's parents told Chloe that Felicity's in hospital. Chloe went to see her first thing this morning. She spoke to her about what happened, and Felicity said she noticed a black car with tinted windows following her and reckoned it was Mr Ex. She freaked out and drove faster and faster until she lost control and hit something – thank goodness it wasn't another car or person. But her car flipped over, and she's got multiple injuries. She could've *died*.'

Panic and guilt coursed through me. 'How is she now?'

'Last news I received from Chloe is that Felicity's stable and doing well now. But it'll take her a while to fully heal from the injuries.'

A strangled sound escaped my throat.

I'd known Felicity for as long as I could remember and, despite everything that had happened recently, I loved her deeply ... I couldn't bear to even imagine the horror of her dying while we weren't on speaking terms ...

'Felicity's OK, Karim,' Abeo said gently, sensing my anguish. 'But the rest of us have decided it's time to put our foot down. We're going to release a video explaining how Mr Ex is tormenting us. Shall I pick you up?'

'Of course. When are the rest of us allowed to see Felicity?'

'Her parents have asked for some space right now. Chloe has told Felicity to keep us posted about when the Wongs are happy for us to visit her. We should all go to see her together. This is bigger than any of our stupid disputes and power plays.'

'I agree. The past is the past. I'm here for whatever Felicity and you guys need.'

After we hung up, it took me a while to calm myself, to get my breathing back to normal. The Exes were my family. Regardless of everything that had happened between us all, if they ever needed me, *really* needed me, I'd be there in a heartbeat. No questions asked.

When I'd stopped shaking, I picked up my phone again and looked through the calls and messages. I had nine missed calls from Zara and several anxious messages. I called her back. She answered straight away.

'Where have you been?' she immediately asked.

'I'm so sorry. The event went on till the early hours! I was going to call you when I got back home but my battery was dead and I knocked out waiting for my phone to switch on.'

She took a deep breath, then said, 'Did you see what's been posted about us online?'

'No, what's been posted?' I asked, panic pounding in my ears like the wail of a siren getting louder.

'Mr Ex released photos of us kissing. They're *everywhere*.'

It seemed my deal with Mr Ex no longer stood; instead of waiting for the exclusive wedding photos I'd promised in exchange for him leaving Zara's identity anonymous, he'd released footage featuring her. It made sense; this was better gossip, and my family photos would eventually find their way to social media anyway.

I felt helpless, nauseous. There was no undoing it when something leaked on to the internet, which meant there was nothing I could do to help her now. If only I'd been able to protect her from all of this . . .

'Or maybe you did know,' she snapped, 'but you didn't care very much because it doesn't affect you like it affects me.'

'Zara! Are you serious?'

'Yes, I am.'

I'd never heard such venom in her tone. It was unsettling.

'I can't believe you'd even say such a thing.'

She scoffed. 'And I can't believe you'd peacefully knock out after something like this was posted about us last night. It took you *hours* to get in touch with me.'

'You know yesterday was a big family event for me,' I replied defensively.

'Maybe you should've just focused on your family instead of getting your hands on me.'

'Yeah, maybe I should've.' I instantly regretted saying that. 'Look, Zara, I admit it was my mistake. I should've been more careful. I honestly thought we were alone. I've liked you for so long and it felt so *right* between us last night. I guess I got swept away in the moment.'

'It *was* so right between us last night,' she said quietly, her voice breaking a little. 'But everything's all wrong now.'

That hurt more than I wanted to admit.

She cleared her throat and continued, 'I still can't help but feel you don't actually care. Maybe it's even good for you in some ways – everyone can see you're moving on.'

Her harsh tone pricked a nerve. 'Why on earth would I want something like this to be out there? I certainly don't need the extra clout or views, if that's what you're suggesting.'

'Thank you for reminding me what a great big influencer you are,' she said sarcastically. 'Perhaps I should be pleased that people are even associating me with the incredible Karim Malik. What a privilege for lowly old me.'

'That's not what I meant,' I replied irritably. 'Are you just going to twist and misinterpret everything I say right now? If that's the case, maybe we should just speak later.'

'Are you not going to do anything about the situation?' she practically shouted.

'There really isn't much we *can* do because it's already out there,' I replied, my voice also rising. 'Stuff like this dies down naturally with time. It's not even big enough that I need to put out a statement.'

She gasped, clearly offended.

'Zara, there's a lot going on right now,' I said. 'One of my best friends had a car accident last night. Felicity's been dealing with blackmailing and *real* pressure online. The crash nearly took her life.'

Zara was silent for a while, and I thought perhaps she'd calmed down a bit. I hated this rift that was forming between us. I wanted things to go back to normal, but I could sense that would be difficult.

'*Real*, huh?' Zara asked darkly. 'Well, you should know that my parents have disowned me and kicked me out of the house because of the photos. I'm staying at my friend's place. And on top of that, everyone on the internet is hell-bent on reminding me that I'm an ugly little nobody. How's that for *real*?'

My chest tightened. 'I'm so sorry, Zara. I had no idea –'

'How could you have known? You weren't even there for me!'

'What can I do?' I begged.

'Apparently nothing. Oh God, I'm really starting to see how your privilege makes you blind to all of this. This will never affect you because you're a man, so you'll never be labelled a *shameless slut*, and you're wealthy, so you'll never have to worry about shelter, and your family loves you unconditionally, so they'll always forgive your every mistake.'

I let out a deep breath. 'What do you need from me? I'm really trying here, Zara.'

'*This* is you trying? You know what? You're exactly the entitled rich prick I thought you were the first time I saw you. I wish we'd never tried to share our worlds with each other. I wish I'd never kissed you. I wish I'd never even met you.'

Then she cut the call.

When it Gets Hard to Handle the Heat, Fan Out the Flames

There's nothing to heighten drama and emotion like a near-death experience. #PrayForFelicity is trending, as it should be.

I'm aware that my announcement may have been nerve-wracking for her and possibly played a role in her erratic driving. But the news about the Wong family's bankruptcy and charity fraud would have come out eventually anyway – the truth never stays buried for long. But, of course, since I was the one to shed light on the gross mishandling of charity money, I'm being crowned the evil bitch of the internet (still not the worst title you guys have given me. Keep trying, darlings, and get more original!). And generally, I would wear it proudly, but I care about mental health (and staying alive) too.

And that's why I've decided to shed my Prada flannel suit, throw in my Versace lace-ups and call it a day. It's time for me to don my D&G silk robe, cake on a Chantecaille Gold Recovery Mask and reflect on life while sipping a hot cup of tea. And yes, for once, I genuinely mean tea. Perhaps I'll even go for a stroll around Hampstead Heath with that trending self-help book in tow. Your boy really needs it right now.

Many of you wild keyboard warriors are labelling *me* an awful person who should die instead. Be glad that I'm thick-skinned and know my worth, or else I might drive rather recklessly too, and things would get *really* dramatic. Besides, how on earth would you guys manage without my fashion discount codes and advice? Duh?!

I'm certainly not the only one who sheds light on the goings-on in the lives of London's top influencers. There are gossip blogs and websites across the world delivering the exact same news, some in tones much darker than mine. Even *the royals* can't escape gossip scandals, for crying out loud! I mean, it's all freedom of speech at the end of the day. What are we going to do? Never let anyone make a single disagreeing comment or joke at another's expense ever again? Sorry to break it to you, but that's wanting to get rid of British humour altogether. And that shit will survive anything, including war, depression and months (probably even years) of miserable weather. I have a sense that this is going to be a long, complicated and exasperatingly political discussion . . . ew.

As for now, may I remind you that this isn't the time to play the Blame Game. It's time to come together in support of mental health causes (important links and resources will be provided across my social media platforms). Truth, gossip and scandal all have their own place, but people's well-being trumps it all. I never thought I'd say it, but it's time to fan out the flames because it's getting a little hard for everyone to handle the heat. Including me. Lastly, I'd personally like to apologize to anyone I've ever hurt.

You guys do know that under all this designer garb & spirited sass I'm just one of you, right?

Yours Faithfully,
Mr Ex

Zara

47

I survived another day.

Saliha's family showered me with warmth, encouraging pep talks and delicious Bangladeshi food. I smiled and nodded and reciprocated the tight hugs, but I was constantly aware that it was my own family who should've been comforting me in this way.

'Just look at this tragedy, Zara,' Saliha piped up, pointing to the TV, making me snap out of my reverie. 'If there's anything we should be crying about, it's *this*.'

We were lounging on the sofa with Saliha's parents, watching *Kal Ho Naa Ho*, a heartbreaking Bollywood romance film. It was a classic. They couldn't believe I hadn't watched it before.

'When your weekend includes seeing Shah Rukh Khan, you know it's going to be a good one,' Uncle Begum said enthusiastically, then turned to me. 'You're going to remember this movie for the rest of your life. I'm glad we're watching it with you.'

'Just wait till the next song comes on,' Aunty Begum added with a sly look. 'I'm making us all get up and dance to it.'

Saliha cheered and I covered my face with a hand.

'You and I never got to finish movies in the past,' Sal said, cuddling into my side. 'It's great that you don't have to run off before your curfew. I like that we get to keep you.'

I never felt like a burden here. The Begums made me feel cherished, loved. It was an effort for me to hold my emotions in.

'It's *so* lovely having you here, Zara,' Aunty Begum said warmly. 'Our home feels alive again! I thought having five children was enough, but three of my daughters are married off and busy with their own children most days. And my son is living out at university. The house was starting to feel so empty.'

'That's because this one,' Uncle Begum said, pointing at Sal, 'prefers to sit quietly and scroll through her phone rather than socialize with her parents.'

Sal gave him a hard look. 'I talk to you plenty, Dad. Can't be having our dramatic heart-to-hearts every day.'

I didn't think Sal realized how lucky she was . . .

The way they spoke to one another – it was so wholesome. As busy as her older siblings had become in their lives, they always came back to their parents' home with love and joy in their hearts. It was true that the Begum household was becoming quieter as the children grew up and moved out, but on the weekends that they all got together again, their laughter could be heard from the end of the street.

My chest ached. Because as much as I loved being in this house, it wasn't my reality. It was Sal's.

'This is really nice,' I whispered to Sal. 'It feels like . . . family. I know I've said this a million times already, but thank you so much for everything.'

'If you thank me again, I'm going to pinch you really hard.'

I laughed, then jumped as my phone started ringing loudly.

It was Aisha baji. I'd ignored her for long enough. It was time.

'We'll pause the movie until you're back,' Uncle Begum assured me.

When I was in Sal's room, I answered the call, dread ticking inside me like a bomb.

'What were you thinking, Zara?' Aisha baji cried.

All the emotions exploded at once – shame, sadness, anger.

I sat on Sal's bed and took a deep breath to steady myself for the onslaught on my character and life.

'You have no idea how awful this is,' she barked. 'It's making you and our whole family look so bad.'

It went on and on. And I decided to zone out for most of it. Apparently, my family didn't understand that this was something I was going through in a far more gruelling way than any of them, that it was *my* face that was plastered on the internet, that the last thing I needed was for them to make me feel any worse than I already did.

'I've spoken to Mum, and she told me that Dad kicked you out. His reaction is understandable, but don't give up hope. Maybe if he sees how sorry you are, he'll let you come back.'

'*His reaction is understandable?*' I spat. 'You're the last person I'd expect to say that. Especially since you've been the most affected by his shitty patriarchal views.'

Silence.

'Would you like to know what *I* want? What *I* think is best for me?' My voice sounded so mature and calm I barely recognized it. I sounded like a woman. 'To never go back to that house.'

Aisha baji must have noted the change in my tone too, because she didn't even bother to argue with me on my decision.

Shortly afterwards, I called Farhan bhai, finally responding to his endless missed calls. I beamed with pride when he told me that Jashan had catered incredibly well and that their schedule was booking up quickly now, but I could tell from his voice that he wasn't able to celebrate wholeheartedly because of everything that was happening with me. He also told me off for my lewd, irresponsible behaviour, but in a gentler way, and he tried to make sure I was doing OK. I got off the phone to him quickly, feeling a fresh wave of shame. He'd expected better from me, and his disappointment was crippling the little self-confidence I had preserved till now.

Mum and Dad hadn't bothered to reach out, to find out where their daughter had gone, and I wasn't the least bit surprised.

Imran tried calling multiple times, but I wasn't answering his calls or messages any more; Saliha had mentioned that he was now texting her for updates. Karim, on the other hand, hadn't tried to get in touch once. I decide to block his number, taking away his ability to reach out even if he wanted to.

I took a moment to calm my breathing, my fingers digging deep into Sal's soft duvet.

Speaking to my siblings had been exactly as I'd expected: they'd only worsened my panic. They had reminded me that I would always be connected to this incident now. Things lived forever on the internet, which meant I would never move on from this . . .

Monday came, and it was back to school.

I didn't know whether it was better to be left with my dark thoughts in Sal's room or to deal with the gruelling gossip at school.

Sure enough, the moment I entered my first class, everyone's eyes seemed to latch on to me. The whispers hissed around me like snakes . . .

She kissed Karim Malik.

If she can get with him, I bet I can too.

How could he leave Chloe Clark for her?

The first few lessons of the day passed by in a haze, as did everything else. I simply wasn't mentally present in my life any more. Saliha would nudge me again and again to get my attention. Perhaps it was a survival mechanism, so that my sadness wouldn't destroy every single part of me. Apparently, there was still something inside me that longed to live.

'Hey, Zara,' Imran said, cutting the lunch queue so he could stand near me.

No one reprimanded him. They simply didn't have the guts to. He was a good friend to have for times like this; people could gossip as much as they wanted behind my back, but they wouldn't dare to cross me if I had him by my side.

'Hey,' I replied simply, then looked away, signalling that I wasn't in the mood to talk.

'How's it going?' he continued, not taking the hint.

I shrugged dismissively.

'Good. What about you?' Saliha said kindly, making up for my rudeness.

'All right. I was wondering if I could speak to you, Zara?'

'Maybe later,' I replied, not appreciating the keen eavesdroppers around us.

'Sounds good.'

I finally looked up at him properly.

He was wearing a green bomber jacket and a black beanie hat with his hood lifted over it. He looked like the perfect model for a JD ad. He'd never looked at me with such tenderness before. I felt the sudden urge to run my fingers through his neat black beard, across his sharp jawline.

I looked away quickly, blinking the images away and scolding myself. I was in the midst of dealing with an international gossip scandal because of being intimate with Karim Malik, and here I was, unable to control my thoughts for another guy mere hours later . . .

What on earth was I doing?

We got our lunch and entered the hall.

I could sense everyone's gaze fixed on me. I wished it could be like old times, when barely anyone noticed me. My eyes were red and swollen from all the crying, my hair was a greasy mess, and my face was devoid of all life and colour. I looked exactly as I felt, and I didn't want *anyone* to look at me.

I'd noticed some people taking sneaky photos of me during lessons, and it had pushed me further into an anxious spiral, thinking of all the people online who'd be dissecting me in my depressed state. But I'd deleted all social media apps from my phone – the less I knew, the better.

Saliha guided me to a table. She sat next to me on one side and Imran on the other. They chatted away like normal, catching up on everything from A levels to gyming to university prospects. Thankfully, neither of them mentioned anything related to Karim Malik.

After some time, Hania came and sat opposite me, her sister and friends joining her. It was becoming a full table. My insides clenched with discomfort.

If these people had come here to get the latest gossip directly from the source . . .

'Hey, Zara,' Hania began awkwardly. 'I hope you're doing OK. I'm sure you already know that I've been through something like this before. Obviously it was on a smaller scale, but pretty much *everyone* in my life saw my photos and heard about the incident. I just wanted to let you know that people do move on from the gossip. Your life isn't over. Just hold on.'

She stretched her hand out across the table. I looked at her and a painful lump formed in my throat. I reached for her hand. She squeezed it and, to my surprise, I felt a little better. Hania had been through exactly what I was experiencing and had made it through to the other side.

It was a moment of solidarity and sisterhood that touched my soul.

'At least you got caught with Karim Malik,' she continued. 'I kissed a prick from our ends who got so dramatic when we broke up that he burned the teddy he won for me at our local funfair.'

Saliha snorted first. And soon we were all laughing.

I felt loads lighter.

The rest of lunch went by surprisingly pleasantly, as did the remaining lessons. I was getting used to the stares and whispers, and realized they didn't have as much power over me when I had such a good support system.

At the end of the day, Saliha and Imran walked me home. It was like having bodyguards.

'Can I speak to Zara alone?' Imran asked Sal.

Saliha looked at me. I nodded. She handed me her house keys and then turned to Imran.

'Don't keep my roomie for too long, and definitely don't annoy her.'

When she was out of range, Imran chuckled. 'Gettin' revenge for the time I iced you out, huh?'

Despite myself, I smiled. 'No, it's nothing like that. I'm just not in the mood to speak to anyone much these days.'

We walked in silence for a while. Imran steered us to the local park.

Despite the glaring December chill, it felt refreshing to be outside. So many of my childhood memories danced before my eyes: sitting on the seesaw and swings with Aisha baji, running around wildly with Farhan bhai, him teaching me how to ride a bike, having a picnic on our floral blanket and eating Mum's special homemade kebab rolls with my whole family.

It was another life – another girl.

If I had known back then that my family would disintegrate in the way it had, I would have treasured every single moment deeply. But I had experienced it all with the innocence of a child who believes things will always be the same.

'There's something you should know,' Imran said. 'I've had a crush on you since that time I found your library card last year. Dunno if you even remember that.'

I turned to him with raised brows, surprised that he even recalled the moment that had stayed with me.

'I do remember. I didn't realize you did.'

Imran smiled. 'A part of me wanted to start talkin' to you then, but somethin' stopped me.'

'What?'

'Not sure exactly. Maybe nerves?'

I punched his arm playfully, feeling the solidity of his biceps. 'Yeah, right! I've seen how you chat up literally every girl. That sounds ridiculous coming from you.'

He ran a hand over his beard and grinned. 'I'm being serious. The way you looked at me just felt like you were able to see right through me, like none of my moves would even work on you. It felt . . . different.'

'So, different scares you?'

'Nah, it doesn't scare me exactly. It's jus' outside my comfort zone. But I had it in my mind that I'd get to know you at some point.'

'And that point is now?'

'I'm hopin' so,' he replied, looking uncharacteristically vulnerable. 'I'd really like to.'

The nerves in his voice were obvious, and I found it endearing. Light rain began to fall. I felt it settling on my cheeks and forehead. Instead of answering him, I asked, 'Do you mind the rain?'

He shook his head. 'We're Londoners, ain't we? We're used to it. Do you?'

'I'm starting to really like the rain and this cold weather. It's grown on me.'

'Now you wanna tell me your personality's too dark and depressing for me to get to know?' Imran said with a smirk, removing his bomber jacket. 'That I won't be able to handle it?'

'You really won't be able to.' I frowned and let him place the jacket over our heads to keep us safe from the rain as it got heavier.

We were in our own little cocoon, locked away from the world and its light. I looked up at him and swallowed.

'I understand your darkness,' he whispered, 'and you understand mine.'

This could have been it, I realized. My first kiss. If I hadn't met Karim, perhaps this is how it would have happened ... and perhaps it could have gone perfectly right ...

I found myself laughing. 'I'm in the middle of an online love-triangle scandal with two of Britain's top influencers. If anyone captures photos of me standing like this with another guy, literally two days later, my reputation is truly done for.'

He shrugged. 'Reputations are overrated.'

We grinned at each other. And I felt it. The electric chemistry, the deep understanding, the broken pieces of our souls reaching towards each other to heal.

He took a small step closer and leaned down to kiss me.

The trauma of what had happened last time caused me to jerk back. Imran instantly tensed up too.

I took a deep breath. 'I know everything online is making it look like I'm open to casually making out, but I'm not. I don't really do this . . . stuff. That was actually my first kiss and I –'

'It's OK, I get it,' Imran murmured. 'You may have had your first kiss with that guy, but your last will be with me.'

My breath hitched at the confidence and fire in his voice. I knew exactly why he was saying this because I'd experienced such certainty before. It had felt so right with Karim – but I'd learned the hard way about getting swept away with emotions.

'Look, Imran. You may think it's the right time for us, but I don't. I'm going through so much in my life at the moment.'

Now that we were all alone, I felt comfortable enough to finally touch his face, to trace my fingertips across his smooth cheek, his coarse beard, working my way down the jawline I'd admired so many times.

I loved the feel of him.

'Can we just be friends? That's what I need right now.'

He nodded, and I could tell that he truly meant it. 'No more icing out, OK? And maybe we can start studying together again.'

'No more icing out,' I promised. 'And yes to studying together.'

We looked into each other's eyes for a long time, and I felt like I could've stayed right there forever, hidden from the world under his jacket, wrapped in his charm and magnetism and warmth.

He'd heard me speak truths I'd never shared with others, he'd been there for me when no one else had, he'd shown me my life had value when everyone else had made me feel worthless, and it had bound me to him in some inseparable way. Whatever our futures held, I knew he'd always own a small piece of my heart.

'I'm visiting my dad's grave now,' he whispered after a while, removing his jacket and letting the light and soft rain touch us once again. 'Will you come?'

'Of course.'

He held my hand and led the way.

Karim

48

'You're sure I can post the *My Side of the Story* video on The Exes' channel?' Chloe asked nervously.

'Of course,' Abeo replied, placing a hand on her shoulder. 'I really respect the way you've reclaimed your story. Everything finally makes sense.'

'It needs to go on our main channel,' I agreed. 'There are too many rumours going around, Chlo. Everyone needs to hear the truth and see that we support you.'

'And this is the perfect way to do that,' Sanjay added.

We were in Sanjay's Notting Hill flat-slash-studio. We'd been there for an entire day and night, having napped on the sofas in between all the work: preparing the script for our video, and then shooting and editing it. It felt like old times, even though the circumstances were far from the reckless pranks and banter that usually accompanied us filming together.

Our video highlighted all the ways in which Mr Ex had attacked us over the years. The cyberbullying, the stalking, the offensive remarks, and everything in between. We'd included as much evidence as we could – anonymous texts, photos he shouldn't have had access to, screenshots of his taunting uploads.

It was important to inform everyone that Mr Ex was the reason Felicity had been so stressed while driving. This was our way of breaking him – even if we couldn't figure out his identity, he was about to get cancelled. We'd been worried about him releasing more of our dirty secrets in retaliation, but at this stage that would only prove our point about his vindictive nature and how desperately important it was that he got cancelled online. Besides, getting justice for Felicity was more important than our fears right now.

Chloe had also filmed a video separately, in which she explained her side of the story, her truth. And it was just as important to share that with the world.

'Shall we look through it one more time before putting it out there?' Chloe asked us all quietly.

Abeo clicked play on his laptop. We crowded around the sofa he was sitting on and watched the clip of an uncharacteristically casual and make-up-free Chloe sitting on her bedroom floor and talking to the camera.

'I know you guys have a lot of opinions about me right now,' she began. 'A lot of *nasty* opinions. Chloe Clark sleeps around, ruined The Exes because she doesn't value friendships, got an abortion like it was nothing –' Her voice broke, and I felt my own eyes fill with tears. 'But I can't tell you how far from the truth that is.'

She exhaled deeply before continuing. 'I love my friends so much; I care about everyone in my life, and I most *definitely* cared about the fact that I was pregnant. And I still do.

Sometimes I care so much about it all that I can't handle it, and I need to switch off from it, escape from all the emotion and how much it can *hurt*.

'The truth is that I just wasn't ready to be a mother. I'm so young. How could I possibly raise someone when I'm still raising myself? I wouldn't have been able to provide that child ... my child, with a healthy and stable life. I knew that down to my core, and I just wanted to get out of that situation as soon as possible.'

Chloe wiped away her tears. 'As awful as the abortion was, the aftermath was just as bad: I did whatever I could to forget, to move on, to erase my past. And nothing worked – not the drinking, not changing partners, not losing myself in work. I'm ashamed of everyone I hurt while I was so desperately trying to heal the wound in my heart that may never fully close, but I'm going to do everything I can to better myself and earn their forgiveness.

'I'm also sorry to myself – to the old Chloe Clark, who was just a scared young girl trying her best. I'm not going to be so hard on her in the future. And I hope that maybe you could find it in yourself to give her a break once in a while too.'

When the clip finished, Chloe uploaded it.

'I don't know if anyone will forgive me for my behaviour,' she said, her voice thick with emotion. 'I don't even know if I'll be able to forgive myself. But it means everything to have you guys back.'

We all embraced her, and stayed in a huddle until her breathing evened out and she was ready to stand. Then the doorbell rang and Abeo went to grab the Chinese takeaway he'd ordered for everyone.

'Let's upload everything after dinner,' Abeo said, tearing into the bag of food that smelled delicious. 'I think we deserve a break.'

We settled down around the living room with our food and ate in silence for a while. We were famished, emotionally exhausted, still tense with worry about how Felicity was doing.

'Do you think we're missing anything important in school?' Sanjay asked.

'Mocks are coming up, so probably,' Chloe replied. 'It's cool though, I'll get the girls to –' She froze, her eyes wide with realization, then sighed irritably. 'I still can't believe those bitches had the nerve to ditch me like that. There's no way they're going to share any notes with me.'

Abeo laughed sarcastically. 'But honey, the whole purpose of what we're doing is to tell people they should stand up to their bullies.'

'Oh, shut up,' she exclaimed, but there was a smile in her eyes. 'To be fair, after seeing how everything panned out, I'm rather pleased I made their lives a little difficult.'

Sanjay shook his head, chuckling. 'Ah, Chlo, I don't think you'll ever change.'

'That sounds like a lyric from one of my songs,' she chirped. 'Can't wait for you guys to hear the whole album.'

Abeo kissed his teeth. 'Just as long as there aren't any off-key notes like that time you tried to sing Mariah Carey.'

She pretended to stab him in the eye with a chopstick and he shrieked and rolled around on the floor as though she'd succeeded.

We all laughed. Something that had been a little broken inside me these past few months started to heal. It was good to be back to normal with my best friends; I hadn't thought it would be possible after the summer we'd had. It felt like throwing on my favourite old jumper and finding it still fit me just right.

'Have you guys noticed something?' Sanjay asked thoughtfully. 'Mr Ex has *a lot* of stuff on us, but he hasn't really released most of it. It's like he doesn't want us to hate him. He just wants to feel in control of The Exes, like he's a part of it.'

'I've noticed that,' Chloe pondered. 'Even his name reflects just how much he wants to be a part of our clique. He doesn't hate us, or else he would've destroyed us already. I think he craves to *be* us. Which is even more creepy, if you ask me.'

Abeo clicked his tongue. 'If only we figured out who it is. But he kept us so wrapped up in our own messes that we barely had a chance to hunt him down.'

'I can't believe we nearly lost Felicity,' Sanjay said quietly. 'All because of the stress of Mr Ex.'

'Mr Ex will get what he deserves,' I said coldly. 'We're about to destroy his career.'

'I'm not so sure about that,' Abeo countered. 'The internet is a weird and twisted place, as we all already know. A lot of people assume that if you're a public figure, it's justifiable for you to be criticized or harassed, so I have a feeling Mr Ex will still get some support.'

'It's true,' Chloe chipped in. 'I've experienced it repeatedly. If I call out those who bully me online, I always get comments where people suggest I'm the one to blame because I "put myself out there".'

'These anonymous keyboard warriors honestly think they can get away with anything, don't they?' Sanjay said, looking disgusted. 'It all comes from a place of insecurity and hate. And bloggers like Mr Ex are the worst of them – profiting from it all.'

'This time will be different,' I stated confidently. 'Felicity is so loved online, one of the most followed influencers in the world, and she nearly *died* because of Mr Ex's harassment. There's going to be a huge backlash.'

'Let's find out, shall we?' Abeo murmured, playing our video for us to review one last time.

After we'd checked it through, he hit the upload button. This felt different from anything we'd put out there before.

'I know this is a horrible situation because Felicity's unwell,' Sanjay said, 'but I like that we're together. It's like we're the original Exes again. When we were just a bunch of best mates uploading fun videos that we genuinely enjoyed making.'

'The pranks and vlogs we made in the first two years of our channel will always be my favourite,' Abeo mused. 'I randomly flick back to them and watch for hours. I love that we've basically recorded us growing up.'

I smiled. 'It's crazy to think how much we've captured of our lives over the years.'

Chloe's voice quivered as she said, 'This situation with Felicity has made me realize that your lives and happiness are worth more to me than anything else.'

Abeo stood up and initiated a group hug.

We came together and held each other closely. I didn't want to let go, to face reality. It seemed they all felt the same, because we stood there for a long time with our arms, emotions and breathing intertwined. Even when a ping alerted us that our video had gone live, we remained entangled in the silence. The fact that we had each other again was infinitely more important than any video we could ever upload.

Chloe's phone started ringing, and she was the first to break away from the hug.

'It's Felicity,' she cried, and then said into her phone, 'Oh my God, yes! We'll come now!' She turned to us and pulled her car keys from her pocket. 'We're finally allowed to see her.'

I was tense the entire ride to the hospital. I didn't know how on earth I was going to face Felicity.

But the moment we entered the ward and I set eyes on her, the only thing I knew was that I was *so* grateful she was alive and well. I tried not to focus on the fact that there was a thick cast on her right leg and bruises littered across her face.

We encircled her bed, and I could sense we were all bursting to speak to her, to say about a million different things because we'd been so afraid that we'd never get a chance to talk to her again. It was just a matter of who broke the silence first. But it seemed to stretch on and on, as though none of us had the guts to say the first word.

By the time the first tear fell down Felicity's face, we were all crying. Words weren't needed today. I kissed Felicity's cheek. When she smiled at me, I could finally breathe easier again.

I sat near her, just savouring the sight of her.

'You're not allowed to drive ever again,' Abeo said eventually, and we all laughed.

Then we cried some more.

After some time, we began to speak as normal. The chatter between us was a rhythm I would never forget; even if I hadn't experienced it in a while, I could always fall back into it as easily as singing along to an old classic.

I asked Felicity if she wanted anything to eat, and that prompted everyone to give me a long list of what they wanted. I stepped out with a grin, promising to be back soon with sushi, cheeseburgers and pizzas.

Chloe followed me out. 'I drove here, so it makes sense if I come with you, right? Unless you'd rather go alone, of course. I could just give you my car keys.'

I wasn't used to seeing her so awkward and unsure of herself. She really was changing . . .

'There's a lot of stuff to pick up, so it'll be nice to have a hand.'

She beamed, and we headed towards the car park together. This was a day of making amends, and I planned to do exactly that. With everyone.

Zara crossed my mind, and my throat tightened. I'd hurt her so much and I had no idea how to make things right with her. All I knew was that I wouldn't feel calm inside until I'd found a way.

'Would you like to drive, or shall I?' I asked.

Chloe flicked her hair dramatically as she got into the driver's seat, making me chuckle. After putting her seat belt on, she paused.

'Chlo? Are you OK?'

'Not really. Can I talk to you about something?'

'Of course.'

'You're my soulmate,' she began, her voice already breaking. 'And I know things between us have always been intense, but life just isn't the same without you.'

She reached for my hand, and I let her hold it.

'I wish I could go back and change it all,' she continued. 'The way I handled the abortion and how I chose to move on. I thought being with someone else would take away the emptiness inside me, but it only made it worse. You're my person. Only you can fill this empty space inside me.'

'No. *You* are your own person,' I said firmly. 'You don't need anyone to complete you. Never give anyone that power over you.'

Tears trailed down her face and I brushed them away with a soft hand.

'You're about to start your dream career, Chlo. *You* are going to accomplish everything you've ever dreamed. You may want me there, but you don't *need* me.'

She grimaced cutely. 'Urgh. You always know the perfect thing to say.'

I put an arm around her and let her sob her heart out. She needed this closure. So did I.

'The girl you were caught kissing at your brother's wedding,' she said after a while, moving back. 'Who is she?'

It hit me that I didn't know how to respond with a label. I decided to go with the simple truth.

'Zara Khan. She's really important to me.'

Chloe smiled. 'I could tell. The way you held and kissed and looked at her . . . it was . . .'

The unspoken words lingered between us: *it was like how you were once with me.* The heartbreak on her face gave me chills. I had to look away. This was hard. I wished I could just get it over with, like ripping off a plaster, but it didn't work like that when it came to real emotions. It took time to work through them. And although our relationship had felt contrived at times, a show for social media, it *had* been real. We had been in love for real at one point.

'I just hope I haven't messed things up with her,' I murmured. 'We had a bad fight and I feel like she'll never forgive me.'

Chloe waved a hand dismissively. 'Oh, you're the most irresistible man I've ever met. Trust me, she'll forgive you.'

'I'm really counting on it.'

'She seems like a sweet girl from the photos I saw, and the Chlarim gang has been quite nasty to her. I feel so bad.'

'The Chlarim gang will eventually settle down and get over us.'

'I just hope I do.'

I shifted uncomfortably. 'What's going on with you and Sanjay?'

'We weren't right for each other. I'm just glad he's forgiven me. Even though I really don't deserve it. I don't deserve having any of you guys as my best friends.'

'We love you, Chlo. Despite all your crazy bullshit and drama.'

She laughed loudly, but when she turned to me, she looked a little sad.

'This may be a selfish thing to say, but I have a track record for selfishness now, so what the heck. As toxic as Chlarim fans can be at times, there's one thing I have in common with them: I believe we're meant to be. Regardless of who we date, I think we'll find our way back to each other in the end. Right?'

There was such hope and conviction in her eyes that I didn't know how to tell her there was only one girl I now envisioned a future with.

So I didn't say anything at all.

Zara

47

I entered Saliha's driveway to find Mum lingering near her doorstep, phone pressed against her ear.

'I'll call you back soon,' she said in Urdu, hung up, and then gave me a death stare. 'Why are you so late?'

'I don't have to answer to you any more,' I replied in our mother tongue, digging in my pocket for Saliha's house keys. 'You kicked me out, remember?'

'Stop ruining your life,' she hissed. 'Don't you have any self-respect? After all the things you've been doing, I thought you would've died of shame, but here you are carrying on as normal.'

'What kind of a mother are you?' I responded dully, sick of this. 'One that wishes death upon her child because they made a mistake? Don't all children make mistakes? You had *three* children. Now you have none. Notice a pattern here? I don't think I'm the only one to blame. In fact, if things at home had been better, it's unlikely that any of this would've happened.'

'Yes, yes,' she cried sarcastically. 'Of course, your parents are the only ones to blame. The ones who've been working day and night to provide you with a roof over your head and food in your belly.'

I rubbed my temples. 'It's not enough to do just that. You need to give your children unconditional support and love, let them make their own life decisions and mistakes. Otherwise, there's no point in working so hard to run a house for them because they'll want to leave to find a real home the first chance they get.'

She laughed derisively. 'So we should let you do whatever you want, huh? And what do we get in return? Insolent children that make us look bad in front of everyone we know?'

Mum looked around the street pointedly, as if eavesdroppers and gossipmongers were hiding nearby. I wished she'd just stop already. For her own sanity as much as mine.

'Maybe if you stopped caring so much about what people think, you'd finally get to have a *family*.' I paused as I reached Sal's doorstep. 'You're childless. And we're all orphans. What can be sadder than that? To lose your children without them dying. And to feel like an orphan while your parents are still alive.'

She was speechless.

I opened the door and left her there with her mouth hanging open.

After sharing warm greetings with Saliha's family, who were watching TV together in the living room, I went up to the bathroom and locked myself in. As lovely as the Begums were, as grateful as I was to have shelter here, this wasn't my home. I was a guest and I couldn't stay forever. And the truth was that I did miss my parents, that I'd always, always love them.

My strength slowly crumbled.

I curled into a ball on the floor and cried. I hated talking back to Mum like that. I knew I'd hurt her, and I didn't want to cause her any pain, but I just couldn't hold in how I really felt any more.

Although I hadn't planned to, I found myself carrying out ablutions in preparation for prayer. After all that had happened, I didn't feel pure or good enough to stand in front of God, but I wouldn't let that hold me back. After all, sinners needed God too. Probably more.

Since Imran's dad's funeral, I hadn't prayed. I hadn't felt the urge or need to. But something inside me was pulling me towards it. Perhaps I knew it was the only place I'd find peace right now.

I went into Sal's room and grabbed her prayer mat, faced it in the direction of the Kabaa and stood on it. I used my phone to check which prayer it was time for. Isha – the last prayer of the day. And, without overthinking, I started.

As I recited the words about God's forgiveness and guidance, emotion broke out of me so suddenly that I was barely able to keep praying in the set routine I'd learned as a child. But I kept going, fumbling and weeping my way through it. I realized I was crying because this was my one safe space: in front of the one true judge, I felt no judgement.

When I finished praying, I remained kneeling on the mat and made a decision. I either had to hang on tightly to my family or let go of them completely. This limbo was unhealthy for all of us.

I phoned Aisha baji first.

'Dad has told you to come over tonight with your whole family. It's urgent. He should be home soon, so please come as quickly as you can.'

She pestered me for answers, but I hung up quickly and then called Farhan bhai with the same message.

I remained seated on the mat, praying for strength and guidance, right up until I heard Dad's car pull in. Then I stood and walked to the window so I could get a glimpse of him. His face was grim as ever, even when he was alone; his brows furrowed heavily, as though he was always angry at the world. It looked like an exhausting way to live – in fact, it was no way to live at all.

'Zara? Is everything OK?' Sal closed the door behind her.

'Yes,' I said, turning to face her. 'I'm just going over to meet my family tonight. We have a lot to discuss.'

Her face fell. 'It's going to be safe, right? Your mum … hit you.'

'Don't worry.' I smiled reassuringly. 'It'll be fine. I need to do this.'

I turned back to face the street. Sal came to stand next to me, an arm curling around me protectively.

'When all of this is over,' she said, 'you *have* to tell me what happened between you and Imran after I left.'

I nudged her, smiling deeply. 'You're the queen of gossip. Who knows, maybe you'll replace Mr Ex someday.'

'Hell no,' she replied tightly. 'I'm officially a hater now. OK, I'm not saying I'll *never* stalk his socials again, especially since *you've* started making an appearance on them, but I'll do it with my eyes squinting in outrage and disgust.'

Although my insides were churning with nerves, I laughed a little.

Farhan bhai's car pulled up at the same time as Aisha baji

came into view. Farhan bhai had brought Morowa and Zain. Aisha baji had come with Abbas and Saniya, but her husband was nowhere in sight, which was a relief. He wasn't really family.

'It's time.' I sighed, and Sal gave me a little squeeze before letting go.

'I love you,' she reminded me.

'And I love you.' I gave her a quick hug and left.

Before either of my siblings could reach the front door to knock, I slipped past them, murmuring my salaam, and used my keys to let everyone inside. As we entered the living room, Mum and Dad stood up and looked at us in complete and utter shock.

'What is the meaning of this?' Mum demanded.

Aisha baji looked confused. 'Zara told us that you needed us urgently.'

'We didn't invite any of you over. Nor do we need anything from you.' Mum glared at me. 'What is this so-called urgency, Zara?'

'*This*,' I responded loudly in Urdu, gesturing to the space between us all. 'It's been years since we all gathered like this. And we're a family.'

Dad made a disapproving sound.

'I know I've made mistakes,' I began, 'but we all have. I know that Allah has forgiven me – he's forgiven us all – so why can't we forgive each other?'

A cynical laugh escaped from Dad's mouth, wounding my heart. 'Is that really what you think? That Allah would forgive you for your shameless actions that are plastered all over the internet?'

I looked him dead in the eye, something I'd rarely had the guts to do in my life. 'Yes, I really do think that. When you ask for forgiveness from the heart and your intentions are right, God forgives. *This* is our faith. So, here's my question to you: if God has forgiven me, if He doesn't consider me to be a worthless, shameless girl, why do you?'

Dad looked dumbstruck.

He'd always used Islam as a tool to control us. It seemed he'd never imagined me using it as a tool to question him.

'You all need to get out of my house,' Dad roared suddenly, then looked at Morowa with disgust. 'Coming to this country has corrupted you. You've all been led astray by the Devil. Allah's curse is on people like you.'

Morowa flinched. She couldn't understand the language we were speaking, but it was obvious enough how Dad was talking about her. Zain was in her arms and cooed cutely, but it didn't seem to melt Dad's heart at all. It left me burning.

'No, Allah's curse is on people who are racist, sexist and full of ego.'

'Don't you dare,' Dad screamed, pointing at my face. 'You're such a rude and disrespectful child. The worst of my children. At least the others admit their mistakes.'

'I don't admit to any mistake,' Farhan bhai said. 'Marrying Morowa was the best decision of my life.'

Dad's eyes widened so much it frightened me. He muttered some swear words in Urdu and made to leave.

I blocked the door and stood firm. 'No one is leaving this house until we're either a family again or we choose to stay away from each other for good.'

He attempted to pull me out of his way, but I stood my ground and shook my head.

'Running away isn't going to work today; only the truth will.' I looked at his enraged face, searching for some real emotion in it. 'I've felt so miserable and alone in this house for so long. It's exhausting. Can't we at least *try* to communicate?'

'Why would I communicate with someone who has no self-respect?' he spat at me.

'How can you hate us so much, Dad? We're your *children*. We're sorry if we've hurt you but –'

The slap came so suddenly I didn't have time to prepare. My neck twisted to the side sharply.

'Dad!' Farhan bhai shouted.

'I have nothing to say to any of you,' Dad hissed. 'Get out of my way before I strangle you to death or burn the house down with all of you in it.'

Aisha baji's sob cut through the ensuing silence, and then I was crying too, no longer able to keep myself together.

'Fine!' I screamed. 'If you prefer violence so much then just kill me. I'm not going to do it, so if you want me dead so bad you should just do it.'

I opened the door, raced to the kitchen and came back with the first knife I could get my hands on.

'Take it,' I cried, thrusting it into his hand. 'This is what you want, isn't it?'

'Hai Allah,' Mum breathed, touching her temple as though she felt like she was losing her mind. She wasn't the only one.

'It's impossible to live with you,' I raged. 'And it'll be impossible for me to live without you. Because despite everything, I love you. I want to work hard and accomplish things for you. I want to make you proud. I want to be there for you as you grow old.'

Dad's grip on the knife tightened but his lower lip quivered. I didn't know whether it was with anger or something else, but it opened something inside me – a window of hope. Perhaps the man I'd always seen as devoid of all emotion also felt things such as sadness, loss, fear.

'What is it that you're holding on to so tightly?' I asked. 'How much you care about what your family in Pakistan are saying? What the people in our community here think of us? Is honour and respect seriously more important to you than the life of your *family*?'

'These are the words of a selfish fool who thinks only about their own filthy desires,' Dad barked.

A sinking feeling began in my stomach and expanded throughout my body. My own father would always see me as impure now, and there was nothing I could do about it. I felt stupid for thinking I could communicate with him and bring our family together.

'Whatever we are,' Farhan bhai said, 'we are your family. Your so-called relatives in Pakistan are not even there for you when you need anything. *We* are. We will always be there.'

'I don't see my son doing anything for me.' Dad wheeled to face him, and I suddenly felt stupid for having handed him a knife.

'The only one keeping this family apart is you,' Farhan bhai shouted, a finger at Dad's chest. 'Your obsession with your so-called honour and people who don't really give a shit about you are the reasons you're going to grow old alone.'

'Oi!' Dad shouted.

Farhan bhai scoffed. 'I'm not a child any more. I'm not scared of you, even with that weapon in your hand. I just feel sorry for you. You're so misguided and you'll never change.'

My brother took a step forward, and the face that I'd always seen relaxed and happy was twisted with hate.

'The closest I'll ever be to you again is probably when I perform your ghusl before your burial. And I might not even do that. I doubt any of your relatives from Pakistan would bother to make the trip, the same relatives you've been sending all your money to, money that was meant for raising your family *here*. They wouldn't even use *your own* money to attend your funeral; if that doesn't open your eyes to how one-sided your relationship with them is, I don't know what will. What a way to go – to be buried by strangers.'

Dad jerked as though his son had just slapped him.

This had hurt him deeply, and we could all see it.

Perhaps it was the fact that Uncle Sayyid's funeral had taken place so recently that made the reality of this so raw, so unbearable. Farhan bhai's words were a reminder of how far we were drifting from each other, how close we were to becoming strangers permanently.

Farhan bhai turned to me. 'I don't want you staying here with Dad waving a knife around. Pack your things. You're coming with me and Morowa.'

'She's not going anywhere,' Mum said firmly.

'I thought you wanted me gone,' I replied, staring at her in disbelief. Then understanding struck. 'You don't want to be all alone in this house, do you? You want your children here with you. Why don't you go ahead and just tell Dad?'

Mum looked at Dad, and I recognized fear in her eyes.

'Why are we all afraid of you, Dad?' I cried. 'How the hell are we supposed to love you if we're so scared all the time?'

He looked down at the knife in his hand. Or maybe he just couldn't meet my eyes any more.

Aisha baji approached Dad, and I was instantly overcome with protectiveness. I didn't want Dad hurting her in any way; she'd suffered enough.

'Baji,' I warned, but she ignored me.

She kept going until she was standing right in front of him. Gently, gradually, she removed the knife from his hand and threw it on the floor violently, as though she was throwing away a lot more than just that, and then she hugged Dad and cried into his chest like I'd never seen anyone cry before.

And then Farhan bhai was hugging Dad. And then Morowa and Zain were. And then Saniya and Abbas. And Mum. And me.

We made a circle of love around him, a cocoon of vulnerability, refusing to let him go, to let his honour and ego tear us apart, to let his hard heart remain hard forever.

Dad was always so strong and stoic, so I didn't have the courage to look up and watch him cry. But I felt his shoulders shake, I heard his sharp intakes of breath, and when I reached for his hand I felt him hold on so tightly I was sure he'd never let go.

Karim

50

'How are *we* the ones getting hate?' I exclaimed, flicking through the comments section of our latest video, which had been online for twenty-four hours now.

Abeo snorted. 'I did warn you guys.'

We were in Chloe's family townhouse in Belgravia, sitting in a circle on the living-room floor eating Ladurée macarons and drinking Yorkshire tea.

'This is ridiculous.' Sanjay grimaced. 'I have no faith left in humanity.'

Chloe moaned irritably. 'Mr Ex is getting hate too, but I swear we're getting it just as bad. Looks like we're all getting cancelled.'

'We're *not* getting cancelled,' I replied. 'If Mr Ex can brush this off, and he's the one to blame for it all, we can keep going as normal too.'

Chloe placed a freshly manicured hand on her forehead. 'I really want to get the police involved, but I'm under strict instructions from Felicity not to. I think Mr Ex has more stuff on her family.'

Abeo let out an angry exhalation. 'We were so convinced we'd finally expose his identity this year. But it's nearly Christmas and we're still at square one.'

'At least now we know it's not one of us,' Sanjay said. 'None of us would hurt Felicity like this.'

Chloe snorted. 'Did you seriously think it was one of us?'

'I actually thought it was you at one point,' he replied tightly.

'Mr Ex got inside all of our heads,' Abeo exclaimed. 'Even I suspected all of you at one point or another.'

'Maybe it doesn't even matter who he is,' I said. 'He's just a twisted stalker with far too much time on his hands.'

'You can say that again,' Abeo agreed.

'We're going to uni next year and we'll all move on with our lives,' I continued. 'Mr Ex will be stuck in the same place, criticizing us in his pathetic way, and I'm sure a large chunk of the internet will continue to do that too. But it's our choice whether we focus on that or the amazing things we've achieved through our platforms.'

'Financial freedom,' Sanjay said, counting off on his fingers. 'Insane work opportunities. The ability to share our talents with a large audience. Being able to collaborate with top industry professionals. Enjoying each other's company while creating great content.'

'It's true,' Chloe said with a warm smile. 'The good definitely outweighs the bad.'

I breathed out. 'After experiencing all of this pressure and hate online, we should talk about the reality of being internet sensations and how it impacts our mental health. We could start some really important conversations.'

'One hundred per cent,' Abeo said enthusiastically.

'Nothing can stay a secret forever,' Sanjay said, and his eyes flicked to Chloe. 'Everyone is eventually going to find out who Mr Ex is and he's going to get what he deserves.'

'It's true,' Chloe murmured. 'We just need to stick together through it all.'

'It can be frustrating sometimes,' I said, 'but I actually *like* that our friendship is also our brand. It means that we have to be friends forever, to stay in touch regardless of wherever life takes us.'

'I'll cheers to that,' Abeo said loudly, extending his teacup forward.

We grinned as we clinked our cups.

As I walked home from Chloe's, I decided to call Zara.

Now that we'd given each other some space to cool off, and things between The Exes had settled down, it was finally time for us to talk.

I pressed call, but it wasn't going through. She must have blocked my number. I didn't have her on any social media; we'd wanted to keep our relationship separate from my internet presence, which was inextricably linked to The Exes and copious gossip, drama, lies. But now I had no way of reaching out.

From the way I'd treated her, I wouldn't be surprised if she never spoke to me again. She'd basically told me our kiss had destroyed her relationship with her parents and left her homeless, and I hadn't known what to say or do. I hadn't been there for her at all.

I found myself taking a stroll through a rather damp, cold Hyde Park, thinking everything through.

It wouldn't make sense to go to Zara's house. I didn't even know what number she actually lived at. More importantly, it would be chaotic to just show up on her parents' doorstep – the guy who'd kissed their innocent daughter in front of the entire world in the *flesh*.

The smart thing would've been to have given her the keys to my spare apartment in Chelsea, to ensure she was safe with a roof over her head. Why hadn't I thought of that straight away? I'd been so fixated on Felicity's accident . . .

When Speaker's Corner came into view at the edge of Hyde Park, quiet and vacant, an idea came to me.

I'd seen so many people standing there to speak their mind, exercising their freedom of speech on topics ranging from politics to religion to art. And there was something I craved to share with the world today.

I pulled my hood off my head and waited.

Within seconds people began to recognize me and gather around. The crowd seemed excited to see me, but thankfully they didn't come too close. They knew that when someone stood here, the words they shared mattered more than anything else.

'Hey, I'm Karim Malik. Which you might already know.' I laughed awkwardly. 'The last few months of my life have been . . . hard. And I want to talk about it openly.'

The crowd grew large quickly, and pretty much everyone had their phone out. I cleared my throat and went for it.

'I'm a member of The Exes. In case you haven't heard of us yet – we're British influencers. Our YouTube channel is . . . er, quite popular.'

Some people from the crowd cheered and I smiled.

'This is a little different for me. Usually I talk into a camera, and it's either a prepared script or everyday chatter. But today, I want to tell you a little about what's really going on in my mind – the mind of a seventeen-year-old with a huge following online.'

A light spatter of rain began, but everyone stayed put.

'The truth is that I'm . . . lonely. Despite all the fans, family and friends, this has been the loneliest year of my life. And I was so afraid to admit that before, but I'm not any more.'

I paused to let it soak in just how much I meant that.

'Being online also feels exposing and painful. It hurts whenever I see a hateful comment about my personality, my skin colour or my religion. It hurts when my mistakes are displayed for everyone to judge. It hurts when I feel like I just can't handle the mental pressure of saying or doing the right things all the time. It hurts when one of my best friends nearly dies because of that same pressure.'

I paused to get control of the emotion breaking out in my voice.

There was such a loud, appreciating cheer from the people around me and I felt steadier.

'As a public figure, I know this is all part and parcel of the process. I've known that since I was thirteen, when I first started creating content as a job. I was a minor then, and I still am now. But I don't want to carry on going through life in the same way and pretending I'm fine. I'm no longer afraid to admit it when things affect my mental health and relationships.'

A round of applause broke out, and my spirit soared.

'I know that speaking honestly about my experiences can start some important conversations and raise awareness about the truth of what it feels like to be a young person online today, so that's exactly what I'm going to do.'

The cheers were extra loud and encouraging this time. It was empowering to see that so many understood what I was trying to communicate.

'Zara, I just want to talk to you directly for a moment. I know you don't really want to hear from me right now, but I just hope you know how sorry I am, and how much I care about and respect you.'

I felt a heaviness lift off my shoulders, my chest, my heart.

'It's not fair how you've been treated. It hurts me to know that people in your life have been awful to you because of your association with me. I'm sorry that I haven't been there for you in the way I should've been. You're so special to me. I've only been able to weather the last few months because of *you*. I wish the world could know your heart because it's so beautiful. Everything about you is beautiful.'

After quickly exhaling, I decided to just say it.

'In case you don't give me a second chance, I need you to know this. I love you.'

The screams that ensued were almost deafening.

This news was going to be trending everywhere soon, and I had no idea how to feel about that.

But it was my truth, and it felt good to let it all out.

'Thank you for listening, everyone. And thank you, Zara, for giving me the opportunity to know you. To fall in love with you.'

When people came forward to greet me, to talk to me, I didn't feel the urge to pull my hood up and run away like I usually did. I stayed for a long time and spoke with strangers about mental health, love, tolerance and the future.

My heart felt full.

But nothing gave me happiness like when I saw Zara's message. She'd seen the video.

And she wanted to meet.

A Christmas Miracle: The Exes Reunite
After Days of Distressing Drama

A snow-kissed London is one for the postcards.

If anyone's got the holiday blues, I recommend braving the chill and going for a stroll through Parliament Square: the Houses of Parliament and Big Ben appear even more picturesque under a powdery glaze. The hustle and bustle of dull scarves and coats will likely serve as a much-needed reminder to check out my tips for a trendy winter wardrobe. There's nothing quite like entering the new year with a fashion glow-up (Vivienne Westwood's check-print coats are still trending and I recommend nabbing one before they disappear off the racks for good).

It's been a dramatic and distressing first semester. I'm still deciding whether it was in a good or bad way. Let's just say I'm glad the Christmas holidays have arrived so we can all relax and recharge. I'm about to indulge in some festive feasts, glitter-infused make-up looks and brow-arching Bottega Veneta gowns. Think Gatsby flamboyance meets British Drag Queen brilliance.

The Exes haven't been active on their socials for a while now, and still their following continues to grow. Whether you love or hate them, there really is no stopping their stardom. For the past few weeks, they've spent ample time together and it's been so nostalgic to see! The Exes have been sighted visiting Felicity at the hospital regularly, eating at their fave Michelin-starred restaurants, and partying in style throughout parts of Europe that decorate extravagantly for the holidays.

So, the Christmas miracle we all hoped for this year has come to pass – The Exes are officially back on track. And I must admit it's all very impressive: if their bond can survive the trials of the past few months, it can survive *anything*. Take notes on how to keep things tight with your besties, folks! It seems the famous quintet have decided to enjoy the pleasure of each other's company without any cameras or publicity. If you ever wondered whether they're truly best friends behind the brand, now you have your answer. Which begs the question: is offline the new online?

Perhaps The Exes are trying to make the most of their last few months together at St Victor's School before they go their separate ways in life, pursuing their dreams, chasing different academic and professional careers. Everyone in Year 13 has officially submitted their university applications now, and I for one can't wait to see where they all end up!

Now over to the Magnificent Maliks – with a wedding that lush, they're certainly relevant again, perhaps more than ever before. Azad Malik and Sana Qureshi's baraat and walima functions were just as exquisite and iconic as the mehndi – although there certainly wasn't *half* as much drama or 'indecency' this time (probably because our Dark Fairy was notably absent!). All The Exes were there, and they entered with such flair they almost stole the show (Felicity rocked her cast so well it almost looked like a fashion statement). Most pieces from Fouzia Faris went out of stock globally after The Exes were seen flaunting those outfits. It seems the Maliks have taken the art of throwing British South Asian weddings to a whole new level, and their splendour will serve as inspiration for many years to come.

I'm going to end on the note we've all been obsessing over – Karim Malik's very public confession of love for Zara Khan. It's gone totally viral and is the most popular sound on TikTok right now: *I wish the world could know your heart because it's so beautiful. Everything about you is beautiful.* I adore the romantic content you guys have been posting to these words; love is truly in the air this winter. In all their time together, Karim never spoke about Chloe Clark this way; it seems our Dark Fairy has a tighter grip on his heart than any lass has managed before. Zara Khan may not have a public presence, but if she's going to continue being in Karim's life (and it certainly seems like it) I'm sure we'll be seeing a lot more of her . . .

I'm officially off to enjoy my holiday somewhere lush and lavish. I'm taking this time to reflect on many things, including the direction of my online presence. I know I've made some mistakes this year, and perhaps got a little carried away . . . but change is on the horizon. You'll hear from me again in the new year. Try not to miss me too much. Or do – I like the thought of you pining for me.

Merry Christmas & Happy New Year to you all (yes, even the haters).

Yours Unfaithfully,
Mr Ex

Zara

51

At Tower Bridge on New Year's Day, I leaned against the blue railing, taking in the view: soaring skyscrapers, a cloudy grey sky, the murky waters of the Thames.

It lifted my spirits.

As the cool winter air surged, I settled deeper into my wool scarf.

Things at home were the best they'd ever been. I'd moved back in after our family meeting, and we'd spent the next few weeks trying to build our communication and trust.

Now that the winter holidays had begun, I was able to spend ample time with everyone. Aisha baji had moved back in too, and Abbas and Saniya had transformed our house into a *home* again, filled with silliness, freedom and the laughter of children. Farhan bhai and Morowa came over often now. They'd been around for dinner yesterday: we'd played Ludo and Jenga, listened to Farhan bhai's favourite Bollywood songs on full blast, and Morowa had baked the most delicious chocolate cake in human history.

Although they still weren't the most expressive, Mum and Dad were glowing in a way they'd never done before.

They were happy.

We all were. At last.

I'd redownloaded all my social media. The gossip was still there, as were the judgements and taunting comments. And I hated the mere thought of seeing aunties and uncles at a community event, but I was dealing with it all. With time and the support of loved ones, I could feel myself becoming stronger, and I chose to focus on that more than anything else.

I was learning to be optimistic and strong-willed, and I liked this new Zara. It felt like the new year was truly bringing a new start this time.

I suddenly felt Karim's presence next to me.

'Happy New Year, Zara. It's so good to see you. You made me wait long enough.'

'Happy New Year to you too,' I said, giving him a small smile. 'Thank you for giving me the space I asked for. I needed some time for myself and my family. It just felt right for us to meet at the start of the new year, when everyone is ready to leave the past behind.'

He looked around, absorbing the beautiful view. 'Why did you want to meet here?'

'There's a place nearby that does the best hot chocolate I've ever had.'

We fell quiet for a while, and I got the sense that he didn't know where to begin.

He'd said so much to the world, declared his love openly for me, and yet here he stood at my side, unable to say any of it. The silence stretched like a rubber band, and I decided to snap it.

'You really hurt me.'

I turned my whole body in his direction and took him in properly. He was wearing a grey hoodie with a black leather jacket over it. It looked like something Imran would wear. I tried to push aside the thoughts of him that were creeping into my mind, but, as always, it was impossible. We spoke all the time now, and he'd become a very close friend. He'd really been there for me through all of this stuff with Karim.

'I don't even know how to apologize, Zara. But I'm so sorry. I wish I could go back and do things differently.'

His dark gaze caught mine, and suddenly all I could think about was that kiss . . .

'I'm glad it happened,' I said. His brows creased with confusion, and I smirked. 'That kiss – and everything else between us. I'm sorry I said all those awful things on the phone. I didn't really mean it. I was just hurt.'

Karim grinned. 'I've got to admit it – angry Zara's quite frightening.'

I snorted and elbowed him in the chest. Something had felt very wrong until this moment, but now that we were together, face to face, reconnecting, things felt OK. *Better* than OK.

'So, about Speaker's Corner,' he said sheepishly. 'I hope I didn't terrify you by professing my love for you in front of the entire world.'

We laughed awkwardly.

I looked down and played with my scarf. 'Erm, it did catch me a little off guard. I hadn't expected it. In fact, after the way we left things, it seemed like you'd never even *think* about me again.'

'Zara, I think about you all the time. I didn't know how to reach out to you, so I shared my truth in whatever way I could.' Karim paused to take hold of my hand, and my fingers intertwined with his instantly, naturally. 'There's no pressure from my side, by the way. But whenever you're ready, I'd like to know how you feel too.'

'I have strong feelings for you,' I said. 'Whenever we spend time together, I just want to stay with you forever.'

His answering smile warmed my heart. 'Oh, I know the feeling. So . . . does this mean we're still kinda . . . together?'

If I rejected Karim now, everything we'd gone through would have been for nothing. The hope in his eyes was too potent, too familiar, because it was the same hope *I* felt for us.

I found myself nodding. 'I want to keep getting to know you. Just so long as your overbearing fans don't start making weird names for us. Karizara sounds awful. Like some strange new curry flavour.'

He chuckled, picked me up and swirled me around, making me giggle, reminding me of the first time he'd ever done that. My favourite memory. When he put me down, I looked up at him and felt a little giddy at how *much* he made me feel.

'But can we take things slow? There's just so much going on with my family, A levels stress, university stuff. Unwanted social media stardom.' I paused to roll my eyes, and he chuckled. I silently added *my feelings for Imran* to the list. 'At this stage of my life, I need to figure *myself* out.'

'I understand and respect that completely. But just so we're clear, I meant it. It wasn't something I said on the spur of the moment. I really have fallen in love with you.'

I blushed deeply. 'It's too soon for the L word, don't you think?'

He shook his head. 'I *know* how I feel about you. But I think it's good we're taking it slow. I want to be the best version of myself for you, and that might take a little time too.'

A fluttery sensation sparked in the pit of my stomach and leaped its way across my entire body. There were so many girls the world over who wanted Karim Malik's heart, and here he was handing it over to me so casually . . .

It was almost too good to be true, as was the fact that I'd survived the past few weeks.

'Deep down I think I always knew something like this would happen if I started living my life and taking risks,' I said. 'And, as crazy as it sounds, I sort of needed it to happen.'

Karim's brows shot up.

'It's been quite liberating. I mean, the worst that could've happened to me – to my reputation – *happened*. And I'm still here. I survived it. And my family not only survived it but became closer after overcoming it.'

'I really didn't realize how deeply it would affect you, and you were right in pointing out that that was because of my privilege. The privilege I have as a wealthy, liberal man in the South Asian Muslim community. I'm sorry I didn't understand this then.'

'There are some things I guess you just won't understand about me. About my world. And there are certainly things I will never get about you and your world. I mean … who on earth knew it was such a faux pas to wear the same outfit as someone else to London Fashion Week?'

He grinned and shook his head.

'On a serious note, when I heard what you said at Speaker's Corner, I realized things are difficult for you too. I guess I just assumed you'd be desensitized to all the gossip and online pressure after all these years.'

'I don't think you ever become desensitized to it, but you do learn to deal with it. I guess we've both been judged for a long time. For me, it's online. For you, it's your family and community.'

I linked my arm around his and squeezed. 'When you put it like that, I guess we have a lot in common, regardless of how different we are.'

Karim sighed. 'Maybe we just need to choose our own happiness, you know? Screw everyone else. They're going to talk regardless of what we do.'

'Exactly. My parents are finally understanding this too.'

'Just so you know, I have an apartment in Chelsea. If you're ever in need of your own space, it's right there. I hope things keep getting better with your family, but just in case.'

He extended a hand to me, and a black key lay in his palm.

'Everything at home is great, Alhamdulillah,' I said, touched by how he was trying to take care of me. 'I'm not going to move into your place.'

'But you want to though, right?' he asked, raising a brow suggestively.

I nudged him playfully, my heart racing. 'I'm glad that I met you. I'm glad that you were my first kiss, despite everything.

I'm glad that we shared our worlds with each other. It's been the best experience of my life.'

'And it's only the beginning.'

With the way he looked at me, I believed him.

'How are things at home for you?' I asked.

He sighed deeply. 'Azad's wedding events have been exhausting. I'm still recovering.'

'From the events?' I asked with a sly look. 'Or from breaking the internet with the most dramatic kiss this city has seen in a while?'

We laughed, bending over the rail, snickering into the cold wind. It felt good that we were able to let loose, even about this.

I took a deep breath. 'I can't believe all the things we've been through in the past few months. What do we do with ourselves now?'

'We follow our dreams,' he said, and I loved how simple he'd made it sound, like everything would have a way of falling into place.

'There's something I have to tell you,' I said in a serious tone, turning to face him. He was instantly equally serious. 'The last person to get to the end of the bridge is paying for our hot chocolates.'

I watched his face split into a grin before I bounded away.

And then we were running.

The wind tore at my face, its roaring at my ears finally blocking out the whispers. Somehow I knew that when I next heard them, they'd have no power over me.

Karim's wild laughter matched my own. And I didn't care how I looked, only how I felt.

There was so much we were running from, leaving far behind us, dispelling right into the cold, rain-speckled day. Without even asking him, I knew he could feel it as well. This exact emotion I was filled with right now, he was too.

We were running from the slander and hate and expectations.

And racing into a new chapter we had chosen for ourselves and would continue to choose every day.

Together, we crashed and soared into possibilities, breaking through every barrier, flying past every hurtful comment and moment.

Our faces wide, eyes filled, hearts thundering, we bounded into a new year.

A new life.

Turning Tides & Terrains: A Summer to Spark a Sobering Switch

The end of another academic year, or should I say *era*. And the start of something new . . .

The days of St Victor's School are officially behind for those who completed their A levels this year. Exam season was stressful, fraught with late nights, anxious study sessions and worries about the daunting, unknowable future. The partying and holidaying afterwards were intense and non-stop, borderline sickening. But the results are officially in, and every student raced back to London to collect them! Where is everyone off to? I hear you ask. Well . . .

Chloe Clark decided higher education was not on the cards for her. Not that she'll need it for her choice of career. I'm sure you've all already heard her first song, the hot new single – 'A Woman's Body'. It's raw, fiercely feminist and unapologetic. It speaks of her journey through a rocky relationship, an abortion and an eating disorder. And people are eating it right up (no pun intended, I swear). I'm going to be completely honest here – I'm a fan. That girl's voice is exquisite, and I can't help but play her song on repeat. Move over Billie Eilish.

Sanjay Arya is hopping over the pond to the States; he'll be majoring in Art at Yale University. Some of his artwork is already worth hundreds of thousands, so perhaps he's on his way to dethroning Damien Hirst; I can certainly imagine his work in the National Gallery or Tate Modern. He's been working incessantly on a new collection over the past few months (maybe he just needed some motivation, a little *push*). He hasn't tried to get with any more of his mates' old flames – I guess he learned his lesson about playing with fire.

Felicity Wong is well on the road to recovery (again, pun unintended). Her casts are off and most of her injuries healed. She announced that she plans to start posting content again soon, but it'll be more light tempo stuff since the doctors have warned her to take it easy. Less krumping, more crimping. Felicity has decided to take a gap year to fully recover for the dance auditions for the Juilliard School in New York. We can only imagine how much her following is likely to grow if she focuses on her socials full-time!

Abeo Okon will be studying fashion design and development at the London College of Fashion and is already in the midst of creating an iconic fashion brand inspired by his West African heritage. Rumour has it

Fouzia Faris herself is on board to give him advice about materials, style and design manifestation. Also, he's newly single. It took him long enough to realize his ex-boyfriend simply didn't have the flair to keep up with him. Here's to hoping he'll stumble across Mr Right at some point . . .

Karim Malik is heading over to the University of St Andrews, as per family tradition. Our heart-throb will be studying computer science (is this a sign that he wants to go into the family business in the future?!). I don't know about you guys, but I can totally imagine him fitting right in over there: wrapped up in sophisticated wool overcoats against the Scottish elements, making heads turn in lectures with eloquent observations, and perhaps even donning a kilt every now and then.

Just a side note – Zara Khan is the only person Karim congratulated online via a sweet Instagram story, which stated how proud he is of her acceptance into Queen Mary University for dentistry. As private as these lovebirds are, it seems things are going strong. But they're going to be in different countries in a few months, so who knows whether they'll be able to go the distance . . . I guess time will tell all. For now, it's nice to see them supporting each other's dreams and ambitions. We're all a little young to think about forever – all we can really do is plan our next step. And that's exactly what our favourite quintet are doing.

The Exes have recently stated they'll be continuing to share their separate journeys with us via social media, and whenever they have a chance to shoot together, we'll be enjoying that content too. So, although they may have left St Victor's, it's certainly not the last we'll hear from them. But this will be the last you hear from me ... with regard to them. You may have noticed their presence decreasing on my blog in the past few months, and that's intentional. From now on, if you want an update on what's new with them, I'd recommend going straight to their verified accounts.

This is because school's out and so am I. Don't get too excited, I'm not referring to my identity or sexuality (the first will always be a secret and the latter has been out since forever!); this is about the sobering switch I've got planned – an internal glow-up, if you will. I am so out of here. The drama, bitchiness and toxicity of all this gossip?! The Exes have turned over a new leaf in this regard and it's inspired me to do the same. I think there comes a point in everyone's life when they have to make a choice: to remain as they are or change for a better future. I want change, to seize the chance to focus on global fashion, beauty and viral trends while uplifting others instead of tearing them down. You may never know my identity, but I think you're about to learn a little about my heart.

But if you're ever *really* curious about who I am, just know that I'm that guy you saw sipping coffee in a cafe around

Soho; I'm that guy crossing a street in Notting Hill who made you turn twice to take note of his outfit; I'm that guy on the Tube pretending to read the newspaper when I've really got half an eye on you.

So, I guess I'll be seeing you soon.

Yours Unfaithfully,
Mr Ex

Acknowledgements

I wrote multiple books before this one; it was heartbreaking that none of them got picked up, but now I understand why. *The Exes* was always meant to be my debut. So, as strange as it may seem, I'd like to start by thanking the many rejections and failures that led me here. And I'd like to thank myself for taking all the rejections and failures, and transforming them into something beautiful that I can be proud of.

Hannah Schofield, my incredible literary agent, was the first person to ever read the whole book, and she changed my life with her offer of representation. I'm so grateful for her kindness, enthusiasm and hard work on *The Exes*. Many heartfelt thanks to India Chambers, my wonderful editor at Penguin, who enriched this story profusely. Thank you to my amazing copy-editors Shreeta Shah and Mandy Woods. A warm thank you to the talented Malaika Qadeer for the stunning front cover – you've brought Karim and Zara to life so charmingly. My wonderful film agent, Luke Speed, has truly widened my vision for *The Exes*; I'm so thankful to have him in my corner.

There really are no words or ways in which I could ever thank my wonderful, supportive family. But I'm going to try. Thank you, Mama and Papa, for *everything*. You'll always be the biggest blessing in my life. I know I wasn't always easy to raise – thank you for your patience and unconditional love. I hope you know that it's because of your hard work, prayers and countless sacrifices that I've been able to achieve anything at all in life.

To my lovely sister and best friend, Shanza: thank you for that pep talk when I was about to give up on writing; I wouldn't be here without you. To my incredible nephews, Zakariya and

Adam, you are the light of my life. As irksome as my brothers, Noman and Faizan, can be at times, I cannot imagine my life without them (I know you guys secretly love my feminist lectures and extensive political monologues). Thank you for always celebrating my achievements as though they are your own (I promise not to pretend I don't know you when I'm rich and famous). A warm thank you to my sisters-in-law, Heera and Waseema, for their excitement about my novel. To my adorable niece, Amal, your cute cuddles make everything in the world feel OK again. Thank you to all the other Iqbals, particularly Chachu and Aunty, for being so supportive. I have been blessed with incredible in-laws; I'd especially like to thank my beautiful mother-in-law, Aunty Faiza, for all her support and prayers.

Dear husband – I've adored love stories since I was a little girl, and I always wondered what my very own one would look like. I wish I could go back and tell myself not to worry so much, and to stop growing cynical as the years went on, because, for a while there, I started to think that maybe dream guys and epic love stories only exist in romance books and movies. You are proof that that is not the case: you are my dream guy and epic love story. You're the reason I'm able to write love stories from the heart.

A massive thank you to *you*, dear reader. Thank you for taking your precious time to read my book. It means the world.

Finally, no amount of gratitude will ever be enough, but still: thank you to the One and Only, without whom there is nothing. Wherever life takes me and whatever I do, I realize again and again that You truly are As-Salam, the source of all peace. Alhumdulilah.